I0607518

Meridian

STONE & CHAINS

AURELIA T. EVANS

Stone & Chains
ISBN # 978-1-80250-503-0
©Copyright Aurelia T. Evans 2022
Cover Art by Kelly Martin ©Copyright December 2022
Interior text design by Claire Siemaszkiewicz
Totally Bound Publishing

STONE &
CHAINS

Dedication

A warm thank you to Melanie Marchande for her watchful eye.

Chapter One

Abby closed the book, glancing between her two charges. "I think that's all for now. I'll be back on Wednesday for Chapter four. That'll be exciting, won't it?"

There wasn't enough tea in the world to get her through reading aloud another two Chapters, although she loved the young adult fantasy series and wished she could read it forever. Her charges, about the same age as Abby herself, never complained that they were too old for the reading material.

Abby smiled and patted the two hospital beds on either side of her. Two young women—one of them quite pregnant—reclined supine, their monitors beeping softly in a steady rhythm. Neither of them could tell her if they enjoyed the books, but it wasn't about the stories so much as the women knowing someone was there to do more than give them sponge baths and prevent bed sores.

The pregnant woman's baby was getting more human care than the woman herself, out of the belief that Maggie wasn't really there anymore after the car accident that had put her in the extended care ward. Then there was Kara on Abby's right, who had simply lost consciousness one day and never awakened, cause unknown.

Coma patients still experienced the world around them, just not in the same way that they did when conscious or even when asleep. Like infants in the womb, the lost sometimes remembered it like the shadow of a dream, but it was still *something*. They knew the difference between caring and concern versus the cold, clinical indifference and abandonment they often experienced in a hospital environment. Just as most people didn't like the reminder of mortality from the elderly, they didn't like the stark blankness of the comatose.

But Abby felt their presence in the way some sensed the passing of a ghost—except she experienced it as warmth on the back of her neck instead of a chill. And that warmth was the reason she came to the hospital several times a week in the middle of the night to read to her two friends, although they'd never formally met.

No handsome doctor was going to wake them up with a kiss. All they could really depend on within the mortal realm was divine intervention and an overworked, underpaid woman who wanted to give them some kind of connection, even though she couldn't help them any more than that.

Abby was tired, always tired, pulled between day life and the night shift, making money and helping people. There weren't nearly enough hours in the day for everything she needed to do, so she depended far too often on free coffee refills in twenty-four-hour restaurants. There were other things more important to her than sleep, and it was easier to get out of the house more often when her bedroom—which was actually just the storage closet under the stairs—barely held the bed, and she shared living space with two other girls who didn't share her hours.

Still, life could be so much worse. She could be trapped in her own head like Kara and Maggie. Abby tried never to forget what she'd been blessed with. She'd been born with so many gifts, gifts she couldn't keep to herself, even if she tried. Volunteer hours and night shifts meant she didn't have much of a life, but Abby could live with that if she could give other people the life she didn't allow herself.

And here in Meridian, she felt like she could finally put down some roots after these last two years of seemingly aimless wandering from city to city.

She felt like she might have finally found what she'd been looking for.

"Life could be worse," Abby whispered into Kara's ear before kissing her cheek. Kara's skin was cold from the hospital air, but underneath the surface was the heat of life, and within that life, there was still hope.

She sent that hope to Maggie as well, and to Maggie's eight-month pregnant belly and the baby within. "Stay safe."

Abby carried mace and a switchblade in her purse to go to and from her night shift at the Cemetery Grove clinic downtown, but just because Kara and Maggie were in a bright hospital ward and supervised by security cameras didn't mean that they were safe, even if the only thing they weren't safe from was their own minds—what dreams and nightmares haunted them, the kind of horrors that machines couldn't measure.

* * * *

As she left the hospital, Abby had to adjust to the darkness of three o'clock in the morning. Most people feared this time, especially in Meridian, but Abby refused to let the late hour—or early, depending on perspective—make a coward out of her.

She was used to the night. She'd kept a vampire's hours for years now, ever since graduating from nursing school. After a while, the underworld that rose to the surface in the dark didn't scare her so much as the crowd during the day. She kept a hand in her purse in case the wrong person came up to her, but after months in Meridian, she hadn't been approached by anyone except a sex worker asking for ten bucks. If a person looked like she knew where she was going, the other night people didn't bother her. And the day people walking around at night figured she was one of the night people they were supposed to avoid.

On the way to the Cemetery Grove clinic, Abby passed by the Gothic-style church of the famed Cemetery Grove itself, a sprawling plain of headstones.

Meridian was a place deeply inspired by age and wisdom, although it held neither within its city limits and had barely even been a city until about thirty years prior, when two enterprising architects—Christian spiritualist Angela Cabrera and Bartholomew Vega, a reclusive man who some said was a Satanist, others a demon worshipper and others an occultist, although no one really knew for sure—had decided to make the old outpost of a ghost town the site of their own private religious war.

Whatever deeper battles they had waged then, they'd warred more publicly with the weapons of development. Vega had built and nurtured a strong financial industry that had risen to the skies in conscious mimicry of Dallas, just a little over a hundred miles away. In the undercurrents of the mini–Wall Street of investment and private equity arose complementary booming industries of law and medicine, even a thriving media stream.

As practical as he'd been, he'd taken the black and brown glass functionality of the modern skyline and twisted it further. There were rumors of spells sewn into fiberglass, runes etched in cornerstones and keystones, secret passageways through walls and basements and parking garages, bodies and blood sacrifices soaked into the concrete foundations. Under different circumstances, the rumors might have cast Vega out of his own creation in the interest of optics, but he'd ultimately been deemed essential, a necessary economic evil.

On the other side of the aesthetic spectrum, Angela Cabrera was an accomplished artist who had established a well-regarded sculpture and architecture firm in the heart of the developing city that managed to draw a radically different element than Vega's clientele but nevertheless made its visible mark on the city even more obviously than Vega's aggressively functional shibboleths.

She hadn't built all the houses of worship within the city limits — and because this was Texas, there were many, of all kinds of religions and creeds — but she'd been responsible for the designs of about eighty percent of them. She'd also provided concepts for a number of restaurants, apartment buildings and the model homes of high-end neighborhoods. Once the city had realized that her particular brand of modern Gothic was a tourism goldmine, Cabrera had gotten the last laugh when a significant number of Vega's buildings had been remodeled with architectural details designed by her and her artistic acolytes. Because of Cabrera,

Meridian became the second-weirdest large city in Texas, with an art scene that rivaled Austin, Dallas and San Antonio, especially with its Old European slant as opposed to contemporary or Spanish-colonial influences.

Even Cemetery Grove, one of the roughest neighborhoods in the city, had been touched by the ambitious, generous, artistic Cabrera hand. The cemetery was attached to the cathedral of the First United Methodist Church. Its gray marble swept in ivy whorls, the rose window lit from within and edged with statues hidden among the flora, cherubs peeking through the leaves, grander human-like angels flying among the turrets, two true cherubim on either side of the jutting, jagged steeple. And along the edge of the roof lining the length of the sanctuary, grotesques screamed, smiled and mocked above and below the gutters, although most people just called them gargoyles, whether or not they spouted water.

The cathedral was as good an example as any of Cabrera's style, a mix of the divine and dangerous. Unlike Vega's buildings, the rumors that followed Cabrera's work were of hidden reliquaries and talismans, words of God written into the foundation, spells and prayers etched in secret rooms that housed valuables protected by riddles and more statues.

The cemetery itself, one of five within the city limits and definitely the biggest—which made it another popular tourist destination, in spite of the rough neighborhood—was surrounded by a wrought-iron fence designed with Cabrera's signature whimsy— curling thorny vines threaded between the bars and tipped with spikes on the end to discourage intruders.

At one point in her life, Abby hadn't known why anyone would want to break into a cemetery. Sure, a bouquet of flowers wasn't cheap, but where would you resell it? Aside from that, a person couldn't find anything more than coins and trinkets.

These days, she knew better, especially since she was the one jumping the fence.

One wouldn't expect such a new city to have so many gravestones, but the somewhat clandestine origins of Meridian had yielded another side effect other than a roaring nightlife and eye-catching architecture. As expected with a rise in new gangs and other criminal enterprises that ran through the sewers of white-collar business, Meridian boasted an unusually high homicide and suicide rate. Armed robberies and other forms of theft, on the other hand, were unusually low.

Per her research, experts, baffled though they were, blamed the gargoyles for both.

Well, it wasn't *that* simple. Some places in the world were just haunted by death. But although the gargoyles were meant to protect the city, their dark drama sometimes inspired dark extremes, self-fulfilling and self-sustaining prophecy.

The bodies had to go somewhere, and St. Theresa's wouldn't take the suicides. Cemetery Grove took the ones no one else wanted and sponsored its own potter's field on the other end, which meant that, although it was attached to a Methodist church, it interred all sorts.

Abby landed on the other side of the cemetery fence. It wasn't her first trespass. She'd learned how to avoid the finials.

What a place to call home.

Still, it was where her father lived. Now, if she could only find him.

She'd tried other cemeteries, and she was a third through this one. She wasn't even convinced that he'd settled in a cemetery, but the way the gravestones were arranged made it easier for her to keep track of where she'd already been. If he wasn't in a cemetery, she'd have to start bringing binoculars out with her to look at all the Cabrera-treated buildings in Meridian, and that could take nigh unto forever.

Still, she had a feeling, and following her feelings usually led her in the right direction—even if the right direction sometimes meant slowly traveling through half the country before finding what she was looking for deep in the heart of Texas, of all places.

Anywhere but Chicago would have been random, but something about Texas made it extra random to her. Still, Meridian was certainly where she'd go if she were a statue. At the very least, she'd be in good company.

She switched on her flashlight. Police didn't come down here unless they had to. If she needed to hide, a number of mausoleums would do the trick.

Abby continued down row forty-two. She passed her dim beam back and forth, the light catching and chasing off the dramatic shadows of the grave columns and wings. In this cemetery, gargoyles guarded the columbariums and mausoleums, while angels guarded gravestones. Walking through them, especially at night and under the cloudy slate-colored sky, was like walking through time. The light passing over them gave the illusion of movement.

And sometimes it might not have been an illusion.

Most of the stone angels were women, their soft, stylized breasts pressing against classical sheet-like gowns. Abby didn't understand why angels always seemed to be Greek. During the Renaissance, it had been de rigueur, but plenty of artistic periods had passed since then. What if a few wanted to be medieval for a change…or cyberpunk? If she were an angel, she would rather be naked than in a toga, but Cabrera hadn't been quite *that* classically inspired. There was certainly an appreciation for the human form, but none of Michelangelo's liberality. This was, after all, a church graveyard in Texas, in a country where Justice needed her breasts covered for a president's speech.

"Think of the children," she muttered as she passed by a child's grave, over which draped a chubby, weeping cherub.

Her flashlight beam found a tombstone for *Abigail Santana*, which was the very definition of irony, because over the "In Loving Memory of" stood a male angel with wings outstretched, his gentle face like so many stone angels in the cemetery, agonized by human folly and the finality of mortality, but his hand grasped the hilt of his sheathed sword—ready to defend.

Abby stepped back, sat on the edge of the tombstone behind her and primly rested her hands in her lap.

"Hi, Daddy."

The father she'd known was far more likely to wear board shorts and polo shirts than the partial toga draped over him now. If she'd wanted to check that it was really him, she had the last picture of all three of them together folded and slightly crumpled in her wallet—Abby eight years old and sitting on her daddy's lap with her little shoes on Mommy's shirt while Aunt Sharona took the photograph.

But stylized features or not, she would have known him anywhere.

She waited patiently with the flashlight beam fixed on his chest, enough to illuminate all of him.

With a sound like chalk on concrete, the angel shifted his weight, tilted his head, then opened his eyes. He was still made of smooth gray marble, early signs of ice damage in the porous areas of his skin, but the details sharpened to form the even more recognizable visage of her father's face.

"Hi, honey." The back of his mouth was closed-off stone, but sound came out, nevertheless. "I knew you'd find me eventually—although I would have preferred if you hadn't been looking."

"Are you kidding? Mom worried sick about where you went, and everyone was badmouthing you about just walking out on your wife and kid because your family didn't think we were good enough. I know it's all lies, but it tells on Mom. She didn't know where you ended up. I wanted to be able to tell her."

"Looking for me instead of focusing on school... I'm sure your mama had a few things to say about that, not to mention your gramma."

Abby smiled wryly. "I finished school, got my nursing degree. You're hardly one to talk about following through. Besides, shouldn't you know what I've been up to, guardian angel and all?"

"Stone angels aren't guardian angels, and guardian angels as such don't exist. You should know better."

Abby narrowed her eyes. "Then how'd you know everything about me those four years in that cemetery in Chicago like a decent cursed angel father?"

"Your mother visited me more often than the once-a-week trips you took. Made me seem much more omniscient than I was, and your amazement was worth the deception."

"Okay, you look like my father, but you're right, I *should* know better. I should have checked before we started." Abby hopped off the tombstone and approached the creakily jerking angel. "When I was four years old, what did I want for Christmas and didn't get?"

"A puppy." His serene smile offset the carved sorrowful expression. "You were convinced Santa would bring you a puppy you wouldn't be allergic to. You wanted to call him Patches."

"There are labradoodles now, not that I could have one anyway. And when I was seven, what part of my body did I scrape during that bike accident?"

The angel laughed. "I believe that would be your floral-clad buttocks. I had to carry you home in my arms with my jacket over you so no one would see your underpants."

"You are a monster," she said, "but you're definitely my dad."

A demon with knowledge of her family deliberately trying to impersonate her father could conceivably know those details, but that was an awful lot of trouble for a demon to go through for little old her.

"You're too easily pleased," the angel replied, as though he knew the direction of her thoughts. "But how about this? You were born with a caul, and your mother turned to me with accusation in her eyes, screaming why her daughter didn't have a face. I couldn't stop her crying when the doctors pulled off the caul and revealed you to be perfectly, beautifully human."

Abby lowered her eyes. Mama had told her that story when Abby was seventeen, about to go to college and start looking for her father during breaks. The story her father shared sounded more familiar than how her mother had explained it. She thought her dad might have told it as a fairy tale when she was a child, more fanciful at the time, in a tale about a princess and a dragon.

"I knew you would look for me, and I knew you were coming." Her father eased himself down to sit on his stone, where Abby tentatively joined him. "Not you, specifically, but that someone was searching the cemetery for a specific angel. I sensed it might be you, through the part of me that is you."

He gently stroked her hair. He had to compensate for the hard stone of his hand by not petting too close to her scalp, with none of the warmth or dexterity of the father she remembered.

"How'd you know someone was looking?" she asked.

"Like people, I only know what I hear, and like other stone angels, I only hear as far as other stone angels whisper. I know about grave robberies, family drama at burials, church scandals, grief, gifts to the dead, pranks played by irreverent children, but only because there are so many of us here and we're all desperate for whispered entertainment in the evening."

"I've never heard them whispering," Abby said.

"Because they don't whisper when you're here. That's how we knew you were here in the first place — because we couldn't hear anything."

"So, when you become stone angels, you devolve into a quilting circle? That's almost...cute."

"We have nothing else. It's fortunate that we are so many, that we can hear the doings from blocks away. We don't even hear Our Lord anymore, only what is spoken within the walls of the church. We are otherwise locked to our foundations and must communicate like trees. It's a lonely, trapped existence — one I didn't want you examining too deeply at ten years old when your mother was still telling you stories of guardian angels. But you're old enough to know now, honey."

Not the deadbeat dad that her mother's side of the family thought him, instead a man with a stone heart and an angel's wings, a man who Abby remembered through the haze of daughterly nostalgia and her mother's bitterness. Her mother didn't hate him for disappearing on her, but she could never quite conceal her pain that her time with him had been cut so short, even if she'd known it was coming.

It had taken Abby well into her early twenties to understand that her father's capacity for love was not only greater than she could remember but that he'd also known exactly how little time he would have with the two women he loved the most. And because Abby finally understood this, she also understood her mother's bitterness that he had fallen in love with her and that she'd fallen in love with him just as completely, when heartbreak was inevitable from the start, and he'd known that all along.

That was a grown-up thing to understand, though. For most of Abby's life, he'd just been her daddy, a father she missed so terribly that she'd devoted most of the free time in her adult life to find him.

After all that time, she'd expected finding him to be...more. She'd thought she would be happier to see him. But since he'd disappeared, her father had transformed from the God-like angel she had believed him to be—a cross between Santa Claus and Roma Downey—to a very limited entity, all the more limited by this curse, the consequence of loving a human and coming down to be with them—and by choice, if Abby's last name was any sign of his acceptance of those terms.

He wasn't a god. He wasn't even an angel anymore. He was little more than a man made of stone. It made her heart sink like one to realize that, after all her searching, she might never truly find the father who'd left her.

But although he wasn't the man she'd expected, what hadn't changed was how he looked at her. His eyes were carved from marble, but there was no mistaking the familiar love in them, mingled with the sadness of their last year, those visiting hours in the cemetery — the sadness of a father who didn't want his daughter to see her idol fall.

"Getting older sucks, Dad," she said with a sigh.

"It can't be all bad, Abby baby." He nudged her with a winter-cold knee. "Tell me some good news. Tell me about what you're doing with this nursing degree. Tell me how your mother is. Tell me if you have a nice boy in your life. I want to hear everything. Not all at once, although I wish we could. Maybe in daylight so that I can see you better, even if I can't reply. Just visit me until you have to leave again. That's all I ask. I've missed you so much, my girl."

"Well, you don't have to miss me anymore. I work at the clinic just over there, actually. They're the only ones that accommodate my hours."

She pointed southeast, where in daylight her father might have seen the threadbare awning. She thought she caught the gleam of the OPEN sign on the window.

"You work *here*? You *live* here?"

"I've been a little aimless since graduation, but yes, I signed my first six-month lease with some girls on a house that probably needs fumigating — "

"You can't live here."

Abby raised the light to the darkened expression on her father's face. "What?"

"You can't live here. I would never have allowed such a thing to come to pass." His stone brows drew closer together, and he returned his hand to the hilt of his sword.

"Well, at a certain point, you wouldn't have been able to stop me."

He'd been out of her life for fourteen years, talking to her for less than fourteen minutes, and he already thought he could tell her what she could do and how to live. But he'd missed the parts of her life when he could still do that.

"I'm not joking, Abby. This city is a dangerous place."

"Spare me," Abby said. "Aunt Sharona already gave me the 'cities are dangerous' talk when I decided to live in the UChicago dorm."

"Not cities. *This* city. Meridian. The city of the war between worlds. *This* is not a good place. It is a center of spiritual warfare that started long before the architects, and I won't have my daughter caught in the crossfire between demons, humans and the Powers. Abby, return to your mother. Live in Baghdad or Benghazi—anywhere but here, where all the gates are open and all the gloves are off. Don't stay."

"I told you, Daddy, I have a lease—and a job that I actually enjoy, even though it takes two years off my life every month I do it."

"Break the lease and find another job. This is no place for a sweet girl like you. I don't want to be trapped here, unable to help, while my Abby exposes herself to this corruption." Her father rose to his full height, pulling the sword halfway from its sheath in preparation for battle, even though he couldn't tear himself from the stone.

Abby set down the flashlight to stand as well, crossing her arms, although she wasn't quite as intimidating as an avenging angel, even one who could only move his limbs as fast as an arthritic tortoise. "I've already been exposed—side effect of my work. And I wouldn't go as far as to call myself sweet. Altruistic, maybe, although saying so just took 'modest' off the table. But as they say down here, I ain't going nowhere."

"Abby, I'm not joking. I don't want you anywhere near here. Every night you breathe its air, the greater the risk that you will cross paths with those who would take your life — or worse. Don't stay, or so be it, I'll..."

"You'll what? Brandish your sword and threaten to call my mother?" Abby picked up her purse from where she'd propped it against the gravestone, then slung it over her shoulder. "Look... I'm not some innocent flower anymore, Dad. I know that's not what you want to hear, but you couldn't protect me, even if you wanted to. I've seen some of what this city has to offer, and I've seen worse elsewhere, okay?"

"Then you haven't seen what this city truly has to offer."

She retrieved the flashlight. "I think it's time for me to go. I'll try to come back when I can. I take the night shift, but at least you'll know that I'm just a few hundred feet away four nights a week."

"And the other three, my baby girl?" he asked, rigid where he stood.

She leaned in and stood on tiptoe to kiss his cold cheek. "Just a few hobbies. Those days, I sometimes even see the sun. I'll be back later, yeah?"

"Abby!"

Facing away, she stared down at the amorphous darkness of her sneakers.

"I love you," he said. "I missed you."

"I missed you, too, Daddy."

Chapter Two

She'd led her father to believe that she had to go to work, although she hadn't said it in so many words. Abby justified the lie of omission by telling herself that she didn't share with her mother what she did in her spare time, either.

Some things you just didn't need to tell your parents, especially when one of them was an angel.

Abby pulled her jacket more tightly around her and zipped it up. Most native Texans were donning scarves and coats and multiple layers, complaining about how cold it was the same way they groused about the heat— although Abby thought she'd likely more than agree when summer came along and she had to endure triple-digits on the regular. However, she didn't understand why people broke out the Uggs in sixty-degree weather and called high forties freezing. Her lips weren't turning purple in just the jacket and jeans.

Rather than heading for work or home now that the search for her father was over, Abby headed to Threshold instead.

It was a dirty name for a bar, but the bar itself wasn't bad. Next to the Holy Grounds 24-hour coffee place a few blocks over, it was her go-to watering hole.

And in its own way, stopping by Threshold now and then was kind of part of her job — the non-paying one.

Threshold was one of two bars that welcomed demons and the humans who conjured them, whether intentionally or unintentionally — mostly those aligned with the Vega faction, but sometimes a few artsy types getting in touch with their darker sides by rubbing elbows with the locals of another spiritual plane.

Abby guessed her father would have a few words to say about his little girl doing some of the rubbing.

She pushed open the swinging door to the bar.

Truth to tell, the ambience was a little rough, but the clientele wasn't too bad. It was open to all, so everyone was on their best behavior. Abby had witnessed more fights in all-human bars. Beings didn't have much to prove here. They saved their beatings for the alleys and sewers. Here, they just wanted to get their drink on and shed their responsibilities, whether the corporate rat race or the torture and torment of the innocent — which, of course, sometimes overlapped. It was in everyone's best interests to keep to one's own company or companions rather than risk being kicked out by the golem bouncer, Larry, who didn't give a flying fuck who or what he threw out when the bartender and owner, a witch named Miranda, told him to.

Abby wasn't quite a regular yet, especially after that week where she'd worked Darcy's night shift in addition to her own, plus mornings, and she'd thought that if she drank a drop of alcohol, she might fall asleep where she stood. But Miranda recognized her and started on Abby's rum and Coke before she asked. Abby smiled and settled onto her bar stool, considering the clientele reflected in the mirror, then briefly checking behind her to make sure there weren't any vampires in the mix.

"You're new."

Abby glanced up from her first lightheaded swallow.

A man in a black leather duster, gloves to match, ivory scarf and something dark green underneath leaned against the bar stool next to her. His dark eyes were warm, crinkled up in such a way that made his smile all the more effective. Short black hair spiked so perfectly that it had to be natural rather than moussed that way.

"Depends on what you mean by 'new', but any way you spin it" — she lifted her drink and swirled it in the glass — "I wouldn't say I was new to anything. I've been drinking since before I was legal, I've been to Threshold enough that I don't have to ask for my usual and I've been in Meridian long enough to see the seasons change."

"New to Threshold, relatively speaking." With more than two words passing his lips, his English accent became more apparent. Abby wouldn't know Cornwall from Kent, but it sounded vaguely like what she'd expect from a Londoner. "I've seen you a few times. You like this side of the bar. Back to the door, so you're not paranoid, but you keep an eye on the mirror. People watcher, or are you looking for something in particular?" He pulled his gloves off and tucked them into the pocket of his jacket. Then he nodded to Miranda, who brought out the bourbon. The witch had a knack.

Abby took a heartier sip of her drink and set it down sharply on the wooden bar. The ice that clinked against the side of the glass wasn't the only thing that was cold. "Not interested."

"Not interested in what? I haven't even made my proposition," the man said, unchilled. "I only wanted to say hello, pay for your drinks, maybe ask if you wanted coffee." He slid his hand deliberately over the bar to brush his fingers against her hand holding the glass.

She jerked away, drink sloshing. "That's what I'm not interested in. If you try to touch me again, incubus, I'll cut off your hand."

The man's smile broadened. "Did I leave my wings on?" He checked behind his shoulders as though he didn't know damn well where he'd put them.

"You think I can't sense incubus charm from only a foot away? If you absolutely insist on continuing this pointless conversation, you better put your gloves back on, because you're not laying a finger on me." With her left hand, she tightened her grip around the mace in her purse. It was as effective a deterrent against an incubus as any man. It was her switchblade that wouldn't be much use.

Miranda slid him his tumbler. "You know better than that, Charles."

Grinning at both women, he made a show of taking the gloves back out of the pocket and pulling them on again.

Abby told herself that her reaction to the sight of his hand entering the supple leather was just incubus magic—incubus magic and the great gaping hole between now and the last time she'd been with a man. And she sure as hell wasn't going to fill any holes with an incubus, not unless she wanted to join her father in the cemetery in a six-feet-under kind of way.

"I wasn't looking for takeout, sweet thing—just company. I've had a feeling about you for a while, had to come over and see if I was right. And I am. You're nephil offspring."

"I'm not nephil. My dad's an angel." Abby slid off her seat, even though that robbed precious inches from her height. She was reminded of that unpleasant fact when the incubus looked down his nose at her the way a serial killer might consider his victim. "Not that it's any business of yours."

Charles' laugh was as smooth and warm as his smile, with an edge like knives under floorboards that Abby wasn't sure a pure human would hear but certainly raised the hairs on the back of her neck and down her spine.

"If you're sired by an angel, love, you're nephil offspring. We're all fallen angels down here. Some of us just fell further from grace than others."

"My dad is *not* nephil." Abby hooked the strap of her purse over her shoulder and flashed a glance at Miranda. "Can I pay you back next time I'm in? You know I'm good for it. Company's gone stale, not to mention rude."

Charles paused Miranda's nod by raising his hand. "Already said I'd pay. Don't go, love. If cold truth offends your sensibilities, I'll call that creature an angel. But it's not right, you going through life so naïve. Someone had to break the news."

His teeth were perfect—too perfect—and set in a firm jaw that simply didn't exist on this side of the silver screen. There was no doubt that he was a full-blooded incubus—and that this face, this figure, this voice, this accent were all chosen. His real face, the one that she couldn't see but sensed like light on the other side of closed blinds, would be quite different. She couldn't trust a word the silver-tongued devil said any more than she could trust his appearance.

Then again, it wasn't exactly the nature of a lust demon to tell her something she *didn't* want to hear.

"Was it devastation or the shattering of innocence that you were going for tonight?" But she climbed back into her chair to nurse the rest of her drink, hoping he'd had his taste of baiting her for the evening.

"Devastation." He spoke the word like a kiss to her neck, rough, dark and hot as coffee in his throat. He toasted her before swallowing half of his tumbler. "But shattering has a nice ring to it as well."

"Look... I'd like to drink the rest in peace, if it pleases Your Highness."

He rested his elbows back on the bar as he gave her a closer, more lingering, appreciative onceover. With any other man, it might have felt slimy, but Charles had the benefit of his charm to make it flattering, in spite of herself. "Is that really the only reason you come here? This city isn't lacking evening entertainment, even at this hour. You just happen to tempt your palate in an establishment like this by mere coincidence? I don't think so. You come here for the demons, sweet thing."

"So what if I do?"

"You can't learn a thing about us by just sitting at the bar alone."

He nodded to Miranda for another bourbon, then signaled for another rum and Coke for the lady. Miranda checked with Abby, who shook her head. She'd be fuzzy walking home as it was. On these streets, especially near a demon bar, it wasn't recommended to stumble drunk into any dark alleys.

"You seemed reluctant to satisfy your curiosity on your own," he said. "I thought I'd break the ice, so to speak."

"Didn't think I could make up my own mind?"

"A woman like you, uniquely equipped to see us for what we are, it would be a shame to keep your distance indefinitely, with blood so near to our own."

Although the intense warmth from his bundled body seeped through Abby's jacket, he didn't remove his duster in spite of the working heater in the bar. But she also didn't dare take off her own jacket. It was an extra layer of armor against him — and this *was* a war. She wouldn't make the mistake of forgetting that.

"Blood isn't what you want," Abby said, stirring her ice.

"And what is it that I want?"

"Blind nuns know what you want."

"I like an angelic woman with a precision streak and respect for religious orders." He nudged her thigh with his knee.

Abby took a deep breath. Clothing dampened the effect from irresistible to simply stirring, but the effect also dampened certain pieces of her clothing in the process, and the smug demon had to know it. "I'm no angel."

Charles had somehow managed to lean in close enough that his forearm rested inches from hers. His breath brushed over her cheek and lips, cool only from distance. "Any fool could tell."

"What's that supposed to mean?"

"I thought I wasn't supposed to talk about that," he replied in good humor that belied the coals smoldering sparks in his brown eyes.

He thought he was so smart, insinuating himself into her space for the cologne of his charm to work its way into her system like a pheromone. But she had the benefit of knowing what it was, recognizing her feelings as manufactured rather than natural — mostly.

A few jokes, casual flirting, glancing touches, those dilating irises, his impossible beauty and he thought she'd be putty in his hands? He wouldn't be the first to try, but she wasn't going to let an incubus, of all demons, make soul prey out of her.

Abby pulled back and slid off the stool again. "Save your games for the tourists. Better yet, go back where you came from."

"More fun here. Leaving so soon? Reality get too much for you?"

She poked his jacket. It really was good leather. "Nothing that you show me is real, and nothing that passes your lips is anything close to reality."

"Is that so?" He remained slouched against the bar, his hands draped casually over his thighs to frame the front of his jeans in a way both deliberate and unconscious, as though he'd done it so many times he barely tried anymore. "How about this? You're a night nurse at the clinic down the way. You live like an invisible houseguest with two other women. You came to Meridian from Chicago, but you didn't follow a straight line. And when you're not getting tipsy with the demonfolk, you enjoy extra-large coffees."

Under her military jacket, she locked her knees to keep herself upright and conceal most of the trembling. "You been stalking me, Prince Charles? I swear, if you've been feasting on my roommates, I'll rune their windows so quickly that you won't know which holy hell hit you first."

He pulled a smartphone from his pocket. "Your social media profile could use more security if you don't want a man to know those things after five minutes of a basic search. You forgot to take your badge off after your shift last week."

"Oh, so you're only stalking me a little."

"Don't flatter yourself so much. You have your own little charms, and I look forward to getting to know them better, but other prospects keep me well fed and otherwise occupied. Besides, you're awake during most of the hours I feed, and I'd only be able to read your mind in dreams."

She hadn't had any sex dreams lately. Well, that one a few weeks ago, but it hadn't involved a chiseled Sino-European man, and she'd awoken rejuvenated rather than drained, so she was pretty sure that one had just been her dreaming with her clit.

Even so, she was going to rune the door frames as soon as she got home, just in case.

"I haven't had the pleasure of invading those particular Elysian fields...yet." He touched the tip of his tongue to his lower lip as he looked her over again. "However, flatter yourself just enough that I did my research. A predator's nature is not entirely to blame when you present such a lovely feast."

Abby released the mace but didn't relax. Just because he was still seated and casual didn't mean he couldn't attack at any moment. An incubus's power was strongest in dreams, but they had a fair bit of power in the waking world as well.

"Cute trick, pretending *I* was leading *you* on when I barely knew you existed until today. Oldest trick in the book, actually, but I don't think I even own a skirt, and you'd be hard-pressed convincing people I was just too sexy in my jeans, sneakers and a jacket that covers my butt."

"I'm wearing even more than you. Tell me you feel nothing." He lingered his gaze on the place between her legs also covered by her jacket. But he knew exactly what he was doing to it by looking her over like a chocolate-coated candy cane again and again. She resisted the urge to pull her jacket more tightly around her. She wouldn't give him the satisfaction.

"You may think I'm naïve, but I'm not that naïve, and your little tricks don't fool me, so there's no point even trying. Maybe I *am* a little curious about how the other half lives, but I don't need your help. And if you try to get into my house while I sleep or if I find out that any of my roommates are lethargic and moaning in their sleep, I'll get my DIY flamethrower and torch your ass before you can lie to me again. Do I make myself clear?"

"Oh dear, have we got an amateur hunter on our hands? I'd recognize that righteous fire in your eyes anywhere, love." A fountain of laughter bubbled from between his lips until it filled every corner of the bar. "Better watch your backs, bats and ghouls. A pint-sized hunter wants us all to know a new sheriff's in town."

Abby couldn't help the blood rushing to her cheeks as other patrons laughed with him.

"I'm not a hunter." Perhaps the way she stood her ground instead of fleeing quieted the more raucous laughter. "I'm careful. And not prepared to take any crap just because I'm pint-sized."

"Precisely what a fellow wanted to know." Charles toasted her once more before throwing his head back to display the ripple of his pale throat over the scarf. When he slammed the glass on the bar again, he was still laughing at her, but behind his eyes instead of for all to hear. "Dead careful, by the way, walking into the devil's den to entice the locals."

"I just like the way Miranda makes my drink. Last I checked, this was a demilitarized zone. But if I'm unwelcome as nothing more than a temptation that you just can't help but give in to, I can check out and tempt you no more."

"I enjoy the temptation. Besides, I appreciate a girl who does more than lie in her bed and passively let me in."

"You're sick." She adjusted her purse strap to head out then pushed open the door.

He shrugged. "I am what I am. It's you who hasn't figured out who you are yet. But you're just starting to get interesting."

Chapter Three

As soon as she was out of view from Threshold's front window, Abby sprinted, her sneakers slapping against the pavement as she ran around the corner. Then she slowed down and caught her breath, heading for the open mouth of the alleyway between the streets.

She didn't approve of stumbling drunk into alleys. Walking into them with purpose was another thing entirely, even if she was a little fuzzy-headed.

Demon hijinks rarely took place within the walls of Threshold, but this alley was fair game and one of the most dangerous in the city. It was hard to find the specific statistics on criminal activity for such a narrow area. Abby suspected that someone had buried the information, which had made it difficult but not impossible to recover during her research. At least half of the terrible things done in and around the alley were put down as 'missings' or 'unknowns' rather than murders, kidnappings by demon-worshipping cults or consumption by the kinds of wild beasts not found in any forestry database. Abby patrolled Cemetery Grove at least once a non-nursing night as a rule, and she saw more action in this alley than anywhere else.

She'd told the incubus the truth, technically. She wasn't a demon hunter. She didn't have the physical strength for it, nor a witch's magic to compensate.

Abby had few illusions about what she was—a five-foot-nothing skinny woman, with some muscle tone but not exactly a bodybuilder. Like every other human being, she had no good natural defenses and had to depend on the brass knuckles she kept in a pocket sewn into her purse on the other side of where she kept her switchblade, and even then, she didn't use them to get *into* a fight.

Like she'd said, she wasn't naïve. She hated fighting demons. It was just a nasty side effect of what she really wanted to do, which wasn't destroying evil so much as saving the victims. In the clinic, she helped people one way. On the streets, she helped them another.

But right now, she just needed to help herself for a moment.

It had been foolish to engage an incubus like that. Charles had been on home turf, and if he'd set his sights on her, the last thing she needed to do was give him attention and make him think it was worth his time. An incubus on her ass was the last thing she needed.

Although it sounded better and better the more she thought about it.

"Damn, he really put it on me," she murmured to the gargoyles that lined the top of the alley. She could only imagine the show they'd had over the last few decades from their vantage point. And they were about to get another one if the tingling against the thick seam of her jeans got any worse. Abby's eyelids fluttered, wanting to close, as she pressed the heel of her hand against her mound. It really had been a while. She barely had enough time to sleep, and she had even less for taking care of nuisance non-necessities like her sex drive. It gave an incubus the advantage, because it wasn't like they had to try that hard.

Well, they were usually hard when they tried, but that was a state with which incubi were intimately familiar. They could be pretty focused while full-boned.

Just need a little. She unbuttoned her jacket and slid her hand under the waistband of her jeans and panties. *Make it quick. Just one little...*

She licked her lower lip, remembering the way that Charles' tongue tip had touched his. No extended titillation or tantalization this time.

She really shouldn't have been doing this when any person or demon could interrupt her. How was she supposed to explain herself? *"I dropped a popcorn kernel down my shirt, and it went down my pants?"*

Abby had actually used that excuse once, except that time it had been completely true. She'd produced the kernel for the scandalized college staff member. This time, the hot little nub she'd found couldn't be revealed to a passerby without a felony charge.

Still, it was four-something in the morning and, as far as she could tell, the alley was empty, except for the usual assortment of dumpsters, a stray cat and the kinds of things a stray cat would hunt.

Abby caught her lower lip between her teeth and reached into the scooped neckline of her practical knit tee. There were buttons, but they were decorative. She pushed the fabric down to cup her breast under her bra. The nipples had been tight, sensitive and hard against the bra cup for a while under the incubus' influence. She flinched slightly when she rolled one between her fingers, her gasp close and intimate in the alleyway, as though she were all alone in the confined space of her bedroom under the stairs instead.

In her mind, she could still see Charles and that annoyingly attractive scarf framing his damn fine leather jacket. Although she hadn't seen anything underneath his clothes, she could imagine that he was right here in her imaginary bedroom, sliding his scarf off, the collar of his shirt spread to show the hollow of his throat and the line of his collarbone. Then his jacket fell to the floor before she knew it, because she'd been so focused on the hollow that called her to kiss and lick, to make skin contact and set his natural aphrodisiac in motion.

He gave her the dark crinkle of his eyes and that devastating smile as he posed so casually that it had to be deliberate.

She moved her fingers faster over her clit, squeezed and rolled her nipple with her other hand.

Charles had only undone a single button of his well-fitted shirt before Abby fell back against the concrete wall to hold herself up as a long-delayed orgasm wracked through her, spreading heat in her belly and wetness over fabric. Air rushed harshly through her nose in a hyperventilating rush.

Abby wiped her hand on the front of her underwear and warned herself not to put off taking care of certain needs for so long next time. Some denominations frowned on these kinds of things, but scratching itches like this really helped in her line of work. A person always had something that they lacked in life, and demons found those weak spots pretty quickly. If an incubus had decided to make her a project, it'd be easier dealing with him if she ensured her sexual needs were satisfied.

Sure, he could have just been flirting-slash-tormenting her and nothing more, but incubi had obsessional tendencies that could lead to very real physical cravings, and although they could control themselves, they weren't really known for their self-restraint. Being the bullseye for an incubus was hot in theory, but now that she'd rubbed out her frustration, reality set back in, along with the knowledge that incubus obsessions rarely ended well.

A muffled cry came from the other end of the alley.

Streetlights illuminated silhouettes at the mouth, a hooded man in red robes and a smaller figure struggling against two shadows that were either demons or basketball players, but it wasn't March Madness, and one of them wore a headdress no basketball player would ever get caught dead in.

"No rest for the wicked," she muttered, reaching into her purse for the brass knuckles, one for each hand. They were plated with etched sterling silver, so she guessed they were technically silver knuckles. She didn't care about the etched part. They'd just come that way when she'd bought them from the same demon-hunting hole in the wall where she bought her holy water.

Her jacket flapping at her waist like a cape, she ran down the center of the alley toward the cries of the girl who'd managed to lose her way in the worst part of town. Only the Good Lord and the devil himself knew why girls kept doing that around here. If there was a conjuring charm for young virgin women attached to the alley, Abby had yet to find it.

She wasn't interested in staying hidden. She wanted the demons to know she was coming. And she wasn't saying anything ignorant like 'Hey, get away from her!' or 'What are you doing?' Her silence would clue the demons in to the fact that she understood perfectly well what they were doing, and she was coming at them anyway.

As she got closer to the demons and their prey, the hooded man hissed at them, "Don't you dare lose her." Then he melted back into the dark street.

The demons pushed the girl behind them, one of them holding her arms so she couldn't run.

If they'd expected a demon hunter attack with a crossbow or a broadsword, they'd have been sorely disappointed. However, if they'd expected her to leap up with all her running momentum and glide down at them like a flying squirrel six feet in the air with her fists poised to strike, then they would have been right on the money—although what were the odds they'd expected that?

Her wings were little more than focused swaths of smoke that emanated from her shoulder blades, but they held her as though solid. Although she couldn't sustain flight like an incubus or an angel, she could float, and the smoke sometimes scared the demons whose perception of her could shift from tripped-up hunter to some kind of avenging power—a warrior angel or maybe another demon getting in on their action and not above taking a little demon blood for her trouble.

She slammed her knuckles into the chest of the left demon and into the headdressed head of the second. The first demon grunted, the place where she hit him pitting in like a sinkhole where the silver touched his skin. Her right blow, however, glanced over the headdress, tearing it away from the second demon's face. Underneath, he still wore a human form, while his brother-in-arms was already transforming with the spicy scent of brimstone.

"Get your own." The transforming demon's voice roughened from the fire that burned within.

"She's not demon, half-wit," the one with the headdress snarled at his partner.

"Just a concerned citizen." Abby struck the human-looking one in the abdomen. He stumbled back with a surprised *oomph* as his transformed brother's skin smoldered into a dark blood red that went with his human-faced partner's black, pointed goatee.

Wonderful. Traditionalists. Luciferian acolytes, which was a bit ironic, because the one they liked to call Master would never sully his own altar with the kind of virginity the demons' victim was supposed to be good for.

Abby raised her fists again, swallowing back a wince. Silver knuckles made breaking through demon flesh easier, but they didn't actually lessen the impact of the blows against her hands, which meant she occasionally broke fingers. But broken fingers could be dealt with. Souls were a different matter. "Let's make this easy. Let the girl go and no one has to get their innards roasted."

"The sow is ours," the transformed demon said.

Abby lunged to punch him in the stomach, which was the easiest target from her height now that she wasn't floating like a butterfly. He knocked her arm away before the silver could reach him.

His human-faced partner backhanded her against the alley wall, then grabbed the girl by her blonde hair and bared her neck to Abby. "She walked into our net of her own free will. She's ours."

"That's not how free will works, and you and I both know it. A girl *can* change her mind. Get with this century." Abby wiped her nose. Blood smeared the silver. Good thing she wasn't demonic, or that would really sting—the silver, not her nose, which definitely stung, throbbing like an infected tooth. But it wasn't broken. She'd live a little longer.

Of course, 'longer' was a relative term.

"You want her?" the human-faced demon growled, shaking the girl's neck almost hard enough to snap it. "Then come get her. We'll just have one more for the altar."

"Oh, I'm all gamey and spoiled. I'm more of a Beelzebub kind of brisket."

"Sounds tasty to me." The blood-skinned demon lolled his tongue out like the unwinding of a scroll. It unfurled to his chest, dripping with saliva and steaming in the cold. The girl in the human-faced demon's grip screamed, but no one outside of the alley would hear it. Even if someone heard, they'd pretend they hadn't, and eventually she'd stop and the lies they told to themselves would become truth. People were people, and Cemetery Grove was no place to venture out of your door after midnight unless you had horns, wings or a tail.

People still did, of course, or else Abby would have much less to do on her nights off. It wasn't always foolishness or random chance that got people caught, either. Abby had to give people the benefit of the doubt, because she'd fallen for a few lures herself by demons who didn't know what they were getting themselves into. Tonight and the moisture drying against her thighs were a case in point.

"You're not as useless as you think, but even if you were, that would just mean we wouldn't have to keep you alive to bring you to the altar." The human-faced demon slashed thick claws at her, but Abby ducked and somersaulted on the grimy concrete. A little dirt was better than being gutted. That's what showers were for, and for all the flaws of where she lived, the hot water worked.

She spread her wings again to facilitate a quicker rise to her feet. "That's a little fast for me. Shouldn't you buy me dinner first?"

"This one banters. Delightful." The human-faced demon kicked at her, but there were benefits to being a short person fighting tall demons. She ducked again, then flew up and connected with his chest. He roared as the silver knuckles plunged into the furnace of his caving rib cage. Abby hissed, withdrawing her hand as fast as she could.

The blood-skinned demon slurped his tongue back into his mouth. "I'll eat her intestines all the way up to her throat."

"Charming. You would both be such a hit with my parents." Abby caught the first demon's leg before his boot struck her stomach. She couldn't stop his momentum or flip him onto his back like a ninja, but she kept him from kicking the breath completely out of her.

The human-faced demon grabbed her hair with the same grip as the blonde girl. Abby shrieked at the tug against her scalp.

"Why continue this pointless charade, child?" he asked. "Who do you think you're fooling? You can't win this contest. You are small and annoying and know a little about us, but the smoke and mirrors of your blood cannot help you. Amateur."

He shook her like a bad kitten when Abby tried to burn his wrist with her silver. She was pretty sure he took out a good chunk of her hair in the process, but now was not the time for vanity. Now was the time for panic, because smoke and mirrors were basically the primary weapons in her arsenal.

The blood-skinned demon was drooling, spittle hitting the pavement with a skillet hiss.

A mighty crash behind them made the demons whirl around. Abby and the sacrificial lamb were almost flung right into the creature blocking the entrance of the alley with its massive, leathery wings. Light glowed dimly through the membrane between the bat-like skeletal structure, but Abby couldn't discern much more of his features in the darkness, just that he had a demonic sort of anatomy, and that rarely boded well.

"Either of you have any intention of sharing?" the creature said.

The blood-skinned demon wiped his mouth with the back of his hand. "Who the hell are you?"

The human-faced demon edged behind the first to protect their catch. The blood-skinned demon was more brawn than brains anyway. He bared his teeth in a fierce grin.

Just because the creature was demonic didn't necessarily mean that everyone in the alley with brimstone in their blood would get along. All demons served the same Master in the end, but there were lots of principalities to whom they owed allegiance before they got to the big devil man, which was where the trouble usually started. Even demons had religious differences, and like humans, sometimes the results weren't pretty.

"You wouldn't know me." The creature pulled his wings in, letting in the light.

He still looked like a demon, but the streetlight shone over him just enough to illuminate his features and backlight his face and shoulders, and it was the strangest thing. His wings moved like flesh, but shadows developed in the tiny pits of texture in his skin. It honestly looked just like…weathered stone.

There was only one kind of demon Abby knew of that was made of stone, and they weren't technically demons at all. With the angels, they practically ruled the roofs of Meridian.

Gargoyles, like the ones that lined the rooftops above… Except this one was right in front of them, living and breathing—at least Abby assumed that's what the heaving chest was doing, although in places like this, not all living things breathed and not all breathing things lived.

"Let the women go." The creature even sounded like stone, air rasping wind against a broken window.

"So you can take them for yourself? These sows are ours," the blood-skinned demon snarled.

"You really don't know any other lines, do you?" Abby said.

The human-faced demon shook her again. She flailed her legs to offset the whiplash.

The gargoyle crouched and tilted his head up at the demons. The golden streetlight caught in his eyes, a pure dark red, the same color as the transformed demon, but they didn't glow with hellfire. That was slightly promising, but not any true indication of whether he was friend, foe or enemy's enemy. Not all the gargoyles of Meridian were Cabrera-carved, and even if they were, that didn't necessarily make them good. Their place in the angelic-demon pantheon was still a bit hazy to her.

"You really want to let the women go. They're not worth the bad day you will have if you don't," the gargoyle said.

"Piss off, traitor." The blood-skinned demon lunged, claws out to rip stone as though it were putty.

Abby tried to touch silver to the human-faced demon's wrist again while the gargoyle distracted him, but he realized what she was doing soon enough to fling her hard against the brick wall.

She cried out again, but not only was her breath stolen, a snap quaked all the way through her. Brick pieces rained upon her as she landed on the alley pavement. The blood-skinned demon slammed into the gargoyle, who barely moved from where his feet attached to the ground. The gargoyle bellowed in response and shoved back against the Luciferian. Both of their mouths were open, sharp teeth bared at each other, but neither backed down. The girl in the human-faced demon's hand screamed as he tossed her over his shoulder to free both hands for tearing but keep his sacrifice close.

Although bits of stone grated from the gargoyle's body when the demons struck him, the blows hardly seemed to faze him. As Abby watched, the empty parts filled in as though there had been no blow at all. Convenient ability, like the way the gargoyle could plant his stone roots into the ground and become a part of it as surely as the gargoyles above were a part of the roof.

Speaking of being attached to the ground, Abby's legs weren't moving.

Well, this sucks.

The blood-skinned demon and the gargoyle continued to trade blows in the uniquely pointless fashion of most demon brawls. It took special magic or specific targets to vanquish immortals, so a vast majority of their violence amongst each other was a fruitless exhibition of strength. Physically speaking, they were equally matched, even when the human-faced demon joined in, and therefore at an impasse while the blonde girl over his shoulder shrieked from her skin burning where the demon's insides had been exposed from Abby's silver knuckles.

In the meantime, Abby had to observe all this from the dugout. On the bright side, now that she was injured and out of commission for any kind of battle, the demons weren't paying attention to her anymore.

On the less bright side, she seemed to be completely paralyzed below the waist, a new sensation for her, in the sense of no sensation at all.

She didn't even feel pain beyond the initial snap, and that had been gone just as fast. All she felt was a whole lot of nothing. In her unofficial line of work, Abby had experienced her share of broken bones. She'd never had a broken spine before.

Keep them busy. Whether the gargoyle wanted to keep the sacrifices for himself or he was trying to rescue them, either one worked in her favor if it gave her some time to get her shit together.

Shit like broken vertebrae and spinal nerves.

Paralysis didn't hurt, but putting the shattered and severed pieces together again certainly did, because then she *could* feel. Abby shouted into her jacket sleeve as she knit her spine back together—an apt comparison, since thousands of knitting needles were currently embedding themselves into her spinal column. She bit through the jacket material and into her arm before the worst of it was over and she could wiggle her toes again.

It was a useful power to have. It wouldn't save her from death, since the healing needed her will to drive it, but it had been a lifesaver at least twice and a body saver the rest of the time. Abby wouldn't do this fool's errand of a hobby saving people if she couldn't heal herself from what the demons did to her ninety-nine-point-nine percent of the time. That point-one percent was going to eventually kill her, but then she wouldn't care anymore.

Abby crawled to her feet just as the gargoyle flared his wings, stabbing the human-faced demon in his broken chest with a bat claw as he kicked the blood-skinned demon's abdomen. The blood-skinned demon doubled over, giving the gargoyle a chance to put it off-balance, tumbling it onto its back. Then the gargoyle drove his foot into the blood-skinned demon's chest, smashing bone and cinder and flesh all the way through. Abby heard the crackle of stone attaching to the pavement on the other end, rooting the demon to the ground. The blood-skinned demon wracked with agony like a live beetle mounted in a shadow box, but it wouldn't kill him. That was the real torture of it.

"Let the girl go or I rip out your brother's heart and feed it to the corvids." The gargoyle curved his wing claws, ready to strike the human-faced demon in less than a second.

The human-faced demon held the girl against his shoulder all the more closely. "There are more important things than survival. You have no idea what you've interrupted, twixt dweller. I may not be able to get this girl to my Master, but I can still score him a victory. I can bleed her out and drink from her beating chalice faster than a wrecking ball could crush you."

The gargoyle plunged his hand into the blood-skinned demon's chest. It writhed against the stone, twice impaling him. "I said let her go. Does it look like I'm bluffing?"

"Neither am I, little bat." The human-faced demon yanked the girl down from his shoulder. Her head hit the pavement, and she crumpled at his feet. "This one is meat for the beast, and if she can't be for my Master, that doesn't mean I'd let good meat go to waste. I'll certainly not hand her over to you."

"Do it!" the gargoyle shouted.

"How did you think this was going to end?" The human-faced demon smiled as he pulled out a sacrificial knife from within his robes.

Then he sliced the girl's belly open.

"No!" The gargoyle stabbed his wing claws at the human-faced demon, but the demon broke through the thin, porous membrane of the wings with one punch. The gargoyle continued to slash at the human-faced demon's features as he ripped the blood-skinned demon's heart out of its chest, which did away with that particular flesh sack.

Abby was more concerned with not rebreaking her back and the way the girl's intestines threatened to spill out onto the concrete. The girl's body shook with pain, even though she was unconscious. Abby crawled over to her to grab her hand and hoped the human-faced demon wouldn't notice her underfoot.

The gargoyle hooked his claws into the human-faced demon's chest, lifted him up, then whipped him against the other wall, which helped.

Abby surreptitiously dragged the girl away. She rested the girl's head in her lap — not because it did the girl any good, but because, in keeping her on her back, the girl's intestines would stay where they were supposed to be.

The gargoyle removed his foot from the blood-skinned demon's chest to face the remaining demon. With the demon to compare, the gargoyle was about human size, but his wings were massive. He had to have amazing strength to hold them up, especially if they were really made of stone and that wasn't just skin texture.

"You don't know who it is you thwart, little bat," the demon said. "A reckoning approaches. You shall be found wanting. Do you even know for whom you fight?"

"A reckoning is always approaching. Apocalypse has been nigh since the beginning. Death is inevitable, devil, even for demons, and I know for whom I fight. Do you?"

With his partner unmoving and mostly dead on the ground, the remaining demon stepped up his assault, but the gargoyle became more vicious, too, and met the second demon and his slyer technique fist for fist, tumbling in and out of shadow and light. If these had been human men, the alley would have been littered with teeth and blood and their faces would already be puffy masses, but here, the mouth of the alley was dusted instead with ash and gravel. Blood trickled like rocky lava through demon veins, and gargoyles apparently didn't have blood to pour.

"Hey!" Abby shouted, clenching her fists where she stood.

The demon paused in his pummeling of the gargoyle and twisted around, although he maintained a grip on the gargoyle's shoulders as he struggled against the wing hooks in his chest.

The demon went rigid when he saw the sacrifice he'd gutted stumbling out into the street, holding her head against the migraine from hell. Abby sympathized, but it was necessary for a headache to dig a hole where her memory of the event had been. The girl wouldn't have to remember any part of this horrible night—a bonus, along with her life.

"That's impossible," the demon said.

"Really? *That's* where your suspension of disbelief fails?"

"I promised you that bad day," the gargoyle said. He met Abby's eyes and, tightening his grip, nodded as she ran toward the demon.

Abby spread her wings to lift herself high enough to push her poisonous silver knuckles against the back of the demon's neck.

The demon bellowed as his flesh and bone dissolved under the silver onslaught. All too soon, the demon's head toppled and rolled to the center of the alley, the face frozen in a mask of shock. Abby pulled back. The silver steamed, but it wasn't hot enough to melt. However, her knuckles felt like they'd been beating a brick wall. She'd only focused on healing her broken back.

Now that the demons were both on the ground and the gargoyle wasn't showing any sign of picking up where the demons had left off, Abby could assess the damage to her person—singed skin, pulled-out hair, bruises on her back, assorted scrapes and scratches that weren't nearly as delightful as assorted chocolates, a swollen cheek, a bloody nose and hairline fractures in her knuckles.

Her fingers took some coaxing to release the silver knuckles. Even then, she cried out at the movement.

The gargoyle's wings billowed like a cape as he tightly furled behind his back once more. He was much less imposing without them outspread. "I'd ask if you are all right, but you seem to have things well in hand."

"I would have been finger food if you hadn't tagged yourself in." She focused on her hands first. Her healing magic was like her wings, a similar charcoal smoke invisible to humans. It curled and wafted over and through her fingers to settle into her skin, with a scent vaguely like a memory of woodsmoke and stone. She closed her eyes as she addressed the injuries to her face, inhaling the smoke through her nose. Then she wiped her bloody but healed nose on her sleeve. Now was no time to be a lady. "Thanks for the help. I think I took on more than I could handle."

"You only say that because you didn't have to handle everything. You were more than capable, had I not interfered."

"What gave my stunning, capable heroism away? The flailing or the hair-pulling?"

"I saw what that demon did to you, yet here you are, with almost no wounds to show for it. I'm only glad to have been of service. It's not often I encounter a human with those kinds of abilities." He shook out his wings, baring the delicate membrane that was still repairing itself like tarmac in a pothole.

Abby reassessed her bodily integrity and found it mostly sound. Anything that still ached tomorrow evening could be dealt with, either with a heating pad and naproxen or a little healing push. It was best not to overtax herself with things her body could fix without her help, aches and pains notwithstanding.

"I'd say I've never met a gargoyle before, but that would be a lie," she said. "However, I didn't know they were alive."

"Alive. How generous." The gargoyle sighed, bringing a hand to his bare, grayish chest. "My heart beats, but I don't know why, because it doesn't move anything through me. I experience the rush of excitement or fear, yet I have no veins for blood to rush through. I endure mind-numbing boredom during the day as I wait for night to fall so I might have a few hours of precious freedom, yet I have no brain. It's all stone."

"It looks like flesh." She nodded to where the gargoyle held his hand against his skin. The stone gave, pliable, as though there was subcutaneous fat and muscle underneath, all the flexible parts that moved over inflexible bone — except his flesh was smooth, occasionally porous where the elements had worn parts of him away that he didn't or couldn't replace. Abby had never seen anything like it. Well, she'd seen plenty like it, since the city was almost literally covered with them, but this was different.

"I can be pierced, yet no blade or bullet can harm me. I crave no sustenance, and I suffer no starvation." The gargoyle crept forward, expression suggesting shyness rather than predation, so Abby remained wary but cautiously optimistic. "As long as the sun doesn't cross the horizon for its rays to touch the stone of my skin, I can move about the city. When I do, I do what I can."

"Sounds nice, fighting without having to worry about dying." She inspected her jeans and jacket. The rips in the knees of her jeans could pass for fashionable outside of work. Fortunately, her jacket had weathered the fight with nothing more than smears of grime and ash. It was a good jacket. Abby could sew her spine together and anything connected to her on the cellular level, but she couldn't use a sewing machine to save her life. That's what discount stores were for, although she'd dropped a little extra on the jacket for durability.

"Immortality is an overrated pleasure," the gargoyle said softly. "And I do have weaknesses, few though they are. However, I am not fool enough to share them with a stranger, even one like you."

"So you feel like sharing your bitterness instead?"

The gargoyle ducked his head with a self-deprecating smile. There it was, the confirmation Abby needed. A demon could play at humility, but they never quite managed it.

"I thought someone as breakable as you, someone who has to mend her own wounds, might understand the disadvantages of imperviousness," he said.

"I guess I do. So, you do this kind of thing often—swooping into alleys to save damsels and gentlemen in distress?"

"What else am I supposed to do with my nights?" he asked dryly. "And you?"

"On my nights off."

She tried to make her hair more presentable, but she thought that if she had a mirror, she'd know for certain it was hopeless until she could get it trimmed. Her stylist was going to have a fit when Abby told her she'd torched it while absentmindedly wielding a straightener, but her stylist would have more of a fit if Abby told her she'd torched it on a demon's brimstone insides. That was the thing about fighting the forces of darkness— It made a person seem clumsy and silly to people who walked in the daylight. If she had a boyfriend, people would probably give him some disapproving glances. There were benefits to being single. When you said you ran into a doorknob or fell down the stairs, people generally believed you.

"Is this your roof?" Abby glanced up at the gargoyles edging the buildings. Now that she'd asked, it sounded kind of rude to make that assumption that just because he was a gargoyle, he had to be one of the gargoyles from up there.

"No. I belong to the church by the cemetery." He pointed in the direction of the FUMC across from her work.

"No kidding. I go by there all the time, and you don't look familiar to me."

"Don't feel bad. I stand there every day, and you're not familiar to me, either," the gargoyle said with a crooked grin. "Although now that I know you, I think I'll notice you."

"Well, I'm not usually there during the day. Maybe that's why we've never run into each other. We keep the same hours. What I can't figure out is how I've lived in Meridian and worked in Cemetery Grove for months, saving who I can, and I've *never* seen anything like you, down on the ground or up in the air. I'm familiar with the angels, but they all seem earthbound. Those wings don't exactly look conducive to flying, though." Abby eyed his textured wings with some skepticism, although she'd seen stranger things than soaring stone creatures.

"No, they don't look it, but I fly as well as you do."

The alley filled with wind like a storm through a breezeway as he buffeted the air with his wings and raised himself from the ground up one story, two, three, toward the rooftops. Abby conjured her wings again but struggled against the relatively dead air he left behind to climb after him.

She dropped onto the flat roof, panting. "For the record," she gasped in a crouch, "these don't work nearly as well as you think. They're not substantial enough to trust over long distances."

Although she'd crashed onto the surface of the roof, none of the other gargoyles on the edge moved to see what was happening behind them, just like most angel statues never moved when she could see them. It was hard to tell whether they couldn't move at all, whether they couldn't when a human was watching or whether they just chose not to.

Obviously, this gargoyle in front of her was an exception — perhaps on all levels.

"I apologize for taxing you. From what I saw, they were good wings."

"They have their moments." Abby rolled her shoulders to shrug off the phantom ache of them now that they had disappeared. "But they're barely more than an idea, better kites than wings. I don't complain. They were pretty darn cool when I discovered I had them. And that's a story you don't get to hear because Mama doesn't like me talking about that day."

"You were a handful, weren't you?"

"You have no idea. I did, however, mean well. Are you sure that those demons didn't hurt you? I can try to fix it my way. I've never tried my healing on de— On people who aren't human before."

"You're being polite," the gargoyle said. "You're wondering if I'm a demon, if I'm to be feared and slaughtered like all the others you have slain in your hunt."

"Actually, I don't hunt. Easy mistake to make when I'm killing things with silver. I'm not much for the slaughter side of things. Most of the time, smoke wings and the silver scare them off, then I get to do my saving bit, which is the part I prefer."

In Abby's experience, when they were seen and recognized for what they were, demons were usually cowards. They derived most of their power over humans from camouflage, darkness, seduction, sneakiness and lies. Confrontation wasn't their strong suit. They preferred to run when a hunter came at them with the accoutrements of the mystical trade. As immortals, many without souls of their own, they feared death more than humans did.

"I won't beat around the bush here, though," she continued. "I *have* been wondering, and I'm still not sure what you are, besides the obvious. But the obvious isn't always right, and deceiving appearances aren't unique to demons."

"I am a demon. Anyone who looks at me knows what I am."

Abby backed away.

"But please... *Please*." The gargoyle gestured Abby to a bench arranged against the roof access. The bench didn't look like the most comfortable place in the world, but the tenants of the building kept the area clean. There was an outdoor ashtray and trash can and everything.

The gargoyle didn't join her, gave her plenty of space to escape if she chose to, but Abby appreciated not having to depend on her legs, which were suffering the shaky aftereffects of adrenaline. Besides, he'd earned the opportunity to explain himself, after saving her and all.

"I'm a demon," he said, "but I am what I am today because I no longer allow my demonic origins to rule me. There are consequences to everything. A demon was once an angel, an angel who made a certain choice. Although not all angels are given the dubious gift of free will, those who do all too often fall. And it was fun—for a while."

He lowered his head, the dark red of his eyes bloody in the shadow.

"But then things changed. I changed. And when I renounced my fall, reparations had to be made. It is much worse for us than for you. Humans must rely on faith, of which they are never certain. Angels have no faith. Those of us with free will who fell did so with the knowledge of what we abandoned. And so I must make my reparations until penance for my grievous error is paid."

"For how long?" Abby was captivated, and not in the same way she'd been with the incubus. No woven spell settled over her head like a sheer veil. The gargoyle really did have a marvelous voice for someone without vocal cords. A bit dramatic, but demons tended to be. They could see the greater scale of good and evil from their perspective — and the weight of even the smaller things.

"I don't know. Whatever the number, it is beyond your conception. It's like trying to imagine what is beyond the universe."

"What *is* beyond the universe, by the way?"

"Did I not just say that you cannot conceive of it?" A small smile belied the tone of irritation. "Some of these" — he swept his hand to indicate the line of gargoyles facing away from them on the edge — "are just stone, adornments only. But some of them are recanted demons. Only a few of them can move, and fewer still can leave their foundations. It's only within the last twenty years that I've been able to wander the world at night. In every state of our stone, we are protectors, guardians. Those blessed to come and go freely in the darkness must fulfill that duty more directly. That's what I was doing when I found you and the demons with their sacrifice. It is what I must do until I reach the next level of my penance."

"Which is?"

"I only know what came before. I cannot see the future as the Creator does."

"You and me both, brother."

"And what penance do you seek?"

"Pardon?"

"The reason why you risk your life and soul to fight demons," the gargoyle said. "You were given gifts, no question, but I sense no calling."

"I told you, I don't fight — or at least I try not to. I'm a rescuer, not a hunter or a soldier. I'm there for the victims, not the ones who make them that way. That's my gift." She held her hands in front of her face, inspecting the flawless skin where her knuckles had been bruised, bloody, broken and slight burned before. "I'm not on the spiritual frontlines. I'm just the nurse. That's what I've wanted to be my whole life, it's what I am now and it's what I try to be in spiritual battles as well as the everyday ones waged inside my patients. *That's* my calling. I'm afraid you kind of caught me out of my element."

"You might have been out of your element, but you did very well. I was impressed."

"Sometimes you have to beat away the bastards to get to the damsel in distress," she said with a shrug. "It can be that way in the clinic, too, and it means I sometimes hate people. I mean, I'm allowed and expected to hate demons, present company excluded, but I'm supposed to love people, and being a nurse can make that difficult."

"What's important is that you continue striving to achieve what is difficult," the gargoyle replied.

Damn if she wasn't blushing, but at least it was dark. "Well, when you put it that way, I sound very noble."

"And if I told you that you were?" The gargoyle glanced at her with his face in odd shadow. While his form was generally human in appearance—with the obvious exception of bat wings—his cheekbones and brow jutted out sharply in stylized grotesque, not quite horns or ridges but close. His ears ended in an elven point, the lobes slightly longer than average, and his canines were longer and sharper as well, like a vampire, although none of the vampires she'd encountered even had smoke for wings. Those little oddities added visual interest in the absence of any accessories against his bald skull, somehow delicate-looking in spite of being made of stone.

Now that she was looking, there was no way to ignore his bare torso above the stone cloth over his waist and thighs. Angels and gargoyles weren't known for being carved with an abundance of clothing or a love of modern fashion, but it took real confidence for a gargoyle with his level of mobility to fly around in the classical equivalent of a kilt.

Which brought up the question of what was underneath. The drape had been carved onto him but moved like fabric, just like his stone skin still moved like skin. Abby guessed he didn't have much in the way of underclothes. That just wasn't how he'd been created.

She'd have to look up at night more often.

"I think you don't know me well enough to say that with any kind of conviction," Abby said. "That, and being treated like some kind of hero is making me uncomfortable."

"True heroes rarely wish to hear they're heroes." He finally joined her on the bench, which groaned under his weight. He wasn't as heavy as an actual hunk of stone, but he was a large man and clearly denser than one. However, the bench held and didn't snap into kindling, which would have made things even more awkward.

"Really, could we change the subject?"

"I do not even know your name," the gargoyle said. "If you don't yet trust me, if you believe I secretly wish to do you ill, you don't have to…"

"Abigail Stone. Abby." She stuck out her hand for him to shake.

He grasped it. "And I am Zekiel."

"Wow. You're so warm." She bit her lip slightly as the way that had just slipped out. "Sorry. It really is like skin, isn't it?"

"At night, despite my appearance, I am flesh, more or less, as much as stone." He released her hand and quickly stood, flustered but concealing most of it well. Abby knew how he felt. "I can clean up the rest of the mess in the alley, but now that we're acquainted, I'd like to ask whether you wish to accompany me tomorrow night to continue this spiritual battle in better company than none."

He asked her to fight demons the way a boy would ask a girl to a dance. She wondered if he'd bring a corsage.

"I can't do tomorrow night," she said. "I'm working. But I can do the next, after two."

His smile out of the shadows and into the moonlight was as beautiful as it was fierce. Abby liked it.

* * * *

When she got home, Abby poured herself a generous glass of Zinfandel. Instead of turning on the shower, she ran herself a bath and dug out one of her bath fizzies from the back of her assigned drawer. Cary had bubble bath in hers, but breaching bathroom drawer trust was even more egregious than taking a soda or swig of milk from another girl's refrigerator shelf. A person couldn't live on bread alone, and Cary and Melody understood that, but the Good Lord forbid anyone touch their bath products.

If Abby could have had her way, she would have turned on some Celtic music and drifted off on the good vibes, but it was five o'clock in the morning and Cary and Melody would kill her if she woke them up with Enya at this ungodly hour.

She'd have to make do with wine, a lavender fizzy and hot water on her aching muscles. New ally aside, it had been a rough day.

She winced at the firework display of bruises around her lumbar vertebrae visible in the bathroom mirror. The slight discoloration around her nose and cheek would fade on its own, but the ones on her back were alarming enough that she reminded herself to tend to them a little more in the bathtub.

As soon as the mirror had steamed over, she lowered herself with a moan into the hot water. The lavender fizzy hissing between her legs, she sipped her wine before lolling her neck against the edge of the bath and closing her eyes.

She steps into the orchard. Thousands of tiny lights glitter from fragrant apple trees, lighting her way. She runs, her white dress like clouds swirling around her legs. Summer warms her skin, and a sheen of sweat cools in the breeze that curls through her hair like fingers. Everything moves in slow motion, and so does her delight, extending until it is an endless sea of excitement stretching in all directions.

The excitement slowly swells into pleasure as she approaches the gazebo, a glowing oasis of white light in the center of the orchard. Under its roof, a swing draped in white rocks back and forth, beckoning.

She is helpless to resist and runs up the steps into the arms of her lover, a dark figure reclined in the swing, waiting for her. He envelops her like a swath of shadow, but that shadow is comfortable and welcome, like the dome stretch of the night sky.

Their lips meet. From within her abdomen rises delicious heat from how good it feels to be with him, more profound than simple arousal. They fit, his firm chest against her full breasts framed in the thin cotton of the dress and without the bra she usually wears. Her nipples press against the material, and as he draws her over him, they rub against his chest as though just as desperate for his touch as she is. Only he can touch her just right. Only he can pluck the strings of her pleasure and make her sing. Only he can draw such tension to an exquisite peak before taking her through the climax of the song that he conducts.

Every part of her body yearns for him, seems to reach for him – her breasts and their painfully tight nipples, her swollen, sensitive clit and labia as she cants her hips against his, against what burns her skin so sweetly.

All this with just a kiss, his hands chivalrously at her waist and lightly stroking her back. He hasn't even touched her exposed skin. But she slides her palms under his black sweater and strokes up his hard, hot body. His strength entices and excites her more. She straddles his waist, riding her filmy skirts up her thighs to expose the length of her legs to his gaze when she withdraws from the devastating magic of his kiss.

She whimpers the more of his torso she reveals, the more she touches. She cannot get enough of the softness of his skin over the hardness beneath. She knows that his cock will be the same. Her hands seem to hunger for it, but she tantalizes herself instead with his chest. Then, when she pulls his sweater over his head as he looks up at her like a goddess, she shifts her attention to the impressive muscles of his arms.

He clasps his hands and holds them over his head to present the whole length of his upper body and the care he puts into it to her warmer and warmer gaze. The longer she observes, the longer she touches, the greater her need, the greater her desire to be fulfilled. But he always fulfills the promise that remains unspoken between them. He always satisfies. However long she can hold back, the moment of release will only be sweeter.

"My honeysuckle beauty," he murmurs, breaking the stretch of his repose to caress her cheeks, brushing his fingers over her lips. She gasps, her head falling back, and he strokes her lower lip with his thumb, pressing slightly inside. She meets his gaze then and closes her lips around the tip, hollowing her cheeks to suck hot and wet around it. He shifts, the erection in his trousers noticeably uncomfortable in its confines.

Her father would be outraged if he saw her like this, if he knew what she did with this man, the things he sometimes told her to do, the things she sometimes did without being told. She hadn't had him between her legs yet, but oh, he knew every inch of her mouth and had taken her there as well. She'd memorized every ridge of his pulsing cock with her tongue.

It wasn't just what he did with his cock that she couldn't share. There were so many other things he had done, things that made her feel such lovely shame, her cunt wet and open and desperate for him from just a glimpse of his erection.

This is not what she had set out to become, but every time he touched her, she could be nothing else. And it felt so damn good.

She would die for him if he asked it of her, because she knew he would make it feel better than living.

"I don't ask so much of you yet, sweet thing," he says, although he peers at her through heavy eyelids as he plunges his thumb deeper into her mouth, in and out, in and out. She sucks at him as though he were made of cinnamon and sugar.

When he withdraws, he drags his wet thumb down her chin and neck to her sternum. Her breath catches, and she grinds down against him through their clothing, a broken moan escaping her lips. He takes a detour to the strap of her sundress, which he eases down her shoulder, and she thinks she might come. The fabric folds down over her breast, caught at the hard peak.

She tosses her head from side to side, unable to contain the flood within as he deliberately brings his mouth to her breast, pulls the fabric down to expose her to the summer heat, to his gaze, to his mouth made of sin, that mouth that latches upon *her and swirls pleasure hotter than summer, sweeter than the cool breeze. She shudders, her thighs seizing upon his hips, comes in an explosion from within.*

She wraps her arms around him as the orgasm recedes, then returns like the tide, again and again and again as he feasts upon her, until she's screaming.

But somehow, she knows that through it all, she is silent.

Chapter Four

Most of her job at the clinic consisted of blood pressure cuffs, thermometers, vaccinations and writing things down in a coherent, clear fashion that anyone could read, since Dr. Drobny couldn't write legibly to save a life, including his patients'. He claimed to have poor spatial relations, which was the biggest load of crap. He also claimed he'd been that way since elementary school. Abby deeply sympathized with his teachers.

Given that the clinic had only two nurses and one doctor at any given time — if that — Abby had learned to be a jack of all trades, although she well understood she was the master of none...except for the actual healing. She was pretty sure she had the best specialist beat on that one.

However, the hardest part about being a healer in a clinic was how often she *couldn't* use her ability. On the streets, she could save everyone she got her hands on because they were all the basic equivalent of a random sampling, and she could make them forget about her without repercussions. She couldn't do that with patients who came into the clinic.

For one thing, they had to remember that they'd come in so that they didn't do it again. For another, if people started getting better from their physical and psychological maladies at a hundred-percent rate, the wrong kinds of people would start paying attention to the clinic. Abby didn't want to become the center of an inquest — or an inquisition, for that matter.

Also, healing wasn't an endless resource. It took energy. And if she used too much of it, like last night, she got headaches, nausea — all the markers of a hangover. And that was just as far as she'd taken it in the past, which wasn't far. Trying to heal everyone who came into the clinic would blow her head open for sure.

It was sometimes torture, though, not to heal everyone who came in, to watch some of her patients slowly die and know there was something she could do for each and every one of them, but not all of them at once. She had to choose based on a compass in her gut, and sometimes she didn't know whether the gurglings down there were from the Good Lord or just the tacos she had on the way to work.

But the one thing they were? Random. They weren't based on whether she liked the person, although the fact that she couldn't — didn't — heal her favorite people every time made her sick as she watched them suffer. She attended their funerals only when she could get herself out of bed for five minutes after crying for hours. Having a gift didn't mean everything came up roses for her or everyone she touched.

Take Mary Margaret Sanders, for instance, who was presently tolerating the blood pressure cuff with aplomb in spite of the suspicious glance she gave it every time she came in.

A lovely lady when she was on her medication, she lived five blocks down in an alley with four other people with whom she squabbled over territory. The Cemetery Grove clinic provided her with 'sample' medication for the schizophrenia—when they had it, and the clinic's supply was unreliable, given that the clinic's income was unreliable. Donations and grants didn't cover nearly enough, and only a tiny fraction of the people who came in had insurance. A tinier fraction of those who didn't have insurance could afford to pay their bills. Most tried, but the clinic had been set up in this neighborhood precisely to serve those who couldn't afford to go anywhere else.

They recommended the ER for the really big emergencies, but most people were in states of emergencies that they couldn't pay for, or their emergency wasn't urgently urgent so much as depressingly chronic—cancers that would never be treated, only managed, infections where the nurses could only tell people to take antibiotics, keep an eye on it and go to the ER if limbs started dying off, or people like Ms. Sanders, with her on-again and off-again delusions and hallucinations, the severity of which was based entirely on whether she'd been regularly taking her medication...not that the average psychiatrist could tell the difference between her schizophrenia and her second sight.

Abby, on the other hand, could discern between the demons that Ms. Sanders saw when she was off her meds and those she saw when she was on them. That was part of the reason why Ms. Sanders came by the clinic, although Dr. Drobny had warned Abby over and over that it didn't help to indulge Ms. Sanders' delusions the way that she did. But Ms. Sanders was never agitated or violent when Abby humored her, either way. Every time Ms. Sanders left, she was always calm and smiling, cheesy teeth and all.

The pay was absolute crap that Abby could have doubled or tripled by working in a posh retirement home or taking shifts at the children's hospital — or hell, just by taking on more than forty-eight hours a week. Nursing wasn't a flexible profession, so she'd had to accept the job that would give her that flexibility more often than not.

But Abby loved what she did, soul-crushing sadness and all, because she needed to give people hope, a little humanity, even if she couldn't always dole out the healing like she wanted for everyone who walked through their open doors.

"Why do you need the same numbers every time I come in?" Ms. Sanders asked. "You just saw me last week. I didn't get any bigger. I still fit into my wools and my coats and my scarves, don't I?"

"Because I never trust a person to tell me the truth when I ask about their weight," Abby said.

Ms. Sanders cackled. "Smart girl. Next, you're going to have me pee in a cup to make sure I'm not pregnant, right?"

"At your age, probably not, but if you have the burning desire to pass me a urine sample, I wouldn't say no. If you have burning urine that you're passing, then I'd definitely recommend it."

"Nope. I piss just fine. I'd show you, but that wouldn't be nice."

"Much appreciated. Now, how's your med stock, ma'am?" If she'd asked that question with a 'ma'am' tacked on the end back home, she'd get an earful. Down here, she sometimes got an earful if she didn't.

"Could be better. Want to top me off there, missy?" Ms. Sanders pulled out an old amber prescription bottle from her pocket.

"How long has it been empty, Mary?"

"A few days. Hard to tell."

Abby gave Ms. Sanders a knowing stare over her file. Ms. Sanders met it with a stubborn set to her rotting, caving mouth. Abby knew for a fact that Ms. Sanders also helped a few other people who lived near her block with her medication, people who couldn't or refused to come to the clinic. It didn't really help any of them to spread the meds around and miss doses on the regular, but Abby couldn't force Ms. Sanders to keep her pills to herself any more than she could force the woman to take them when she didn't want to.

"Well, you're in luck. We have another two weeks' worth in stock set aside for you," Abby said. "Anything else we need to talk about? Any symptoms that 'you' are having lately?"

"That about covers it. I've been having a cough lately, but it's this damn weather. Haven't seen that much mucus since the snail population up and revolted last fall."

"How about the demons, Mary?" Abby set down the file and sat across from Ms. Sanders. "You had any demon-botherers by your home?"

Ms. Sanders had been off her meds at least a day, but she'd been fairly lucid through the appointment, and when she was lucid, Ms. Sanders was one of Abby's best informants on demonic activity on the outskirts of the Cemetery Grove neighborhood. The homeless were vulnerable not only to crime and the elements, but few missed them when a cult or a demon needed quick organs or blood for a spell, conjuring or sacrifice — or sometimes just food when they weren't picky where it came from.

"Why do you call them demon-botherers, girl? Do you mean they bother demons, or the demons bother me, or they bother me because they're demons, or they bother me because they think I'm a demon? Which I'm not. The whispers tell me I am, but I'm not."

Another good sign, that she could distinguish between what the whispers told her and the truth.

"I mean has anyone or anything come into your territory and bothered themselves up a demon? Or has a demon or two come in and bothered you?" Abby said.

"The ones I can't see, the ones that aren't real? Or do you mean the ones I see that other people think aren't real, but you're just as crazy as I am about them?"

"Second choice."

"You're off the deep end, girl, but I guess it's not much stranger than people who believe God is in the sun," Ms. Sanders said. "We've had a few red robes running through the alley. They look like priests — or altar boys dipped in blood. And sometimes, when I'm supposed to be sleeping but see them go by, something large walks through behind them. I don't see what it is, but not because it's not there. I don't look. I don't want to see."

"You don't have to see," Abby said gently. "But do you only hear it?"

"I seen its shadow," Ms. Sanders whispered, leaning in as though to tell Abby a secret. Her breath was bad, but Abby had become accustomed to foul smells from both her jobs. "It reaches the top of the second-story windows. It lumbers through, but I don't look, because

I don't want to witness that kind of evil." She crossed herself, although she was Lutheran. "This ain't one of the ones that I never see, the ones that you tell me aren't real. I wish this one weren't real, either."

"These altar boys in robes, do they wear anything other than the red robes? An amulet or stole? Or are their robes embroidered or dyed with a mark on them?" She thought of the man with the two demons. With the exception of the headdress—which didn't have a denomination, to her knowledge—the demons had been dressed in black but otherwise normal clothes. She hadn't seen enough of the man who'd been with them to determine anything but the color of his robes, but maybe Ms. Sanders had seen more. If red robes alone were a pattern, Abby didn't recognize it, and she certainly hadn't witnessed anything large enough to lumber.

"I didn't see nothing." Ms. Sanders clamped her mouth tightly shut and crossed her arms. Abby knew she wasn't going to get anything more out of her.

She didn't keep Ms. Sanders sick on purpose in order to maintain this particular line of information. On the contrary, Abby suspected that the reason why her gut never told her to help—no matter how loudly her mind and heart told her to—was *because* Ms. Sanders was still a valuable source of intel, which was the worst feeling. But there was no guarantee that in curing her schizophrenia, Ms. Sanders and the rest of the world would even realize that she was cured. Psychic abilities had been all too often misdiagnosed. Her mind would have cleared, but all the demons and monsters would remain, and perhaps nothing at all would change except for that clarity.

Abby could only trust that whatever drove her gifts in this particular lane knew what they were doing.

"All right, Ms. Sanders. Tell Jaspreet to get you your sample refill. I wish we could give you more, but we really can't."

"Don't worry, girl. We all get by with what we have. It's the holidays. Get yourself a latte or a fruitilicious or whatever they're calling those froofy drinks today." Ms. Sanders climbed down from the examination table. "Something hot — and think of me."

"I'll do that."

Ms. Sanders spread her arms and wrapped them around Abby's waist before she could respond. "Thank you for believing me," she whispered. "No one ever believes you when you're crazy, even when you're telling the truth."

"Tell me about it. Try to stay warm."

When Abby had first earned her trust, Ms. Sanders had directed her toward a very confused Anglicized Kali cult forming in the warehouse district a month ago. Then she'd informed Abby about a dracul — not a dragon of medieval lore but an actual hellfire dragon demon — passing through the city looking to wreak havoc. He'd taken human form, but his disguise had been useless against Ms. Sanders' unique neurological state when she wasn't hallucinating. Then there had been the five loner demons that Ms. Sanders had given her one at a time, the ones who'd believed that the homeless population was an easy all-you-can-eat buffet. In each case, Abby had sent anonymous tips to local demon hunters. Then she'd made sure to be hidden but on hand for the victims whenever she could.

And that was just in Ms. Sanders' territory. It was all too easy for Abby to get overwhelmed by all the things she had to accomplish, all the people she had to save. She often had to remind herself that she wasn't trying to save the world. She wasn't watching harbingers and battling demons for the purpose of extermination.

Not least because it was impossible. Not even a highly sophisticated secret society that infiltrated all levels of the world's infrastructure could do anything to eradicate the big man on hell campus, nor could they stop the real Apocalypse, the one with a capital A — the end of the world to end all ends of the world. They could stop the little ones set in motion almost every day by ambitious demons seeking to cripple humanity, but the Last Battle was never intended to be won by those with souls. Humans were the battlefield, not the soldiers, and Abby wasn't going to make a bit of difference in that outcome.

All she could hope for was to rescue a few people and help them live a little longer to make a tiny difference in the lives around them. She'd wanted to save people, save them from suffering, long before she'd learned about her healing powers.

She remembered her daddy lying on the couch while she pulled play medical equipment out of a plastic doctor's bag. She would knock his knee with the reflex hammer, then listen to his heart with her stethoscope. Her mother had eventually needed to hide the bandages to keep her from using them to fix every imaginary boo-boo.

Once she'd found out about her powers, it had only confirmed that this was what she'd been created for.

Still, the account of a red-robed cult moving into the north side of Cemetery Grove was disquieting and deserved a looksee. She'd have to ask Zekiel whether he'd heard any bushes rustling in that neck of the city. If it was a group of people or demons involved, she could definitely use his help.

It was nice to have a demon-hunter ally in this city who she didn't have to hide from. Most of the people in the hunting business tended to be action-oriented, Type A personalities, some natural leaders and some natural loners—neither of which Abby cared to hang out with on a regular basis. They tended to treat people like Abby as pit crew rather than actual people. They also had no sympathy for those who chose not to fight the same kinds of battles. Much as she valued their work, she preferred to maintain her anonymity with them.

Zekiel was different.

All the demon hunters she'd known before had been categorically human. As a demon himself, he could have been as cynical and jaded as every other hunter she'd met, but as an ex-demon, Abby guessed he had more reason than anyone to believe there could be light in the darkness, that what a person—human or otherwise—did could make a difference and that the fight was worth it.

Abby might not have always taken up a sword herself, but she believed the same.

As far as the description of the cultists, red robes weren't enough to go on. Most demon cults tended toward red, black and gray, occasionally purple or green. No one could accuse them of being original. Then again, demons weren't all that original, either. They'd been writing things in blood, desecrating the sacred, committing sacrifices, conjuring vermin, making scratching noises, murmuring in the walls, hiding in shadows, screaming things in dead languages and making inappropriate sexual advances for what felt like forever.

It was possible that if the cult had a symbol either on an accessory or anywhere on the robes, Ms. Sanders just hadn't seen it. She hadn't been looking that closely, and her vision wasn't the best. But the symbol declaring their allegiance could have also been hidden, an amulet worn under the robes or an image tattooed to their bodies. Either way, investigation was necessary before running in guns a-blazing or before pointing other hunters in the right direction.

Abby finished her notes in Ms. Sanders' file and stored it in the cabinet.

The waiting room wasn't exactly full. They were an all-hours clinic, but after midnight—even in a neighborhood like this, where some of its inhabitants were nocturnal by necessity—things usually slowed to a steady but trickling flow, regulars checking in rather than dire emergencies.

She should have gone out to the waiting room and called for the next person, but she sat on the examination table for a moment before putting out new table paper. Her back hurt, her head felt as though it had been stuffed with cotton balls and she was tired… always tired.

Work never stopped. In spite of how fulfilling it was and how she needed to keep doing it, it always seemed to take more than it gave.

* * * *

After a twelve-hour shift, Abby sometimes went on complete autopilot. It wasn't until she reached the Threshold door that she realized where she was.

She was so muddled that she hadn't gone to the cemetery like she'd planned, but now that she was here, it was hard to turn back. She hadn't promised her father a tomorrow — or anything, really. And for some reason, facing him again made her nervous. With her tired enough to make it all the way to Threshold without any sense of where she'd been during the walk, she'd leave herself too vulnerable to questions he might have for her that could lead to outrage. The man would probably wrap his hand around her wrist and never let go. Unlike Zekiel, her father *was* stone in his transfigured form, and she was pretty sure she wasn't strong enough to shatter him.

Now the question was whether she should enter Threshold, knowing that Charles and those who'd witnessed their altercation might be there again.

Under the OPEN sign on the door was a faux woodcut poster that read, "It's five o'clock somewhere." And it was five o'clock right now. The sun was just on the wrong side. Abby was pretty sure Miranda had sold something important to some kind of entity so she never had to sleep.

Abby was half tempted.

She pushed open the door and strode to the bar to climb onto her stool. She wasn't going to let an incubus intimidate her away from her watering hole of choice. Abby smiled at Miranda and raised her finger from the bar to get a glass of her usual.

"So we didn't scare you off." Charles kept a respectful distance, slipping onto a stool with a chair between them. If she didn't know any better, she'd believe it to be some kind of truce.

"Please." The first swallow of her rum and Coke was nice and zingy. She immediately felt more relaxed and herself. "If jerks were enough to scare me off, I'd have been terrified right off the planet."

"Touché. May I purchase your drinks again?"

"Glad you asked this time. Absolutely. If the jerk wants to pay, I never say no. As long as it's clear you're doing it out of the generosity of your heart and not for what I can do for you later—'cause I don't have a price like that."

"Of course." Charles put twenty down on the bar and passed it to Miranda.

"And certainly not that price," Abby muttered.

Honest folk often had to scrounge to save, but Abby had never met a poor demon. They always seemed flush with something valuable, even when they resided in modest dwellings. Sometimes a lavish home just wasn't their personal vice.

There were perks to being evil.

"Have you ever given thought to the price you would accept?" Charles asked. "Purely hypothetical, of course. I don't plan on filling out a blank check."

Abby considered her drink for a few minutes. He didn't rush her, nor did he fidget as she thought.

"It doesn't come down to price," she finally said. "I mean, part of it is about the money, but it's also circumstances. If it's not a person's aspiration to become a working girl, it's usually a matter of not knowing what else to do or being forced into it, but I assume we're talking voluntary here, and I just don't see myself in those circumstances. I've got people. I've got a safety net. I have an in-demand profession. That means if I did decide to sell myself, it'd have to be for more than a million dollars—and still not to you. What point is a million dollars if I don't live to see it?"

"Fair enough. How was your night?"

She looked up from her drink. "What are you doing, man? I mean, really, what's the game here? There's got to be a reason you're doing this."

"Doing what?" His innocent expression didn't fool her for a second.

"Talking to me. A demon doesn't just get up one day and think, 'Oh, that girl looks nice and interesting. Let's get to know her as a person.'"

"Sometimes I wake up in the evening with a craving for pizza. Why can't I crave to know a person?"

"Because you don't interact with humans unless you think you can corrupt them. And in here I'm not going to make a deal of it. It's what you are, fine, this is the place to come as you are. But give me one reason I should open myself up to your corruption instead of telling you to get lost."

"Why would I want to corrupt you, sweet thing? You're already corrupted."

"What the hell is that supposed to be mean?"

"I wouldn't have said it if you hadn't opened the door," he said mildly.

Abby spread her hands, at a level of what-the-fuck that transcended indignation. She was human and supposed she had the same seed of sin inside her as anyone, but that didn't irreparably corrode her soul.

"I've upset you," he said.

"And you're doing it on purpose."

"Believe it or not, Abigail, demons sometimes just do things they *want* to do. It's not all a grand plan, some great conspiracy about the state of your grace. I like riling you up, because your eyes get this quality... But I didn't set out to bring up your origins. You told me not to. You seem intent on talking about it, though, so perhaps it isn't me you're so irritated with."

"I'm pretty sure it is."

"Then, by all means, have your drink and I'll stop irritating you, little pearl." He slid off his bar stool.

She almost grabbed his arm to stop him from leaving, but she caught herself just in time. "No. Now you got things started, and I want to know why you think I'm corrupted. Not corruptible, but already corrupted."

She really should let him go, drink her drink and just forget about him, narrowly escape from his interest. But sometimes demonic lies were rooted in truth, which made them even more potent. The trouble was untangling one from the other, if there was anything to untangle.

Charles slowly eased back into his seat. "You sure you really want to hear this?" Even when his mouth was serious, his eyes never lost their smile.

"This is about my father, then."

"On the nose, love."

"I already told you, he's an *angel*. His blood wouldn't corrupt me. I don't think it particularly blesses me either, but it gave me gifts, abilities for the general good. That doesn't sound like corruption to me."

"Your gifts are neutral, no more good or evil than your nose or your hair," Charles said.

"I'd call it a curse if it were bad. Gifts are good things."

"You've never received a gift you wanted to return? How lucky you must be."

Maybe it was her exhaustion meeting the rum, but he had her there.

"Your daddy isn't an angel," Charles said. "He *was* an angel. He fell to earth, so he's nephil. There's no getting around it, love. I am what I am, a nephil who became an incubus. I can't tell you what he has or will become, but what I do know is that he's fallen, otherwise he wouldn't have been able to breed with your mother. There are rules, Abigail. He broke them. The price for copulation with the earthbound locals is to damn yourself."

Charles swiveled around so that he rested his crossed arms on the bar. Even his smiling eyes were sober now — happily sober.

"I can't believe that," Abby said.

"It's not a matter of faith. It's fact. Your father made a choice, just like the rest of us."

"No." Her father was in a cemetery watched over by angels. He wasn't a grotesque or a gargoyle. He looked like the man she'd known, just with wings where before he'd had nothing but smooth skin over his back. He wasn't fallen. He wouldn't have done that to himself, damned himself for just ten short years as a human.

"Your father wouldn't happen to be made of stone these days, would he?" Charles asked.

"What the hell do you know about it?" Her face flushed, the skin prickling underneath, and her eyes hurt.

"I know you love him very much. And I would like to have known your mother. If she was anything like you, I think I might understand why an angel would fall for her. Shhh, love."

He reached across the gap between them, brushing the hot, awful, humiliating tear down her right cheek with his glove. He didn't hit her with the full impact of his charm, keeping his promise not to touch her with his bare skin, but she still closed her eyes, gasping against it and struggling with the obstruction in her throat that pricked like an arrowhead whenever she swallowed.

"But he left her behind, didn't he? Only ten years — not even a grain of sand in the vastness of an angel's lifetime. Not many years for a human, either. He only had ten years with her. How many did he have with you? Seven? Eight? Then he disappeared. And in his absence, a gaping hole right here." He tapped her chest over her jacket, neither lingering nor trying to cop a feel in the process. "Tell me, Abby. Does goodness leave this kind of damage behind? This kind of ache?"

Lord help her, she couldn't answer.

She knew so little of what her father was. Her mother had known that her father was an angel before he'd disappeared, but Abby hadn't known until her mother had told her, after her father had been bound to a cemetery closer to home. And when it came to research, there was far more information about demons than angels, because angels tended not to manifest on the mortal plane, whereas demons made that plane their playground.

Many things took fathers away from their daughters other than being whisked away by mystical forces to serve as a stone cemetery angel. War, disease, random chance, chaos, conquest…

"Does goodness leave this kind of damage behind?"

Charles tilted his head to maintain eye contact as she leaned over the bar, weighted by the emptiness in her chest that she'd thought had closed up with scar tissue and purpose. "You don't have to answer me right now. It's a lot to take in. And I might be able to help you with that, if you'd like."

"How the fuck can you help?" She managed not to break into sobs in the middle of the bar, but suddenly feeling thirteen years old again did nothing for her state of mind. That hadn't been the most wonderful time in her life—a time of feelings too big for her small body, of awkwardness, of physical changes in asymmetric fits and bursts that she'd never been quite ready for, of questions that had swelled against her skull without answers to relieve the pressure.

She was twenty-seven, for heaven's sake. She was supposed to have left that all behind. But the past had a way of trailing like the frayed remnants of a worn dress, tripping her when she—or someone else—stepped on the train.

"Whether you accept it or not, you have a little demon in you," Charles said.

"And you want to see if you can put a little more demon in me." She sniffed back her feelings and clenched her teeth. "Fat chance."

"In a matter of speaking, and I don't mean in the delightfully literal way."

"Then lose the cryptic. Tell me what you want. That's all I needed to know in the first place."

"I want you to come home with me."

"What kind of brainless do you think I am?"

Charles continued as though she hadn't spoken. "Once we have a little privacy, I want to help you learn more about what you are."

She scoffed. "I'm insulted that you really believe I'm that gullible."

"My most potent feeds are when they're unconscious, Abigail, and I don't want you unconscious for this. The moment I met you, I could see your spirit, love. It's rich and powerful and just itching to be released, because you only know half of what you're capable of. I'd teach you the other half right here in Threshold, but I don't think you'd be any more comfortable showing them" — he gestured to their surreptitious audience — "what you've never allowed yourself to know than you're comfortable showing them your tears."

God above, he was working his charm on her. It didn't feel like it. She didn't experience the surge of pleasure, a shiver under her skin, the way she did when he touched her through clothing. But he had to be using it, because now she was confused. Confused, because for the first part of her life, she'd been the daughter of a mother and father, and the rest of it, she'd been the daughter of a mother and an angel. But now she wasn't sure that was entirely true, either.

Which meant all these things she'd thought had come from God — the calling, the power, the gifts, the premonitions, the blood in her veins that carried her father with her — might not have come from God at all. She'd believed herself on a holy mission, but what if she'd been on the wrong track this whole time?

"Let's not make a scene," Charles said. "Come with me. We don't have to go far. I live just upstairs."

"You live above Threshold? Seriously?"

"I like it here. It's mere minutes away from the nightlife if I'm not interested in other people's dreams. I can commute just about anywhere, and anywhere I live, I'm close to a food supply. Might as well live where I want."

"I'm still not naïve enough to leave Switzerland to go into a private residence with you," Abby said. "You like dreams? All you have to do is slip me a roofie or knock me unconscious. Voilà, microwave dinner."

"I've already had my meal tonight."

"Oh, wonderful."

"I'm not going to touch you if you don't want me to," Charles said.

"And I'm supposed to believe you just because you say so."

Charles smiled, sat back and pulled off his glove. "I'll give you a blood oath."

Abby hesitated.

Demons were deceptive assholes. There was no getting around it. They lied, cheated and stole to get their opportunistic selves where they wanted and with whom. They had few scruples, and those they had were enforced upon them, because demons had rules like humans did. Demons just had different rules.

An experienced demon conjurer could paint all the right symbols and call forth a demon who couldn't escape past the lines of the circle, no matter how violently the beast raged.

Demons could pass through the walls of a church, but they cowered from spiritual conviction. The two weren't necessarily connected.

When someone exorcised a demon by its name, it had to leave the host.

And when a demon gave a blood oath, they had to abide by it.

Demons didn't give blood oaths lightly. They weren't like legally binding contracts. There were no loopholes. When a demon gave a blood oath, they swore to uphold the spirit of the oath, not just the letter. If Charles did this, he wouldn't even be able to touch her through her dreams.

Basically, he was promising not to feed on her without her permission, period, and there wasn't any chance of her giving permission. He might believe that he could wear her down until she begged for his touch, but she was prepared against his charm now.

"I'm only going to do this if you promise to go upstairs with me." Charles held up his finger and brought it to his mouth. As Abby stared at him, stunned, his needle-sharp incubus teeth curved over the human ones. They were good for gripping and reminded her of nonvenomous snakes, the kind that bit and didn't let go.

"Mind if I chime in?" Miranda wiped down their part of the bar with a washcloth as an excuse to speak softly near them. "He swore the same oath to me. It was the only way I'd let him take up residence. I've been up there before. It was completely safe, aside from the earth shattering. That man can take you places like a spiritual awakening."

"I'm not sure that helps." Somehow, it didn't imbue Abby with confidence that Charles had done this before. Actually, it kind of cheapened it for her, if she had to acknowledge her vanity. But Charles was a lust demon. If she was going to do this, she'd have to be okay with the idea of sharing.

"I only want to help," he said. "Demons do that sometimes. You'd be surprised. We're not all about apocalypse and destruction, you know. And those of us who are hybrids like you... We take care of our own."

That wasn't entirely true. Demons were just as racist and species-ist as humans, which was either a greater indictment against humanity or some kind of humanization of demons. Abby wasn't sure which was worse. However, she'd witnessed cults and nests sacrificing themselves for their own or their allies. They were just as prone to martyrdom as human zealots.

Abby couldn't shake the feeling that this was all an elaborate trap, Miranda's endorsement included, but she also felt drawn to him — and not just because of his magnetism as a fine specimen of male flesh. The same invisible, indeterminate compass that had led her to accept work in Cemetery Grove also pointed her to Charles — which meant that compass wasn't necessarily a moral one, even though she'd always believed it was, which just made the answers that he offered all the more tempting.

His only condition for giving her a blood oath was going upstairs with him. She could do that, and if she didn't like what she saw or heard, she could leave and his blood oath would still be viable. After all, *she* wasn't promising him anything more.

"Okay," she said. "I'll give you that bone. Make the oath. But the first sign of funny business, you get the funny end of my consecrated blade. Are we clear?"

"And she says she isn't a hunter." Charles bit the pad of his middle finger. In hybrids like Charles, blood rushed much the same as a human's, welling in a bright red bubble.

The whole bar, even the jukebox, had gone quiet.

As the blood slid down, he met her eyes between his fingers. "I promise not to touch you, skin to skin, unless you specifically and consciously request it of me."

Charles slipped his finger into his mouth, sucking off most of the blood all the way down to the base before replacing his glove, obviously not caring if the leather got a little dirty.

She pretended the sight didn't affect her. The quirk to Charles' lips and the sparkle in his warm eyes suggested she fooled no one. He'd elicited exactly the response he'd intended, and he hadn't needed to touch her for that.

"Follow me." He slid out of his chair and headed for the back of the bar, where a set of stairs led away from the bathroom doors.

Abby swallowed down the rest of her rum and Coke.

Miranda took the empty glass. "Just sit back and enjoy the ride. He's good at giving you what you need, not just what you want. Man's practically psychic."

"You know what he is, right?"

"Means he's more than capable in bed—and out of it. Whatever tickles your toes."

"Usually means he kills women in their sleep, too," Abby said.

"But not you. He doesn't just give those kinds of exceptions away."

Abby was halfway off her seat before pausing again. "What did *you* learn from him?"

"That's between me, him and the Goddess, hon."

Chapter Five

Charles lived on the third floor over the bar.

He pushed open the door to what could have been anyone's living room, kitchen and eat-in nook, with screens to cover the bedroom and a balcony with a view of the skyline over the building across the street — not a million-dollar view, but it wasn't cheap. The room itself was clean, dressed for functionality and comfort within a subdued gray-to-blue palette common among men who feared the complexity of coordination, although Charles had already proved himself comfortable with a daring color or two.

"Would you like something to drink or eat? It's free of charge up here." Charles took off his coat and hung it on the coatrack near the entrance, then gestured for her to do the same. She did so with some reluctance, reminding herself that she didn't have to worry about him taking advantage of the lower neckline of her shirt. She'd changed out of her scrubs today, but she was still in her usual casual-practical chic with a long-sleeved knit and jeans, because who the hell was she trying to impress at five o'clock in the morning?

"Water would be nice," she replied.

He even had inexpensive but serviceable water glasses. She'd really appreciate if there was something in this apartment representative of what he was. At least in Threshold, there were other demons in their true physical forms to remind her that some demons wore human faces. But everything about his place and him in it was just so fucking *normal*.

"Have a seat wherever you like," he said.

Abby doubted 'wherever' included the mini-chandelier over the small dining table, but she decided to sideline the snark for a few minutes and settled into the armchair adjacent to the couch. That way, Charles couldn't inch nearer to her and try to get his arm around her or put his hand on her thigh like a horny teenager.

He handed her the glass and slouched on the sofa with the carelessness he almost always exuded, fraught with none of the anxiety that Abby experienced being alone in an incubus' home.

She slipped her hand inside her purse to find her mace.

"You won't need whatever weapon you think makes you safe." Resting against the back of the sofa showed off the lean lines of his body through his blue plaid shirt and dark jeans, drawing the clothing tight against his chest and thighs and calling attention to the muscle beneath. "If I wanted to kill you, I would have done it already. I think I've explained well enough that I have no interest in hurting you, at least not more than you ask for."

"If you think I'd ask for it, you've lost your mind."

Charles shrugged. "All hunters have a masochistic streak."

"I'm not a hunter."

"So those bruises on your face and back aren't from fighting demons?"

"How the hell do you know about the ones on my back?"

"Incubi aren't so different from vampires. We share a good sense of smell for blood, where it flows and where it congeals."

"I only fight them when I have to," she said. "I had to. But I'm not looking for demons to kill like hunters do."

"Your intentions are irrelevant. Your actions make you a demon hunter. You still put yourself into these battles, over and over, regardless of the consequences. And part of you welcomes those consequences." He raised his hand before she could protest. "I don't blame you, love. Nothing like war wounds to remind you that you're alive. Admit it. We're all alone here, no need to keep up a saintly appearance. Admit you get a thrill out of the hunt, the heroics, the hurt...the whole package."

Abby withdrew her hand from her purse, which she set on the ground near her feet. It was a gesture of trust — trust she didn't actually have, but she *wanted* to believe him when he said he wasn't going to harm her here. "All right. Fine. I get a thrill — the same thrill I get from working night shifts at the clinic. It's fulfilling because it's the right thing to do."

"Long hours on your feet, putting yourself at risk of disease with sometimes dangerous individuals, then spending your free time engaging with beings indistinguishable from the monsters of fairy tales, monsters who have no problem pulling your head off your neck like clipping a flower off a bush... If that's not masochism, I don't know what is." His smile was abnormally bright in the dimly lit room. He'd turned on the kitchen light to get her water but kept all the other lights off. Perhaps he preferred the dark, nocturnal creature that he was.

"I think it's a stretch to go from personal fulfillment to sexual masochism." Just because a person worked herself to the bone doing one thing, that didn't mean she wanted to be worked to the bone in another area — just like a person enjoying something spicy at the dinner table didn't necessarily indicate that they'd like something spicy in the bedroom.

"Have you ever tried?" he asked.

"I wasn't interested. I attended a few workshops with my college roommate, but that's it."

"You didn't volunteer?"

"No. I said I wasn't interested."

He narrowed his eyes like a cat. "Hmmm. I'm not usually wrong about these things. In fact, I'm *never* wrong about these things."

"Whips, chains, switches, spankings... I'm okay with other people doing it, but the whole thing makes me uncomfortable, historically speaking. It doesn't turn me on at all."

"Arousal shouldn't be a problem, but that's not what tonight is going to be about." Charles leaned forward with his elbows on his thighs, peering up at her. "Tonight is about what you think demons deserve. You go out hunting them and never stopped to consider what *you* were. Whatever you're fighting against in them, you're fighting it in yourself as well — and you don't even know what it is."

Aurelia T. Evans

"Just a guess...evil?" Abby said. "It's not like it's exclusive to demons, and I know I'm not perfect."

"But you believe yourself closer to perfect, as the daughter of an angel—blessed."

"I wouldn't say that." Figuring out her purpose didn't make her perfect, just satisfied.

"Sometimes *I* did when I was younger, a long time ago. I'm older than I appear—far older—and my father wasn't just nephil. My blood's not as diluted as yours. He'd already taken his demonic form—masked from my mother, of course. He was an incubus, planting his seed. He didn't need my mother to provide an egg. He just needed her to nourish me through the few months it took her to quicken, nurse me, raise me in the scandal of giving birth out of wedlock, then guide me into adulthood before he could show me what I truly was. I was *his* fruit, not hers, although I took on her family's appearance through my youth and embraced it the rest of my life as a demon, because it is familiar to me."

Charles stroked down his cheek, black leather dark against his paler skin.

"My mother raised me like a cuckoo in the swallow's nest. I only had the barest understanding that I was more than I appeared. But I knew some of it, even before my father unlocked the demon in me. When I touched another..."

He breached the space between them and put his hand on her knee for a few long moments.

Abby forced herself to stay absolutely still in spite of the sweet pleasure of his touch, like a burst of fragrant heat from an oven on a winter night. She could only imagine how potent it would be when there weren't layers of leather and denim in his way.

92

"I believed it was a blessing, too," he said quietly. "I had a wife when my father took me away from human life. I thought she was what this gift was for, to allow me the luxury of choosing the most perfect mate, whomever I desired, in exchange for this prize."

Abby thought of the woman that Charles had taken in holy matrimony, only for him to one day disappear, not knowing where he had gone or why and fearing the worst. Abby knew that feeling. "Do you miss her?"

"I did, for a time. She died. I didn't."

"You didn't love her. You just got what you wanted from her. Do you even know how to love?"

"I've had so many lovers since her that I lost count."

"Please. I'm not counting all the people you seduced in their dreams or who you lured into your lair with a touch just to suck all the sexual vitality out of them."

"That does narrow the field a bit," Charles said, amused. "But even without those discards, I have still had a fair number of lovers since. And there was a time when I thought I was human, as well, and I thought what I had then was love. I learned better after I changed. You speak of fulfillment. We serve a purpose, too, you know. Without demons, there is no sin. Without sin, there is no salvation."

"I don't think that's a get-out-of-jail free card to do whatever you want."

"Are you sure?" He swept to his feet, the movement graceful and surprising as he loomed over her, sliding his hand under her jaw to guide her head up.

Heat sluiced down her body as though she'd stepped straight into a hot shower that warmed her from the inside. She whimpered before she could stop herself.

"Don't you want to know what you're meant for? What you're capable of?"

Abby jerked her chin away from his hand. "I already know what I'm capable of. I started healing myself at thirteen, other people at sixteen, but I've wanted to be a nurse since I was five. I've known what I was meant for before some people stop sucking their thumbs."

"Is that why you're trolling the streets with little more than trinket weapons in your purse?" Charles asked. "I'd think that battle is the opposite of your supposed calling."

"I hurt the demons to stop them from hurting other people. Sometimes I get hurt in the process. Acceptable collateral damage, since I can heal most of it."

"Not all of it?"

"I have limits."

"I don't." Charles gestured to the screens that separated his bedroom from the living room. The screens moved on their own, collapsing to the side to reveal the whips, canes and switches hanging on the wall across from the bed. A foursome set of chains had been attached to the wall adjacent to the beating implements. A double set hung from the ceiling, with the option for height adjustment. Another foursome set were attached to the wrought-iron bed frame—and those were just the ones she could see.

That was more like it, much more demonic. Not intrinsically so, unless her college roommate had had a vestigial tail that Abby hadn't known about, but still closer to what Abby had expected from an incubus' lair.

"I'm pretty sure you do have limits." She practically had to bite her tongue to keep from laughing, because it was all a little cheesy but also not amusing in the slightest.

This was no fantasy dungeon for someone who didn't know what they were doing. The whips and chains were a bit over the top, but they weren't displayed against black velvet with ultraviolet light and a disco ball. They were arranged with the same straightforwardness and lack of reverence as the abstract trio of paintings over his living room couch. They didn't need any additional atmosphere to speak for themselves.

"Okay, I exaggerated a little." He raised a shoulder and smiled. "I do have limitations. But you would be surprised how few."

"I thought this wasn't supposed to be about sex." She deliberately eyed the sadomasochistic diorama in the middle of his vanilla apartment.

"Do you want it to be?"

"Okay, now you're just being manipulative."

"I just think it's interesting that your first assumption is that I have those up there for sex."

"They're in the bedroom and you're an incubus. What am I supposed to think?"

"They're in the bedroom because the bathroom is the only other private room in the apartment, and it's too small for my purposes."

"Don't fuck with me, Charles," she snapped, standing. It didn't give her much more height to keep him from using his as an intimidation tactic, but it gave her a fraction of power for a fraction of a moment.

"I told you it's not *always* about sex—and it doesn't have to be tonight. Tonight isn't about pleasure. You don't want pleasure from me. At least, you don't think you do."

"I certainly don't want pain."

"There's more than one way to cause pain. It may not be what you're looking for yet, but it'll be what you're getting tonight."

"Then what am I looking for?" She crossed her arms and dared him to answer, because even she didn't know what she was doing here anymore. Whether her father was an angel or a nephil was starting to feel irrelevant. She'd managed to have a relatively normal life doing good work these last few years, no matter what her father was. She'd been doing just fine without Charles playing devil's advocate and muddying the waters.

"Answers you thought you had," Charles said. "Life isn't clear, love. It's messy and chaotic and foggy, and that's all *before* your demon nature emerges in full. Things don't come together at twenty-five. They fall apart."

"I'm twenty-seven."

"And a healer." He gently guided her away from the living room toward his bedroom, but she stopped before he could compel her across the invisible line into it. The man was good at what he did, but not that good. Not yet.

He ghosted his gloved fingertips over the tight line of her hair. "Tell me, sweet thing, why is it that I can go by your clinic and don't encounter people praising the Lord for your powers? I should be tripping over the healed. They should be fighting to get in during your shift. Instead, I've noticed nothing different in the neighborhood upon your arrival. We haven't become any more or less popular since you signed on. There are just as many colds and flus and sniffling unwashed as before."

"I told you. I have limitations."

"What kind of limitations?"

"I get headaches. They've never been too bad, mostly because I feel them coming and know I have to stop."

"Interesting." He slowly circled her. She didn't want to have her back to him, but she also didn't want to give him the satisfaction of watching her turn around in circles with him, like a wheel within a wheel. "So you can't use your power indiscriminately, then? You have to pick and choose your beneficiaries. I've seen the element that passes through the neighborhood clinic — so many hopeless cases, so many in need of the assistance only you can provide. But you can't give it to every one of them. And what of the families of those whom you don't help? Those left behind suffering in the absence of the one they loved. Those who lose hope, who lose sanity, who lose faith because God didn't answer their prayer for a miracle — a miracle like you. They mourn because of you, Abigail." He was so close to her now that his breath was warm against her ear.

"It's not my fault." She wished it had come out with the strength of conviction. "I save those I can, the ones I get a feeling about, like a whisper. I just *know* they're the ones I'm supposed to heal. I can't give out miracles to everyone or else they wouldn't really be miracles. *I'm* not the one decides who stays and who goes."

"And what of those you do save? How many of them go out and do terrible things? The father given a reprieve goes home to beat his son. The mother is taken three weeks later by a stray gunshot. The ten-year-old boy succumbs to overdose within the year."

"A bad neighborhood only makes it harder to get help for the same shit that goes on everywhere else.

You know better than that. And you know that there's better here, too."

Charles continued as though he hadn't heard her. "The little boy you heal from leukemia grows up to get into a car crash that starts a chain reaction pileup on the highway. The teenage girl you save goes home and violates her body over and over again until it is possessed not by illness but by a demon, drawn to her despair to fill the empty places you left healed. You save people, Abigail, but I cannot think of a less worthy species to save."

"Someone has to."

"You?" he asked softly. "You heal the physical body. But those whose bodies you save can still give away their souls, while those whose souls can yet be saved are left to die, because you do not heal them. Because you hope that the still, small voice in your heart is the Creator's, that you are a vessel of hope. But how can it be true, when you consider the fruits?"

Abby started to speak, but her tongue had never felt so much like lead.

"Kneel." He didn't have to raise his voice for her to hear the command.

Everything that she was outside of this apartment told her to never kneel before anyone. A person who demanded that she kneel deserved the sharpest rebuke for believing her to be less than they were. But Charles didn't see her as less. He considered her an equal — which made her feel like a slimy oil slick beneath his boots.

He rested his hand against the small of her back, bringing her the last few steps into his bedroom, then turning her around to face him. His touch sent flashes of heat through her, but they were negligible compared to the turmoil roiling within the confines of her skull. His smooth words echoed within, resurrecting rooted worries she hadn't realized she'd buried so deep.

What if all the hours of studying, all the people she'd taken care of and healed, all those she'd had to let go, all the people she'd saved and failed to save, the feelings that she'd followed all these years... What if all of those things hadn't really been to follow in her angel father's footsteps? What if they hadn't been to follow a divine plan for her life?

What if they'd been done in the service of the wrong master all this time, and she hadn't realized it? What if the whispers in her heart weren't from God?

What if all this time it had just been about her?

Or worse?

"Does goodness leave this kind of damage behind?"

"All those people," she whispered, as though they stood before her, ghosts crowded into the tiny apartment to heap her with condemnation Abby hadn't allowed herself to consider.

"Kneel," Charles said more forcefully, squeezing her shoulder—a gesture that would have been almost comforting if it weren't for the wet wool blanket of weight that settled over and inside of her—and not from him.

Abby fell to her knees.

Charles beckoned to the shackles on the ceiling. They slithered down and snaked around Abby's wrists, holding them just over her head. Abby slumped into them, bowing her head as though in prayer, but she hadn't felt farther from grace in her life. There were no words in her mind for prayer, no Word in her flesh.

Had it ever been there at all?

"After everything that you've done, what does a woman like you think she deserves?" He stepped past where she knelt and held out his hand to brush the whips and canes on the wall. "These are just my display. I have more implements in the dresser. I think the whips are more than you might be ready for, but this…"

He paused in front of a sjambok, a black peacekeeper switch with a long rod and leather handle.

"Your clothing will absorb some of the impact, but I think this will do." He lifted the switch from its mount. "And of course, you can end this at any time. I don't do safewords here, love, regardless of what you might have heard about the lifestyle. I know how to handle my instruments. I will give you exactly what you need, hurt you exactly how you deserve. But you can tell me that you've had enough, and I'll stop. I'll end this, release you from your chains and you can walk out of here without the absolution for which you came. You'll have spared yourself pain, but you'll have denied yourself…clarity. Pain, ecstasy and revelation have been closely intertwined throughout history. That is what I offer."

He laid the switch over the swell of her ass where she bent over. With his left hand, he touched her shoulder blades, his hesitancy there almost reverent. "I can't see them, but I…"

Abby shuddered under his fingertips, aware of the picture she presented. Her wrists clinked heavily together as she shifted forward more.

"You are not my slave," he said, as though he read her mind. "Shed all history, love, all sense of right and wrong and God and the devil, wings and horns and tails, angels and demons. We are each other. We are now and no more."

Then the switch descended upon her.

He hit her thighs first. She'd expected it on her ass, so he took her by surprise, hitting muscles that hadn't been tensed in preparation. She cried out, bucking and swaying in her shackles. Charles struck her thighs again, five times in a row. He braced her with his free hand between her shoulders to keep her from swinging too far forward.

He not only rained down a kind of pain Abby hadn't known existed, but through her shoulders, Charles' touch made her wings itch, like feathers trying to grow out of her skin, made her just as aware of the folds of her cunt pressing against the seam of her jeans, her legs slightly parted as though ready for another kind of activity. But that didn't distract her from the switch hitting her where she was softest, where she had meat to hit. Even so, after the fifth blow, tears sprang to her eyes, and she wailed again. He spaced out the blows so that she had the chance to feel the sting every time. She was almost sure the denim had split but didn't feel a cool breeze against her skin.

Then he swung the switch up to her ass, transporting Abby to an older form of chastisement, but this was so much worse. It was supposed to be more humiliating than painful, but this was both, striking just short of her bones, sometimes alternating between sides and sometimes striking both at once.

She tried to wriggle away when he struck her thighs again, but he wouldn't let her. He gave her only brief respite, stroking the length of the switch over the places he'd hit her. Her skin burned under the fabric and stung like an echo when he applied pressure. He was giving her a chance to tell him to stop, to tell him that she couldn't take anymore.

But he massaged his strong fingers into her shoulders and neck and down her spine, and although her face was wet with tears and probably looked an absolute fright, she rocked back and forth, up against his hand, back against the stroke of the switch, out of control against the demands of her body. It wasn't about sex, not really, but Charles was what he was. He could be nothing else, nor could she. Her reaction was undeniable and irresistible, adding another layer to this twisted penance — penance for crimes she didn't know for certain that she'd committed, yet she had to make sure that if she had, she paid.

"Is this what you deserve, Abigail?" He trailed his fingertips down the dip of her spine to spread over the flat part of her back above the waist of her jeans. He pressed down as he swung the switch again. It hissed through the air before slapping soundly on her thighs again.

She surged forward, her yell hitched with sobs. She buried her face in her sleeve both to hide herself and to wipe her nose. Clothes could be washed.

Charles swept his hand back up her spine again just as he struck her lower back. The angle protected her spine but mercilessly hit one of her bruises.

He hit her two more times on her back before she buckled, her lower half flat on the floor to escape from the switch and her upper half arched up by the shackles.

"Stop. *Stop*. Don't. Don't hit me again."

"Is this what you deserve?" Charles stroked the switch over her back again. She thought he might have barely stopped from rupturing an organ. She sent out wisps of healing just in case but found nothing more than new bruises. He'd been telling the truth when he'd said he knew how to keep from damaging her—more than surface damage, anyway.

She gazed up at him. "What do you want from me?"

"Your eyes are so green when you've been crying." He tucked loose strands of her hair behind her ear so he could see better. "And tears make your eyelashes glitter."

"What do you want?" Abby repeated, almost begging this time.

"Do you deserve this?" He brought the switch up and held it between them. He ran the rod against the hollow of her cheekbone. "Or do you deserve this?"

He tossed the sjambok to the side and took her face in his hands, which were still sheathed in their black leather gloves. He guided her back to her knees, although she groaned and winced at the ache that reached all the way down to bone. The stinging left behind from the blows stretched out like a swarm of biting insects amid tendrils of heat.

The lips of her cunt were so swollen with arousal that her jeans were more than a little uncomfortable against her underwear. If she'd been home and unbound, she would have had her clothes off in a second, with the 'marital aid' in the box by her bed put to good use to make the ache go away.

Charles' face was inches from hers, his dark eyes fathomless as he gazed at her lips. Abby wanted nothing more than to kiss him, to lose herself in his charm, let him feed until she fell into unconsciousness and dreamed of him, where he could drain the life from her, but at least it would put an end to his question, because she didn't have an answer, didn't want the answer, feared the answer more than she feared the demon.

"I don't know," she said.

Charles ran the tip of his tongue over his lower lip as though tasting her reply in the air. Abby whimpered. She didn't think she'd ever wanted anything so badly as his mouth against hers right now.

"That's what I wanted, love." His soft voice had gone husky. "I think that's a wonderful place for us to start."

"Us? *Start?*"

"Do you want me to touch you?" He traced her lips with his thumbs, and Abby almost leaned in to kiss him, the very thing her body screamed at her to do. To pull him down and crawl over him so that she didn't have to put any weight on her back, ass or thighs, to rub her hips against his to feel him against the place he'd made so wet for him—ripe and full and slick with nowhere to go.

She couldn't answer him. If she told him no, it would be a lie. But if she told him yes, it would give him permission to end his oath, and she couldn't let that happen. The uncertainty beaten into her wasn't enough to give her a death wish.

Instead, she drew upon every last thread of her will and pulled away from him, resting back on her knees. She nearly sat on her heels but remembered the bruises in time to jerk back up.

"No worries, love." He straightened, his good humor washing over the uncharacteristic solemnity he'd adopted during the beating.

"It didn't even affect you, did it?" she said. "What you were doing to me, it meant nothing to you. Were you just trying to figure out how long I'd go before I wised up?"

"I wouldn't be so sure it had no effect. I won't be applying any precious healing powers to *my* bum, that's for sure, but there are other pressing matters that need attending to." He brought the heel of his palm to the front of his trousers.

Abby didn't know how she'd missed it, eye level as it was. Their respective positions weren't lost on Charles, either, from the way that he gazed down at her through heavily lidded eyes. His erection curved in a bulge to the side of the trouser placket. Her mouth watered as Charles squeezed it through his pants, parting his lips slightly in a sigh.

Abby bit her lip, swayed where she knelt. On the one hand, she should demand that he release her. Then she should go home and metaphorically lick her wounds. Everything would seem better with a glass of orange juice after she got some sleep. This enormous mistake would be nothing but a fading memory. Even without using her healing powers, sleep could be an amazing curative.

For everything but the effect of an incubus, that is. Who was she kidding? This wasn't going to go away in her sleep.

If she couldn't kiss him and he couldn't touch her with his bare skin...

As her cunt fluttered over aching hollowness, Abby nudged his hand away from the outline of his cock. She closed her eyes against the flood of stronger arousal that came from stroking his erection through the denim. He was as hot in her hand as her beaten thighs were against her jeans. It only made sense that his power was more potent here. The simple act of feeling him from base to tip, of gripping the hard cock as well as she could through his trousers, gave her as much pleasure as if they were naked and he were kissing her like she wanted him to.

"Yes, ah…" Charles gasped as she nuzzled her cheek against his cock, moaning before she could stop herself.

Her shackles no longer had any purpose other than symbolic. Perhaps that was why Abby didn't ask him to remove them. They were heavy against her wrists as she held his thighs and rubbed her face over his clothed erection, imagining there were no barriers between them. As her pleasure climbed higher, she pressed her own thighs together to create some kind of friction against her clit and folds—nothing as good as what she could do with her own hands, but she didn't want to let him go.

His sexual magic coiled tighter and tighter in her lower belly, and he murmured a litany of encouragements. Her moans grew more unrestrained, her hips making little jerking movements until she couldn't take it anymore. She parted her lips and mouthed his cock, licking the denim of his trousers.

Abby cried out when Charles thrust against her mouth, his head thrown back from his climax. She panted, her mouth pressed desperately to his cock as though it were she who drained the pleasure from him into her. Nothing in her drained into him—that much she was sure of—although she couldn't determine what else she might have given him.

Her soul?

Do I even have a soul?

Abby tightened her grip on his thighs as she rode out her own orgasm, long and hot and sweet as the cock against her cheek. She thought it would never end until

Charles grabbed her hair and yanked her back, his smile showing too much of his teeth as he laughed breathlessly.

The shackles fell from her wrists. Charles helped her to her feet, offering her a strong shoulder as she staggered, her legs not quite ready to hold her up. He didn't comment on the fact that she hadn't healed them yet.

He caressed her cheek again before they left the bedroom. "There are special things in store for you, offspring. Just wait and see."

Chapter Six

Where is he?

It was after four in the morning, and Abby was in the self-same alley behind the apartment where Charles had reduced her to something she hadn't known she could be.

It wasn't that he had made her weak, because he hadn't. Charles had woven his magic, but she'd had power of her own as well as power that he'd voluntarily given to her.

The problem had been lack of will — a dread uncertainty, a shaken faith.

Abby wished she'd woken up the next evening for her retirement home and hospital reading rounds with all the questions that the incubus had posed to her answered, her shields fortified against him for the next time he tried to pierce past her armor.

Instead, she'd awoken with a whimper as she moved the limbs that had kept still while she'd slept, skin stretched tight over swelling. When she'd switched on the light and checked the full-length mirror she kept on her 'bedroom' door across from the closet rod and boxes that served as her wardrobe, she could point out each individual blow that Charles had applied. She checked her vitals again, but there were only the welts and bruises and the way her body protested the abuse.

She'd still decided not to heal them. So many times, Charles had asked her what she deserved, the pain or the pleasure. Abby still didn't know, but she did deserve to go through the rest of the day with these bruises on her body, since she was the one who'd invited them. When she fought the forces of darkness, that was different. Under those circumstances, she wasn't setting out to get hurt, and she wasn't planning on getting hurt tonight, either. But last night, she'd had opportunity after opportunity to avoid the pain and accepted it anyway.

So now she winced as she leaned against the wall, her lower back slanted away from the brick, and waited for a gargoyle to show up before a demon did—and before Charles learned she was out here. Now that she was aware he lived just above Threshold, it made her wonder whether he'd ever seen her fight before. All he'd have to do was come out onto his balcony. It wasn't like Abby had ever considered the people in the buildings while she was getting stabby with demons who didn't know when to quit. She'd only really paid attention to the gargoyles looming on the edge. For all she knew, Charles had first seen her here rather than Threshold or the clinic and decided then that she was someone he needed to pursue.

Abby hadn't known how much she needed to see Zekiel until he swept down from the roof, diving like a falcon. He spread his wings to stop in midair, then lowered himself to the ground in a parachute of stone leather.

"I didn't know if you were going to show," she said.

"I was delayed by geography. I cannot ride around in a city bus to get to where I need to be more expediently."

"No problem. I'm betting gargoyles don't have easy access to phones, either."

He smiled. "Nor to a public computer with Wi-Fi. Flying isn't as fast as one might expect. An owl may course the skies on silent wings, but I must avoid detection. And I will admit, I have not had a partner in many, many years. I've rarely had any place that I needed to be at a certain time."

"How long has it been?" she asked.

"At least a century. Yes, that sounds about right. I transformed into a gargoyle in the nineteen-aughts, and that was when I left my partner of that time."

"If you don't mind my asking, what kind of demon were you before? It didn't really occur to me that you weren't always like *this*. I mean, you said that you'd transformed, but..."

Zekiel lowered his head, drowning his eye sockets in shadow. "I would rather not speak of those days. It is something I left behind at great personal cost. I am no longer that demon, that kind of man. I do not wish to remember it."

"Hey, sorry. I didn't mean to dredge up bad memories. It doesn't matter to me what you used to be if it's not what you are anymore."

"It isn't."

"Okay, then." She squeezed his arm in encouragement. She honestly hadn't intended to get a good feel of the muscle under the stone texture of his arm. "If it makes you feel any better" — which would be pretty damn difficult to do, because he felt amazing — "I have a few things I want to forget tonight, too. So why don't we just do what we do and do it well?"

"In His name," Zekiel agreed.

On any other night, Abby would have repeated the response, archaic though it was, but she was uncomfortable saying it when the demon she'd allowed to shame her was so close by, his questions unanswered — and when a man she was lusting over was right in front of her, however innocent that appreciation was.

"One of my patients mentioned something last night about some activity going on where she lives, and I wondered whether you'd heard about anything happening at Cabrera and Sixth."

Zekiel furrowed his brow. "No. I don't know of anything particular occurring at that intersection. Nothing noteworthy, anyway. However, there's always something. We can begin there."

"There's nothing more pressing elsewhere?"

"Doubtlessly so, but I don't know of it. Shall we fly?"

"How about I meet you there? I run faster than I fly, and I'm less winded afterward."

"Nonsense. I can carry you," Zekiel said.

"That's just a little too Superman and Lois Lane for me."

"Not like that," he said with a laugh.

"How do you know Superman?"

Zekiel tilted his head in amusement. "Close personal friends, the two of us. We fly around all the time."

"No, you nut. I mean, how do you know about the character?"

"I sometimes watch television through people's windows. I didn't mean holding you in my arms, although I could do that, too. It would be much better if you were to wrap your arms around my neck and your legs around my waist, riding on my back."

"Instead of riding your front that way?"

"Y-yes, well, it would be better on my back."

Oh, if a gargoyle could blush.

"If you say so," Abby said, trying not to giggle. "It won't impact your wings' range of motion?"

"It will, but I can adjust. They are powerful enough to hold my weight and yours."

"Of course they are," she muttered. Hard to imagine a hero who couldn't hold a distressed damsel's weight. "We can try."

He crouched with his knuckles to the concrete, then extended his wings.

She hadn't climbed onto someone's back since college. It always reminded her of sitting on her father's shoulders when she was younger. She wasn't too much bigger than the last time her father had carried her. She'd stopped growing in fifth grade, for which she would never forgive her mother—which doomed her to hell for eternity right there.

"This is ridiculous," she said as he gripped her calves.

"Magic and physics, my dear. Magic and physics."

"I'm not sure which makes me more nervous."

"Where one is deficient, the other takes over. Have no fear. I will not let us fall."

A few minutes later, Zekiel was flying as Abby made every attempt not to strangle him to stay on. She kept adjusting her grip because of her sweaty palms.

"Sorry," Abby said in his ear. "I didn't know I'm afraid of heights when my wings aren't out."

"Hold on as tightly as you like," he called back. "I don't need to breathe."

Don't mind if I do.

When she was absolutely certain her arms wouldn't unwrap from his neck, she took a moment to appreciate the size and strength of his wings. No wonder his shoulders were so broad. And under her, he was warm enough to keep the winter night from chilling her through with the buffeting of the wind around them.

Not to mention that, after what she'd done with Charles the previous night and with the continued ache over her thighs from being spread over Zekiel's back, she couldn't help but think about her teasing him, except it wasn't so much of a joke anymore.

Zekiel wasn't an incubus, but that didn't mean he wasn't an extremely attractive man underneath the granite façade. A strange man, sure, but Abby had seen stranger. Given more time, she might get to know Zekiel better — and Charles as well, unfortunately — but she thought she already knew enough about the character of each after seeing the fruits of their labors. They were both attractive, and she wanted to kiss them both, but she could only kiss one — if he would let her.

Another time. A kiss wasn't the best prelude to spiritual espionage. It would break their focus, and focus was essential when a gargoyle was flying from rooftop to rooftop.

"That's...tacky?" Abby said as they approached Cabrera and Sixth. "Has that always been there?"

Gargoyles, angels and demons — Meridian architecture had a collector's collection of them, but they were usually human-sized or smaller. The demon statue squatting on top of the warehouse was unlike any of the statues that Abby had ever seen from the ground.

It was massive, easily ten or twelve times the size of an especially large person, and its head had been covered by a folded drape of fabric like the cloth that covered Zekiel's waist. It couldn't have been intentional by any sculptor, because it obscured what would have made the demon identifiable. Instead, with the demon bent over, hiding all distinguishing features, it made for quite a boring statue, which made it all the more interesting in her and Zekiel's line of work.

"Who the hell is that?" she asked.

"The demon is unmarked."

She could hear how troubled he was, even over the billowing of his wings.

He brought them down on the far side of the warehouse roof, away from the demon statue in case it animated at the sound of Zekiel's landing. He furled his wings once more after Abby slid off him.

"He was not here three nights ago," Zekiel said.

"That's not encouraging."

"Something truly is happening."

"Clears everything right up, Captain Obvious."

"I meant that your hunch that something bigger was going on, based on your friend's observations, was correct," he amended.

"I'll say."

They stayed near the edge of the roof as they made their way toward the statue on foot. In Meridian, even the warehouses got the artistic treatment. The flat edge was lined with a short wrought-iron fence that doubled as decoration and deterrent. A deterrent for what was the question. Parkour wasn't exactly epidemic, and there were fire escapes from lower floors providing potential access to the building. So why was the roof protected?

Wrapping his hand around the grip of his sword, Zekiel approached the statue. The demon appeared even bigger from the ground than the air. Abby doubted mace or a switchblade would make much of an impact. Even her silver knuckles wouldn't be much use, little more imposing to a demon of his size than a mouse wielding a needle.

"You know, I've seen demons the size of basketball players trying to pass in the human world, but I thought demons this big didn't manifest," she said.

"They usually don't. There's no reason for them to manifest when acolytes do their bidding in the physical realm. The greatest damage is done behind the scenes. But I can't determine why this one is here until I know who he is. Different demons have different desires, different motives." He prodded the demon's thigh. It made a sound like stone on stone. Zekiel shook his head. "The demon is dormant."

"Mary thought she heard and saw something massive slouching through the alley down there. He's not dormant all the time."

"But he is now. I'll hear the stirrings of his waking before you do, if he indeed wakes and is the demon that your friend observed."

"I hope so. Otherwise, we have two of these things in Meridian, and that just makes everything more dire, doesn't it?"

"Two demons of this ranking in one city...yes." Zekiel lowered himself to his knees to inspect the platform on which the demon crouched. "Unfortunately, he is as impenetrable as he is dormant.

There are protective spells carved into the base. He'll only be vulnerable when he's awake."

"That's not very vulnerable."

Zekiel shook his head in agreement.

"What does this mean?" Abby dealt with small-timers, small potatoes. This kind of demon and its impact on the physical and spiritual planes were beyond her ken. Being born of an angel — or nephil — didn't give her innate knowledge of demonic hierarchy in the world beyond the world she knew.

"It could mean a number of things, but I do not wish to alarm you with the wrong one," Zekiel said. "I would rather watch the acolytes in action, if they are still in the warehouse below. Tonight, we must observe."

"And act, right? We should act if something starts happening, some kind of ritual that involves violence. This is too big not to act. Literally."

"It might be too big to act." Zekiel stopped in front of the roof access door and turned to her. "If we go in —"

"Oh, we *are* going in."

"If we go in, you must promise that if I advise you not to make yourself known, you will stay hidden. This is a reconnaissance mission. If they are doing something terrible — more terrible than usual — timing is everything. It is unfortunate for a soul to be snuffed from this plane, I know, but we may jeopardize more than just our lives by interfering at the wrong time. They might kill us, or worse, and their nefarious plan would continue unchecked. Do you trust my wisdom if I tell you not to save something?" His dark red gaze pierced her.

Abby crossed her arms. It wasn't in her nature to just sit back and accept demons hurting people. But she did have to just sit back and accept some of her patients' suffering and death. Zekiel was telling her that this time it would be his decision instead of hers.

"Fine," she said. "We're just figuring out what they're doing, not interfering if it's not helpful. But if you tell me not to save them, I refuse to be okay with it."

"I accept your terms," Zekiel replied solemnly. "There are benefits to being made of stone."

They headed down the stairs, which was more difficult for Zekiel than either of them anticipated.

It was hard to tell if the warehouse was an abandoned one that had been inhabited by opportunistic acolytes who had banished the squatters—in which case, Abby took personal offense to some of her patients losing a roof over their heads—or whether the warehouse was one specifically purchased for the acolytes' occult activities—in which case, Abby still took offense, because that was a waste of perfectly good real estate. At the very least, it seemed well maintained, although not so well guarded if Zekiel could sound like a rock rolling down the stairs and no one came to investigate.

She needed to get him some shoes or towels to duct tape to his feet. Anything to give him some stealth while walking on metal. It wasn't so noticeable on concrete, and he was amazingly quiet in the air, but once they discovered Zekiel's noisy limitation, Abby took point, scouting a hall before beckoning Zekiel forward. It was easier as they made their way toward the heart of the warehouse, but then Abby reached the edge of the third floor and peered into the open room from between railings.

Whatever kind of manufacturing that the warehouse had been responsible for in the past, all indications of previous use had been gutted, leaving the main floor open and available for the giant inverted pentagram that been painted in the center.

Abby held up a hand to stop Zekiel from advancing. Red-hooded figures milled about the main floor. They were just talking with each other, not acting in any official capacity, but they could start at any time, and when they did, any clinking or clanging would stick out like a cymbal.

"Slowly," she whispered to him.

Zekiel abandoned the mesh walkway in favor of clambering over the railing like a chameleon.

Impressive, and much quieter.

He blended into the shadows and continued to cling to the railing as he settled next to Abby. She was glad she'd chosen a gray palette for her clothing today as well. She might appear a bit bland out of scrubs, but bland urban camouflage was better than dead every time.

"Can you hear them?" She didn't know whether gargoyles had super hearing like a bat just because they were created in their image, but it didn't hurt to ask.

Zekiel shook his head.

"Can you tell if they're human or not?"

He shook his head again. "I think most of them are human, but it's impossible to tell, especially if they've adopted a human guise."

Abby didn't know which would be better, a cult of demons or a cult of demon worshippers. Both were a hassle and left bloodstains on the floor when hit with sharp objects. Either way, there were too many of them for a two-on-two-dozen battle to go very well.

She lowered herself to the mesh floor and crossed her legs, leaning forward against the metal rail as she tried to listen to their conversations from two stories above. It looked like they might be there a while, and she was surprisingly good at getting up from that position if they were caught—with or without the muscle aches from a beating, which made sitting a lot more uncomfortable than usual.

She only heard snippets, but those snippets were strongly suggestive of these acolytes being a mix of human and demon. Some of them talked about their families and jobs, while others spoke of their latest possessions or how many humans they'd corrupted that week. It was surreal listening to mixed fellowship like this—like a Muslim-Baptist potluck.

Abby glanced up at Zekiel as the conversations drew to a close and the red-hooded acolytes quieted and formed a loose circle around the inverted pentagram. She reached to tap Zekiel's calf but paused, distracted by the shadow underneath the covering over his waist and thighs. She felt like a teenage boy getting a chance to look up a girl's skirt, a dizzying mixture of thrill and guilt.

It wasn't like she could see anything, really, except for the glimpse of the back of his strong thighs and the faintest suggestion of curves above and his scrotum between.

A flash of heat from crown to abdomen surprised her with its intensity, and she quickly looked away.

But she was a grown woman, for heaven's sake, and she wrapped a hand around his calf. He twitched a bit at her touch. She pressed her finger to her lips without looking at him, trusting that he would see.

What was she thinking anyway? He was a gargoyle. The man knew how to be quiet and still.

And he had rock-hard calves, even without being made of stone.

The leader stepped forward with a leather-bound book in his hands, written in red ink that was doubtlessly blood of some kind. No demon ever had his book anonymously self-published. It was always parchment handbound in leather that still smelled like the animal it came from. Demons were more traditionalist than a Catholic mass.

From the part of the warehouse ground floor that she and Zekiel couldn't see, women came out to join the red-robed demons and humans, although they were without robes—in the sense that they were without clothes at all. Two flanked the leader. The others stepped between at seemingly random intervals, although the brief distraction to the red-robed people they joined suggested intimate familiarity, and the smooth protrusion of each of their bare abdomens suggested the rest, because almost all of them were visibly pregnant. Two of the women weren't pregnant to Abby's eye, but they could have been in the early months...or still trying.

"Oh my God." Abby tightened her grip on Zekiel's leg.

"No. There are too many, and we do not yet know their intentions," he whispered back.

"Screw their intentions. There's only one reason a demonic cult keeps women like this alive."

"They're clearly here of their own will."

"That's not what I meant. They're—"

"I know what they're for," Zekiel said grimly. "But there is no immediate danger. We cannot interfere. You promised."

Abby couldn't hear much more than the hum of the collective chanting. Few clear words came through because the high priest spoke too quickly, but she suspected it was in Latin—harder to understand from a distance, although she had a working knowledge of enough Latin to grasp a Black Mass or ritual spell. Just another form of traditional grandstanding, since speaking it in English would have worked just as well. When a person was invoking their demon, presentation was half the sycophancy.

The high priest closed the book and rested it on the podium, then gestured for two of the demons—or likely demons by their stature, both headdressed like the human-faced demon from the alley—to retrieve something that looked suspiciously like an old dentist chair, the black vinyl polished to a glossy shine.

Once the demons had arranged the chair in the center of the pentagram and returned to their places, the high priest raised his hands, palms forward and glaringly pale in the spotlights against the blood-red contrast of his hooded robe. The chanting abruptly ceased.

"The time draws nigh."

Abby immediately recognized the rasp in the man's voice, although she'd only heard it once and she'd been distracted by the demons and the girl. But with all the naked women around the circle, she wondered whether virgin sacrifice had actually been on the menu or whether they'd had more insidious plans.

"We have waited for our Master. We have waited and we have been patient, as a mother is patient." The priest laid one of his pale hands on the pregnant belly of one of the women.

The woman swayed where she stood. Abby couldn't see her clearly enough to tell if she was drugged or enspelled, perhaps even possessed. One could always tell by the eyes, but three stories up, Abby was too far for that kind of detail. However, there was no mistaking the smile. Ecstasy like that could be the province of magical influence, but also religious fervor. The woman could have been a victim, but she could have just as likely been an acolyte herself, thrilled to serve her Master in a way that she was more qualified for than the male demons or humans in the congregation.

Whether coerced or voluntary, the woman covered the priest's hand with her own. "Now?" She sounded almost childish, but the way she slid the priest's hand up to her breast wasn't.

"Not yet, my dear. There are other ways you can serve until the quickening." The priest brought her to his side and kissed her cheek from under his hood, then guided her to the chair. The same two headdressed demons quickly darted forward to bind her ankles to the custom stirrups retrofitted onto the chair. Then they bound her wrists to the arms of the chair and laid her back.

The priest stepped forward between her legs. Although he remained fully clothed, he pressed himself against her. Certain angles, certain shadows, indicated that he wasn't unaffected by his proximity or her nudity, nor did her seven-month-pregnant belly dampen his desire. He caressed it as though it were a crystal ball and he could see within.

"Day by day, night by night, we ready ourselves for the Reckoning, for the days and nights of sacrifices before us. We prepare for blood and make full the flesh." The priest groaned as he rubbed himself against the woman, who did not at all appear as though she needed to be bound. "The altar remains unstained, the Master remanded to stone, but we call him to us. We call him, and we give him a taste of the sacrifices to come."

The priest reached into a deep pocket. At first, Abby thought he would stroke himself through his clothes, but instead, he pulled out an empty syringe, which he uncapped with his teeth, then brought to the woman's belly.

Unless this man was a doctor, he had no business bringing a syringe anywhere near a pregnant woman, much less her womb. He inserted the needle into her belly without an ultrasound or sterilization, putting both mother and baby at risk, but Abby got the impression both were replaceable in an acolyte's eyes, even if the mother was an acolyte herself. But neither were replaceable to Abby, and a bad amniocentesis could go horribly wrong with an ignorant touch.

The woman's ecstatic smile gave way to frowning discomfort. She strained against the padded leather bindings, which at least partially explained why they'd bound her, beyond the same aesthetic presentation that put the acolytes in robes over a pentagram, chanting in Latin.

Abby tightened her grip on Zekiel's leg even more.

"There are over twenty of them down there, some demons themselves, not counting the unclothed women," Zekiel whispered. "She chose this."

"We don't know that. We don't know what he's doing. He could be hurting..."

The priest pulled the syringe out and held it up. It was full to the top with amniotic fluid, far more than would be removed in a typical sample, but although the woman panted and clutched the ends of the chair arms tightly, her smile returned, albeit with the grimace of pain.

Still holding the syringe high, the priest resumed the chanting, but this time from memory, and the acolytes raised their voices to join him in typical chorus replies of '*Carpe noctem*' and '*Veni diabolus*', which were as common during occult rituals as 'The Lord be with you' and 'Hallelujah' in a church service.

The priest pressed on the plunger in the syringe, spraying the amniotic fluid in a fountain above him.

It never fell back down onto his robes or even into the pentagram.

Oh shit.

The warehouse trembled with a clatter of stone, metal and concrete. Both she and Zekiel stared up at the skylights to the roof. They couldn't see anything, but something had fed on the fluid offering and something had shaken the very foundations of the warehouse, and it didn't take twenty-one questions to figure out what.

"It's awake," Zekiel murmured.

Abby looked away from the skylights back down to the cult. And stared straight under the red hood of an acolyte to the demon eyes beneath.

"Intruders!"

Chapter Seven

Chaos ensued below as the acolytes broke the circle and ran red toward them, with the advantage of knowing their own territory. Abby climbed to her feet as fast as she could.

It didn't matter how much noise they made now. Zekiel thundered over the grating like a giant, and Abby ran behind him. His massive, furled wings were a hindrance. He couldn't open them even a little to give himself more balance. He had to adjust for the weight by running crouched, his head down. He gave a gravelly shout as he rammed his stone skull into the stomach of an acolyte, sending him flying.

"Go!" Zekiel pointed her past the fallen acolyte in the direction they'd entered the warehouse.

"Wait! We're going *toward* the roof where they just woke the demon?"

That gave Zekiel pause. He shook his head. "No, you're right. Find a window with a fire escape. Get to the alley. I will find you out there. *I* will go to the roof and lure them away. Go *now*!"

Abby bit her lip as she scurried past the acolyte, who still gasped fruitlessly on the walkway. She looked back only once to see Zekiel drawing his sword.

She found a nook in which she could hide in shadows as the acolytes ran past to follow the clang of Zekiel's ascent to the roof. She waited until the last set of boots had run past her, then waited a few beats longer in case of stragglers.

Her heart pounded in her ears as she crept out, staying low and glancing to the right, where everyone had gone. Three acolytes convened at the intersection, but to the left, she couldn't see anyone else coming. If she had, she would have had to take out her switchblade. As it was, Abby retrieved one of the silver knuckles from her purse and clenched her fist around it. It wouldn't burn holes through the humans, but it would hurt like hell, and if they were demon-bothering with an aperitif of amniotic fluid in preparation for a more dire harvest, they deserved whatever limited hell she could rain down upon them.

No, she couldn't think about where this cult was headed, because her nose was stopped up, the contents of her throat thick and she still needed to run.

Now.

She darted in the opposite direction from the acolytes. She'd made it to the other end of the building before someone shouted, "Hey!"

Crap, crap, crap. Abby abruptly turned to the left and hoped as she entered the dark corridor that it wasn't a dead end.

It was a dead end.

She pounded the blank wall in front of her, then peered through the darkness to either side of her, feeling along the walls for a door. The first one she found, she yanked on the doorknob and darted in, then closed the door as slowly and quietly as she could so that they couldn't follow her sound. There was a little light in the room from a window — a blessed, blessed window, because it led to a fire escape.

A commotion on the other side of the door compelled her to lock it. Then she worked on getting the reluctant, rusted window to open. She was about to punch out the glass, but the window finally groaned up.

Climbing out was easier said than done for a short girl. With one leg mostly out and the other in, she was straddling the sill when an acolyte busted through the door.

Panic constricting her chest, Abby rolled out and fell onto her arm on the fire escape platform. She clambered to her feet, then punched the acolyte under his hood before he could climb after her. From the lack of singeing, he was human, and his nose was not going to be happy in the morning. He stumbled back, clutching his face and shouting for the rest to join him.

She pushed away from the window and climbed down the fire escape ladder, checking the skies for Zekiel.

She couldn't find him.

"Wait till I get my hands on you, girl." A new acolyte above her launched over the side of the fire escape, sliding down the ladder without bothering with rungs.

Abby had to jump for the next platform, her belly hitting the railing. The demon on the other side of the hood smiled widely, his needle teeth gleaming and the mouth a little too wide. He was barely more than an arm's reach away.

"Such pretty eyes," he said. "I could use them in my collection."

"Now!" Zekiel shouted, diving from the other roof and swooping toward her.

Abby didn't—couldn't—give it a second thought. She leaped into the air and spread her own wings to slow her descent so that Zekiel could get underneath her. For a second, their wings overlapped, which was the oddest sensation Abby had experienced in a minute—like recalling a dream of feathers against her cheek, although her wings were smoke and his were stone.

She landed on his back and immediately grabbed onto him like before. The demon acolyte swore after her. Two acolytes in the window tried to cast a spell at them, but Zekiel flew too fast and swooped into another alley, staying below the roofline until he could get around a taller building to climb the skies once more.

When he was sure nothing followed them, he turned around to return to Cemetery Grove.

Neither of them spoke until they'd landed on the gargoyle-lined roof across from Threshold.

"That was way too close," she said.

Abby couldn't remember the last time she'd seen a demon cult that large, just like she'd never seen a demon as large as the monument on the roof. She'd braved a cult of ten before. At most, cults and covens stayed around a baker's dozen—for the symbolism. Any more than that, rifts tended to form. For most people who joined demon cults, cooperation and talking out differences weren't high on their list of priorities. But between the high priest and the harem, she guessed an established hierarchy and ready sex made for more cooperative followers.

"When I reached the roof, the demon was gone," Zekiel said.

"Then we're back to square one. We don't even know what they've unleashed or why, and now they know someone's checking up on them." Abby struck the roof access wall. It hurt, but not nearly enough.

The only silver lining she could find was that she'd been wearing her silver knuckles the whole time and hadn't burned a hole in Zekiel's shoulder. So he was unequivocally an ex-demon, with an emphasis on the 'ex'.

Then she stared at her own hand with the silver knuckles still on.

That filthy son of a bitch.

He'd really had her going, making her think she was a demon when she wouldn't be able to use silver like this if she were. She might just have to introduce Charles to some shiny metal next time she encountered him.

"Are you all right?" Zekiel asked.

"Yeah. Just some demon yanking my chain and me being a fool, letting him. It's nothing, and now I'm embarrassed about it. What's important here is that we have a cult that's hellbent on killing kids that they're growing themselves, and we just ran away from it instead of stopping it. What if one of them miscarries? What if one of them goes into labor early? We might not have seen all their women. We have a little time, but we don't have a lot, and those women—girls, really—either have no idea what they've gotten themselves into or they're under a hell of a spell. And Zekiel, this demon wants *children*..."

"Was it a good decision to run? No," he said quietly. "It was the right decision, though, the only decision we could make that would have you standing here in front of me now. And that's important, too."

She leaned back against the wall, rubbing her face with her hands. "Should I punt this over to the demon hunters I know, have them put together a hunting party or something?"

"I'm uncomfortable telling others until we know who the demon is. We might send them to die if they do not know the tools they need."

"It's what demon hunters *do*. This is *their* specialty, breaking up the worst of the demon cults, slaying the dragons."

"I *am* a demon hunter," Zekiel said with as much gentleness as he could muster.

"Well, I'm *not*. I'm the medical unit. I'm the one who's supposed to save the ones who can't save themselves—those women, their..."

Zekiel enveloped her in his arms and let her rest her head against his shoulder as she let it all go. "We have a little time—but it is still time."

There were always people she couldn't save, whether on a sacrificial altar or in the examination rooms of the clinic. Sometimes God told her who to heal with a feeling, other times by circumstance.

No. No, she could have done it. Charles was right about that much. She still wasn't sure about those feelings or where they came from, but she would never know whether she could have saved the women and the babies growing inside of them, because she hadn't tried. Sure, she hadn't failed and died in vain, either.

But when she'd first learned about her power, she'd thought she would be able to save everyone, that with her abilities she could actually make a *difference*. What was the point of having this gift if its yield was as random as life already was?

Zekiel stroked her hair and didn't say anything as she cried. That might have been because he didn't know what to say and found the whole situation awkward as hell with a woman he'd only known for two fraught nights, but it was still exactly what she needed from him at that moment. Anything else he could have said would have either been wrong, trite or cruel. Saying nothing was perfect.

"You know, when I thought we'd be in this position, I imagined it differently," she said, with a laugh she didn't want but coughed out just the same. She wiped her face on her sleeve again.

"How did you imagine it?"

She pulled back. She was sure she looked a state, but Zekiel didn't recoil in horror, so it probably wasn't too horrible. And really, that didn't matter. He wasn't looking at her reddened eyes or her tear-streaked cheeks or her wind-crazy hair. He stared at her lips.

It could have been twisted, but it wasn't. They could have died, but they hadn't. That's all it came down to. They were alive in a world where people died every day, sometimes horribly and for evil reasons. But they *were* alive, and even though they didn't know what to do about the demon and its cult, there was still a chance to do *something*.

That something might involve getting their heads cut off by an angry demon cult, but the angry demon cult would have to wait until after she kissed him.

Kissing him—like touching him—was nothing like kissing stone. When she closed her eyes, she could have been kissing any warm-blooded man, his bare chest under her palm, his skin hot and his lips soft and hesitant against hers.

Abby withdrew slightly. "Is this okay?"

"Is it..." He encircled her waist with his strong arm and pulled her up against him, pressing his lips more firmly against hers. She whimpered, her body practically melting, awakening all over like lights turned on in a dark house.

He buried his other hand in her hair, which confirmed that her crazy hair wasn't a problem, because it wasn't going to look much better after this, and that was just fine with her. Zekiel tilted her head to the side and parted his lips in silent query to which she enthusiastically assented, yielding her mouth to the deepening of the kiss. She clung desperately to his neck to hold herself up. The sheer largeness of his body overwhelmed her, suddenly so much more imposing than it had been before, but in all the ways that made her skin hum with electricity as he tasted her, touched her, deliberate and unrelenting.

She'd always liked a man much bigger than her, which wasn't difficult. She thrilled at the helpless feeling, the good kind. She had little power in this position—on her toes, bent over his arm, her head back, dependent on him to keep her balanced, especially when her knees had stopped working. But she had a few kind weapons on her side as well.

Such as the way she met every thrust of his tongue with her own, the way her broken moans made him shudder under her hands and tighten his grip on her, the way she canted her hips against his. His covering was thick, but she felt the stirrings of his arousal against her leg, which hit her with a shot of warm pleasure low in her abdomen.

She sighed as he tore himself from her mouth and kissed over her cheek to refocus his intense attention to her neck under her ear, biting gently and sucking at a place that made her eyes roll back.

The best part was that she could touch him, and that almost everywhere she touched, there was nothing but skin. There didn't have to be layers of fabric between them for her own safety. His heart beat under her palm, and when she stroked his nipple with her thumb, he groaned against her throat.

On any other night, Abby might have stopped with this, making out on a rooftop with a gargoyle, mapping the planes of his extraordinary chest, rubbing his shoulders, teasing down the terrain of his abdomen. But last night and tonight combined into a potent and surprising aphrodisiac. She couldn't stop, didn't want to stop, didn't want him to stop doing those things he was doing to her neck that would leave more marks she didn't want to get rid of.

She lowered her hand beneath the waist of his covering, its texture like cotton. In a déjà vu moment, she stroked him through it. Her fingers quivered at the sensation of his girth only because she craved what she had in her grasp. It had been too long, and what Charles had done with her had whetted her appetite. An incubus was incapable of truly satisfying. That was its nature.

But this man and what he had... Abby thought he could satisfy quite well.

"Abby, I..." Zekiel groaned as she strengthened the grip of her strokes.

"I've been wondering what you had under there, if you'd been carved with that in mind. But it seems your Creator—whoever he or she is—is the very picture of generosity."

"Are you sure that— You wondered?"

So cute when he was flustered.

"Can you take this covering off, or do we have to hike up your skirt?" Abby asked.

"I, um, it can be removed, but…"

The gentleman protested, but he seemed more concerned about her than the prospect of sex with her, which encouraged Abby to shed her dirty jacket. She was too hot in it anyway, especially as close as she'd been to the furnace of his body.

Then she took a few steps back until her shoulders hit the brick wall. With her gaze locked on his, she unbuttoned her jeans and pulled the zipper down. Slowly, so that he could protest for real this time, she pushed her jeans over her hips, then down her legs, where she toed off her shoes and removed her jeans entirely. From this angle, he wouldn't be able to see anything left over from last night, and she wouldn't have to think about it, either.

"Better come over here quickly, Zekiel, or else I'm going to get cold again." She stroked her fingers over the front of her panties, teasing her folds. Biting her lip, her face heating in the shadows, she reveled in the intensity of his gaze as she slid her hand underneath to touch herself without any barrier. She had just brushed her fingertips through the wetness from her cunt when Zekiel darted forward, his fingers intertwining with hers under the fabric then pushing hers out of the way so that he could take over.

Abby had no way of knowing how long it had been since Zekiel's last opportunity to take care of a woman. She had the impression from his abnormally sharp focus and from her experience with other crusader types that it had probably been a lot longer than her. Also, unlike many demon hunters who engaged in one-night affairs if they needed release, often the kind they could pay for, Zekiel's unorthodox appearance likely kept him from picking up women of convenience.

However long it had been since his last, he'd lost none of his skill. He was patient and as unhesitant in touching her as he was hesitant to speak, seeming to know *exactly* how to touch her with minimal trial and error and *exactly* when to continue stroking her clit with his thumb as he slipped two fingers into her cunt to placate the thrusting of her hips.

"You are such a beautiful man." She spread her fingers over his abdomen, relishing the velvety texture in spite of how rough it appeared. She couldn't figure out which part was the illusion, the heated softness of his skin or the pocked stone that should have been freezing under her palms.

Either way, he was a fine specimen, the carving as idealized as any she'd ever seen. Considering he'd turned into a gargoyle and was supposed to have an element of horror to his visage, she wondered how lovely he'd been before the transformation.

"Beautiful, oh yes, beautiful, right *there*..." She gasped as he curved his long fingers to beckon at that place inside her that made her clench around him and moan high in her throat.

Zekiel kissed her cheek with delicacy that belied the forceful thrusts of his fingers, drawing her to some pinnacle that seemed so much higher than anything else, higher than the tallest skyscraper or steeple. No matter how close man tried to get to God, no one would ever be closer than Zekiel brought her, soaring until her wings spread smoke to either side in a burst of ecstasy.

That had never happened to her before. Then again, she'd never been with a man with whom she could spread her wings and not feel alone.

Zekiel pulled his fingers away before she could reach her climax. She groaned in blissful frustration and punched his chest.

"That is so not okay," she said, laughing, more giddy than amused. "Man, what a night."

He stroked her cheek with his thumb, brushed her lower lip and without a word in response, leaned back down to recapture her mouth. He was more forceful this time, with more purpose, sliding his hands down over her breasts, then grasping her hips to lift her up for her to wrap her legs around his waist once more — but this time from the front, as she'd teased. Abby moaned high in her throat as he shoved her against the wall. She winced at the reawakening of her bruises along with her lust, but she didn't say anything, and she didn't think he noticed.

He had no trouble holding her pressed to the wall with his body, no strain, petite as she was. She liked that she didn't have to cling to him, that she could appreciate the musculature of his body with both hands. And she liked the creaking groan that wrenched from his throat when she rocked over his erection.

"Abby, I...you... It's been such a long..." He was breathless, voice deep, rough and needful in her ear. She arched at the sound.

"You and me both, brother."

He shoved his fists against the wall on either side of her head as she continued to press her folds against his clothed cock, nestled tight between her and his abdomen. The force broke some of the bricks behind her wings. She gasped again from the odd, ghostly sense of him going through her, with the scent of rosemary, the whisper of feathers and the desire for more, almost as though it reminded her of something lost in the past—perhaps not even her own.

"I want inside of you," he whispered into her lips before kissing her again, kissing her until she thought she might do anything he wanted, kissing her until she thought she'd come from his mouth alone. But that would leave him unsatisfied, and her cunt so desperately wanted something inside of her right now, too.

Abby hitched herself up and stared down at him expectantly. Then she pressed her lips to his temple until she heard the harsh metal clang of his sword and a rustle of heavy fabric hitting the ground. The latter made her shiver from something other than cold. She didn't think she was ever going to be cold again with the dizzying fire coursing through her, the best kind of fire, the kind that accompanied epiphanies and ecstatic revelations.

He pushed her panties to the side, a momentary discomfort—one she decided she could tolerate when the head of his cock probed at her entrance, then slid into her. They groaned in unison as she sank over him, gravity forcing him in all the way to the base.

"Abby," he murmured with prayerful reverence as he thrust into her again. "So..." He still couldn't finish a thought. She didn't mind at all.

His wings spread as well, giving him extra balance to speed up. The way their wings overlapped seemed to take them higher, although they never left the roof. He drew a moan from her every time as he brought her back to the skies. She bounced over his rigid cock, shaking from each internal stroke and the way that her clit pressed against him whenever she tilted her hips forward. He was tireless, his fanatical fervor now focused entirely on surrounding his cock with her pussy, which clenched around him, the sensation contorting his chiseled face with what looked like torturous pleasure.

Abby took that face in her hands and kissed him again. Any thought of the rest of that night or last fled from her mind, leaving behind blissful emptiness that Zekiel eagerly filled. Temporary though it was, she reveled in it, wished it didn't have to end, despite how good the impending ending promised to feel.

"Faster. Almost there." She threw back her head and guided his mouth to her neck once more.

Zekiel suddenly stiffened.

At first, she thought he'd reached his climax. She anticipated the twitch of his cock inside of her, his wrenching groan as he came.

But a few seconds passed and he didn't come. He didn't even move.

And he was getting cold.

She opened her eyes and looked down.

The flesh that had been warm, pliable and soft—the flesh of a man—had turned completely to stone.

The lights that illuminated the roof around the shadow cast by the roof access building had hidden the early signs of dawn, but now a fog of sunbeams stretched over the city and glowed on the edge of Zekiel's outstretched wings.

He was hard as well as erect inside of her, his mouth immovable from her neck. She was effectively trapped against the wall by a statue.

"Dear Lord." She wrapped her arms around his neck and laughed helplessly against his shoulder, her body wracking with it, until the convulsions around his cock reminded her that they were both unsatisfied and, after being brought so close to the edge twice already, she really needed release.

"I don't know whether you can hear me," she whispered into his ear, "but I sincerely hope you don't mind."

She had to do most of the work this time, riding his cock that stayed hot from her own body's warmth until she brought herself back to the peak. She reached between herself and the statue and rubbed her clit as she ground down over his cock and panted her climax. It wasn't the same as if she'd shared it with Zekiel, but it got the job done.

Now she could turn her attention to other important tasks — like extricating herself from his embrace.

This time, it was useful being as small as she was. It took some creative maneuvering, but once she'd risen herself off his erection, she eased herself out over his leg and under his arm, squeezing through the gap between his torso and the wall.

"Oh, you poor, poor thing." She covered her mouth to stop the laughter again as she took in the sight of him. It was funny, but if he was aware of what was going on, he probably didn't think so and wouldn't think so until he got some perspective from distance and time. "Again, I don't know if you can hear me, but I'm so very sorry, and I'll try to make it up to you."

Abby grabbed her purse, then pulled on her jeans, jacket and shoes, glad that his discarded covering hadn't overlapped with any of her possessions, otherwise they too would be trapped on the roof to which Zekiel and his covering and sword were now firmly attached.

"I wish I could do something about this." She gestured to his erection. Under other circumstances, she would have draped her jacket over it, but it was far too chilly to go home without a jacket on. "I have work the next two nights, twelve-hour shifts, and they kind of kill me. But I promise we'll get a chance. I know you'll find some way to contact me if you learn anything new."

Glancing again at the salacious tableau that Zekiel now presented — with his bare backside to the wind and his erection unmistakable to anyone with binoculars or who came up to the roof for a smoke or wintery lunch break. Abby again fought the urge to giggle. After the last two nights, it was amazing she could still laugh at all.

"Oh man," she muttered as she ran down the stairs, "he is going to be so pissed when he wakes up."

Chapter Eight

Zekiel was pissed.

He usually took the time during the day to 'sleep'. His eyes were usually locked open, but he would drift in a meditative state that occasionally unraveled into dreams. It had been centuries since he had slept the way a human did, when his thoughts would simply cease. Sometimes he missed it, that peace.

Over ten hours touched by the rays of the sun. Over ten hours that he could not sleep. Over ten hours with an excruciating erection, his pleasure captured just short of his climax without hope of relief before the sun set, the wetness of Abby's arousal with which she had coated him cooling and evaporating.

Over ten hours of remembering Abby in his arms.

He had laughed in his head with her. The sun hadn't caught him off-guard like that since the early months of being able to move at night. And although he couldn't speak or give her any indication that he was still there, the way she had finished herself off with his statue self would have taken him the rest of the way if he hadn't been a slab of stone.

There weren't many things associated with his life as a gargoyle now that Zekiel would call hellish. There had been a few at the beginning of his transformation when he hadn't been able to move for decades, just while away the hours, days, months, years with memory and repentance within his mind. It had been a different hell after he'd been granted movement, then freedom, when he'd needed to adjust to an existence driven by a will not entirely his own. As a demon, he had been encouraged to do anything he willed, anything that gave him pleasure. Self-denial had taken an especially long time to learn.

But this day, trapped in a so-obviously-unfulfilled body without any recourse until nightfall... Zekiel could safely call it a kind of hell.

So, in the midst of that hell, Zekiel tried as hard as he could—because he *was* as hard as he could be—to think of anything other than the pressing need jutting unabashedly toward the brick wall.

He started with a moment-by-moment memory of what had happened at the warehouse, combing over the details of the demon statue that he had been able to see. It seemed to follow similar rules to that of a gargoyle, in that there was a time when it was dormant and a time when it awakened, but it wasn't bound to sunset and sunrise as Zekiel was. Its size suggested that, under ordinary circumstances, it did not walk among men and instead ruled over minions on a more spiritual plane. But it wished to enter the physical realm, or else it would not have had its visage carved and animated with the promise of innocent blood.

There was only one reason a princeling demon would choose to enter the physical realm — an apocalypse, an end of the world as the inhabitants knew it, to rule a hell on earth.

Zekiel wished the choice of sacrifice narrowed down the number of demon princes that the statue could be. However, since he and Abby had only witnessed a single offering, not even a sacrifice, they could not infer that a child would be a typical sacrifice, a convenient one or merely one in a specific sequence. Even if the demon preferred children, that still pointed to at least a dozen demons with whom Zekiel was familiar, not to mention all those with whom he wasn't.

He sometimes had to remind himself that, although he considered his sins less terrible than some of his brothers', he had cut his own swath of death and destruction in his time. He was no better than this demon prince just because he'd been of a lower rank and less violent or hateful. Perhaps 'contemptuous' was the better word for what he'd felt — contemptuous for humanity.

Zekiel had known women like Abby before. Well, never one quite like her, but she was definitely a member of a class of women who shared certain traits. There had been a time when he hadn't appreciated them. He valued them much more since his transformation into the gargoyle, but none of them had ever left him in this present unpleasant state — so consumed with her that he'd forgotten what he was, lost all words, abandoned his control and cast his attention from the skies instead to the sweet shadow of her skin. It was difficult, though, for him to explain to himself why this woman was so much different. There was no denying that she was special, but that was no reason to trip about and fumble like a dewy schoolboy, getting caught with his metaphorical and literal pants down, as though he hadn't been turned to stone every morning of his ex-demon life.

The quality that stood out most was that she still cared. She cared about the people around her — people who Zekiel would have once despised, used and abused because he cared not a whit for any of them. They had been beneath him in their weakness and multitude. Such an attitude would be alien to her.

True, she was young. Perhaps after the three-hundredth sacrifice she tried and failed to save, she would feel less charitable toward her species. Perhaps she would start seeing the capacity for that kind of depravity in every soul, including her own. If a subtler demon got the best of her after gaining her trust the way that Zekiel had, perhaps she'd lose that attractive innocence that had melted his resolve. She had trusted him far too soon. He knew what else was out there, what he could have done to her by now if he'd still been one of them.

That innocence was so rare in the professions she had chosen.

Then, mixed with her compassion and innocence, courage — courage to do the right thing, even when it was dangerous. Courage to plunge in and kiss him, to shed her clothes in winter and trust him to keep her warm. Courage to make herself vulnerable. And in spite of the fact that Zekiel thought she'd offered that vulnerability too freely, he also knew she hadn't given it indiscriminately.

He'd visited her the other night at her work before he'd gone on to his. Even after one night in her company, he'd wanted to see her again. He hadn't lingered long, just enough to witness her with some of her patients, watch her smile and light up like a Christmas wreath, even when one of the patients unleashed a phlegmy cough on her. Instead of recoiling, she'd touched his forearm. A human wouldn't have been able to see it, but he had — the tiny points of black-edged light sparking from her skin and sinking into the man's arm as the darkness under his eyes had lessened.

Abby was a healer. She had adopted that title through and through, outside to inside, profession to persona. She still had time for such purity to crack, but Zekiel did not believe it inevitable or, if it happened, irreparable. And it wasn't just disease that she healed. He hoped she never realized how quickly she had spread that healing inside of him to make him forget that his heart was made of stone. She reminded him why he had accepted the transformation and become a demon hunter in the first place — not just to save people like her, but because there were people like her who did their own saving as well.

Although the pleasure was akin to torture when stretched over the span of hours, she had been only the third woman who had sparked his sexual interest since the transformation. Part of it was her teasing, part of it was her eyes and part of it was the freshness of her beauty — unadorned, unenhanced, yet it filled his vision with light. Zekiel couldn't understand why all were not as blinded as he was.

The swell of her breast captivated him as much as the strength in her fist, the gentle drape of her hair brushing her shoulders, the coiled energy in her lithe thighs.

Thinking about her like this was not helping.

Zekiel exhaled in relief as the sun set enough to leave him in shadow once again, releasing him from his stone prison cell. He immediately wrapped his hand around his cock and wrung it with the desperation borne of hours. As a gargoyle, he didn't chafe, and he needed to come *now*.

"Well, well, well, you look in quite the state."

Zekiel dove for his sword and whirled around. It humiliated him to be seen by a stranger with his cock this erect, but his feelings on the matter were irrelevant. He deserved humiliation. The mission took precedence over everything else, and most human beings wouldn't have responded so cavalierly to a hard-pressed gargoyle on a roof where he did not belong.

"Oh my, it looks even worse from the front. Need a hand?"

Zekiel cautiously lowered his sword. "What on earth are you doing here, Charles?"

Charles ran his gaze over Zekiel's gargoylian body with amusement he didn't bother to conceal. "I sensed you. At first, I thought it could have been some bad Mexican food throwing me off, but then the feeling just stuck around...so I followed it." He leaned his shoulder against the brick wall and smirked. "Just in time, it looks like."

"You shouldn't be here."

"It's a public access roof. I'm allowed to be up here, same as you. And is it a crime to want to see an old friend? I haven't seen you in... What's it been?"

"Over a hundred years," Zekiel replied evenly.

"How time flies. I could have sworn it was only seventy." Charles pushed himself away from the wall and took a step closer, joining Zekiel out of the darkness and into the beam of the roof's light. "By the way, mate, as a friend, I have to say that you look simply terrible. Really, you disappear for a century and just go downhill from there?"

"And you look the same. Don't come any closer."

"Why? I'm only going to give you that hand."

"No."

"No kind words or even a kiss for your old partner?" Charles narrowed his eyes as he really took in more than Zekiel's hardened state. "Why, that's cold as stone, mate—which is exactly what you look like, like you took a gander at a gorgon but turned away before she finished the job."

"That's not what happened." Zekiel picked up his cloth, trying to cover his nakedness.

Charles raised an eyebrow. "It's nothing I haven't already seen a million times, Zekiel. And I don't believe a slip of cloth like that is going to hide your need. Come on. Let me help you."

Zekiel didn't respond or stop tying his covering.

"What's wrong? What changed that you won't let me…"

Zekiel buckled his sword back around his waist and raised his gaze to meet Charles' eyes.

Charles tightened his jaw, tireless good humor finally finding its limit. "You haven't put on your human disguise. And you don't just look different, you feel… What happened?"

"A demon can change."

"But who would want to?"

"I did."

"So this is the change?" Charles gestured over his body. "You turn to stone every morning and come to life every night, never able to hunt and losing every smile you once had? You did this willingly?"

"It's my punishment."

"Your punishment?" Charles scoffed. "What demon hunter or witch did you piss off?"

"No one did this to me." Zekiel never took his hand from his sword. The sadness that settled over him like a mantle at seeing his old friend dulled the urgency of his need, although his erection still tented the fabric in a way made even more ridiculous by the sudden solemnity between both men. "I chose it."

"What fool would choose this?" Charles poked Zekiel's arm. "Feels fleshy enough, but it wasn't a few minutes ago, was it? It really was stone." Revelation widened his eyes. Then he just looked annoyed. "Oh, devils below, Zeke, what did you go turning yourself into a gargoyle for?"

"I didn't want to be a gargoyle."

"You just stopped wanting to be a demon. You bloody fool. I can't believe it." Charles stormed away, pacing between the silver darkness and golden light. "I can't imagine what would convince you to walk away from the *perfect* existence. Hell, do you know how many men would kill for the life we had? Always a nice place to stay, a single touch got us whatever we wanted, we had our pick of anyone we desired and we could always do what we did best with our partner — sometimes without adding anyone else into the mix. All those nights in our bed and other people's beds... Did we bore you? Did it mean nothing?"

"It isn't a perfect existence," Zekiel said.

Charles stalked back to him with such agitation and even hatred in his expression that Zekiel tightened his hold on the sword, ready to do battle if he had to. And he didn't want to, because it hadn't meant nothing. It just couldn't mean anything anymore.

"Bollocks," Charles snapped. "It's that and more. A hundred-thirty years in the world and it never fails to excite me. Maybe you just needed a break. You'd been going at it longer than I had, after all. Things have changed, though, since we were in the game together. More of them indulge their fantasies while they're still awake. They're not nearly so repressed that you have to go into their dreams to see what they want. I'm telling you, Zekiel, this is an incubus' time to feed."

He spread his arms and spun around toward the multicolored glitter of the skyline. When Zekiel approached Charles and peered over his shoulder, he saw what Charles saw for the first time in a long while — potential, rather than the ever-encroaching darkness.

"It's a veritable feast," Charles said. "Tell you what. Let me show you what you've been missing. I have a few appetizers, a damn good selection of entrees and a hell of a fine piece of dessert that I've been cultivating, and I'm more than willing to share. What do you say?"

"I think you should leave now." Zekiel lowered his gaze when Charles faced him, incredulous.

"You aren't the incubus I remember. Nothing like him, except for that cock trying to drill a hole through your skirt."

He grasped Zekiel's shoulder. Charles' touch affected him, but no differently from what it had done when they'd both wielded that incubus charm together. However, Zekiel's first instinct was to jerk away from Charles' touch. It would be best not to tempt himself with all the memories that flooded back as Charles lightly massaged his shoulder.

"No, I am not the demon you remember," Zekiel said. "I'm not a demon at all. I relinquished everything."

"Not a demon," Charles said softly. "Have you looked in a mirror lately? You're still demon, just with the consistency of a concrete slab. You can't shed the demon, love. It's etched into the lines of your face and the glory of your wings." Charles stroked the pointed ridges of Zekiel's cheekbones, the horn-like protrusions on his forehead. "It's what you are. And the Big Man hasn't taken that away. I wouldn't have felt the incubus I knew if He had. I think you're still in there, Zekiel, no matter what crusade you think you've taken up. And might I add that the Crusades didn't end up so well. You're going to find yourself on the wrong side of history, mate."

"You know that's not true." Zekiel brushed Charles' fingers from his face and shrugged away from the hand on his shoulder. "In fact, you know for a fact that, in the end, I've chosen the right path."

"There's still time to have some fun before Daddy makes us all go to our timeout corner," Charles said, grasping him again. "We had less than twenty years together. That's not enough to do anything, really. I can make it fun for you again."

"Fun was never the problem." Zekiel threaded his fingers through Charles' to force them away, but Charles refused to cooperate, as he always had.

His stubbornness had been one of his most infuriating and attractive qualities when they'd hunted together. Zekiel had been content with average fare before he'd met Charles. But Charles had convinced him to do all kinds of things that he had never done or wanted to do before — every one of them amazing, even the dangerous ones that set hunters on their tails. There was nothing more adventurous than a demon who had just learned what he was, because everything was a novelty, the freedom and power addictive. With Charles, Zekiel had experienced a renaissance. Feasts that had been routine had become exhilarating, because Zekiel had shared Charles' exhilaration.

Twenty years, they'd hunted together—not very long for demons, but those years stood out as exceptional in Zekiel's long memory. He had been the elder of the two, yet Charles had taught him more about the full breadth of what it meant to be an incubus, had injected his existence with pleasure Zekiel hadn't believed possible, even as a sex demon.

In some ways, Charles was the reason why Zekiel had repented.

The highs that Charles had given had brought him too close to the sun, an incubus Icarus, a moth who had learned too late that the light would scorch him and send him plunging when reality finally set in.

And it had. One day, he had blinked and could see all the things he hadn't before. He'd seen what he had become—and, worse, that what he had become was what he truly was. He could never forget what he was now. As Charles had said, he could see what he was in every reflection.

A demon. A monster. A beast, one among many that should have been destroyed, as foretold.

"I told you, Charles, you need to go. *Now.*" Sometime between his trying to back away and ease Charles off his body, Charles had gotten awfully close, his leather jacket swinging against Zekiel's erection.

"Why? I think I'm the perfect one to fix this particular problem. I can't imagine being so desperate for a wank that I'd forget an impending dawn. Truly, mate, you shouldn't be having this problem. There are ways to deal with it, so many filthy, nasty ways. I shouldn't have to tell you that."

Zekiel kept his lips sealed about Abby. If he told Charles that he'd ended up this way because of a woman, a woman for whom he genuinely cared, Charles would fixate on her in a heartbeat, find some way to worm into her life, into her relationship with Zekiel, into her dreams, until he had consumed her entirely. And by that time, maybe he would have wrangled Zekiel into joining him, defiling the very woman whose virtues he'd extolled to himself all the blessed day. Already, he sensed himself falling into the same behaviors and feelings as Charles tilted Zekiel's head up, his smug, knowing smile a mere few inches from Zekiel's lips.

"I have renounced what I was," Zekiel said, although without the conviction he had hoped for.

"Easily fixed. Last time I checked, which is about now" — Charles lifted the hem of Zekiel's covering to expose his erection once more — "you aren't dead."

"But you could be."

"What's that supposed to mean?"

Zekiel had always liked it when Charles had been rough, but when Charles wrapped his hand around the shaft, he squeezed a little too tightly. The morning-coffee warmth of his smile had taken a chilly turn, his teeth sharper than before.

"I mean that I did not transform into a gargoyle to simply turn to stone during the day and bemoan the mistakes of my prior life when I awoke."

Charles pulled Zekiel's cock with firm strokes just short of painful, yet so excruciatingly wonderful. "The next thing you'll tell me is that you've become a man of action. Shove off, Zeke. I sometimes had to drag you with me to get you out of the house."

"I kill what we were." Zekiel wrapped his hand around Charles' to still it over his cock. "What you are. I've been given a mission."

Charles laughed, abruptly releasing Zekiel's cock and bracing himself against one of the gargoyles on the edge of the roof to steady himself as he caught his breath. "A 'mission'? Oh, hell help me, who do you think you are, an archangel? You've been given a *mission*? From *God*? He breathed life into dust to create humanity, but he touched you and turned you to stone. God wants nothing but your misery. I wouldn't be surprised if he had you walking around with that boner like a repressed, self-denying monk all the time. The Creator hasn't given *you* a mission."

He spun around and shoved Zekiel, startling him. Charles' face contorted with anger, but not hatred this time, or else Zekiel really would have unsheathed his sword. Charles shoved him again with preternatural strength, slamming Zekiel into the wall where he'd punched his fists. This time, Zekiel was the one with his back to the wall and Charles was the one who slammed his fists into the craters that Zekiel had left behind.

"He only wanted to dole out your punishment early. He wants *nothing* to do with you," Charles said through clenched teeth. He brought his hand between them and wrung Zekiel's erection again, brought it to full mast with his deft touch, as though the century behind them had been nothing more than a brief interlude. "He doesn't want you, but I do."

His gaze locked on Zekiel's, he knelt at Zekiel's feet, smiling with more sincerity now, although his teeth were sharper than ever.

"It's been too damn long, love." The velvet of his voice wrapped around Zekiel's cock even more effectively than his hand. "Let me take care of this for you — for old times' sake, if nothing else."

"I shouldn't—"

"Of course you shouldn't. That's the fun." Charles lunged forward, engulfing Zekiel's sizable cock in his mouth and taking it all the way down as though he didn't have a gag reflex — because, of course, he didn't.

Zekiel cried out, jerking his hips and shoving his cock deeper down Charles' throat. Charles moaned, twisting over the base as though wishing he could take even more in. He dug his fingers into the muscles of Zekiel's ass, rubbing into the tension that he had helped create...and Abby.

Zekiel tried to remember Abby and that this erection had been because of her, that it was *hers*. Charles' mouth where Abby had been only tainted the memory.

Zekiel should have yanked him off, rebuked him before cutting off his head. To do so would save every woman and man upon whom Charles latched himself like a lamprey. He loved what he did too much to give it up any time soon. He needed to be stopped now, while Zekiel had him in his grasp.

A grasp that formed a fist in Charles' hair so that Zekiel could piston his hips into Charles' mouth, all while Charles made obscene, wet moans every time, his teeth pricking Zekiel's shaft. Zekiel cursed as he punched the wall again, so fucking close to coming, but Charles wouldn't let him. He sucked hard from base to head, then licked his lips once he'd pulled back from Zekiel's erection completely.

"There's the demon I remember. You even smell more like him now." He mouthed down the shaft, savoring the taste as though he'd poured melted chocolate down Zekiel's cock—which he'd done before, so Zekiel had the perfect point of reference that replayed in his mind.

Charles licked lingering circles around the ridge of the head before swiping his tongue against the slit, where pre-cum gleamed.

Clenching his teeth, Zekiel jerked Charles' head back. Charles laughed as Zekiel rubbed his cock over Charles' face. He playfully licked what Zekiel gave him but closed his mouth when Zekiel tried to force himself inside again.

Zekiel groaned in frustration. He would prefer for Abby to be here for this—maybe then his mind would not be so muddled with nostalgia for what had been and could be if he let himself slip back. It hadn't been all bad. Some of it, things like this, had been fantastic—because he hadn't had to care. Carelessness so easily transformed into recklessness, and recklessness became violence, because he'd never had to worry about hurting Charles.

Zekiel yanked him up. Their mouths clashed, meeting as though there had been no time apart. Zekiel grabbed the collar of Charles' leather jacket and held him close as Charles pinched Zekiel's nipples and sucked hard on his lower lip. He gasped as Zekiel replaced his cock with his tongue in Charles' mouth, plundering and dominating him as though he were the elder demon once again, with the proverbial leash around his young apprentice.

Just as Zekiel groaned and bucked at the jolt of pleasure that Charles sent through him—not as potent as it would have been for a human being, but a marvelous aphrodisiac between two incubi—Charles laughed again, his face bright with color from their combined heat.

"You feel that?" Charles took Zekiel's cock in hand again and had to catch his breath. "I feel it, too. I knew you were still in there." He caught Zekiel's nipple between his teeth then soothed the brief pain with his tongue.

As Charles sent his charm through, Zekiel also sensed something leaving him and going into Charles, like it used to when they would get lost and frantic in their own magic, the sheets tangled in knots around their legs and Charles underneath him or above him. It never really mattered, as long as they kept contact. They could feed off each other for hours.

"Let me come, damn it."

"I don't know. I don't think I've gotten enough out of you yet," Charles said, stroking and twisting Zekiel's erection to the edge. "What do you think I am, an incubus who can get sex whenever he wants? Who knows when my next opportunity will be?"

"I have needed release all day. *All* day. Please. If you don't, I will destroy you and do it myself."

"You sure you don't have to flagellate for a few more days as penance for your wickedness?" With his other hand, he cupped and caressed Zekiel's scrotum, teasing the wrinkled flesh behind and hinting at more he could do.

"For God's sake…"

"Not for His. But for yours, I suppose I could give you some relief." Charles lowered himself to one knee and surround the head with the firm, hot suction of his mouth once more, milking him roughly with his hands until Zekiel came, fucking Charles' face and flooding his throat with cum that was eagerly swallowed down.

Zekiel sagged against the wall, all the wretched tension from the day relieved in an instant. He felt so much more like himself once more.

Of course, that just made everything more complicated, because Charles licked his lips with a pointed tongue and stood again, graciously rearranging Zekiel's cloth so that it once again covered him, waist to knees, no more erection pushing it outward.

Zekiel knew he should not have permitted it, but when Charles slid his hand over the base of Zekiel's skull and drew him down for a slower, more searching kiss, Zekiel relented. He held his old partner against him, aware for the first time of the bulge in Charles' pants pressing against Zekiel's abdomen. Charles teased Zekiel's tongue with his sharper teeth then withdrew with a satisfied grin.

"Thank you," Zekiel said. Ambivalence aside, it was only polite to show gratitude for being given what he had begged for.

"My pleasure. Now I have a few needs of my own to fulfill. Are you sure you aren't interested in joining me for dinner?"

"I'll give you tonight." The distance that returned into Zekiel's voice made Charles stiffen in a less enjoyable way. "For old times' sake, I'll let you have tonight. Next time, I might have to kill you, because I know you, Charles. I know you won't listen to me, because when have you ever listened to me? Even so, I suggest you don't try to see me again, if you value your life."

Charles took a few steps back, then rearranged himself to appear as though he hadn't been urgently kissing or sucking off a desperate gargoyle. "My, aren't you an unpleasant sort these days? Fuck 'em and leave 'em didn't used to be your modus operandi with me."

"It's no worse than the way we treated all the men and women we discarded." Zekiel crossed his arms and spread his wings slightly, in case he had to fight or flee. But if he were honest with himself—and he had an obligation to be—he didn't want to kill his old friend. Charles had no truly malicious intent. He was a destructive, insidious libertine who suffered no discernable consequences and thus never had any reason to stop. Zekiel understood, because he'd been the same way once.

Heaven help him, he was still immensely fond of the young incubus, and death was not something Zekiel wished for him—not when there was still hope. Slim hope, foolish hope, hope that would be a long time in coming to fruition, but hope, nonetheless.

"We were brothers, Zekiel. Partners." Charles assumed his fully human visage, smile bright and not nearly as sharp as before. "You were more than just my lover. You were mine and I was yours. Let me know if your God gives as good as I gave you."

"I give you tonight." Zekiel advanced on Charles, who retreated with a kind of confused fury.

"I'm not letting this go. And I'm not just letting *you* go. You wait. You'll come crawling back to me. You'll crave what you left behind."

"I did crave it," Zekiel replied softly. "For decades. I still miss it some nights. But I have since found another purpose, and I can never go back to what I was."

"Of course you can. You fell once. You can fall again."

"You can never truly return to what you were. It is a consequence of time." Zekiel placed a hand on Charles' shoulder. "I will pray every day that you come to understand."

"Ew." Charles shrugged Zekiel's hand off as though he'd put a rat there. "Save your prayers. Enjoy your crusade. Look me up when you come to your senses. Just leave the blade at home. I know we enjoyed it once, but with all the talk of killing me, I might misinterpret the gesture, and I'd hate for you to bring a knife to a gunfight."

Charles pulled open the roof access door, then locked it behind him, perhaps to keep Zekiel from having second thoughts and chasing him down. Zekiel could have kicked the door down without difficulty, but instead he contemplated the doorknob for a few minutes with the sinking feeling that he should have killed Charles where he'd stood.

Chapter Nine

Out over the waves is the most beautiful sunset in the world. She has never seen colors like this except in retouched photographs and advertisements, pictures she's never trusted. Now she barely trusts her own eyes, but the terrycloth under her belly, the sand gritty under her elbows, the salt of the surf and the coconut of the sunscreen all assure her that this is real.

Everything tells her that it is, but she cannot shake the suspicion that it's all a dream, too perfect to be true.

Her reservations fade when he settles beside her and presses his lips to her shoulder, sending a jolt of arousal so powerful through her that she has to close her eyes to the once-in-a-lifetime view.

"Sorry. I didn't mean to be so late."

"It's all right," she says. "As long as you're here now. Never leave me."

"I would never abandon you. I certainly wouldn't want to miss you looking like this, now, would I?" He slaps her left buttock, half exposed by her bikini bottoms, and she laughs. It's true, she's rarely this exposed to him, and he has been *very understanding about going slow, especially when all the little things overwhelm her so quickly. She never knew that love could be like this, that sometimes all it took was a touch to crash her through a blissful climax.*

He kisses cold shivers over her shoulder and breathes her in. "Eager tonight, are we?"

"It feels like it's been forever."

"It's only been one night."

"Like I said, forever."

"It's nice to be needed as much as I need you." He guides her gaze from the deepening sunset to him and kisses her lips lightly.

She's the one who leans in for more, parting her mouth to invite him to take her, to take all of her. The sunset suddenly seems unimportant.

She'll buy a postcard.

"You are so beautiful," he groans into the kiss.

"How can you tell with your eyes closed?"

"I've memorized every inch of you."

"Not every inch."

That opens his eyes. She moves her elbows back to expose the tanned swells of her breasts that she presses together with her arms for a dramatic shadow of cleavage. She's already overheated from the day in the sun, lightheaded, but her heart beats faster and warms her further when he's captivated by the sight. He swallows as though his mouth goes dry.

"Well, go on, soldier. Open your present." She glances pointedly in the direction of her back, where the bikini top's string ties are.

He trails his fingers down the dip of her spine, tugs at the loop of the tie to tease her before sliding lower. He stops at the waist of the bikini bottoms – a whole new thrill and profound wish.

"What's the occasion?" he asks.

"Does there need to be one?"

He grins. "I accept gifts all three-hundred-sixty-five days of the year."

"I figured."

He shifts closer, propped up on his elbow so that she can see the whole beautiful expanse of his bare chest and abdomen, the trail of dark hair leading from his navel to under the waistband of his swim shorts.

This is more than she usually sees of him, too. Not much left to the imagination. They might as well be naked, the both of them, right here on this public beach, although there isn't a soul around. She has never understood what twisted social rules allow this much skin on display around water but forbid lingerie on city streets. Not that she was complaining at being able to stare at him now, memorizing him the way he claims to have memorized her.

"Are you sure?"

"Yes," she whispers. "I don't care who sees."

"No one will ever see you but me."

His possessiveness is a promise. She beckons him in.

He captures her mouth once more. Her breath catches as he deftly undoes the tie to her top and the strings fall to her sides. Only her arms hold the front over her breasts, but his kisses become more sensual and insistent, as though he's drinking from her, and eventually she finds herself on her side against his hot body, his erection cradled in the valley between her thighs and her breasts bare to his gaze when he pulls back.

"I've now seen the most beautiful thing in all of creation," he murmurs. He doesn't touch her, although her nipples wrinkle and tighten from desire that he will. His gaze warms her further, almost tangible as he appears to commit the sight of her bareness to new memory.

"You're not finished." She feels as though someone has stolen her breath as he glances lower, the place she knows he wants to press his erection, and she wants him to, doesn't want anything between them anymore. "I'm ready."

"Yes, I think you are."

He caresses her from the hollow under her cheekbone down to her breasts. She gives a soft cry as he circles her nipple with his thumb, scraping the nail lightly against the nub until she's panting. She wants to lie back and spread her legs for him, let him have it all, anything he wants. Nothing he does will ever hurt her, not when every little thing he does gives her more and more pleasure. She knows there must be an end…or a plateau. There should be a point where the pleasure must at least level out. But he always finds new heights.

"You have to make me ready first." He nods to where he's long, thick and straining against the front of his shorts.

Her mouth waters, although she has never seen him or had a cock in her mouth. She struggles not to seem too excited or willing. She doesn't know why she worries about appearances when no one but him watches her, and he won't judge her for how much she wants him.

She sits up. He appreciatively eyes the sway of her breasts from the movement. She doesn't know if she's ever felt so desirable as when he looks at her. Her fingers shake when she takes hold of the waistband of his shorts.

He lifts his hips as she works the shorts down his thighs. She struggles to breathe at the sight of his thick, flushed erection curved against his hip. It's almost as though it stretches toward her, pleading for her touch. But he stops her before she can, and she blinks back tears. She thought he would let her. He said she was ready.

"That's all I needed, sweet thing," he says. "Just seeing you like this, having you strip me, I might come if you touch me. Time for you to lose your last barrier, too, love."

She reaches to do it herself. It's just a strip of cloth. It would take three seconds for her to be rid of it, but he slaps *her hand then pushes her onto her back and straddles her legs. His cock bobs from the weight of his arousal but remains rigid above her, dripping pre-cum.*

"Let me."

She groans because she knows he's going to take his sweet time. He smiles as he takes the end of the string ties on the bottoms and slowly pulls them up.

"I can't — " She tosses her head on the towel, lifts her hips toward him, but that doesn't hurry him at all. The crashing of the waves roars in her ears. She might go crazy before he finally sees all of her, before he's finally inside her as she has dreamed for so long. She wants to be his, and she doesn't want to climax before he's taken her. Her whole body screams for his cock to slam into her. She doesn't care about kindness or gentleness anymore. All she wants is for him to rip her bikini bottoms off, pin her to the ground and shove in. She doesn't think that's a lot to ask for, yet he pauses before his work frees the knots on her last bit of clothing.

"It's late," he says with a toothsome grin. "Maybe we should go home."

"Don't you fucking dare. I'm ready for you now. I'm ready for you to fuck me. Just please, please, please fuck me with that big cock. Fill me with you, please."

"Such language. Does your father know you talk like that?"

"If you don't finish this now, I'm telling him you took my virginity. He owns a gun."

He laughs, hearty and rich and vibrating all through her. "Even I know that's not true — and not the part about your father owning a gun."

"Yeah, well, he doesn't know that. It's been torture waiting this long for you. I don't want to wait another second."

"I had to be sure you were ready." He strokes his thumbs under the fabric strings at the crease where her legs meet her hips.

For a moment, only a moment, her stomach dips, not with arousal but with déjà vu, sure that she's had this conversation before. But when she tries to grasp the memories, they slip away like water through a sieve. He raises an inquisitive eyebrow.

"I've been ready," she replies.

He pulls the strings, revealing her like the present she is. His mouth is wet as he brings his hand between her legs, slicing a finger through her folds and dipping into the slit. She arches her back in the hopes that he will enter her, but he pulls his hand away and brings the fingers to his mouth, clearly relishing her taste. Her cunt clenches, pleasure shuddering through her. She feels full to the brim like ripe fruit, but hollow where she needs him most.

She growls. "Stop teasing."

"But it's so goddamn fun."

She grabs his shoulders and pulls him down, wrapping an arm around his back to bring their hips tight together. A bead of sweat slides down her forehead into her hair. It's a warm evening and he's even warmer, but she wallows in the heat suffusing her. She almost shudders into a climax at the way his cock rubs against her swollen, tingling clit.

"Who's teasing now?" he whispers against her neck.

"Inside. I need you **inside**." She doesn't exaggerate. She thinks she might actually hyperventilate if she doesn't get his cock into her pussy right the fuck **now**, and it only gets worse as she strokes his back and he kisses her neck, palms her breasts, slides his cock through her folds. Her hips have stopped listening to her. They move of their own accord, bucking as though begging for him where he might actually listen to her, because weren't cocks supposed to be more demanding than pussies?

If only it were so. She wouldn't have to be frantically frotting with him as his laughter rumbles through her.

"You want me inside? Everywhere? All over you?"

"Everywhere. Everything. I'm yours."

"That's what a man wants to hear." And he slips his cock into her as though he's done this with her a thousand times, that's how right this feels. She screams with the gulls when she can get a gasp in edgewise, holds on to him as though clinging to life itself, unable to do anything herself. Her body has forgotten anything other than his.

He makes no complaints, the muscles to which she clings like warm, velvet-bound stone. He spreads her legs with his thighs, pumping into her with the full measure of his strength and desire, plumbing fathoms into her body and igniting her like a thousand stars in the evening sky. The thickness of his shaft and the ridge of the head seem to reach places that have never been touched or that she has never been aware of. Her world narrows to his skin sliding smooth over hers with sweat and lotion and softness and his cock stroking through her wetness, which smears over her thighs and scents the air.

It occurs to her that he usually smells of cinnamon and sandalwood, but now he smells of nothing.

"Is this what you wanted?" He pants from exertion but still goes strong — oh my, yes — inside of her. Tears join sweat at her temple.

"Yes," she whispers. "Yes. Yes. Yes! Yes!" Once she starts, she cannot stop, because he's riding her forward, momentum catapulting her body into its orgasm. She clings to his cock as he comes with her, sucking at her neck and his hips flush with hers.

When his cock stops twitching, she goes limp, boneless, unable to do anything more strenuous than blinking. It alarms her at first, but he smooths his tongue over the place he's bitten her, and he keeps his cock, somehow still firm, inside of her until she drifts off to sleep.

* * * *

There was no getting around it. Abby was distracted, and her night patients noticed—many of whom were tired after their day shifts or, as night wore on, tired because they had to get out of bed to see a doctor when they didn't even want to be wearing pants.

"You've already taken my blood pressure," Jorge Martinez said.

Abby held up the blood pressure cuff and racked her brain to remember doing it, but she failed miserably.

"I'm sorry, Jorge. It's been one of those days." Abby checked her notes. Yes, there it was, slightly elevated blood pressure, but nothing worrisome, which made sense because he'd come here with a persistent, productive, hacking cough and fever. Abby didn't need a doctor to know that Jorge had a nasty case of bacterial bronchitis sitting uncomfortably on the edge of pneumonia, although Dr. Drobny would still have to put in a perfunctory appearance, just to reassure himself that his degree still had purpose in the same facility as a healer who diagnosed by touch.

Not that Dr. Drobny knew, but he usually trusted her instincts without much pushback. A doctor couldn't be too arrogant working here. He wasn't paid enough for pride. None of them were.

"Tell me about it. Give me some good news," Jorge said, practically croaking his words, because that was the best he could manage.

"Good news is that Jesus is alive and so are you, sweetie," Abby said.

That got her a crackling, phlegmy laugh that turned into another cough.

"The bad news is you probably have a bad case of bronchitis. We'll consult with the doctor, but we both know he just consults with me, right? A course of antibiotics will clear the worst of it right out."

"I have work to be doing and bills to be paying. What the fuck do these antibiotics cost?" Jorge muttered.

"Let's not think about that until we get the doctor in here. And ideally, you shouldn't be at work at all, Jorge. You'll pass it on to everyone else and make them miserable, too." She set her hand on his on the examination table—a firm grip instead of a flirtatious one so that her signals couldn't be mistaken.

"I know, missy, but at least we'll all be miserable and *paid*."

"I'm contractually obligated to tell you to stay home and drink lots of fluids. You need some good vitamin C. I'd write a note if I thought it'd help."

She hoped that their conversation masked the magic that passed from her palm to the back of his hand like fireflies.

"Not in the real world, missy. But I gotta say, you're a balm for the soul. I feel better already. Must be that pretty smile of yours."

Maybe she didn't hide her impact as well as she'd hoped, but he didn't seem to connect his feeling better to her contact, so she patted his vascular hand and took up his file.

"All right, I'll get the doctor for you. I'd say he'll be right with you, but we both know I'd be lying. We do, however, have out-of-date magazines in the corner."

"You're a treasure." When he grinned, his teeth were surprisingly white against his dark, leathery skin.

"Comments like that are my reason, Jorge. Have a good night, and say hi to your wife and son for me," she said around the door frame before heading back to the reception desk.

Although healing usually stole some of her energy, it never left a hole inside of her. She experienced a brief flush of fever that subsided like the pull of tide, leaving only the thrill of charity, not to mention the joy that she actually got to heal someone today.

Dr. Drobny caught her before she reached reception. "I heard some of that. You really have been distracted lately."

"Lately? I thought I was only distracted today."

"Today is lately."

"I'm not perfect. It was bound to happen sooner or later. I'll do better."

Dr. Drobny bit his lip, but the smile crept through anyway. "Abby, you're doing fine. You're allowed to have an off day as long as you keep doing your job, and you are. I just wanted to say, in a completely non-harassment way, that you're not just distracted. Darcy's been asking me all night whether I know who your boyfriend is. You're glowing."

Abby recoiled, only partially exaggerating. "Goodness, I hope not."

"Not that kind of glowing. All I'm saying is that we're happy for you, Darcy's desperate for salacious details, I'm very much not and try not to let it affect work overly much. Deal?"

"Deal. I'll get my act together by tomorrow."

"You better," the doctor said. "Room three?"

"Possible bronchitis."

"That's been going around, and everyone's waiting too long to come in. I heard him in the waiting room. Cross your fingers it hasn't become pneumonia yet." Dr. Drobny edged past her in the hall as Abby continued to reception.

"So, spill." Darcy nudged Abby as she took her next file. "Who's the lucky guy you've been getting some from?"

"Not in front of patients," Abby whispered.

Darcy rolled her eyes. "Like they couldn't all hear you and the doctor in the hall."

"You don't know him. Mrs. Lowry, please save me from office gossip."

Mrs. Lowry picked up her feverish four-year-old daughter, who she'd wrapped in a blanket, but she cracked a weary smile, nevertheless. "Glad to be of service."

Abby peered at little Hannah's brilliantly flushed face. In her blue eyes, Abby noticed a gleam like the glow of a candle. She offered Hannah and Mrs. Lowry a reassuring smile. "Let's get you all better, sweetie, okay?"

Off day, but this was going to be a good night.

* * * *

She was still smiling as she passed the torch to the day shift and stepped out of the front door, choosing not to change out of her scrubs first. The morning crowd could handle her in orthopedic shoes and professional coral-colored pajamas.

The sight of the cemetery across the street, even with the beautiful clarity of morning's light against the headstones and iron, sobered her.

After all these years of searching and finally finding him, she still hadn't gone back to see her dad.

It wasn't like he was going anywhere, unless he'd reached the end of his tenure in Cemetery Grove. He'd been here for fifteen years already, and there didn't seem to be rhyme or reason to whether he stayed or went. Abby doubted he would have disappeared in a few days, though.

She should visit him again, but she didn't want to get into another fight about whether she should stay in Meridian. This last week was an excellent argument both for and against, to be honest. But she could always steer the discussion away from her living situation. Catch up. Grab a hot chocolate, sit on the lap of the corpse whose grave he protected and have a good, old-fashioned conversation with her father, something she hadn't done in forever.

So why wasn't she crossing the street and jumping the fence or waiting for the cemetery to open?

Abby wanted to see him again. She really did. Just…not right now.

Maybe some of the cemetery angels, knowing who to look for, had sent whispers back to him of what she'd been doing. That would really get her a lecture about safety and how no incubus was ever safe and how fighting demon cults with delusions of apocalypse in the company of a gargoyle certainly wasn't safe. either, and that he didn't want to have to preside over her funeral. She could practically hear him now.

Although she hesitated at the sidewalk, fidgeting with the hem of her tunic under her jacket, she turned right, away from the cemetery.

Maybe tomorrow.

Chapter Ten

Abby didn't even bother getting a drink this time. She just surveyed the barroom, judged that Charles wasn't in it, then nodded at Miranda and went upstairs to the residential part of the building.

She only got one knock in before Charles opened the door, pulled her in by the lapel of her jacket, then closed the door with his body flush against hers. He took her by such surprise that Abby clutched at his upper arms to ground herself through the fronts of arousal that poured through her. What really slayed her was that arousal this powerful was actually *filtered* through their respective winter layers. She hadn't had time to put up her defenses, mental though they would have been.

"It's later than I anticipated, sweet thing. I got all my work done, but what am I supposed to do with the rest of my time? Wait and watch the clock for your return?" Charles asked, more frustrated than Abby suspected he wanted to sound.

"Um, I have a job with actual hours." It took every ounce of her willpower to put her hands on his chest and push him away. "I'm not going to sneak out just to scratch an incubus' itch. What? You don't have enough outlets?"

"I'm saving myself for you."

"Spare me. In fact, I was coming here to tell you that you're so full of shit. I'm not going to stick around and be your punching bag anymore."

"I thought you enjoyed that."

"It's not about what I enjoy or not."

"So you admit you enjoyed it. You admit you have a little bit of darkness under that squeaky bright and clinically clean exterior."

"Everyone has a dark side," she said, "but I'm not conceding to your theory that I have a masochistic streak. Being what you are, you could probably make anything feel sexy if you wanted, even things that don't normally push my buttons."

Charles ran a hand through his hair and acknowledged the point with a nod. "I do take requests, but I occasionally switch it up with my more vanilla usuals, too, I'll give you that. However, I think you're putting too much of your pleasure on me. After all, I'm not going to have as much control without touching you." He threaded his gloved fingers through hers. "Or without taking the reins of your dreams, of which I've yet to have the pleasure."

"I do appreciate that." She still hadn't heard any untoward moans from her roommates, and she was no more or less tired than usual, so she believed him.

"How much do you appreciate it?"

"Really, don't you get enough from your victims?"

"I'm an incubus. Insatiable, remember?" Charles unbuttoned his coat and hung it on the coatrack, although Abby didn't know why he'd been wearing his coat in his own home. Maybe he'd gone to get a snack while he'd been waiting.

She hated thinking of people in the same terms as he thought of them, but it helped her focus less on victims she couldn't help at the moment. When dealing with a demon directly, his victims were a distraction.

"And I *have* been waiting for you, imagining the things we could do tonight," he said. "I've found myself unusually inspired."

"Must be going around," she muttered.

Charles perked up. "Have a few fantasies you wish me to fulfill as well?"

"More like a farewell, in the vein of the aforementioned 'you're full of shit'."

"And how, pray tell, am I full of shit?" He backed toward the bedroom. The screens blocking it had already been pushed back, the shackles on the wall opened in anticipation of her arrival.

"Telling me that my dark side, if that's even what you showed me, is that of a demon because I'm the daughter of a nephil."

"It's the truth."

She scoffed. "The truth coming from a demon. I don't know why I ever fell for it, really. You're good…but not that good."

"There's nothing to fall for. You believed me because, deep down, you know it's true. What makes you think I'm lying?"

"It's what you do. That's what an incubus is, Charles—one giant lie. You manipulate dreams, for heaven's sake."

"Dreams are sometimes greater truth than reality, love, and they can be just as real. That doesn't change because it's only in the mind. The soul reveals itself — the good, the bad and the despicably disgusting. It's all there, with no shame to bury it into the recesses of your consciousness. I'd wager I would learn more about you in three dreams than I have in three days."

Charles sat on the bed and beckoned to her, but she crossed her arms and stayed by the front door. He shrugged, then unbuttoned his shirt, which immediately put her on edge. That was a lot more skin for him to reveal, given that he'd been completely clothed for the last session. He was that many more square inches of dangerous to her, and not just because what he revealed was a sculpted masterpiece that shouldn't have been real outside of a stone carving. Zekiel was this pretty, but it was different when he was actually made of stone. Abby had to keep telling herself that Charles' appearance wasn't real, either, any more than his words. It was all illusion, from the pale marble of his chest to the incredible ass in those jeans.

So, damn it, why did she practically melt when he tossed his shirt on the bedspread and lay back with his arms over his head in a luxurious stretch that a feline would envy? The action displayed to the best advantage the delicious vee of his hips narrowing to under the low-slung waist of his dark jeans.

Abby put as much distance between them as she could, which meant flattening her back against the door. She swore he exuded sex, which meant he was probably emanating the full measure of his charm — at least she hoped so.

Reminding herself that her reaction was mystical rather than natural wasn't helping, however, with the way her loose scrubs suddenly seemed too restrictive and decidedly unsexy. He didn't seem to mind. He peered at her with those warm, smiling eyes as though she wore nothing at all.

"Well, you're not getting into my dreams," she said. "And you're not getting me. Not anymore."

"Is that so? I notice you're saying a lot of things about how my lies have no power over you. Yet you came here, and you're not leaving. So why don't you come over here, sweet thing, and get a dose of the truth." He stroked a gloved hand over his chest. She was momentarily enchanted by the twitch of his abdomen as his breath caught from the stroke of leather over his small, tight nipple. "We'll clear up all the little lies you've been telling yourself. Don't judge yourself too harshly. You're awake. Everyone lies when they're awake."

Abby refused to budge. She didn't trust herself even a foot closer to him. "You're not putting me to sleep."

"Of course not." He smoothed his hand down over his abdomen, over the dip of his navel and the dark hairs that trailed under his jeans. Everything seemed to lead there in the end. The lines and folds of his jeans didn't quite conceal his cock, thick and curved over his thigh.

"And you can't possibly expect me to think more clearly over there," she said.

"It's about thinking less clearly. Trusting what you feel."

"Are you serious?"

"How hard do you think I'm trying to seduce you?" Charles asked with a laugh. "You think I'm breaking out all my wiles and using every magical trick in the book? I'm not doing anything, Abigail. A little of what you're feeling is simply a byproduct of my existence. I can't help that. But the rest is all you, love. You're so sensitive. It only makes sense that like calls to like."

"Stop that!" Abby closed her hand around the doorknob but couldn't bring herself to open it. Why had she come here at all? More than that, why had she walked away from her *father* to come here? It wasn't as though she hadn't known what to expect.

"Tell me, nephil offspring, what makes you think you aren't what you are?" He lazily stroked over the placket of his jeans, but his attention was all on her.

"This." She pulled out her silver knuckles.

"And you say you're not a hunter."

"They're for self-defense. And they don't burn me. If they don't burn me, I'm not a demon."

"The first twenty years of my incarnate life, I could touch silver, too. I can't anymore, but my mother had a silver ring, and I never burned myself on it when I was her child. I was human enough, until I wasn't." He pushed himself up onto his elbows. "Come to bed, dear, and I'll show you."

"No. You're not getting me over there again. I'm not letting you confuse me."

"You're already confused. Now, stop brandishing silver. You're human for now, but you won't be forever."

"I'm older than you were when you changed," she said.

"You're also a better woman than I was a man," he replied with a grin. "You can prolong your time as a human, but you can't stay human forever. And I'm willing to bet that if you were completely human, you wouldn't have lasted this long with all the things that you do. Am I right?"

"Demon hunters last without demon blood all the time."

"Do they, though? No. Their lives are cut short, or they remove themselves from this world on their own. You still have ties to people who don't know what you do, what you are. But you only maintain those ties because you don't know what's waiting for you on the other side. Let me show you."

Abby gave a surprised yelp as she slid across the carpet, tripping out of her shoes. Her purse and jacket slipped off her arms. Then he flew her the rest of the way into the bedroom. She flipped around in midair and slammed against the wall. The shackles there closed around her wrists and ankles, holding her spread-eagled.

"No!" She yanked fruitlessly against the shackles. "No, damn it, let me go!"

"We're not done here, Abigail." Charles stood from the bed. "Tell me, love, do you have wings?"

"What the fuck does that matter?"

"It's a simple question. Have you discovered your wings yet? You already know some of your magic, but as the child of a nephil, you might have also discovered the joys of flight."

As he went to the dresser, he revealed his back. Like the rest of him, it was flawless, without even a mole or freckle or scar—except for the two giant gashes over his shoulder blades. The gaping wounds, cauterized and jagged as though broken tree branches instead of torn flesh, shocked Abby into stillness and silence. She'd never seen an incubus without his wings before.

Charles turned around with a pair of scissors in his hand. Her expression must have taken him by surprise, because he hesitated. "Ah. I take it you see right through my illusion."

"What the hell happened?" Abby asked.

"That's what all fallen winged angels look like, love. Perhaps you haven't had the opportunity to see them so exposed. Rest assured, though, my wings are intact—just not this particular pair." He glanced over his shoulder, then back at her. "Would you like to see?"

She nodded.

"Fair's fair." He held up the scissors. "I'll show you mine…"

Abby squirmed in the shackles as Charles approached her. "You don't need scissors to see mine."

He quirked an eyebrow. "Really? Unexpected…and irrelevant. I was really looking forward to cutting those clothes off."

"Excuse me, these are *my* clothes."

"I'll buy you a new pair. I'll buy you three, although it's a shame to hide your body in these."

"I'm not going to wear a negligee to a clinic," Abby said in annoyance, but she didn't do more than shift slightly when he brought the scissors to the bottom of the tunic and made short work of it up to the collar. She felt like a corpse at a coroner's office being prepped for autopsy, not just of the body but the soul.

"I understand the inclination to minimize the number of heart attacks in your waiting room." He snipped the neckline of the shirt and caressed the line of her jaw with the cold metal. "But is a tailored slack too much to ask?"

"Do you *want* me to tell you how often I get various biohazardous materials on my clothes? I don't need the dry-cleaning bill."

"Fair enough."

He cut down each of the sleeves, tossed the ruined tunic to the floor, set the scissors aside, then feasted his gaze on her almost-bare torso. He could nearly encircle her waist with his large hands. She took after her mother in that respect—petite, skinny, but with a solid helping in the back and front. Those who had never seen her graze sometimes made the mistake of thinking she didn't eat.

Abby pulled against the shackles for another reason altogether when Charles slid his hands from her waist up to the jut of her ribs, his thumbs brushing the undersides of her bra.

She wasn't sure whether what she felt for Zekiel was love, but she thought it could grow into that. What she felt for Charles was very much not love. She was supposed to be fighting evil side by side with a noble, worthy warrior struggling for redemption that Abby now found she needed as well. She wasn't supposed to be letting evil undress her or slip that exquisite leather under her bra cups to palm her breasts in his hands.

"I wish I could feel you," he whispered. "I wish I could know if your skin is as soft as it looks. I hate feeling everything through a barrier."

"Tough," she said, biting back the similar wishes that threatened to spill out of her. "You still don't get to touch."

He brushed his nose against her hair, inhaling. "If I had my way, oh, the things I would do to you. I have the stamina of twenty men, love. I could pleasure you all night."

"Until you drained every last ounce of life from me."

"You'd be surprised how long I can make a woman's energy last. Now, show me. I want to see who you really are. Oh, wait, a few more things." He took the scissors and snipped the front of her bra.

"Hey! Those don't come cheap, you know." She wrenched against her bindings out of principle, quickly realizing that he was cutting her clothes so that they were completely useless, and she had nothing else to wear home except a jacket that barely covered her ass.

"I already told you I'll pay for three more. I can shower you with pink bags for the next year if you find yourself wanting—and blue boxes, too, if you desire," he said, patiently cutting through her panties and scrub pants. At that point, she had to stop resisting, because the impressively sharp blades were awfully close to important blood vessels and useful limbs.

"It's not about reparations. It's about you cutting up my clothes in the first place."

"I assure you, my plans for tonight will make it well worth the sacrifice."

"What part of 'no' don't you understand?"

Charles set down the scissors and looked up with a mild expression from where he knelt at her feet, as though he wasn't mere inches away from her naked pussy. "Oh, I'm sorry," he said, not sounding sorry at all. "I was under the impression that your 'no' was in reference to being a demon but that you came here for what I'm doing right now. Would you like for me to set you free and let you leave the apartment? Or will you end this charade and admit that I turn you on more than you'd like, so you'd rather paint me as the nefarious villain than confess that you might have a little villainy in you as well?"

"You just have an answer for everything, don't you?"

"You want to know who has the answer for everything? The one who's telling the truth. Lies are too much work."

"As a demon, you could probably pass any polygraph."

"Could you?" he asked.

"Shut up."

"If you were truly so affronted by my taking your clothes off like this, I think you'd really be getting mad now, but you're losing steam. Could it be that your doubts have returned?" He ran his smooth, gloved hands up her legs as he stood. "Show me your wings, Abigail."

He cupped her breasts on the way up, catching the nipples between his fingers, but when he took her face in his hands, he was surprisingly tender.

"Show me your beauty."

His breath swept warm over her lips, and she almost raised her chin for a kiss. Her eyelids fluttered shut, but she shook her head and opened her eyes wide again to his beatific smile.

She clenched her teeth and called her wings forth.

Smoke erupted from her shoulder blades around where Charles' wings had been torn off. They spread out farther than the width of the room. Technically, she could have sent her wings into the other apartment to the left and the balcony on her right, but she kept them curved along the bend of the walls. Sometimes they actually paid attention to the laws of physics, although they defied all laws of biology.

Charles stroked through the feather smoke, marveling at how his fingers went straight through. The contact sent a shiver down Abby's spine. She was suddenly very aware of how hard her nipples were in the cool air.

"Magnificent," he murmured. "Can you use them? In any way other than looking like the most majestic, beautiful fallen angel on this earth?"

"Please stop that." Abby could accept compliments on her healing powers and her memory for medical vocabulary, but she'd never enjoyed a man extolling shallow virtues, especially when he exaggerated. She detested sweet nothings. They were only more lies. "I can fly short distances. I glide and sometimes use the wind to lift me up. I can't fly like you or a g— bird, at least not for very long."

"And of course they're black smoke," Charles said, still touching them as though petting a ghost.

"Because I'm black or because my soul is?" Abby snapped. "You know, there are good things in the shadows, too. Demon cults aside, evil doesn't usually walk around in black cloaks and snake tattoos and emblazoned skulls and leather jackets. Evil's far more likely to wear an Armani suit, have the face of an angel and wear white after Labor Day like a boss. Just because something's black doesn't make it bad."

"I wasn't being philosophical, my dark beauty. I was thinking they're a lot like mine."

Charles closed his eyes and hunched his shoulders to show her his wings unfurling from the gashes in a burst of feathers as coal black as his hair. They were more substantial than hers, displacing the air around him in a rush of wind and rustling like thousands of ravens instead of hovering silently like wisps of smoke.

"If you were only human, you wouldn't see them at all. Face it, love. There's more to you than meets the human eye. I noticed it the moment I first saw you, when you walked into Threshold for the first time, blinked at the faun in the corner, then asked for a rum and Coke. You gain nothing in denying it. You only deny yourself. That's the lie, Abigail, far greater than any you think I've told you."

He furled his wings to frame him with their mammoth darkness.

"For instance, you say you don't want me to seduce you, yet you arrived without my coercing you in any way, and you don't deny me, even when I ask if you want to leave."

He brought his hands back to her breasts, kneading them lightly, caressing the outer edge of the areolae with his thumbs until she pressed her thighs together. He stayed gentle, unlike the last time, from which she still had bruises, greenish-yellow now, on her back and thighs. She could decide whether she healed herself on purpose, but she had no say on how fast she healed the rest of the time.

Because he stayed gentle, her skin zeroed in on the texture of the leather, the tingling hum that emanated from his touch, vibrating pure erotic delight wherever his warmth seeped through the gloves. His gaze caressed her just as warmly, as though he hadn't seen a woman's body in years. She couldn't shake her sense of the uniqueness of his regard. It must have been a cruel side effect of an incubus' charm, that every victim believed she was his only.

"If I am not permitted to touch you," Charles said, "we'll just have to improvise."

One of his dresser drawers opened by itself. Out poured a thin, shiny purple piece of fabric about the size of a generous shawl, but it wouldn't do much to keep a girl warm. It floated over Charles' shoulder, rubbing over his neck and chest like a cat. Then it flowed down and spread over her, molding itself to her body, stimulating her already hypersensitive nerves, the silken sensation lightly caressing every part of her it covered. It brushed her nipples like lips, massaged her arms and shoulder and abdomen, moved like warm water to her thighs. then slipped between, cupping the contour of her folds and dipping into the dampness that it found there.

Abby threw her head back, hitting the wall with a dull *thunk*. She'd never had something so sumptuous on her skin before, preferring cotton on a daily basis and settling for cheap fabrics if she had to dress up. She wasn't the best judge, but if she had to guess, this one piece of fabric probably cost more than her whole scrub collection.

"Until you let me in, this is the next best thing." And he pressed a kiss to her shoulder through the silk.

She closed her eyes as her whole body tightened with delicious tension. She couldn't feel the subtle texture of his lips, but the thin fabric gave her the closest approximation of what it would have been like for him to kiss her with nothing at all between them. It did nothing to impede the wet heat of his mouth as he kissed down to the peak of her breast to take her nipple between his teeth and tease the tip with his tongue.

And through it all, he never stopped moving his gloved hands over her, even where the fabric didn't cover. All over, her skin tingled as though stepping from a cold room into a hot bath. Her toes curled when he slid his hand between her legs, stroking ever so softly over her folds, which swelled with rushing blood as though to coax him to touch more.

Abby managed to open her eyes again and peered down from under heavy lids where he knelt before her once again. He grinned up at her, but there were lines of concentration on his forehead as he watched her reactions to the heel of his hand pressing in insistent rhythm against her clit.

Charles removed his hand from where he'd been tormenting her other nipple and opened his jeans, freeing his heavy erection. He gave a relieved sigh, smearing pre-cum over the thick, darkly flushed cock. Abby couldn't stop the high moan that passed her lips, although she strangled it as soon as she could.

"If I plunged this cock in that pussy of yours, I think you'd scream loud enough for the neighbors to hear. They probably wouldn't complain. I suspect some of them listen through the walls when I have visitors, especially visitors as delectable as you. What fantasies do you think you might inspire, sweet thing, if they knew even a fraction of what you let me do to you?"

"I'm not letting you do that—or *that*." She tasted bitter regret as potent as bourbon when she denied herself his cock, its unabashed carnal presence promising deeper pleasure than she'd already experienced at his hands.

"Pity. But I can enjoy you in far more ways than just one—or five, or fifteen. How many times would you like to come tonight? It's not often a woman has an incubus at her disposal. What do you wish of me?"

"I have simple tastes." She wriggled against the shackles when he ground his hand against her clit and stroked along the sides of her folds in encouragement.

"Only because you haven't tried enough of the complicated. Perhaps another time. We're only beginning to acquire that taste, aren't we?"

"You really sound like a douche when you use the royal 'we'."

Charles withdrew from her, sitting back on his heels. His wings draped like a cloak behind him. "What are you afraid of? Your words are cold, love, but *you* are not."

"That's what I'm afraid of," she muttered.

He shook his head. "That's the best part. Giving in. Learning who you are after everything's been stripped away."

Then he rushed his hand up her leg under the fabric so that two of his leather-clad fingers plunged into her cunt with no other barrier, curling forcefully inside of her in exactly the right spot. He'd been so gentle before that the merciless thrust of his fingers startled her again, and she cried out, arching her back, yanking against the restraints, but not to escape. Her body was an electrical storm of pleasure, and he impaled her in the center of the supercell as she tightened around his fingers.

"You're so afraid that if I touch you, I'll kill you like any of my victims. But why would I kill kin?"

"There's the whole part where you're lying," she managed to get out.

"I'm not lying." He fixed his gaze on her expression as he plundered her cunt, beckoning every pleasure her body could create. She shook as he stroked the place inside of her that left her breathless and almost in tears the more that he rubbed against it.

Abby didn't think she could keep herself together when he leaned in, as though to pray, and closed his mouth over her clit through the fabric, assaulting her with the sensation of silk, suction and his hot tongue on the sensitive flesh. She literally feared that she might explode like the sun if she didn't come, brought to that desperate peak and not permitted release. Her wings stretched, faded then recoalesced in and out to the rapid beat of her heart. Her cunt clutched fruitlessly at his fingers as they continued their relentless thrusts.

She was moaning loudly enough to wake the dead, but she couldn't help it and didn't want to.

She didn't want to want him. She wanted Zekiel on his knees in front of her, making her feel this way, but he wasn't. She'd come here of her own free will to have Charles do this to her, make her forget herself and everything she had to do when she wasn't here. There were consequences, but she didn't have to think of them as long as the film of silk separated their skin and filtered his charm.

Yet even without the full measure of his magic, he had her like this, bound and writhing within her infidelity, not just to Zekiel but to herself.

When he pulled his mouth away from her clit, she almost sobbed, and she realized that tears streaked her face.

"A thought, Abigail, before we conclude." He licked his lips with relish. "You're a healer. You think that means you're the daughter of an angel, because you were given such a benevolent gift. But have you ever tried turning it the other way? Think on that while you're coming."

His first reaction was confusion, but he didn't actually give her time to think at all before working his mouth over her clit again and quickening the pace of his fingers inside of her, as though he truly could feast upon her. But she felt nothing leaving her to enter him. All she experienced was the climax of the pleasure storm inside of her, her wings somehow turning darker on either side of her with the sudden tightening of her entire body. She clamped her undulating muscles and frantically pushed her hips down over his fingers as she flooded the leather. Then she slumped in her restraints.

Charles pulled the silk off her with his teeth and let it drop to the ground.

Then he stood, bringing his mouth almost too close to her ear. "I want to come on you. I want you to feel *my* pleasure. It's within the terms and spirit of the oath, no more powerful than my touch through the fabric. May I?"

Abby raised her head. She didn't tell him yes, but she couldn't convince her tongue to tell him no.

With his clean glove, Charles pressed fingers against her lips, then kissed the leather, an oddly sweet gesture.

He closed his eyes when Abby's dampness on his other glove joined with his pre-cum to lubricate the tight, firm strokes he gave his cock. Each downstroke exposed the gleaming head under the foreskin, the upstroke squeezing out another drop. He grasped Abby's shoulder, almost pressing his forehead against hers but holding himself back. His wings opened just enough to surround the both of them with comforting darkness. The clean smoke scent of her own wings filled the close air around them.

His breath hitching, he moved his hand faster and faster until it was almost a blur. He opened his eyes to look into hers just as he came. The hot jets of his cum struck her breasts and belly. As they seared her, they seemed to sink in with a slow burn that intensified into a second, slower, smaller but still-intense orgasm, her exhalations paired with breathy moans when she couldn't hold them back.

The shackles opened.

Abby stumbled forward, fully naked. Charles backed away to accommodate her. His wings pulled inward, furling and furling until they had furled themselves into nothing once more. Abby's had stuttered out like a candle after she'd climaxed a second time.

She just stood there—unable to cover herself, filthy with tears, sweat and cum, ashamed and wholly satisfied at the same time, wanting to go home but not knowing how.

Charles wiped the tears from her face and nodded her toward his bathroom. She shuffled in like a sleepwalker. As she waited for the water to heat up, he brought in one of his shirts, which would practically be a dress on her, and a belt to make it seem intentional. The ensemble would be cold for early winter, even for her, but she had her jacket, and home wasn't too far away with the help of public transportation.

He also handed her a pair of black lace hipster panties that weren't hers. "They're clean."

She was too tired to detail all the things wrong with wearing another woman's underwear, because she'd foolishly left herself with little choice.

Charles left the bathroom.

Abby stepped under the shower spray. She was halfway through soaping herself off when her legs trembled so hard that she had to sit down under the hot water with her arms around her knees to cry.

Chapter Eleven

Because Abby was working another overnight shift, Zekiel had one more night and day to find out if she'd decided that his abrupt and quite rigid departure from their amorous activities had been grounds to end any further attempts, although he knew he could do much better for her.

It didn't help that the time away only made him think about her more. He dreamed about her as he drifted into the next sunset, his semiconscious mind full of vignettes of seeing her half-naked, fighting demons, waving him to follow her in the warehouse, her wings outstretched over the gargoyle-lined roof.

When he emerged flesh from stone with the sun beneath the horizon, he had to stroke himself off again. This time, he tried to keep Charles out of his mind, but he couldn't stop himself from remembering, his thoughts of one unfortunately entwined with the other.

However, once he relieved his aching pleasure, he turned on his statue's platform and took to the skies.

The previous night, he'd returned to the warehouse they'd found, and as expected, the demonic cult had abandoned it, preferring their secret rituals unintruded. The giant demon, too, had not returned to the roof, and Zekiel hadn't been able to see any similarly massive statuary on the surrounding buildings. However, there were still things to learn from what they had abandoned. He'd been preoccupied then by a lean, slimy, particularly nasty pestilence demon climbing out of a nearby sewer to pick at the weak living and newly dead, demon and human alike—the mystical equivalent of a cockroach and one of the many causes of missing persons in the city, because no one could find the bodies once the pestilence demons were done with them.

Now, Zekiel entered through the roof access once more. He didn't worry this time about the noise he made on the stairs or on the platform around the warehouse's open center, where the inverted pentagram had been painted on the concrete floor.

He flew down to inspect the symbols around the edge, passing his hand over each glyph. He didn't have an encyclopedic knowledge of every symbol for every cult, but he sensed the power that had been painted into them. Biologicals, animal and human, had been mixed in with the medium, humming even without the acolytes to draw upon them. He found symbols for fertility, which didn't surprise him, given what had been added to the paint as well as the presence of the pregnant women—either captive or acolytes themselves. But fertility symbols usually served female demons, and what had been on the roof and the spells marked on the floor felt undeniably male, given some of the other symbols under his palm.

Aurelia T. Evans

Fertility in service of male conquest... The promise
of blood, the promise of children... And this symbol,
which he'd never seen before but felt like the foul,
blackened decay of necrosis—corruption. Not the
corruption of politicians or rock 'n' roll. This was
deeper, hidden, insidious, the corruption of abnormal
cells and black mold and oil slicks—the worm in the
center of the apple.

If a growing demon cult with its own breeding
program and a Master seeking incarnation with the
blood of the innocent wasn't bad enough, new disquiet
crept into Zekiel's stone chest like winter damp.

He wandered away from the circle, searching not for
ritual clues but more insight into the acolytes
themselves. Those women hadn't entered the circle
naked from their homes on the cusp of winter. As he
expanded his own circle, Zekiel found all kinds of
indications that the warehouse had not just been a place
of ritual.

Some of the demons appeared to have made
themselves a nest in the darker corners—which meant
the cult really had no compunction what kind of demon
they brought into the fold, since no self-respecting
chaos or sex demon would live in a warehouse that
hadn't been renovated into lofts.

But there were also signs of humans living in some
of the empty rooms. Disturbances in dust suggested
beds and carts on wheels, which Zekiel couldn't
explain, but they had also left behind an old working
fridge, where fruits, vegetables and meat were going
bad, and in some trash cans, he found vitamin bottles.
Demon cults weren't usually associated with such good
habits, but this one had a vested interest in maintaining
the health of the women—or perhaps just the babies

inside them. One might assume that a sacrifice was a sacrifice, healthy or not, but corruption preferred to find a foothold in the most wholesome innocence it could sink its claws into, and this cult had devoted itself to that discipline.

It was the prenatal vitamins and fresh anchors screwed into the wall for shackles that the acolytes had taken with them that deepened Zekiel's disquiet into dread.

He ventured further into the warehouse, following the stench of pestilence amid the medical scent of sterilization—bleach, iodine, medical lubricant and antiseptic. It was not necessarily unusual to smell the two together. Pestilence swarmed in the sewers under hospitals. But aboveground, mingled with that of human and other demons, fresh pestilence drew him through a dark corridor into a dimly lit room, where it joined with the less profound corruption of physical decay.

Zekiel might have assumed that this demon had simply found someone's discarded corpse and had taken advantage of the easy meal, except the demon wore the same red robes as the other acolytes.

It was hard to tell if the woman had been pregnant, but she was without clothing, so unlikely to be a squatter. A victim, either way. Whether willing or not to serve their Master, she probably hadn't signed up to die.

Because Zekiel had made no effort to conceal his footsteps or the scrape of his wings on the floor or door frame, the pestilence demon jerked up from where he consumed the woman's organs. His face was covered in congealed blood and bits of flesh to join the crackling mask of his previous feeds. The demon cult was either desperate or confident enough in their doctrine to accept a pestilence demon like this one, given their general lack of hygiene and the odors that accompanied it. Zekiel didn't need preternatural abilities to flinch from the foulness emanating from the woman and from the one who had gutted her.

"You," the demon snarled.

Zekiel spread his wings to their full extent, filling the room from wall to wall. "Demon."

The demon stood from its feast. Blood had joined other stains on the red robes, wrinkled and askew, as though the demon had forgotten who he was and who he served when presented with such an easy feast. Gold around the demon's neck caught in the low light.

The demon's yellow reptilian eyes took in the sight of the gargoyle, processing him piece by piece. Some assumed that they weren't very bright, given their general filthiness and preference for the fringes of both human and demonic society, but Zekiel knew better than to underestimate their cold, calculating cleverness. Their creature comforts were meaner than those of most demons, but their motivations could be unexpectedly complex, sometimes bordering on neutral when weighed upon the grander scale of good and evil.

Sometimes.

Revelation glowed like lanterns as the demon met his eyes. "Traitor."

"Not to you, nor to your Master. Who do you serve?"

The demon shook his head, clicking his tongue. "Not supposed to tell. Supposed to clean up."

"Did she give birth? Has your Master had his requisite sacrifice? Or did something go wrong, and she couldn't be used for that purpose anymore?"

"She's mine." The pestilence demon curled his lips back from crocodilian teeth. "She is mine and we are Legion, but I am only one. And this one will not speak."

"Could have fooled me." Zekiel darted forward, keeping his wings spread low to block the demon's escape through the door, but the demon anticipated him and scurried away from the corpse toward the window letting in the streetlight's glow.

Just like every demon — at heart, a coward. And far more vulnerable than a gargoyle, which was Zekiel's gift in battle.

He jabbed his wing claws into the demon's arms. The demon bashed through the window glass, but not in time. Zekiel ripped through the robe sleeves and into the arm muscles, cutting off the demon's strength as he fought to pull himself over the window ledge. By the time the demon realized he needed to turn around and fight, the fight itself was mostly over, with the demon's arms useless at his sides. All Zekiel had to do was slam his foot into the demon's leg to break it, rendering him helpless, unable to heal fast enough to counter the damage. It seemed cruel, but if not neutralized quickly, pestilence demons fought dirty, because it was often the only way they could win. They weren't soldiers. They weren't even the first choice for acolytes, because they rarely spilled blood for another demon's cup.

"Who do you serve?" Zekiel asked again, the demon's face in his hands. "Tell me, and I might leave you to your leftovers. Who do you serve, and what did he promise for your loyalty?"

"More than you can promise for betrayal that you sold so easily. He will crush you beneath his sole like sand. My brethren shall feast upon the runoff of his table after they finish with me."

Zekiel hooked the demon's necklace under his thumb and held it to the light. "You don't have to tell me. You don't even have to be alive. You'll give me all the information I need."

"Vile, stone-slabbed son of a—"

Zekiel snapped the demon's neck, then braced his foot on the demon's belly to twist the head off completely, with a terrible tearing sound that Zekiel never got used to. He would have preferred to use his sword—a cleaner, quicker cut—but pestilence demons were like cockroaches in more ways than one. Sometimes you thought you'd killed them, and they scurried out from under your shoe. The bigger the mess, the more likely the deed was done.

He tossed the head to the other side of the room, then gathered the necklace from the severed neck before crawling out of the window that the demon had so graciously opened for him. Other pestilence demons, along with the usual carrion eaters, would deal with the bodies. There was little he could do for the woman now and nothing he wanted to do for the demon. All he'd wanted was the amulet.

He angled it to the streetlight to put the imbroglio in stark relief.

Molded into the gold—solid and heavy, not just brass or gold plate—was the head of a bull.

Zekiel closed his fist over the image and lowered his head. "Heaven help us."

* * * *

The night after Dr. Drobny had told Abby she was glowing, Jaspreet had asked whether she'd had a fight, which pretty much summed everything up. Fortunately, tonight was for volunteering, so she tried to recover with some excellent conversation at the retirement center, then lost herself in some young adult fantasy at the hospital.

Maggie and Kara were really excellent company, and not because they were unconscious, since Abby sensed their presence. She found it relaxing to speak without pressure. Neither of them would ever ask her what was wrong or if she wanted to talk about it, which frustrated her no matter how well-intentioned the question. When she wanted to talk about it, she'd talk about it.

"Have a good night, sweetie," Abby whispered to Kara before kissing her on the forehead.

It felt a little warm. Abby checked her stats. She had a slightly elevated temperature, a fraction of a degree — nothing to worry about. Abby checked Kara's chart to make sure the fluctuation was normal. With the confirmation, she set the chart back on the end of the bed, then kissed Maggie goodbye, resting her hand on Maggie's stomach as she always did to make sure the baby was healthy.

All good. Abby could almost forget her problems in the midst of this peace, and here she was, leaving.

Damn Texas weather. It had been drizzling on and off ever since Abby had woken up, and the wind was brisk enough that even Abby shivered when the cold crept under the hem of her jeans. She kept her hood up and her hands in her pockets as she headed down to Cemetery Grove on the way home. She had every intention of avoiding Threshold and the resident above it tonight.

Abby waved to Darcy at the clinic reception desk as she passed by, then turned the corner.

Hands reached from the darkness of the alley and pulled her in. Her purse slid from her shoulder and struck the wall. A gloved hand covered her mouth.

Her first reaction was that it was Charles, for which she was irrationally relieved. But then she noticed that the gloves weren't the same quality leather as what Charles wore, and there were five other beings in the darkness, all wearing red-hooded robes.

The man holding her yanked her jacket hood back and brought the edge of a knife against her throat. "We have a message for you and your traitor."

"And if I'm dead, I'm supposed to give him the message how?"

She winced as the knife slid over her throat—little more than a bad paper cut, but all she needed to do was imagine it all the way back to her cervical vertebrae to understand the threat. Her fingers went numb, and the pounding of her heart reverberated through her body like the footsteps of giants.

"You *are* the message. You could have been useful, but the high priest decided that your use ends here. From us to you, from you to him—the Order of Mokh commands you to stay the fuck out of things that don't concern you. Your interference changes nothing and will only end in more bloodshed. Maybe the traitor will understand better when it's your blood draining down into that sewer."

In a flurry of buffeting wind, like heavy wool in a stiff breeze, Zekiel landed outside the circle that had surrounded Abby in the alley. "If our interference makes no difference to your Master, why provide a message at all?"

The man holding Abby abandoned threats and pontification. He wasted no time slashing Abby's throat.

Message sent.

"No!" Zekiel lunged forward, reaching for her, only to be met by four other red-hooded acolytes who all drew blades.

The man released her. Abby fell to her knees, clutching the gaping part of her neck. She blearily understood that the warm, comforting liquid pouring between her fingers and dampening her shirt was her own blood.

She couldn't feel her hands or her feet, and she was getting cold everywhere else. The pain was negligible, as though all she could focus on was the racing of her terrified heart — which only sped the bleeding — and the stricken despair in Zekiel's dark red eyes.

Abby collapsed to her side.

Knives and swords clashed around her, and the man who had slit her throat joined the fray. Zekiel shouted like a barbarian, meeting each of their blows with three of his own from his sword, his wings, his dense feet, everything in his arsenal.

Her vision was going fuzzy.

Abby pushed the two sides of the wound together and frantically reached inside of herself to grasp the light that gleamed benignly underneath the cage of her ribs — the place where her healing lived.

She usually had time. The falling sands of her hourglass had always seemed a small sacrifice when she could just replace them. But now the sand had turned wet and red and spread in a puddle around her, and she didn't know if she had enough time to heal herself.

It would have been so easy to just let the life bleed out, let the descending shadow take her away. This last week notwithstanding, she thought she'd go in the right direction. She had so much left to do, but she'd *always* have more to do. She'd known from the beginning that her work put her at the same high risk as a demon hunter. Every night she'd survived, she'd only been living on borrowed time.

Instead of Zekiel, her mother or her father, it was Charles' face that surfaced bright and clear in her fading vision. His knowing grin sparked a stab of fear that drowned out any pain.

Because what if she *wasn't* going where she thought she was going? What if Charles' confidence was a reflection of truth too delicious to mar with lies? Or was it possible she wasn't dying at all, but that the demon side of her was stripping the humanity away like shed skin, as though Abby had been the disguise all along?

She couldn't die — not until she knew what she was and that she wouldn't become what she despised.

She doubled down on calling forth the heated tendrils of her healing to her neck, where they'd been trying to sew her together but hadn't replenished her blood fast enough to counter her own beating heart. A different kind of pain pierced through her forehead, like needles behind her eyes, but she'd rather have a healing hangover than an obituary.

She gulped in air as the blood that had been filling her lungs dissolved and the opening in her windpipe closed. Then she rolled over onto her elbows and knees, still gasping for breath. Her heartbeat slowed, but not because there wasn't anything to pump through. The panic was subsiding, her vision clearing, her mind receiving the oxygen it needed and any damage there resolving. Her power lit her from within like a boiler. She felt like she had a fever, but it would cool in the winter air, especially soaked as she was with her own blood.

By the time Abby climbed to her feet, Zekiel had bested three of the five acolytes. The man who had cut her was on the ground and not moving, which was a shame, because she would have liked to hurt him. But just because she couldn't get revenge didn't mean she couldn't help.

She didn't have her weapons on her and couldn't immediately find her purse, not that her slippery hands would have been able to hold weaponry anyway. Instead, she jumped onto another man's back and throttled him from behind. The man's surprise gave Zekiel a chance to slash his sword across the man's stomach.

Zekiel's eyes widened when Abby fell from the man's shoulders and landed on her feet, still covered in blood. However, he set aside his surprise as he applied his blade to the last acolyte standing. All of them had been men rather than demons. Either the cult had deemed them disposable, or they'd expected very little from her. In their defense, if Zekiel hadn't been there, they might have succeeded, since a gargoyle wouldn't have distracted them from her healing herself.

The last man clutched his belly to hold himself together and, brandishing a dagger, screamed, "In the name of Mokh, die!"

The man's head went rolling down the alley and came to a stop in Abby's blood.

Zekiel lowered his sword. "How noble, to lay down your life for your Master. I hope he receives *my* message, though, that I am unimpressed."

He turned to her, but before he could say anything, Abby ran to him. She jumped up, wrapped her limbs around him and thoroughly kissed him, much as they'd ended their last encounter. And in spite of all that had happened between then and now, they picked up right where they left off.

Zekiel expressed his abject relief that she was alive through the low moans that she caught with the slide of her tongue against his. His hands on her thighs were almost bruising to replace what had healed from the beating. He clung to her as though afraid that, if he let go, she would fall back, her throat gaping, and her healing would have just been a dream.

And Abby pressed herself as close as possible to him, entranced by his warmth and strength and the softness of his stone skin, an intimacy of connection absent from all her doings with Charles. When she finally allowed herself some space between them, she still leaned her forehead against his.

All she'd needed was to know that she wanted Zekiel and he wanted her — and not from some kind of twisted addiction or something that they could *do* for the other. Kissing him was like drinking cold, clean water after bad wine.

"I thought you were dead," Zekiel murmured against her cheek. "Are you immortal?"

"Just handy. I would have healed myself earlier and faster, but I was still getting over my throat being slit. I mean, who does that? Usually, they just threaten the hostage until they get what they want."

He hoisted her down, placing her on the ground as though she would shatter. "They did get what they wanted. They were hoping to lure me out, and once they did, you weren't of use to them anymore — or they decided not to use you that way."

"Their mistake." She braced herself against the wall next to the blood pool, lightheaded again from how close she'd been to dying.

"Are you all right?"

"My death just flashed before my eyes. I'll be fine. What did they mean by Order of Mokh? Who the hell is Mokh?"

"Mokh... Must be a bastardization." Zekiel pulled a gold amulet from his cloth covering and handed it to Abby.

She immediately recognized the golden bull. Zekiel's solemner-than-usual expression confirmed her suspicion. "Shit. Child sacrifice. They're breeding for Moloch. Moloch's the one who's incarnating? He's coming *here*?"

Zekiel crouched by the headless body. With the tip of his sword, he lifted away the chain of another gold amulet. Upon inspection of the other four, he found the same talismans. "I think the cult is actually an amalgamation of several, which is why the members are human and both chaos and pestilence demons, and why there are so many. I don't think the ritual we witnessed was by any means the only one in Meridian. There might be several altars all over the city, which would explain how they were able to abandon the warehouse we caught them in so quickly. It would also explain why they considered five acolytes disposable as worshippers — and you disposable in spite of your health and vigor for their cause. And a greater network would explain how they've managed to hide the Moloch statue once again. They probably led him indoors or under tree cover once they determined that I could find him again from the air."

"Okay, I've kind of had a bad few days, Zekiel. I've already regifted myself a pulse, which I'm really grateful for, but give me some good news."

He stood again, tucking the amulets away. Abby put the one he'd given her in her pocket. At the very least, given their weight, they might be worth something for the gold alone.

"Take heart," he said with a slight smile. "Moloch has not yet fully incarnated. Believe me, everyone would know if he had wrested rule over this city. But whether statue or fully incarnated, demons that take form on this plane are far easier to destroy than those who rule from spiritual realms. Form can be destroyed. That's the exchange that they make."

"So, at the very least, we can hit the bastard with a rocket launcher."

"Or we could assemble the demon hunters and let them do what they do in greater numbers."

"I think the rocket launcher would be simpler." She tried to wipe her hands on her jeans but quickly realized the futility. "I look like a Niles vampire. And I got it all over you, too. Somehow, I've got to get from here to home without anyone seeing me and calling the cops about the murder I committed."

"Flying would be best. No one will see you, and I'm already stained."

"I'm going to drip."

"A little mystery is good for the soul."

Abby laughed. It was harder than expected to get herself to stop. "But then how will *you* get cleaned up?"

"Garden hose?"

* * * *

After Zekiel landed in the small backyard, Abby pointed out the mostly unused garden hose. She actually wasn't sure if it worked, but if it didn't, he could just unscrew the hose and use the spigot. She'd invite him in for a shower, but Cary had the main suite, and the bathroom that Abby and Melody shared wasn't big enough for those wings, even furled.

She peeled her clothes off in the shower and shoved them all into a trash bag. She'd been pretty tough on her clothes lately—not an ideal situation for a not-quite-full-time nurse working for an underfunded clinic.

She went through all the hot water and most of the lukewarm before getting all the blood out of her hair. Once she'd dried herself off, she ran a washcloth over the fogged mirror and took her first look at her neck.

If she hadn't known what had happened, she wouldn't have given the scar a second glance—just a thin, pearly line a shade or two lighter than her skin. No one but Zekiel would ever know that she'd had a second mouth in the middle of her throat, and by the time anyone else was close enough to notice, the scar would probably have faded even more than it already had.

As long as her memory of what had happened didn't fade with it. Maybe she hadn't meant to make it a game before—an extreme sport of saving people—but this had been worse than the demon breaking her back, and it had happened in a matter of seconds.

When she failed, it wasn't just *her* soul on the line.

Abby pulled on a pair of lounge pants and a T-shirt. After making sure that Melody and Cary were still asleep, she sneaked to the backyard again. She had to literally bite her lip to keep from laughing. For a hairless gargoyle, he managed a decent approximation of a wet rat.

"I didn't want to say anything," he said, avoiding eye contact. "But now I'm cold. I'm not usually cold."

"Oh my goodness, I'm so sorry." She still had to cover her mouth against the giggles. "I should have thought. Please, come in and I'll get you a towel. The kitchen's tile, easy to clean. Keep it down, though, because I wouldn't even know where to begin explaining you to my roommates. Melody shouldn't be awake for a few more hours, but Cary's sometimes a light sleeper."

Zekiel paused at the threshold of the door. "I can't."

"Why not?"

"I don't enter homes anymore. They are places for family, friends, warmth, light, comfort. I forsook all that when I transformed."

"So you went good and that's why you can't have nice things? You realize that's a bit insulting to me, right? Anyway, I'm not saying we have a waterbed and a fur blanket in here with nymphs to feed you grapes. We're on a first-name basis with our plumber, and we could stand to have more hot water. Get in here."

She tugged Zekiel in by the hand and hurried him to the bathroom. He waited outside until she found him two towels then pointed him to her room for when he was finished.

The tile on the floor just took another towel, and she didn't have to make sure it was completely dry—just dry enough that the heater would take care of the rest by the time the girls woke up. But she had to take her bloody clothes out to the trash receptable, throw the bag in and hope the neighborhood didn't have any scavenging vampires.

Back at her room, she ducked in.

"Ah, I see the flaw in my ingenious plan," she said, closing the door with some creative maneuvering.

She'd factored in his size and his wings for the bathroom but not her closet of a bedroom, which was Abby-size but definitely not Zekiel-size. He hunched under the low ceiling, and his wings crowded the small space she sometimes called her boudoir.

"You know, you can sit down," she said. "You don't have to just stand there looking profoundly uncomfortable."

Zekiel draped his wings around his shoulders like an awkward cloak and eased onto the bed.

"You live in here?" Zekiel asked, his prominent brow all the more prominently furrowed.

She sat beside him. "I don't *live* in here. I sleep in here. The rest of the time, I'm out in the living room or—shock, I know—out in the world. Plus, the rent is awesome for the city, and I get Wi-Fi. What more does a person need? Besides, don't you sleep on a roof?"

"I do not sleep. I simply turn to stone."

"Ah. Yes." She intertwined her fingers between her breasts and contemplated the knot that they made. "So you were awake for that...abrupt end?"

Zekiel betrayed none of his emotions, whether aroused, annoyed or embarrassed. "Yes."

"I couldn't tell if you were or not, so I hope you don't mind what I did. And I didn't mean to just leave you there, um, unsatisfied, but I didn't know what to do, and I had to go home to sleep. I couldn't stay there all day to wait for you to come back, and then—"

Zekiel covered her twisting hands with one of his own and leaned in to whisper, "I took care of it."

Abby exhaled in a rush as Zekiel brushed her hair away from her shoulder, then pressed his warm lips against her neck.

"I was in that state *all day*," he murmured into her skin, sending the vibrations over the surface and into her. "I couldn't stop thinking about you. As soon as I could move, I took myself in hand." He paused for a few beats. "I took care of it."

"We have a few hours before sunrise." She glanced down, shyer than some of her innuendo had suggested. It wasn't as though she'd ever brought a man home with her before, certainly not to her closet. But the room wasn't made for standing or even sitting. It was mostly made for being horizontal. With the thrill of her second chance at life coursing through her, she couldn't think of anything better than pulling him down over her on the bed—in deference to architectural constraints.

"Hours before I turn to stone." He lifted her chin, staring at her lips again.

"But we have to be quiet." She lowered herself to her elbows and worked her way back to the pillows, Zekiel reaching after her the whole way until he was poised over her, his wings obscuring the light of her lamp and rendering him a massive shadow.

She wasted no time pulling her shirt over her head and pushing her pants down her legs. He hadn't expected her to remove her clothing so quickly, given how his whole body stiffened and his chest hitched from catching his breath, although he didn't need to breathe.

"Abby," he whispered. He hovered his hand over her as though afraid to touch, but part of him showed no hesitation. His cock stretched toward her once again through his covering.

She didn't have any patience. She'd been tormented by an incubus who wasn't allowed to touch her. She wasn't going to let the gargoyle get away with the same thing. She needed him. She needed him to touch her, and she wanted him to be forceful and passionate, but more than that, she wanted him to be kind — and she knew he could be all those things.

She pulled at his covering until Zekiel took pity on her and undid it himself with a trick of his fingers. The covering pooled at the foot of the bed, closely joined by his sword. Now there was nothing between her and his lovely cock — the kind of cock a statue should have, not suffering the same diminutive stature as some of the more famous statues. Maybe David was a grower instead of a shower, but Abby still preferred the heft of the cock she took in hand.

It didn't flush like that of a human, but it felt hot, pulsed and twitched like a normal cock, and when she bent down to take the head of it into her mouth, she tasted moisture on her tongue. He hissed, pushing his cock deeper. Abby jerked back to compensate, but once she wrapped her hand around the base, she gained more control.

Zekiel grasped the metal headboard and tried not to jerk his hips too hard.

After she'd bobbed over his cock for more than a few moments, he pushed her away. "No. No, I do not wish for you to do that."

"Why? I seriously don't mind, and you didn't seem to. I like watching you while I'm doing it." The state of his cock certainly suggested that he'd enjoyed what she'd been doing.

He eased her hand away from him, grimacing in what looked like pain and confusion. The confusion turned to tenderness as he settled behind her, his wings trailing behind him and over the foot of the bed. "It's not you. I simply... I would prefer to do other things tonight."

Abby rested back and stretched her arms above her, reveling with feline pride at the way she drew his gaze from her eyes to the peaks of her breasts. "Have anything in mind?"

"Let's start here." He returned his attention to her neck and kissed up to her mouth before claiming her, his arm over her chest until she clutched the back of his neck to guide him over her once more.

When she spread her legs to accommodate him, his cock almost immediately slid through her folds. She stroked the curve of his bare head, encouraging his descent down her neck to the tip of her breast.

At her urging, he closed his mouth over her, running his tongue around the hard nub.

Desire darted through her in an unexpected wave, humming electricity over her skin, and arousal seeped from her with each clench of her pussy. He glanced up at her from where he licked her breast. Then he sucked her nipple almost to the point of pain, but still she fell back against her pillow, her eyelids fluttering shut.

Then she abruptly sat up, almost knocking his head with her shoulder. "What are you doing?"

"What?" Zekiel appeared startled, but there was something else there too, in the way he looked to the side and thinned his slightly downturned lips.

"I've felt like this before. You can touch silver, but before you were a gargoyle, you were an incubus, weren't you?"

Zekiel was the very picture of carved angel agony as he slumped over her lap. Then he raised his head again. "You have experienced incubus charm."

That struck at the heart of the shame that she'd been enjoying not having tonight. She stammered for a moment before deciding to share the truth—with enough deception from omission that the shame didn't quite stop stirring through her unsettled stomach. "A few years ago, I was stalked by an incubus. Suffice it to say, I'm no longer stalked by him. I can tell when my pleasure is being manipulated. What's that about? You haven't been doing that more subtly the rest of the time, have you?"

"No!" He sounded horrified, which placated her somewhat. "I hadn't realized that I still could. There are so many things that I can no longer do. I was recently inspired to try, and I thought... It feels nice, though, yes? I could make it feel so good, and I cannot feast upon you as I once did, so all you would experience is the pleasure."

"Zekiel." She caressed his face then slid her hands down to his chest. *Oh yes, still a good place.* "It might feel nice, but it isn't real. I want it to be real. I feel pleasure whether you charm me or not. Believe me, it's not a chore to just touch you" — she mouthed his nipple and sucked it much as he had done to hers, making him moan as well, threading his fingers through her hair — "and have you touch me."

She took his free hand and, after a moment's hesitation, guided it between her thighs.

"I would, however, love to take advantage of your experience," she said.

He climbed over her once more, his cock heavy on her thigh as he plied her folds and her clit like an instrument until she made the music he wanted to hear. She clung to his shoulders, watching him watch her. For a while, his expression was solemn, as though still disturbed by what he had done—although he seemed overly ashamed about it to her, given what she had to be ashamed of. But when he dipped his fingers inside of her and found her practically dripping with need from skill rather than spells, a smile curved the edges of his mouth.

Abby took his face in her hands. "Inside," she whispered.

She spread her legs more to welcome him between them, then curled them around his broad hips, his thighs strong under her heels. She stroked his cock and brought the slick head to her slit. Her mouth dropped open as though she had to drink the air when he slowly slid into where she was more than wet enough to accept him with ease.

The bed shuddered under her as he spread his wings, gripping his claws on the wooden supports in the closet to steady himself. With his grip as leverage, he pulled himself forward, shoving himself all the way into her. Abby covered her mouth with the back of her hand to muffle her cry.

"You are my light," he murmured before worshipping the flesh under her ear and thrusting into her again and again.

She was too far gone to tell him that she was only shadow. She clutched his shoulders, holding on as he rode her at an ever-increasing pace.

Now that she was aware of what he'd once been, she felt the added sensitivity inspired by his incubus nature, something he probably wasn't even aware of and which was a bare fraction of what a true incubus could do to her. And unlike a true incubus, he wasn't perfect. Her thighs, tight around his hips, were pummeled by the jutting bones of his pelvis. He was dense and heavy, and he didn't always hit the right places.

The important thing was that he didn't have to. He was beautiful, he was hers and he was sweet and good and strong. She loved everywhere that their bodies connected, the way their bellies slid against each other as he entered her and she met him. She loved his moans — spontaneous, natural and so very hot. Just listening to his desire made her wet.

"Shhh," she said with a laugh. "They'll hear."

"I can't… I have to… You…" He shook his head and covered her mouth with his again, caressing her tongue with his off-rhythm to the cock in her pussy, but just as obscenely wonderful. Arousal stretched all the way to her fingers and toes and coiled tighter and tighter around his cock until she thought she must have been squeezing him like a fist.

"Shhh," he mocked affectionately after she cried out into his mouth.

She pulled him down again. "Faster, harder, less talk."

Her orgasm was all the better without an ounce of guilt, all shame driven away before it, knowing that it was well won out of love rather than conquest. She grasped his ass and pulled him into her over and over through the forceful flutter of her muscles around him. His grunt gratified her, and she was glad she'd come first so that she could feel his climax soon after hers, watch his face without the sun turning him to stone, without the haze of her own pleasure.

Zekiel slowly lowered himself to cover her, his weight creaking the mattress springs.

Even a guardian angel wouldn't make her feel so safe.

"I'm not going to be having a gargoyle baby in a few months, am I?" she murmured.

Zekiel laughed into her shoulder. "It's just dew. Stone does not reproduce."

"Good to know." As Abby stroked his back, her fingers encountered the base of his wings. "So, you were an incubus."

"I was."

"Don't worry. I'm cognizant of the verb tense there." She kissed his chest lightly. "If it makes you feel better, I can tell that isn't what you are anymore."

There was silence, comfortable, as their bodies cooled.

Then, "Thank you."

They stayed that way for a while. Zekiel moved to the side so he wouldn't overstay his crushing welcome, but they otherwise remained entwined in each other's arms. The coverlet underneath them dampened, which didn't bother her. It just reminded her of what they'd shared.

But they both knew it couldn't last.

"I must go." Zekiel rose up on an elbow, peering down at her. "I cannot be here when your roommates awaken, and I would rather not get caught by the rising sun in your room or backyard."

"Oof," she said, thinking about what would happen if he turned to stone in her bed. Then she grinned and reached for her shirt and pants. "All right. I hate for you to go, but a new lawn ornament would be a bit hard to explain."

Before leaving, Zekiel tilted her head up and kissed her again, more tender than desperate in the coolness of the dark, damp morning, framed by the back door.

"I'm working tomorrow," she said when she could find her words again.

"I'll continue to keep my eye out for demon cults and giant demons." He stroked her cheek. "Good morning, light of mine."

She leaned against the door frame as he flew over the fence and back toward the city. She hoped he made it to his home or found a suitable roof before dawn.

Abby headed back to her room and sat cross-legged on her rumpled bed. Then she pulled her phone out of her purse and checked the time. Five-thirty.

She selected a number on speed dial.

"Hi, Mama. I don't mean to interrupt your morning meditation, but...I thought you might want to know that I found Dad."

* * * *

He seems distracted.

It hurts to see him like this, glancing around like he's expecting someone to come through the restaurant's front door or from the kitchen, maybe through the windows — someone he doesn't want there but who he can't keep out. He or she hasn't burst in yet, but they've set up shop in his head anyway.

She asks herself whether there's another woman. She tries to tell herself that there can't be, not with the way that he showers her with solicitude, loves her in both word and deed.

It's just that she can't know his thoughts, and she can't be with him all the time. She doesn't even want to. She wants to trust him completely. She loves him. So she says nothing and doesn't check his phone or email, no matter how keen her fear.

The sommelier brings the wine. She shakes her head. The man across from her smiles and accepts. They share a toast, his wine to her water.

They make small talk. She asks about his day. He asks about her doctor's appointment. His day was good. Her appointment was fine. Everything is all fine and good, and she worries that he's going to end the night with chocolate and an abrupt severance, that the last few months have all been for nothing and his beautiful, charming façade shields a colder interior that he will finally bring to light. That she has fallen in love with a lie.

She has given up everything for him. She has no other resources. Her job will only get her so far before circumstances catch up with her and she can no longer support herself on her own — not when her family has disowned her in shame.

He is her center, her foundation, her light, and she fears most of all that he will leave her in darkness.

Although she was hungry before arriving at the restaurant, she picks at her food.

When the waiter brings the molten cake for them to share, her man beckons her to sit beside him instead of across. She cannot meet his eyes the closer they become.

He slips his hand into hers. "Hey. Hey, what's wrong?"

Hot tears fall onto their clasped hands before she can stop them. "It's nothing. Nothing."

And she's not lying, really. She's overemotional. That might be all this is, just irrational paranoia getting the better of her. She's weepy, but her tears are not to be trusted.

"I know," he says softly. He's not responding to the 'nothing' but to what she's not saying, and how dare he read

her mind when she can't do the same. "Hey. I love you. You know that, right?"

"I just…"

He kisses her tears. His lips shine with them before he kisses her mouth. She tastes salt and chocolate, licks his lips, then meets his tongue between them, heedless of the murmur of the crowd, the bell-like clink of utensils on porcelain, the string quartet playing in the background.

He kisses her slowly, calming her desperation and worry with soothing, languid rhythm. Her nipples harden under her little black dress. She isn't wearing a bra, so the cool lining stimulates them further now that his touch awakens her again. He reminds her why she stays. He tells her truth in his touch what she cannot always believe from his words.

A cough interrupts them, and she laughs, staring down at her lap for a new reason. Her man smiles up at the waiter, who presents her with a covered plate.

She's confused. She thought they were going to share a dessert.

She lifts the metal cloche from the plate. In the center of the ivory saucer sits a small black box.

She brings her hand to her mouth with a gasp, her eyes wide.

He leans back in his chair with quiet pride. His grin lights up his face like it always does, and she senses the way that it lights up hers as well.

"Charles, is this really…" But she can't speak anymore. She wipes at her cheeks.

He picks up the box, then drops to his knee in front of her.

The restaurant goes quiet. She feels their gazes, but she has eyes only for the man before her.

He opens the box. The ring is modest, but that's not important in the slightest. "My dear, my love, my sweet beauty, will you marry me and let me make an honest woman of you?"

*She hits his shoulder and laughs through her sobs. "Yes,"
she manages. "Yes. I thought you were going to break up
with me."*

*"Just nervous, love." He slides the ring over her finger.
"If you thought you were free of me, I'm sorry to say I'm
going to be with you for a very long time."*

"That's fine with me."

*He grasps her thighs as he kisses her again, and this time
it isn't rude that he's between her legs and biting her lip in
the middle of a crowded restaurant, because he proposed and
she said yes. Everyone is clapping for them as he strokes the
tops of her stockings, grinning against her lips as though he's
going to pull those stockings down her legs right here in front
of everyone. Her arousal dampens her panties – black edged
with lace, the kind of thing he loves to see her in when they're
alone.*

*He pulls back and looks over that little black dress where
her nipples push against the fabric, then down at the crux of
her legs, and she gets the feeling he knows exactly what's
underneath. Of course, he's seen it all before, but the way he
observes her curls her toes in her shoes.*

*He climbs back up to his seat and pushes her chair in
again, then leans toward her. "Eat your chocolate. Whatever
happens, don't stop."*

*She's glad she doesn't have to stand. Her legs wouldn't be
able to hold her. She knows that mischievous glint, that soft
but commanding tone. He wants to play, right here in the
middle of a crowded restaurant, and God help her, she's
suddenly so turned on that she can barely focus on the
chocolate in front of her. But she does as she's told, as she
always does. If he told her to do something she didn't want
to, maybe that would be bad, but even the things that made
her nervous – especially the things they did in public – he
always made them worthwhile.*

That's why she takes the chance on him. That's why his ring is on her finger. That's why his baby grows inside of her.

He shares the cake with her, taking a few bites here and there until all the conversation around them returns to what it was before the proposal. Then he brushes his hand over her lap. Her napkin falls to the floor.

"Oops. Let me get that, baby. You shouldn't in your condition."

"You know, I think men like you are who my mother warned me about."

"Don't I know it." He disappears under the tablecloth.

At first there is no change. To prevent any suspicion, she continues eating, and he does nothing, just lets the room acclimate to his absence.

Then he jerks her chair forward and abruptly spreads her legs.

She fights not to gasp. The last thing she wants to do is call attention to herself. She wonders whether the waiters know. Perhaps the reason they're not interfering is because they're watching.

She licks her lips free of chocolate cake crumbs just as he slides his hands up her skirt, skimming the tops of her stockings. Air swirls between her thighs and against the damp spot on her panties when he breathes in her scent like the wine bouquet. He hums his appreciation against her shaking thigh.

She tightens her fingers over her fork as he runs the flat of his tongue over her panties. He sucks on the damp fabric, then through the fabric to the folds beneath, slow and meticulous. Pleasure flows languidly through her, as thick as the hot chocolate syrup sliding down her throat.

He removes one of her pumps, like Cinderella in reverse. Then he brings her foot to his lap, where she can feel his erection through his trousers but also where he can dig his fingers deep into the muscle of her instep.

Evil, evil man. *He knows how massaging her feet like that wreaks beautiful havoc on her clit. She can't stop the whimper and hopes that those around her believe that the dessert is really that good.*

She doesn't know what she's going to do when she finishes the cake.

He bites her thigh, making her jump, then laves the sensitive skin there. She's panting now, focused on staying still and keeping quiet, which only makes the pleasure tighter and keener. She spoons up some of the chocolate cake and thick chocolate sauce and takes her time pulling the spoon from her mouth, granting herself one low, luxurious moan as he brings his mouth to her clit with the same sweet, intense, luxurious suck.

She combs her fingers through his hair. Maybe people know what they're doing now, but she doesn't care. She's three months pregnant and newly engaged, and if she's still this happy with her fiancé, it doesn't matter who notices. They might learn a thing or two about how to please a woman.

The deep rubs on her foot continue, and he uses her foot to stroke himself as well, although he isn't stroking to come. He'll be hard through the rest of the night until they get home – or at least until they get into the car. He'll have to walk by most of the restaurant with a bulge in his pants so that everyone can see how lucky she is.

She throws her head back. She feels as though she's been stripped bare. If she had her way, he would take her on that lovely white linen tablecloth, primitive and carnal, their love a compressed rock on her finger and a fierce, furious kiss. She balls her fist in his hair and bucks her hips against his talented mouth as she comes.

She fights to control her breathing. He eases off her clit but continues his massage, sending little twitches of arousal through the aftershocks, and kisses her thighs above the lace of the stockings. His lips are reverent.

But he eventually pulls back, adjusting her skirt and replacing the napkin on her lap. She finishes her dessert and determinedly doesn't look at anyone else in case she actually sees someone watching and fantasy becomes more awkward reality.

He slips into his seat again. "How was your dessert, love?"

"Would you like a taste?"

Instead, she tastes herself as he kisses her. She subtly cups his erection through his trousers.

"I love you," she whispers again.

"And I love you."

For a moment, she thinks he meets the eyes of someone behind her, but when she looks over her shoulder, there's no one there.

"Let's go home," he says.

She has no intention of letting him get that far. This dress and these stockings, thin though they are, are suddenly too cumbersome. Everything little thing he does pushes all her buttons.

He makes her want to keep going forever.

Chapter Twelve

It had taken Abby over an hour to get to sleep after the phone call to her mother, which had ruined any and all calming endorphin rush left over from sex. And that was without revealing that she was in some kind of relationship with a gargoyle. Telling her mother that her husband resided in a cemetery halfway across the country was hard enough—mostly because Abby had admitted that she hadn't seen him again in almost a week without being able to give a good explanation why.

That was *another* thing she wasn't going to tell her mother.

Abby had promised her, however, that she would see her father again soon. But she was sure he was going to notice something was wrong, and she didn't want to explain these things to him, either.

"This is one of those weeks for you, isn't it?" Dr. Drobny said between patients. "Highs, lows, little in between."

"You have no idea." Abby checked the sign-in sheet. "Is that Tony in the waiting room? *Perfect*. The perfect middle of the night to an exquisite end of the week."

Dr. Drobny patted Abby's shoulder. "I'll try to make this next patient quick. And remind me to buy you a drink."

"Yes, please." She sighed, then went into the waiting room. "Tony Danza?"

It wasn't his real name, but it was the one he always used, verified with his fake ID. They weren't supposed to call too much attention to it unless he tried to commit fraud. The clinic was about healing, not judgment.

"At your service, sweetheart." Tony jumped up, full of energy like he always was, although Abby immediately noticed the red eyes and swollen nose. He wasn't just at the clinic to feel up the nurses and steal from the supply closet this time, so that was something.

"Exam Room Two." Abby led him down the corridor and hoped he didn't slap her ass on the way. He didn't.

Good boy. I'll give you some acetaminophen instead of sugar pills this time. She was joking to herself about the sugar pills...mostly.

As per the understood policy with certain patients, Abby kept the door slightly open. Unless Tony had to strip, it would stay that way for the security of the nurses. Tony grinned and closed the door, but as soon as he hopped up on the exam table, Abby smiled back and opened it a crack again.

"Don't trust yourself around me, do you?" Tony said.

Abby continued to smile. "So, what seems to be the problem?"

"I got the sniffles. Can't you see?"

"Tony, a big, strong, brave man such as yourself doesn't come to the clinic for the sniffles."

Some of the bravado smoothed off his face. He fidgeted his fingers between his aggressively spread thighs. "Yeah, well, I think I got a fever to go with it, and it hasn't gone away the last two days. Barry told me to come in. He didn't have to tell me twice when I remembered how good you look in those pajamas." He slid his hand over her waist.

Abby took his hand and returned it to his leg. "Remember when we talked about where your hands go, Tony? That was a no-trespassing zone."

He grinned at his success in getting skin-on-skin contact. With that contact, however, she determined he definitely had a fever and actually had the flu. It probably wouldn't have killed him to wait another three days, since he didn't sample what he sold and compromise his immune system. Dr. Drobny would only tell him to get his flu booster next season and get some oseltamivir from the pharmacy.

"My bad," he said. "You're just irresistible, baby doll."

"I know, but you have to control yourself anyway. You know the drill. Jacket off for blood pressure."

He rolled his eyes. "I came in here for the flu. I don't give a fuck about blood pressure."

"It's procedure. You know that." She secretly took pleasure in his wince as she inflated the cuff. Then she took his temperature.

"You want me to take off my shirt so you can listen to my heart?"

"The doctor does that," she replied. "You definitely have a fever. I'll let the doctor know how you're doing."

"You do that." But he kicked out his leg and closed the door before she could leave.

"Tony, if you do that again, we're going to have to ban you from the clinic." She maintained an even demeanor, trying not to sound scared or angry. She didn't know why she was less scared of demons than people like Tony. Her heart pounded almost as fast as when her throat had been cut.

"Come on, baby. I'm not going to do anything."

"If that were true, you wouldn't have to reassure me."

She reached for the doorknob again, but he kicked her hand out of the way and slunk off the table.

"You don't have to pretend. I can tell what you like just by looking at you — and you like me."

"You're sick...literally. I suggest you lie down and don't move—"

"Mmm."

"While I get the doctor."

Abby saw him coming, but she didn't have enough time to react before Tony shoved her against the wall.

"I don't come here for the crappy ambience, baby. I come for the view." He crossed his arms to pull his shirt over his head. There was a tattoo of a cross on his bicep.

"I could think of a few places with a better view."

"And better security," he replied, advancing.

She'd always read that situations like this seemed like they went in slow motion. It wasn't that way for her. Everything moved as fast as ever, but she was aware of every little detail—Tony's acne scars, the patch of facial hair that he hadn't shaved properly, the cowlick at his hairline, the flex of his biceps under the cross, the chapped lips from his fever that he apparently had no problem sharing with her.

Before Abby realized what she was doing, she pressed her hand against his chest and heard Charles in her head as though he whispered in her ear.

"You ever tried turning it the other way?"

The fever rose to meet Abby's touch, but instead of accepting it into her body, she pushed the magic in reverse, the way she might physically shove Tony away. Shadow rather than light passed under her palm, absorbing into his skin. As with her healing light, the shadow wouldn't be visible to him, even if he weren't trying to look down her shirt.

But then he stumbled back, clapping his hands to his head.

His face contorted as he bared his teeth and clenched his eyes shut, a shout strangled in his throat, where the cords strained and veins bulged out.

Before her eyes, black spots appeared on his nose, scalp, neck, back, even over his eyelids, black spots that bubbled like beetle-filled boils.

Tony couldn't shout, but Abby screamed.

Her knees gave out, and she fell onto the linoleum tile. Her shoes slipped and squeaked against the floor as she tried to escape, but it was a little room and there was nowhere to go.

Blind, Tony knocked against the exam table and the wall before falling in front of the door, twitching with what looked like a seizure, except he was conscious. The muscles of his face continued to writhe in pain as the cancer seeped deeper into his body, maybe all the way to the bone.

She was still screaming when Dr. Drobny burst through the door, which hit Tony's jerking body with a solid thud.

"What is it? Are you okay? What happened? Oh my God!" Dr. Drobny fell to his knees and turned Tony onto his back. "What the f— What happened, Abby?"

"He just— He came in for the flu," she said weakly. Horror turned the screw in her body, her hands and neck shaking from tension. "He closed the door, then this... I don't know what happened."

She covered her face but couldn't cover her eyes. She had to see. She had to see what *she* had done. Dr. Drobny would never know, but she would know what she'd done the rest of her life and deep in her nightmares, both sleeping and awake.

She could have just slugged Tony when he came at her. She could have screamed before he was infected instead of after. But she hadn't. Instead, she'd turned her gift around and done this to him...this abomination.

Dr. Drobny inspected the now-unconscious Tony. The doctor's face had gone almost completely white in shock. He'd never seen anything like this before, and why should he have? There had never been a case of spontaneous body-wide Stage 4 melanoma in the history of medicine.

"I'm going to call an ambulance." Dr. Drobny clambered up and ran to the front of the clinic.

Her muscles protested as she gathered herself together and crawled over to Tony. Abby grabbed his forearm with both hands, deliberately avoiding any of the melanomas, even though they wouldn't be contagious. She reached down into the healing well of her soul and pulled at the strings of the sickness to draw it back into her, to save him, to save her, to take it all back because she didn't want this anymore. She'd *never* wanted to be this.

It didn't work.

* * * *

She stumbled through the streets, blind to the world around her.

"Abby, go home. There's nothing more you can do here, and you look like you're going to faint. I'll call Darcy. Just…go. Have a stiff drink and get some sleep."

She'd forgotten her jacket at the clinic, but she didn't notice the chill, although her fingers were freezing and her palms slick with cold sweat.

"Oh my God, Abby. It's like an X-Files *episode or something."*

Jaspreet had given her a hug and a chocolate bar before she'd left. The chocolate bar was in Abby's purse. She wished she could still have the hug, although she knew she didn't deserve it.

She wasn't just a bad person. She was a demon.

Because although she had been horrified, some part of her had liked it.

She wasn't just a walking cure. She was a walking cancer. When she smote her enemies, they stayed that way. And she was the one who did it to them. The power was hers to command, although for so long she had only listened to what she'd thought were the commands of a higher being. But now she knew that she could wield that power without permission. All she needed was her will, her free will.

"You ever try turning it the other way?"

Charles had not only known that she could spread disease instead of just take it away, he'd known she would eventually do it. He'd known just how weak she would be.

She barely noticed the patrons of Threshold, barely noticed the drink in her hand, although heat sluiced down her throat and into her stomach, barely noticed going up the stairs. The next thing she was aware of with any kind of clarity was throwing open Charles' door so hard it hit the wall.

"Hello, love." He was as shirtless as Tony had been, standing in the middle of the room with his hands behind his back.

"How did you know I was coming?"

"Miranda gave me a ring. She said you looked like you'd gazed into the mouth of hell."

Her tongue was too thick in her mouth. When she tried to swallow, her throat tightened as though squeezed with a fist from the inside. She nodded.

He stepped forward, his brows furrowed slightly in compassion that Abby believed to be genuine. "I see Alice has gone through the looking glass. I'm sorry, love. It's a necessary evil."

"Necessary...evil." Abby jumped as the door closed by itself behind her. "Necessary. No such thing. I'm just... I'm just evil."

Charles tenderly stroked a lock of hair away from her face. "Welcome home."

She jerked back, but she hit the door, and once again there was nowhere to go.

Charles took her purse and tossed it to the side. Then he knelt to remove her shoes. "Still think your daddy's an angel?"

She shook her head, vision swimming. "I don't know. I don't know."

"A stone angel, yes? As effective a removal of wings as my own. Have you ever wondered why the only angels you've ever seen are made of stone? After all, you see the demons walking the earth, see through our disguises, our broken wings. But you've never seen the angels until they've turned to stone."

"Just because I can't see them doesn't mean they're not there."

He stood again. "What a Sunday school answer. It's your proof, sweet thing. You only see demons, including the nephilim, because demon's in your blood, which means they're not angels. They're being punished for falling, Abigail."

"Then why aren't you being punished?" she asked. "Why aren't I?"

"We already fell—a long time ago, long before we incarnated. And we'll be punished again in the end. In layman's terms, your daddy's still being processed, but the proof is in you, the fruitful harvest of his fallen deeds."

He gazed at her, his desire as unhindered by the shapeless scrubs as Tony's had been, except Charles *had* seen what she looked like underneath. "Take off your clothes and get on the bed on your hands and knees. You're not quite ready to descend, but you will be, my sweet nephil."

Their eyes met. He dared her to refuse, to walk away, to go back into a night that was still kinder and safer than this well-lit room.

Abby pulled her tunic and undershirt over her head, unhooked her bra, then removed her pants and underwear. With his gaze heavy on her shoulders like the weight of wings, she squared her shoulders and walked to the foot of the bed. Its rumpled coverlet invited her as the shackles at the four corners clanked up onto the mattress. She closed her eyes and bowed her head.

Warm breath caressed her neck, flowing down her back. The heat that emanated from his gloved hands ghosted over her shoulder blades as though he wished for her wings, but she didn't deserve those wings any more than she deserved her chilled spine.

She thought about all the trouble she could have saved if she'd just left herself partially paralyzed in that alley.

"I didn't waste much time on self-pity when I learned what I was," Charles said. "Then again, my gifts are a bit more fun than yours. Still...I aim to please."

He grabbed her waist and threw her onto the bed. The chains lunged at her wrists and ankles like snakes and snapped around them. Her arms buckled as the chains yanked her forward. She almost fell on her face.

Charles caught her hips before she could right herself and pulled her ass higher, rubbing the rough placket of his jeans against her cunt. She muffled her moan of startled guilty pleasure in the coverlet.

"I don't know when your transformation will happen, but I hope to be there when it does. You'll be the prettiest piece of pestilence this hellish place has ever seen."

He blew cold air down her spine, then followed the path of her shivers with the smoothness of leather, sliding his hand down to grasp her neck and hold her face down on the coverlet. She turned her head so that she could breathe, gasping.

"Did you get to see it, your power?" He thrust two fingers into her pussy without warning. It wasn't as slick as it could be, but his command and rough treatment had made her wet enough to not resist against him. "Or did you turn away?"

"I saw it."

"Say it again."

"I saw it." She whimpered as he twisted his fingers inside her. "It was awful."

"It was beautiful. You won't be able to appreciate it until you finally recognize your calling. Sometimes, art needs time before the artist understands its brilliance."

"You're evil," she said through clenched teeth.

"Takes one to know one, sweet thing."

She hid her face in her arm and pushed back against his fingers, shoving her folds against his knuckles as though begging him to hit her there.

Instead, silk flowed over her back to allow Charles to bend over her, his chest to her shoulders. He grasped her breast as it swung from his thrusts. He squeezed too painfully, but she still wanted to bite her arm against the pleasure wringing hot around his fingers.

Then he withdrew, the abandonment abrupt and complete, leaving emptiness in her cunt and cold skin where the silk fabric floated off.

Abby rose and looked over her shoulder.

Charles narrowed his eyes as he removed his trousers. "Did I say you could get up?"

Abby's heart skipped. She quickly lowered her upper body to the coverlet once more.

"But I do want you to see this."

The silk, red this time, floated up like a bloody ghost. Instead of molding to Abby's body, it clung to Charles like a second skin, groping his abdomen and around his hips. At first, it draped over his erection. Then it embraced itself almost seamlessly around the thick cock, pressing close to the scrotum and thighs.

He grasped his cock through the silk, grunting a little as he stroked the fabric over his shaft. Pre-cum dampened the end. "It doesn't have to be like this. You could let me touch you. There's nothing to be afraid of or fear from me. We're on the same side."

Abby clenched her fists in the coverlet, but she shook her head.

"Damn oath and honor. Very well. I'm going to fuck you, love, and you're going to enjoy it, although it won't satisfy the way that I could with skin and teeth and tongue, my cock stroking your cunt and making you weep. We could make the sweetest kind of music, love."

"Keep your damn promise." But she was fixated on the way that the gleam of silk shifted as he stroked up and down the length of his erection. Her mouth watered.

"You certainly can't tell me you don't want me to break it." He separated her folds with his silk-covered cock and slid through her damp flesh, teasing the entrance and occasionally brushing her clit. "Just the thought of me squeezes the juices from you like a ripe, split peach." He sucked the gloved fingers he'd used to stoke the arousal inside of her.

"What I want isn't good." Like the way she pushed her hips back to rub his cock more firmly against her.

"That's the point." He smoothed his hands up her back and massaged her shoulder blades as though to coax out her wings.

"No," she said, choked more by a sob than by the angle of her neck. It was getting harder and harder to say it. "You can't touch me. Just fuck me. Fuck me like I'm evil."

"Because you are," he whispered.

"Because I am." She buried her face in her arms just as Charles brought the blunt head of his cock to her entrance, dampening the silk even more.

Then, ever so slowly, he entered her. Magic kept the silk fused to his cock instead of sticking to the moisture inside of her. It was like nothing she'd ever experienced before. The damp fabric pulled on the walls of her cunt a little when he moved this slowly, but it didn't matter anymore when he withdrew, then slammed into her again.

He'd promised to fuck her, and that's what he did. There was no love, no tenderness, nothing but the pounding between her legs and the bruising grasp over her hips. He dug his fingers in and pulled her back against him until she whimpered, but that was nothing compared to the slap of his thighs hitting hers or the animalistic groans that wrenched out of his throat from the effort. His heat seeped through the silk and leather, and she could almost imagine that the velvet of skin stroked her cunt instead.

Abby rested her forehead against the cold metal around her wrists and surrendered to the assault of sensation, both uncomfortable and pleasurable. They drew her mind away from the events of the night and into the soft, blood-swollen lips and walls of her pussy.

"Every time you think of me, every time you rub yourself off to the memory of my cock inside you, every time you consider whether to release me from my oath, remember what you are," Charles said through clenched teeth. "One of these days, you're going to come to me and beg me to touch you. We're demons of a feather, Abigail, pestilence and lust. Imagine the diseases you'll spread if you follow in *my* trail."

"Stop. Please stop." But she shoved back to the base of his cock just the same.

"I can't touch your skin, but I'm under it all the same, aren't I? You're mine, whether you know it or not. And I can be yours when you finally embrace what you are as tight and hot as you embrace my cock. I want you, Abigail, and one of these days I'll wrap myself around you and know you better than the Creator ever did. I *will* feel your wings whole and solid against mine."

"No, no, no…" Abby moaned as he thrust in as hard and as deep as he could, his cock twitching with his climax inside of her and triggering her own.

But it wasn't the same as when she'd had Zekiel inside her, when he'd brought her to climax with flesh, stone though it was. She shook and cried out through her miserable orgasm. To have true satisfaction with someone like Charles, there went her salvation and soul, if she even had one.

She would *never* be satisfied with Charles until she let him in. She would always have to come back to him in desperation, because she'd never quite achieve satiation, that blissful end that left her boneless and content the way she'd been with…

Zekiel. Ironic, that he had been an incubus like Charles, but he was her greatest hope for salvation — although he deserved so much more than a demon like her.

And Zekiel wasn't there. It was Charles who discarded the silk and conjured a robe around him so that he could envelop her, still bound, in his arms. He kissed her hair lightly and held her until she stopped shaking. The tension in her burning muscles screamed for relief and release that she couldn't give them.

Instead, she dwelled on the black, boiling cancer, the rictus of pain, the spread of giant bat wings brushing against feathers.

"If it makes you feel any better," he murmured, "I'll bet he deserved it."

It didn't make her feel better.

Chapter Thirteen

Abby wandered the streets in cold darkness, but she wasn't as out of it as before. She wore one of Charles' leather jackets, this one distressed and brown. She usually wasn't for this much cow death, but beggars couldn't be choosers. She'd kept her cream-colored tank top undershirt on and stuffed her scrub tunic in her purse. If she could have taken off the drawstring pants, she would have, but she hadn't worn anything else decent underneath.

She found herself at the gates of the FUMC cemetery, iron chilling her palms.

Daddy, I've done so much since I saw you. I don't know what happened to me.

She wiped away a tear with her fist and swallowed down the lump in her throat. Then she took a step back, waited until a car passed by, spread her smoky wings and leaped over the fence.

She retrieved her flashlight from her purse to find her father's row. With the way things had been going, she wouldn't have been surprised if, after all the days she'd failed to return, he'd been whisked away to another cemetery or rooftop for her to find all over again. But no—Octavius Stone still presided over Abigail Santana's grave, and when Abby sat across from him, he broke his position, life sparking in his face as he met her eyes.

"Abby, I thought something had… I worried when you didn't return. I *told* you this place was dangerous."

If only he knew that it wasn't the place that was the problem. He sounded sincere, though, the distress on his face less stylized sculpture and more the long-suffering anxiety that Abby recognized from her childhood.

Everything that had happened built up behind her lips as though it would spill out any second. Tears pricked her eyes, but she couldn't let her emotions get the better of her. She had to be clear-headed to ask him the only question that mattered, the one that determined whether her whole life had been a lie and only a demon had offered her the truth.

"Are you nephil, Dad?" The open space of the cemetery sucked all the resonance out of her voice, leaving only the naked words.

Her father was as still as the statue that he was. "Who told you that?"

"So it's true." She clicked off the flashlight and slumped on the gravestone, the effort of keeping herself upright suddenly too much.

"No, sweetie. No, it's not true at all. Heavens above, what tales have you been hearing? I can't reach you from here. I want so much to hug you like I used to and tell you everything's all right, but you're so far away from me."

Abby rose to see him reaching for her, stretching his fingers as far as they would go, but he was as stuck as ever to the stone.

"You have to be." Her face grew hot in spite of the cold. "You have to be. You're here, aren't you?"

"In this city? We're here to protect. Come here, sweetie. Please."

"In this cemetery." She grasped the top of the stone against the impulse to run into his arms. "In your stone angel body. You're being punished for coming down here. You're being punished for being with Mama and having me."

"Punished? I'm not being punished, sweetheart. Who the hell told you that you were something bad that I did?"

"Then what would you call this?" Abby gestured to row after row of creepy cemetery angels lining the property. "You can't move, you can barely speak to each other and you were taken away from us. What would you call this except punishment?"

"Consequence."

"That sounds an awful lot like punishment, Dad."

"Oh, Abby." He let his arms fall slowly back to his sides. "It's not punishment at all. I had ten wonderful years with your mother and eight years with you, not to mention two more with you and your mom a few miles from home. But just as a puddle is a consequence of rain, this is the consequence of an angel coming down from heaven to live among humanity rather than fight from behind the curtain. We're not like demons, sweetie. We're not supposed to interact. If we do, whether for love or protection or intercession, there are—"

"Consequences," she repeated, still skeptical.

"Some angels don't have a choice." He settled back on his gravestone once more. "Many of us are bound by the Creator's will, and that's all we do. But sometimes an angel is given a gift, the same gift given to humans—a chance to choose. Some choose to fall, and they lose their light and their wings. Some choose to stay, fighting evil in their own way as determined by the grand strategy. Then there are those like me. I saw a beautiful soul, Abby, and I couldn't resist her. I wasn't stripped of my wings. I still had wings that were just like yours—not as substantial as they used to be. They've returned now, although they're still not quite as they once were."

He spread his wings to their full span.

"They will return to their former splendor in time. I'm not punished by the years served in these cemeteries. It's simply a condition of an angel entering the human world—ten years as a human, many more in service as protector, limited though we are in this capacity. And when my time is finished, I will return to the other side of the curtain. I'm not fallen, sweetie. I can see that this question has been weighing on you. How I wish you'd asked me earlier. Have you believed all this time that you were the daughter of a demon? Oh, Abby, have you believed that you would become a demon yourself? How could you believe that about yourself, with all the good you've done? You're one of the lights. You are *my daughter*."

"Daddy..." Abby stumbled from her seat and fell to her knees in front of her father.

He embraced her, holding her head in his lap and humming soothingly as she cried the poison out.

"It's been such a bad week. And if I'm not a demon, it was all my fault. God, Daddy, I'm so ashamed..."

"You don't have to tell me. As much as it pains me to say that to my own child, I respect your secrets, and sometimes a dad doesn't have to know."

She nodded. She certainly wasn't going to tell him everything. But she needed to tell him *something*. "There's a demon that I've... He caught me, and I took it, hook, line and sinker. I can't believe I fell for it. I can't believe I fell for him."

"A handsome fellow, was he?" Her father rubbed her shoulders. "Charming?"

"He's an incubus. It's in his job description."

Her father tensed, his fingers clenching reflexively.

"No. He swore an oath not to touch me. He hasn't been visiting my dreams—just haunting my happy hour."

"Are you sure he's not visiting? You might not even be aware of it."

"There aren't any of the signs. I runed against it just in case. And I haven't had any, um, vivid dreams."

"Ah. Yes. Good."

In spite of the discomfort, he gently coaxed her up to sit on his lap so that he could hold her as he had when she was a slightly smaller daughter. His stone flesh was cold, but she needed his comfort more than warmth right now.

"He... He convinced me to turn my healing the other way. I didn't even know what I was doing, but I was scared and angry that this man attacked me, and I'd just been attacked the day before, too. I didn't know what else to do, so I pushed disease into him instead of taking it out. I tried to take it back. I tried to use the healing, but it didn't work."

"Do you think a demon or demon-in-waiting would have tried to heal it again?" he asked.

"I don't know. I still don't. I mean, I've built my whole life around being a healer. But if there's more than that, if I can also cause this kind of pain... I don't know what I am anymore."

"Abby, just like me, you have a choice. Your gift, like most gifts, can go both ways. An incubus *could* sow love and instead sows lust. A chaos demon *could* sow order and instead sows discord and strife. It's all in your choices. And a few bad ones won't condemn you to an immortal lifetime of evil. If you *wanted* to be a demon, your decision would have to be deliberate and determinate. Given your distress..."

He stroked her cheek, wetting his fingers with her tears. "You're not a mistake, Abby, neither punishment nor sin. You're my love incarnate, with divine blood in your veins. Even this demon, who introduced such chaos into your life, receives the endless and unconditional love that you carry inside of you, if my eyes don't deceive me. In spite of having to leave you and your mother, seeing you suffer, I'd do it all over again. It's torture to be away from you, but watching your mother from afar and you, the jewel of my heart, never being born, that would have been true torment."

Abby cried with the abandon she'd lost when she was five years old and had decided that crying wasn't pleasant. But in spite of the havoc it wreaked, this was the first time in a long time that the tears seemed beautiful and healing—burning her cheeks and eyes and the back of her throat but pulling something out of her at the same time.

"If only you knew what I'd done..."

"I know a little more than you think I do," her father said. "We cemetery angels whisper, remember, and your work is just across the street. Now that everyone knows who you are, they've kept me apprised of your comings and goings."

She wiped her face with the bottom of her shirt. "Knitting gossips, all of you."

He laughed as he stroked her hair. "You don't know the half of it. No, they simply want to help me know my daughter better, help me protect her in the only way that I can. They saw your indecision when you didn't return to me. They saw your distress. They heard of other things going on in this city, the company you keep, the company you seek. Leave behind the bad, Abby. You had no malicious intent. There isn't a malicious bone in your body. Any forgiveness you seek is granted. You know that."

"But—"

"There will be time for guilt and penance later," he interrupted gently. "You are and always will be my first priority, and I beg you to give me another chance to tell you the whole truth of what you are instead of the abridged version given to you as a child. But I have news, and not just what the angels whispered of you."

She shifted off her father's lap and sat next to him on the gravestone, grabbing a tissue out of her purse to blow her nose. She couldn't undo any of the damage she'd done this week, but the mission came before absolution—although they were sometimes the same thing.

"There is something important I must ask," her father said, "and I hope that you answer me honestly. It has to do with your...other work about which you haven't been so forthcoming. Are you pregnant?"

The cemetery rustled as though swept with wind, although the night was still. The angels around them had abandoned any pretense of not listening and, with rustle and creak of feather and stone, finally turned around to hear better.

"No!" But any color she had left drained out of her as she realized that what she'd done with Charles tonight might indeed have repercussions. Stone couldn't make her conceive, but silk wasn't a condom.

Her father showed uncommon restraint as he witnessed the shades of horror passing over her expression. He managed to hold his tongue when Abby brought her hand to her belly to sense any new life inside. She slumped in relief. She'd have to check for the next week or two, but for now, there was no candle hidden under her bushel.

"I don't think so," she said. "I wouldn't be yet... But I don't think so."

"We know that there's been increased demonic activity, the merging of smaller cults, conversion of different sects to become one greater sect with incarnation in mind."

"It's a Molochian cult. They're trying to bring Moloch into this world. We've had a few encounters with them now, and I'm starting to think they're taking it personally."

"Moloch. Of course it's Moloch," her father said grimly. "He always had such ambition and appetite. We do not know where they're keeping him, but we know that kidnapping, captivity, brainwashing and impregnation has been their method. And we didn't have to hear whispers to feel the time of incarnation drawing near, which means sacrifice—and for the sacrifice to mean something to both elements of this cult, it can't just be human. The demons need to sacrifice one of their children as well."

"If they're kidnapping and coercing, how the hell are we supposed to know who to protect, who to steal back? It's a big city. We can't find a giant-ass stone demon, much less his followers right now."

"The ones they keep with them would be the sacrifices they intend to provide *after* incarnation — a regular supply. The child sacrifices for the incarnation wouldn't be within their sphere, especially with demon hunters nosing around and threatening their operations. They'd keep the sacrifices separate and safe, unassociated with them."

"That makes it even harder. Do you know how many women are pregnant at any given time around here? Just in my limited personal life, I know at least one pregnant woman. I visit her several times a week."

"Then I suggest you visit her again and search for the second."

Abby stood, everything in her belly going tight and cold, as though she finally felt the winter. "What makes you think that my pregnant woman is *the* pregnant woman?"

"Because nothing is a coincidence, and I think the danger you're in indicates that they've realized you're a threat to them, because you're closer than you realize. At the very least, your sphere as a caregiver and healer is a place to start. As much as it kills me to let you go into this danger alone, understand that Moloch is only a little spider in the grander design. There are more powerful beings than he, and all demons are —"

"Cowards. Don't I know it."

"All the more proof that you aren't a demon, sweetheart."

"I love you, Dad." She wrapped her arms around his neck and held him close. Being made of stone did nothing to make that comfortable, but she tightened her embrace anyway.

"I love you too, sweetheart, no matter what," he whispered. "Now, for heaven's sake, stay safe."

"I'll be going into danger, but I won't be going into it alone." She packed everything into her purse. "I need you and all of your friends eavesdropping on us to send out a whisper campaign. I don't know if you know him, but his name is Zekiel, and he's the gargoyle whose better company I've been keeping. Tell him to meet me on the Mercy Hospital roof."

* * * *

Abby ran into the hospital, raised a hand to the nurse heading the extended care ward, then burst into the room where Kara and Maggie were kept. Empty, as usual, except for Kara and Maggie, of course, and the two other patients who shared the room with them.

And the baby in Maggie's womb. Abby covered the eight-month bulge with her palm. The baby was still fine, healthy as the healthiest baby in the world. She caught her breath, sinking into the chair that she used while reading to the two women.

Well, that narrowed her tiny pool of friends with fetuses, especially since she was looking for a pair. She'd have to start looking into the files of the pregnant women she'd met with at the clinic. She doubted Jason or Harold, the patients in the other beds, had buns in the oven. Besides, she'd never sensed anything from Kara.

Abby sat up. She'd never sensed a baby from Kara because she'd never checked. Why would she check? Kara was a coma patient and had been for over a year, longer than Maggie, who had only been in extended care from the car accident for six months. Abby had known about Maggie because her pregnancy was a matter of record. Neither Abby nor the residents or nurses had had any reason to think Kara would conceive, so they wouldn't have ever had a reason to test for it.

In theory, Kara would have started showing by now, but something could have happened — something terrible — that would throw off the typical timeline completely. Kara was a young woman who couldn't stop anyone, and it had been known to happen. The shapelessness of her gown and the blankets shielded much of her shape from visitors. Surely the nurses who cleaned and changed her would have noticed, but Abby couldn't shake the feeling...

She tentatively placed her hand over Kara's belly. It didn't look pregnant to her from her angle, but she could immediately tell how distended Kara's abdomen was from where it should be, and the baby within, alive, healthy, gleamed its spirit at her like black glitter in moonlight.

Kara was pregnant, and what she was carrying was protected, not hidden so much as camouflaged from notice by people who weren't looking for it. But now that Abby knew, she couldn't unsee what she should have seen all along.

And the baby certainly wasn't human.

Abby didn't waste precious seconds on shock. She stormed to the reception desk. "Gloria, has anyone been to see someone in that room, besides me?"

Gloria looked confused. "Maggie's family comes by now and then to check on her and the baby, but otherwise..."

"Maggie's family, do they come as a group or do they ever arrive individually?" Abby wasn't ruling out a demon who could make himself look like a member of the family. He could even enter shielded as a woman.

"They've always come in pairs, at least when I'm here. What's this about?"

"I think Kara's pregnant."

Gloria dropped the files she was flipping through. "What? How can you say... How can you tell?"

"I have a feeling. I know that sounds stupid, but you can do the test if you want. Or just look under the covers. I can't believe no one noticed." She could believe it, of course, but now that she'd called attention to it, the nurses *would* notice. Then the recriminations would start. Abby didn't have time to smooth that wrinkle over. "I'll be right. I'm usually right about these things."

If the night nurses hadn't known she was a nurse as well, perhaps Gloria would have been more dismissive, but she clambered up instead. "I can get a urine sample."

"I need to see the security recordings for their room."

"Abby, if it's true—and we haven't confirmed that yet—we'll have an internal investigation."

"Look... I can't explain why it's important, but I might know who did this. I need to see those tapes." Abby was lying through her teeth and terrible at it, but she didn't know how else to get what she needed unless she had some kind of credible lead.

"What do you mean you know who did this?"

"He might be my boyfriend," Abby said, snatching the first possibility that crossed her mind. "He said some things, murmurs in his sleep, writes weird stuff down in his email drafts and I just… I need to know."

"So you can help him?"

"So I can drag his ass to the police after I'm through with him. Please, Gloria. I only want to help Kara."

"All right," Gloria said, albeit reluctantly. "Let me get the sample first. I can pull up the recordings while I'm testing."

Abby sighed, but that was as fast as Gloria was going to let her at those confidential security recordings without a badge or a warrant, neither of which she could get any time soon without any friends on the force. Besides, she intended to keep this all as far from the police as she could. They weren't equipped to deal with demon spawn, much less those that spawned them in the first place.

"Holy shit!" Gloria exclaimed from the room. "How did we miss this?"

Abby tapped her fingers on the counter until Gloria came back with the sample. Testing would take only moments, so Gloria rolled herself in her chair back to the computer to pull up the security recordings for playback.

"How far back?" Gloria asked.

"Can you just go backwards at four times the speed? I know what I'm looking for."

Gloria glanced back at the test, which had turned positive. "Son of a biscuit eater. I swear, if the father is one of ours, I'm going to raise holy hell. That's just…so wrong. Like, fairy tale princess wrong. But she's clearly been pregnant for a while, and I don't know how… What do you think you'll see on the recordings? They only go back two weeks before they're deleted."

"You think whoever did this stopped just because she got pregnant?" Abby said grimly.

"Gross. And you think you're dating this guy?"

"Not for long."

"But how did he get past all our people?" Gloria asked. "The only one I ever see visit them is Maggie's family and you, and I'm pretty sure you're not the culprit."

"Well, if he's one of yours, you might not think anything of him going in there." Abby stared intently at the rewinding recording. She saw herself and the nurses at their regular times, but no outliers. If the demon was one of the nurses in disguise, this was going to get tricky.

"Wait. Stop." She pointed at the screen.

"What? I didn't see anything." Gloria stopped the video and ran it forward again at one and a half speed. It was a night when Abby had visited, so she watched herself go into the room and read to them for two hours, then leave.

"What'd you see?" Gloria asked.

"It's coming." She leaned in closer. "Okay, stop. Watch in real-time."

"There's no one there, Abby."

A figure with spiky black hair and a black leather jacket entered the room after Abby exited. Then he turned left, toward Kara's bed.

Abby clutched the back of Gloria's chair to keep herself from breaking expensive equipment in fury. Gloria couldn't see him enter, nor could she see the flash of wing feathers through the open door, but Abby could. And because he didn't think he had to hide, he gave the camera a clear view of his face when he left.

She should have fucking known. She'd been busy on the nights when she hadn't been fucking around with him, and obviously so had Charles. When he hadn't been preying on her insecurities, he'd been availing himself of a woman in a coma. And the bastard had infected Kara with his demon seed, which didn't even require her egg for implantation, just a functional uterus.

Abby thought she was going to be sick—or find an ax and cut off his head. Possibly both, maybe at the same time.

"Wait! What's that?" Gloria pointed at the screen, squinting.

Abby was just trying not to see red. "What's what?"

"Under Kara's bed. There's something under there."

Abby darted around the desk back into the room. She fell to her knees and lifted the blankets up to reveal what their shadows had hidden from her view. Then she pushed the foot of the bed to the side when she saw the edge of the mark drawn onto the floor.

She was no witch, so she wasn't positive about the symbology, but it didn't look or feel malevolent to her. There was no denying the faint pentagram pattern, but this one wasn't inverted. If she had to guess, it was a circle of protection, perhaps what had concealed the unnatural quickening. But on a hunch, Abby scrambled over to Maggie's bed and looked underneath it as well. It wasn't exactly the same, but it was similar enough, and the runes had been drawn by the same hand.

Circles of protection, like most kinds of magic, were neutral, used by the benevolent and malevolent alike, and how they protected their subjects depended on the motives of the one who drew the circle. It wouldn't have protected Kara from Charles if Charles had been its creator.

Gloria ran into the room after her and gasped when she saw the protection circles, although Abby doubted Gloria recognized them for what they were. "What the hell is going on, Abby? Should I call the cops? Should I have them moved?"

"You do whatever you have to. I don't think moving them is going to help anything, though." Spell caster aside, Kara and Maggie were probably safer over those marks than anywhere else in the hospital. Abby didn't want to move them from that just yet.

"I'll need to report Kara's pregnancy. The hospital will probably call the police, though. Should I give them your number, to ask about your boyfriend?"

"I'm not sure it's him now. He's not superstitious, and this is just...weird. I'd prefer to stay out of it if it's not him." She climbed back to her feet. "I've got to go. Take care and watch over my friends."

"You be careful, too, Abby, if it *is* him."

Abby ran to the stairs. They were faster than the elevator, and elevators didn't have roof access. She rushed up, but her stomach dropped every step she took, dreading the imminent, inevitable conversation. Part of her hoped that Zekiel wasn't there, even though she couldn't confront Charles on her own.

Well, that wasn't true. She could use his oath to her advantage and chop his head off when he couldn't properly fight back. She'd been dealing with demons long before Zekiel had dropped into her scene. However, she was safer with Zekiel. He could fight the battles she'd never wanted in the first place, and she could save the victim. It was a perfect arrangement.

Except she'd been unfaithful. Sure, she wasn't Internet official with him or anything, but by the time Zekiel had seen her half naked and she'd left him hard after finishing herself off, they hadn't been casual anymore, physically or emotionally. It had happened fast, but that didn't discount the strength of her feelings. What she'd done with Charles had been inexcusable. The only reason she could offer, weak though it was, was that she'd been confused.

Abby wouldn't be surprised at all if she'd just lost herself one amazing gargoyle.

It wasn't any less than she deserved, though, even with her accidentally-on-purpose murder of that man off the karmic table. No matter what her father said about forgiveness, she wasn't going to let that one go. She'd had no business using her power on Tony. If she had to use it at all, she should have used it on the man who'd slit her throat. He'd been a soldier for the dark side of the mystical, so mystical means of fighting back would have been expected and allowed.

Those were her rules of engagement in this convergent city. They'd never been written down anywhere, but they were what allowed Abby to live with herself at night and sleep during the day.

She'd broken so many of those rules this week, she didn't know how she was still herself anymore, much less alive. But it looked like the Creator still had a plan for her. She only hoped that it didn't involve becoming a forced breeder for a demonic cult or dying slowly at their red-stained hands in the name of Moloch — or dying at all before she was ready, alone.

But Zekiel deserved better. And he definitely deserved the truth.

When she reached the roof, Zekiel leaped down from a higher wing.

"The angels spoke to me. They don't usually whisper to gargoyles, so something truly terrible must be happening."

"I told them to whisper," Abby said. "You called them angels. And not just stone angels. They're actual angels, right?"

"Yes. Angels in stasis, so to speak," Zekiel replied, nonplussed. "They usually avoid associations with demons like me, even those on a path to redemption. It's not intended to be cruel. It's just part of the process. Why do you ask?"

Abby's shoulders slumped in dizzying relief. She trusted her father, but without context, Zekiel had no reason to lie.

"Sorry. I've been the victim of a spectacular set of lies, and that's just amazing to hear."

"I'm glad I could be of service."

Abby sat on the edge of the roof. "I need to tell you something. It's going to be difficult, and you're going to be disappointed and furious with me."

Zekiel jumped up and crouched next to her in tentative curiosity. "You can tell me anything. Anything you have done, I have done worse, I assure you."

"In the last week?" She peered up at him with hesitation, wishing her hair was down to shield her from some of his intensity.

Zekiel tilted his head, his stony expression stonier. "Yes. With free will, falls are inevitable. I can only continue to try."

"You might be less forgiving when you hear what I'm going to say." She took a deep breath and hoped her nausea stayed down. "This last week, my divine origins and humanity were questioned. In my own uncertainty, I may have done some things against my better nature. I killed a man—someone who tried to hurt me in the clinic. I could have incapacitated him or just yelled for help. Instead, I took my gift and twisted it around. I didn't mean to, but somewhere deep inside of me, I wanted it to happen, or else I wouldn't have done it."

"It still sounds like an accident, Abby," Zekiel said gently. "I killed hundreds of humans for my own gain when I was an incubus, and it was intentional."

"I lied to you," she interrupted him before he could reassure her any more. "I mean, I didn't outright lie, but I lied by omission. When you confessed that you were an incubus, I told you that I'd encountered an incubus a few years ago, and that was true. What I didn't say was that I met an incubus about a week ago. I thought his lies were truth, but that doesn't mean I'm not responsible. I know what demons are like, especially seduction demons. I shouldn't have let him even talk to me after that first night, but I did. He gave an oath not to touch my skin, so he couldn't feed off me, but that didn't stop him from hurting me or making me feel pleasure or even having sex with me."

Zekiel reeled back. He had to spread his wings to regain his balance, his feet scratching the stone underneath him.

She'd confessed that last part as fast as she could. Now that she'd started, momentum wouldn't let her stop if she tried. "I can't use the excuse that he's an incubus. That would only work if I hadn't known. He couldn't charm me with his touch, so he seduced me the old-fashioned way. He tricked me, but I fell for his tricks, gave in to the doubt that he planted in my brain, calling me nephil and bringing into question everything that I was. Fucking him was like flirting with my dark side, and I chose to do it—not without…consequences."

She had to swallow before that last word, thinking of her father. These consequences, however, were definitely punishment.

"He made me feel good, even when he was hurting me, but he couldn't love me, couldn't give me contentment or satisfaction, only self-loathing. Yet I kept going back, believing every time that I was… I don't know. That I was doing what I was made for. He said that I was a demon and that my demon nature would come out. I believed it. I thought all the things I did this week were because I was what he said I was, even though I didn't want to be, and for the love of all that's holy, would you please say something so I can shut up?" She finally looked up from her lap to brave Zekiel's reaction.

His head hung from his hunched shoulders. "What would you like for me to say? I cannot say that what you've told me does not cut straight to my stone-cold heart." His voice was low and quiet, but she could hear every word. "I also remember how mind-spinning it was to learn that I was a demon, that I had demonic and therefore divine blood within me. I understand how a clever incubus might make you think you had no choice in the matter."

"Okay, I'm kind of waiting for you to start yelling for me to get out of your sight and how disgusting I am. I've done so many bad things."

"It hurts me, Abby. When I first became a gargoyle, I might have only felt that hurt. I would not have seen or heard your pain, your regret, your fear. And a hundred years ago, I might have been the incubus who ensnared you. We are devilishly hard to resist, even to ourselves."

"I'll give you that." She hesitated to touch him when he met her eyes again, but he didn't retreat. She stroked his forearm, and he let her.

"I've already told you that struggle is a companion of free will," Zekiel said. "Have I not said that I too fall and have fallen?"

"I should have known better."

"So should have I." He kissed her forehead and backed up once more, putting space between them and hanging his head again with shame that looked awfully similar to hers. "I cannot rain judgment upon you because I have also strayed into the arms of an incubus since I met you. He was my old partner, in crime and in bed. I'm afraid that old habits die hard, although it is no more of an excuse than yours."

"New habits, too." She glanced at his covering and snorted. "Hard indeed."

"I told you."

"Yes, you did." She wondered what exactly he was hard for. Had *she* been the cause of it, her account of infidelity, in spite of how it had hurt him? Or had it been the memory of his other lover? She decided not to ask, because she wasn't sure how she'd feel about either answer, and he was clearly embarrassed. "I would help you take care of it, if you'd let me, but we really do have something to do besides confession—although we've been doing that pretty well, haven't we?"

"Confession can be good for the soul."

"Even better is confession with a chance at absolution, and we might just get it. You find it a little coincidental that we were both seduced by incubi *and* an incubus got a girl pregnant downstairs — a girl who's in a coma next to another pregnant woman, both protected by some kind of charm?"

Zekiel looked out at the skyline and narrowed his eyes, his firm jaw clenched in anger. "Is that so?"

"My father is one of the angels at the cemetery by where I work. He's the reason why the angels were whispering to you. He told me that those pregnant women have everything to do with what's happening with the Molochian cult. You wouldn't happen to be acquainted with an incubus named Charles, would you? Asian, but his accent is some kind of English, I think."

Zekiel lunged into the air with his wings at full spread. He bared his teeth, exposing the sharp canines. "That grinning, soulless bastard."

"Ah, I see you've met." She covered her face with her hands. "We've *both* been had by the same sex demon?"

"I am more at fault than you. I *knew* him — better than anyone." He jerked his sword from its sheath and pointed it at the sky in the direction of Cemetery Grove. "I will cut off his worthless head and feed it to the demon he's helping to raise. How dare he? How dare he use what I taught him against me? How dare he forget his own misery from when he was taken from his humanity and goaded into becoming a demon? And how *dare* he pass that misery to you?"

Zekiel whirled around. Abby backed away from the fire in his red eyes, but he stared beyond her. Underneath the anger, Abby read anguish. It reminded her of a stone angel instead of the demon he so often appeared to be.

"He saw the light that you were—a healer, a compassionate warrior, a pure heart in the middle of this metal Meridian city—and he told you that none of it meant anything. When I knew him, he was mischievous, yes, but little more than an imp playing games. The craven beast. I'll feed you his heart, my dear, if you desire it."

"Pass on the demon heart, thanks. What we've let him do to us isn't half as bad as what he's done to Kara. She didn't ask for any of this. And Maggie's pregnancy is a part of this, too. My dad said that the incarnation is happening soon. I don't think it's a coincidence that Maggie looks like she's going to pop."

Zekiel lowered his sword until the tip touched the ground. He'd stayed hard through the pumping blood of his anger, but it finally looked like she wouldn't have to deflate him herself before they could get down to business. Thank goodness for an ex-incubus' control.

"I have an idea," he said. "You're not going to like it."

"I'm not going to like anything that a demon cult thinks is a grand old time."

"Do you know where Charles lives?"

"By our alley, the one behind Threshold. He lives above the bar. And he's probably still there, because we were… He's probably still there."

"You'll need to ride on my back. I can explain on the way."

Abby rested her hand on Zekiel's chest to stop him. His muscles twitched at the touch. She stepped closer and brought her hand up to his face, drawing him down slowly enough for him to resist. Instead, he angled his head and met her lips. The kiss was gentle, but it would have been a mistake to confuse gentle for passionless. Zekiel curled his arm around her waist and pulled her in so that there was no space for Charles to insinuate himself between them once again.

"I'm sorry," she whispered against his lips.

"I offer you my deepest apologies as well."

"I'll never let him near me again. I promise."

"Don't make a promise that you cannot keep."

"Zekiel..."

"I would think no less of you. He and I were partners for twenty years, cut short only because I developed a conscience. He was my lover, Abby. We fed off each other. We visited each other in our dreams and in our waking hours. I did not walk away unaffected. It is no different when an incubus has targeted you and gets a taste, even without direct touch—if anything, that makes it worse. He is in your blood as much as mine, and I would not hold you to a promise that may be more difficult for you to keep than you realize." He smiled sadly, squeezing her arms in sympathy.

"At least I can say he never visited my dreams."

His eyes lit up. "He didn't?"

"He said he didn't, and I never woke up with the symptoms. None of my roommates did, either."

Zekiel took her face in his hands. "I can almost guarantee that he tried, even if he didn't intend to feast upon you. Dreams reveal the deepest and darkest of desires, and there's nothing he loves more than sifting through and using those secrets. But if he could not enter your dreams, do you understand what that means?"

She shook her head, but she wrapped her hands around his wrists. His joy was infectious.

"It means that when he tried to get into your dreams, you didn't invite him in. That means more than the world to me, my light."

"But I let him into my conscious mind. That was my choice. He didn't get close enough to wriggle in completely, but..."

"Your conscious mind is subject to all kinds of manipulation and suggestion, by others and by your own lies to yourself. The unconscious mind is different." He stroked her forehead. "It's the most honest part of you, unchained by rationalization, doubt or inhibition. If you had truly wanted Charles, at the very core of your soul, you would have welcomed him in without hesitation." He tilted her chin up and kissed her again. "No matter what happens, I need you to know that I mean that."

Abby understood, and without looking away, she nodded. "No matter what happens."

Chapter Fourteen

No shadow passed across the lit window, but Zekiel sensed Charles' presence as he flew through the alley — because this time he was searching for it. After warning Abby to cover her face, he crashed through the window to land in a crouch in Charles' apartment.

Charles lay on his bed, naked as the day Zekiel had left him and as casual and smooth in his human skin as if he were wearing a tailored suit. The barest lift of his eyebrows was the only surprise displayed.

"You still look good in my coat, love," he said, crossing his legs. "I had no idea the two of you were acquainted."

Zekiel grabbed Charles by his neck and yanked him off the bed. Charles' legs flailed, but he didn't fight back, only smiled.

"Liar!" Zekiel shouted. "You knew. You set out to hurt both of us, because you *knew* we were working together."

"I had no idea, mate," Charles rasped through Zekiel's fist around his throat. "And is that what they're calling it these days?

"Isn't that what we called it in our day, *mate?*"

"There is such a thing as a coincidence, you know. Sure, I was playing you and the girl, but that didn't mean I was playing you both against the other. That just makes it funnier."

Zekiel squeezed until Charles gagged, scratching at Zekiel's hands.

"Stop!" Abby ran to Zekiel and pulled on his wrist. "We still need him."

"Asphyxiation won't kill him," Zekiel said.

"You would know," Charles managed.

Zekiel threw him against the wall. Two whips fell off their hooks on top of him when he hit the ground. Zekiel pointed down at him. "You stay down there. Do not speak except to answer questions. And do *not* look at her. She's too good for your eyes."

"I've seen things about her you can only imagine."

When Zekiel kicked him in the stomach, Charles laughed, even as he gasped.

Zekiel crouched in front of him. "I don't have to imagine."

Charles' widened eyes were the only response Zekiel needed. Despite his jeering, their relationship clearly surprised Charles even more than their professional association.

"You will answer me truly," Zekiel continued. "I'll know if you're lying, now that I know you *will* lie to me."

"What did you expect me to do? You turned over to the other side. You think I'm going to be honest with someone who's fighting against me?"

"You will be honest now."

"Why should I?" Charles jutted out his chin in challenge, still unruffled by the fact that he was nude and Zekiel was made of living stone, nearly invincible in comparison.

"Because I know where your child is."

Charles froze.

"Yes," Zekiel said. "Abby found your breeder."

"You wouldn't hurt her," Charles said through gritted teeth, his black eyes flashing. "And you wouldn't hurt an infant."

"Even more interesting is that the protection spell under her bed is the same spell under the other pregnant woman in that room. This wouldn't happen to have anything to do with the cult that's been rattling chains to raise Moloch in this part of the city, would it?"

When Zekiel said 'Moloch', Charles' panicked anger turned into full-fledged terror.

"So you do possess knowledge of Moloch's rising. You're deep in the thick of it, aren't you?"

"Is that supposed to be a veiled come-on?" Charles said. "Because if you wanted to get it on in front of our girlfriend, all you needed to do was ask."

Zekiel started for Charles' neck again, but Abby guided Zekiel's arm back.

"I don't think 'bad cop' is working," she said softly. "If you're angry, he's just going to bug the crap out of you to make you angrier and do something you'll regret."

"Doing something he'll regret is his specialty," Charles said. "Or haven't you figured that out for yourself?"

"I do *not* regret her," Zekiel snapped.

Having Abby here made this worse. He wanted to throttle Charles until his face turned purple. Maybe if she'd stayed on the roof across the street and he had confronted Charles alone, he might have been able to do so on their own terms. But with Abby present, he couldn't look at Charles without imagining him sucking off the erection that she'd caused. Nor could he look at her without imagining Charles giving her the pleasure that made her so beautiful to him, like it had the night in her room under the stairs.

Forgiveness was divine, but it was also a lot easier than forgetting.

Abby tightened her hand on his arm, and Zekiel reluctantly stepped away. When his legs hit the foot of the bed, anger flared up again. The covers were rumpled. All he could think of was that Abby had been part of the cause, even though it wasn't Abby he was angry with.

Charles narrowed his eyes.

"You don't like that, do you?" Abby said. "You don't like that I can touch Zekiel, while you have to move heaven and earth to figure out how to touch me without actually touching me."

"I *have* moved heaven and earth for you, Abigail, wouldn't you say?"

"I don't need you to move heaven and earth. I need you to tell me about those women you victimized."

"I didn't touch Maggie."

Abby clenched her jaw when he said the woman's name. "No. You just attacked Kara."

"I never attacked Kara." Charles sat up, regaining some of his composure. "Tell her, Zeke. I wouldn't have been able to do anything to Kara if she hadn't let me into her dreams."

"You mean the way I *didn't*?"

Charles tried to maintain an even demeanor, which meant he was making an effort to hide something.

Zekiel crossed his arms. "So you *did* try to enter her dreams."

Charles shrugged. "What can I say, love? I'm just a man."

"And a liar," Abby said.

"Those two usually go together, don't they?" Charles replied with a grin.

"Kara would never have invited you in if she'd known what you are, and she wouldn't have accepted the baby of someone she didn't and could never know."

"Oh, really? You know her so well?" Charles sat back against the wall. "You sign in to read to her. You've only known her when she's lying on her back doing nothing. I know her where she's still present and aware. The things she wants to do with me... Do you want me to describe how excited she is every time she discovers we're having a baby?"

"I'm betting she doesn't want demon spawn. I know you put a cuckoo in that nest, Charles, so cut the domestic crap."

"Hey," Charles snapped. "I wouldn't put my cuckoo in just anyone's nest, all right? I like the girl. That's why she gets to live."

"I'm sure she'd be flattered. So what are the birthing plans for Maggie and Kara? Dual births, dual sacrifices, the key to Moloch's incarnation? Or does it still need to be inside the mother? Is that the despicable kind of desecration that really gets a princeling's blood boiling in all the right ways?"

Charles pushed up the wall to stand. "I can't tell you."

"Can't or won't?" Zekiel asked.

"Won't, if you want to be technical about it. It's part of the deal."

"What deal?"

Charles mirrored Zekiel's stance and crossed his arms. Though he lacked a covering for his cock, he managed to exude the same kind of defensive stubbornness.

"I'll kill your child, Charles," Zekiel said.

Abby recoiled, cutting Zekiel to the quick.

"You wouldn't dare." There was that fear in Charles' eyes again. "Not when there's a chance at redemption. We all know how much you like redemptive arcs."

"Look me in the eye and tell me I wouldn't dare."

Charles must have seen something he didn't like, because he turned to Abby. "Fine. Then she won't let you, will you, love?"

Abby opened her mouth, but no sound came out. Zekiel understood. Infanticide didn't exactly warm the cockles of Zekiel's stone heart, either, but he'd cut a redemptive arc short before. To keep Moloch from rising, he would do whatever he had to do.

"Besides," Charles said, the old petulance creeping in, "even if you kill me, my spells will protect the women and my child."

"And if I intend to kill them for their own protection? Does that spell read intentions? Because my intentions are pure."

"You'd *murder* women and children to get back at me for pawing at your girl? You right git."

"You've stood back and allowed the murder of women and children to keep your child safe."

Abby sliced her hands in the air between them, shaking her head. "What damn difference does it make to you if Zekiel kills the baby instead of the cult killing it, besides compromising the integrity of your own skin with your Master? Don't you even try to go the protective father route. And while we're at it, almost everything you've said about *my* father and my nature is the most beautifully quilted fabrication I've ever heard. You want to talk about protective fathers? My father's a cemetery statue, which is the closest thing this world has to guardian angels, so don't you dare talk about fatherhood as though that's a concept you could even begin to understand."

"I didn't lie to you about everything." Charles gently stroked the open sides of her oversized leather jacket. "If I did, it was only to bring you to the truth."

"Oh, shut up. You were lying to get into my pants. Instead of building me up to make me jump willingly into that bed, you decided to go the other way and make me hate myself, lower myself to your level by making me think I was created for evil things."

Zekiel forced himself to stay back while Charles slowly brought Abby closer to him by the jacket lapels. When Abby had taken over the interrogation, Charles' entire body language had changed. He was respectful without being deferential, confident without being cocky. It was so similar to the way he'd once been with Zekiel.

And that was more troubling than treating her like a victim.

Charles viewing Abby as an equal meant that his seduction might not have been an act. He might truly wish for Abby to accept demonic transformation and join him as his new partner. Zekiel hoped he knew Abby well enough to know that she wouldn't do it, but Charles was even more relentless with those he wanted as more than a feast. He so often inspired obsession as an incubus that it was easy to forget that he formed obsessions of his own. When his advances were welcome—as they had been for most of Charles' and Zekiel's partnership—such obsession yielded some of the most amazing nights in Zekiel's memory.

But when that obsession was resisted...

Zekiel didn't know to what lengths Charles would go to acquire her, but after this Moloch business ended, Zekiel suspected that he would have to kill his ex-lover to save her.

He was willing to kill a thousand demons to protect her light. One wouldn't be a problem.

"I wasn't lying about what you were made for, love." Charles' voice was so warm, it could melt metal. "You have it in you to be one fine-ass pestilence demon."

"But I wasn't made for that."

"Tell that to the man you killed."

Abby's temples danced in fury as she stared up at Charles, her hands clenched.

"I was expanding your horizons, diversifying your options," he said. "You ought to know the whole story."

"You don't give a crap about my story or my options or anything like that. You saw a chance to play mind games with an angel's daughter and you took it. Just another notch on a man's headboard and a tick in the 'damned' column for the incubus quarterly review."

Charles lifted his hand, dangerously bare, as though to slap her, but he caught his palm right before it reached her cheek. Instead of striking her, he cradled it just short of touching her skin. A clueless man would still have sensed the sexual tension between them, and it wasn't from Charles' charm alone. The tension flowed both ways.

"No." Charles' earnestness made Abby shiver. It took everything left in Zekiel's personal arsenal not to tear Charles away from her—or tear her away from him.

"So you were trying to do right by me? Really?" But some of the bite had seeped from her tongue.

He shrugged and grinned. "Well, maybe not *right*."

"What is your child to you, Charles?" She searched his face as though she touched him. "That's what you keep calling it. Your child. Your infant. Not a sacrifice, no distancing language. You say you're protecting your child and the mother. What are you protecting them from? What did the cult promise you? That after they sacrifice this child, you can use Kara for the next one, and that one you get to keep? Or did they promise that this one would be safe, too? How do you keep a sacrifice safe?"

Charles dropped his hand to her shoulder over the leather jacket. "The child and mother's survival is assured. A sacrifice is simplest and most powerful in death, but all that's required in the final ritual is the blood of a demon child. If they're careful…"

"As demon cults always are," Abby said.

"They swore to me."

"Did they swear a blood oath?"

"Swearing still means something between our kind. We lie to you, while you're still mortal, but our word to each other has power."

"That would be a no. And what exactly would you be able to do to them if they went back on that promise? You said it yourself—death is easier. Easier to just kill the child and the silly hybrid demon and keep the comatose mother for further breeding than bother with the safety of a heavy blood donation from a demon infant. They tried to kill me instead of trying to use me. Without my healing power, they would have succeeded. They won't hesitate a moment to ensure the efficacy of the sacrifice you're so willing to offer them in exchange for something as easy for an incubus as access."

Charles didn't respond, but the last ghost of his grin faded from his face.

"If you want to keep that child, you tell us where the cult is hiding Moloch and what they need Maggie and Kara for and when. Then you help us stop him."

"I wouldn't think you'd agree with Mr. Square Jaw over there about doing whatever's necessary, if *necessary* means killing a baby. How would that sit with your soul, Abigail?"

"There's more than one way to take your child away from you," she said. "And it wouldn't sit well with my soul, either, to stand idly by while you victimize my friends worse than you ever victimized me. You planned to sacrifice Maggie and her baby to save yours. Well, now you'll help me save them all to do the same."

She refused to look away. In the end, it was Charles who stepped back.

Zekiel grabbed the discarded trousers from the floor and tossed them at Charles, who caught them against his chest. "Get dressed and start talking."

Charles looked between them again, this time with less amusement. Fear made him seem younger, more human, more like the man who had attracted Zekiel in the first place.

"Sure, love." It was hard to tell which one Charles directed it to.

* * * *

They landed on the roof of the defunct Meridian Public Library. Vega had personally gifted the city with the more modern and technologically advanced Archimedes Library situated nearer the more affluent part of town, and budget cuts elsewhere had closed this one, which had been there before the city's abrupt economic expansion. It now crouched in a valley, a relic of a past no one wanted to remember, not even worth the consideration of the land it sat on—yet.

Abby shed Charles' jacket for easier movement, leaving herself only in her thin tank top in the early winter night. Zekiel wished he'd thought to tell Charles to give her something more practical. Sometimes he forgot that other people experienced the elements more keenly than he did.

"All right, people," Charles said at the roof access door. "I'll go first."

"I am not as foolish as you think, brother," Zekiel said. "We will not give you a chance to send your compatriots some kind of signal that you're being followed."

Charles rolled his eyes. "I know where they keep their sacrifices, and I can warn *you* when you're about to walk into one of their traps, not the other way around. You want to navigate that minefield without me, be my guest. I'll just be on my way."

Abby snatched the back of Charles' shirt. "No way. You swore an oath. And so did you, Zekiel. He'll do his best to keep us alive instead of being sacrifice bait, and we won't kill him after this operation if we survive. He's already proven he can keep an oath, so let's just...get in there and get the lay of the land to figure out how far they've gotten with Moloch and how much longer we have before the end of the world as we know it."

Zekiel reluctantly released Charles to let him take point, then went next so that he could take out anyone unexpected on the way. Abby stayed behind him. His wings meant she had to keep a greater distance than Zekiel was comfortable with, but he understood better than most how she could hold her own.

Vibration paused them all in the stairway down to the second floor.

"Shit. One second. It's Gloria. She's the nurse on duty for extended care, watching over Kara and Maggie." Abby pulled her phone out from her purse, securely strapped across her body, and answered as quietly as possible. "Hey, any news about our girls?"

Her cheeks lost their color.

"Wait, wait, slow down. What do you mean they're missing? With cops and doctors and security guards, how— Did they see who? What about the security cameras? No, I'm all the way on the other side of town with my boyfriend, so we can scratch him off that list. Yeah, keep me updated." She ended the call and shoved the phone back into her purse after turning it off. "Damn it. We might not have found out about Maggie and Kara in time. They've already taken them. We need to get down there *now*."

Zekiel only had to knock out one guard on the edge of the second floor. Charles caught the man as he fell to keep him from making a sound. When Charles laid him down, the man already had an erection. Charles had left his leather gloves on the nightstand, which made him more dangerous to Abby but also to everyone else.

The guard would have a more pleasant unconsciousness than he deserved.

At first, Zekiel believed that the guard was a decoy, that they could not possibly have such lax security, especially in a building so much more easily fortified than the warehouse. Then he better observed the layout of the library and realized that they didn't need many reinforcements at all on the second floor.

One wouldn't assume that a library was ideal to house a cult and its demon prince, but the group had improvised with what they had. The empty shelves had been shoved against the walls and picture window. It looked like a barricade against invasion, except for the way that the second floor had been almost entirely gutted so that the stone idol of Moloch could sit on the first floor and not have to crouch away from the ceiling.

At the moment, the statue was dormant.

It was the perfect place for him to hide, a place that had once been such a siren call to a certain kind of child. But now the books were gone, and the smell was that of a mausoleum, the thin, industrial carpet forever stained with the demon cult's bloody inverted pentagram beneath the dead-center statue of their Master.

Abby, Zekiel and Charles stayed close to the ground in the shadows of the second-floor shelves still standing near the hole's edge. Abby practically lay on her stomach to stay out of sight.

Most of the cult's guards manned the library entrances as well as the area where books had once been checked out. Makeshift bars from old lumber made the checkout desk a prison cell for the involuntary. Spells outside the bars muffled the women's screams so that the chanting in the circle could continue unhindered by the racket. No spells were needed to muffle the pregnant women lying on the rolling hospital beds.

She shook Zekiel's shoulder. "I can cure them," she whispered eagerly. "They have the glow. I feel it. If I can just get to them, I can wake them up and heal their bodies of weakness so we can run."

"The trouble is getting to them, love," Charles said.

"If we interrupt the circle, the ritual cannot be completed until the circle is whole again," Zekiel said. "I can fight every last one of them if I must."

"Yeah, run and stab. That's a great idea." Abby punched Zekiel's arm. "Are you trying to get yourself killed?"

"My life is nothing. I can always be remade. I will sacrifice myself if —"

"Oh, for the love of..." Charles ran almost soundlessly to the stairwell.

Zekiel extended his wings to divebomb down and stop him, but Abby grabbed his wrist and gestured him back to the ground. Either she trusted Charles' brilliant, improvised plan or she just didn't want Zekiel in the crossfire when Charles' plan blew up in his face. Zekiel preferred to assume the latter.

Charles sauntered onto the main floor, cutting the chanting circle short.

The head priest pushed back his red hood. An older man, scarred over his left eye but the good one a cold blue, his face was well-worn, leathered, marked with every one of his sins, especially when compared to the deceptively smooth, ivory, vampiric paleness of Charles. The priest was human, disturbingly human, inside and out. It always repulsed Zekiel how greedy a single man could be, to believe other people's lives were of less importance than his own ill-gotten comforts.

"What are *you* doing here?" The priest's contempt in both tone and twisted expression was unmistakable.

"We've hit a bit of a snag." Charles slapped the back of a demon he passed, breaking the circle and stepping onto the dried blood as though it weren't there.

"The only snag I see here is you," the priest replied. "We didn't invite you here, incubus. You aren't welcome."

"Funny. It seems so impolite to invite only part of the family to the party. Last I checked, I was on the payroll like the rest of you. *I* ensured that your little prosperity-slash-incarnation ritual would go off without a hitch. *I* told you where to hide. *I* distracted the closest thing you have to viable threats to your plans. *I* made the arrangements and protected the women over there so that, when the buns were done, they'd be strong and healthy for your needs. But see, simple hybrid demon me did all of that on the condition that *my* child remains safe. Yet here you are, with my brood without my permission. And you certainly didn't expect me to turn up here tonight, which makes me think your plans for my child extend beyond just blood. If your side of the bargain is broken, then I guess my side is forfeit, too. I'll take my woman and child back, and you can place your bets on a human sacrifice alone bringing back the big guy."

The priest gestured for the tallest demons near him to retrieve Charles. "Get him out of my sight."

But Charles hopped up on the sacrificial altar arranged under the demon prince's mouth and wriggled into place like a toddler climbing on the kitchen counter for the cookie jar. He picked up the knife waiting for a victim and played with the point against his palm. "I wouldn't if I were you. I know I don't look like much, but I'm scrappy."

Both the priest and his demonic enforcers hesitated, afraid of desecrating the blade.

The priest stepped toward Charles on his own. "You peek into windows and attack women while they sleep," he said with an audible sneer.

"And men, in case you were feeling left out. I'm easy." Charles swung his legs on the altar, unfazed by the priest's approach. "Is that what's got you whinging? You want in on this action?"

The priest snatched at the knife, but Charles moved too quickly, bringing the blade to the priest's throat and grabbing the back of his neck. With deliberate slowness, Charles guided him closer, spreading his legs to welcome the priest between them.

"Yes," Charles said softly, "I do taste a bit of jealousy there. There's no need for it, pet. All you had to do was ask."

Still with the threat of the knife on the priest's throat, Charles brought him in for a kiss, sucking with relish on the priest's lower lip. The slide of their tongues made the audience around them hold their breaths from the crackling electricity emanating from their connection.

Even Zekiel lost sight of their purpose as he watched Charles work. It had been such a long time, and he had few moral reservations about Charles spinning his spell around the priest, whose soul was so mired in darkness that he would never seek to escape its morass.

Zekiel also didn't look back to check how Abby was affected by the sight. The truth was that, for a moment, he forgot about her entirely, captivated as he was by his old lover in the arms of another man. His cock grew harder than stone, and he wasn't the only one. The voluntary or coerced women, too, though their desires were more hidden, shifted where they stood, pressing their thighs together and stroking their bodies in the absence of his more dangerous contact.

Charles brought the knife down the priest's throat and used it to cut through the hooded robes. The sound of tearing fabric made the priest moan and clutch at Charles' shoulders. Charles cut about halfway down the priest's front, then worked open the buttons of the man's shirt underneath to leave his chest bare.

The priest threaded his fingers through Charles' hair to encourage him as he left sucking kisses on his journey to the man's heart. Then Charles pressed his hand against the priest's chest and jerked the priest back to him to plunder his mouth.

The priest's skin grayed, color bleeding out from him as rapidly as paint chased by a deluge of rain.

By the time the rest of the cult realized how masterfully Charles had woven his charm, the cocoon of magic that he'd built to protect himself while feeding prevented any of them from stopping him as he sucked out every last drop of the priest's life. It took longer without penetration, but Charles had contact with the priest's core nonetheless, and that core seeped into him now, flushing his cheeks like bourbon.

The demons and men around the circle shouted at Charles and continued their efforts to stop him, but every time they tried, they hit an invisible wall. Only another sex demon would be able to pierce it, but child-eating princelings didn't attract many sex demons. Like Charles, they preferred to keep their children alive.

Finally, Charles yanked himself away from the priest's mouth and let him go.

The priest collapsed dead before the altar.

Charles looked over at where the cult had been keeping Maggie and Kara. They were still there.

"Well, bugger," he said, annoyed.

Now Zekiel understood. Charles had intended the priest's death as distraction rather than an outright attack. Unfortunately, it had been just as much of a distraction for Zekiel.

"I think we were supposed to save the women," Zekiel whispered back to Abby.

His wry statement was met with silence.

Zekiel pushed himself to his knees and turned, peering through the shadows. He whirled back and quickly caught Charles' eye. Charles received the unspoken message loud and clear.

Abby was gone.

Then they heard her screams.

Chapter Fifteen

The surprisingly potent image of Charles kissing another man shot straight between her legs to throb in her clit, but Abby recognized it for the opportunity that it was.

She tried to catch Zekiel's attention, but Charles' spell had mesmerized him — or maybe it was just Charles himself. Abby could believe that. Fully naked or fully clothed, the man was exceptional, even if he was also an exceptional ass.

Finally, Abby gave up trying to shake Zekiel out of his stupor. She crept around the edge of the second floor on her own.

First priority was getting to Kara and Maggie and waking them up. She'd have to do her best to ignore the other women inside the prison. They couldn't incarnate Moloch in their present state, so they had to be second priority. Third priority was everyone in the rescue party escaping with their collective butts intact.

A man yanked a burlap hood over her head.

She screamed as the man dragged her down the stairs, literally so for the last few steps. He yanked her back to her feet, but she stumbled again as he pulled her forward.

"I think we have a conspiracy," announced the man, who was cutting off circulation to her arm. When he shoved her to her knees, she cried out at the splinters of pain that stabbed up her thighs.

"I think you do, too," Charles said, "but that's kind of what cults are, isn't it? Anyway, that particular piece of tail is mine, and it's recently come to my attention you tried to take that away from me as well. Give her to me, make me an oath that my child is safe and we'll call this whole thing even."

"'Even' would be killing your little snack," the man said. "Now that James is demon meat, I take his place."

"My, that's quite the quick succession. Did you all agree to that, or are the demons here just partial to unearned human leadership?"

"I was next in line," the man said, speaking over him. "And you won't ensnare me, incubus. I'm immune to your charms."

"Alas, true. Still, most of your friends seem to carry some latent homoerotic tendencies, and I intend to leverage every single one of them if you don't give me what I want. Otherwise, you'll see more blood spilled before this altar—and not the kind your Master is looking for."

Right on cue, a voice like the roar of a lion filled the giant room to its corners, shaking the thick window glass. "Who dares serve me man?"

The grip on Abby's arm lessened—not enough for her to wriggle free, but her captor was clearly preoccupied by more pressing matters.

Like a waking demon princeling.

She ripped the hood from her head.

A giant stone demon sat up straight across the circle from her, revealing a beautiful golden face framed with cow horns on either side of his head and a heavy ring hanging from his nose. Only his face was gold. The rest of him was the gray, porous stone that she and Zekiel had seen on the warehouse roof. She understood why he'd hidden his face. If the city thought it had a problem with copper thieves, what would one of those desperate souls do to carve the demon's head right off while he slept?

"Sorry." Charles hopped off the altar and backed away. "I didn't realize I was serving my leftovers to the man himself rather than his effigy. If I'd known, I certainly wouldn't have sucked out the priest's life force on your dinner table. My mistake, my lord."

"I know you." Moloch stared down at Charles the way an upper-class lady might consider a yappy mutt biting at her slingback shoes. "How do I know you?"

"I've been keeping your final sacrifices safe and fresh for you." Charles gestured to where Maggie and Kara slept. The steady readings on their monitors showed that they still had no idea what was going on around them, but at least the acolytes hadn't done anything to harm them between the hospital and the library. "I wasn't doing it for free, and I'm afraid your followers haven't done the part that they promised. In fact, they've been right sloppy."

"Sloppy?" Moloch repeated, his speech deceptive in its ponderous speed.

"Confusing my midnight snack for a threat, misplacing my breeder and my child, and didn't you give me your word, my lord? You are bound by the rules of this plane, too, even if you're not all here." Now that he was out of the circle and had a few acolytes between him and Moloch, some of his bravado had returned. But that was all it was, bravado. The gluttonous flush of his feast had already disappeared.

"He swore to keep your sacrifice safe," the new high priest said. "But the woman he's claiming as his is one of the trespassers that infiltrated our last temple with her gargoyle friend. She's already evaded capture twice and killed five of ours in the process."

"Is that so, worm?" Moloch demanded.

"I had no idea she was going after you, much less that she had a partner in crime." Although Charles lied as breezily as ever, panic encroached in his posture and the tension of his hands as skepticism spread over the demon's gleaming golden face. "I thought I was the only partner she had, and now I'm kind of hurt. I assure you, I'll punish her soundly when I get us home…which will be after I'm damn sure my child is taken care of."

"Enough. You have broken your part of the bargain, worm," Moloch said. "I shall enjoy consuming the blood of your spawn—all of it. Cage him. Don't touch his skin, you fools. I've no desire for more manflesh. Bring the woman to me."

Abby struggled against the new priest's viselike grip as he drew her into the circle. "You don't want me. I'm too old for you, too."

"As a sacrifice, yes." Moloch smiled as she crossed the line of the inverted pentagram. As though through unspoken command, the remaining acolytes reestablished the circle behind her. "But you're young and strong. Since you refuse to die, you'll suffice for growing more."

A few of the acolytes chuckled as the demon condescended to mockingly meet her gaze at ground level, feeding on her fear.

She finally wrenched out of the priest's hold. "I am not a fucking Easy-Bake Oven."

Moloch drew back like a mountain giant with exaggerated slowness, a handicap of his stone flesh that seemed to reach deeper than Zekiel's and more closely resembled the stone angels — a comparison they would both probably resent. But it was almost worth it to witness his bewilderment and continue to buy Charles and Zekiel more time — if they figured out that's what she was doing better than Zekiel could figure it out before.

Abby took a deep breath, acknowledged silently that what she was about to do might get her killed, asked for clean-slate forgiveness from the Creator and dove straight in with her best bad-day-big-smile nurse's enthusiasm.

"You know, Mokh-daddy, you ever considered switching over from human children to baby bunnies? Sure, people would hate you just as much, plus you'd have PETA throwing red paint at you all the time, but those horny little devils just keep on coming. There's never a shortage. You could gorge yourself silly on them, and you could have them whenever you wanted. You wouldn't have to wait months for harvest."

"It's not about the feast, as you well know." Moloch stood from his throne, towering over the circle. His shoulders were broader than two of her lengthwise. "It's about the sacrifice. There is no sacrifice in rabbits. But children... Do you have any idea what a mother's grief tastes like to me, woman?"

He crouched until he was almost level with her again. His carved golden eyes were unsettlingly human. She would have leaned back, but the new priest stepped behind her, and she hit his chest instead.

"Mmm, now that's a sacrifice. And if I'm not mistaken, I smell angel blood in that little body. I think I'll quite enjoy the delicacy of children from an angel's daughter."

"Daughter of a what?" She fought to keep her mouth from trembling and giving her away. "What have you been smoking? My mama's a teacher and my dad abandoned us. Angels wouldn't leave so much damage behind. I mean, seriously damaged goods here."

She glanced at Charles, whose lips twitched, although two demon guards had flanked him and kept him from escaping or coming to her aid.

"I know what I smell. And I know what it will do to your dear, doubtlessly bound father when he discovers his grandchildren have satisfied Moloch's appetite, nourishing the devastation of the very race he has lowered himself to love."

"You aren't getting a thing from me," she said through gritted teeth, struggling again to break free, but this time toward Moloch. The priest held her against him just as solidly as before. "You're going back to the hell you came from. You're not going to get all up in the face of *my* city with your perversions and desecrations."

Moloch crooked his finger under her jaw and tilted her head up. "We'll see how spirited you are after you've been seeded and the harvest reaped. Who here wants a taste of secondhand angel?"

A cheer rang out in the library. Moloch laughed as the priest shoved her at one of the demons guarding the imprisoned women, because his cry had rung the loudest. He was a chaos demon, not much taller than a man. His dry, scaly skin rasped against hers as he wrapped his arm around her abdomen and pulled her against him with a hearty, growling laugh.

Abby met Charles' eyes again as the two demons flanking him dragged him to the other side of the prison entrance. The new priest took the fore at the podium as Moloch stepped back to seat himself on the throne once more, stately, preening and as egomaniacal as a Greek god.

Charles gave her a surreptitious nod. Abby tried to look for Zekiel, but if he was in sight, his coloring camouflaged him. She knew he wouldn't leave, but she also wasn't sure what he *could* do, so she couldn't depend on him or Charles to rescue her.

The guard had unknowingly covered her weapons with his arm, but that didn't mean he'd cut off all her options.

Abby gripped the demon's forearm as though she were still fighting to free herself. He chuckled, a sound that made her skin crawl, like the shuffle of a Komodo dragon in the sand. But she gripped him tighter, waiting until the room had gone quiet once more but for Moloch's cavernous breathing and the renewed chanting of the replacement priest. Then she reached deep inside of herself and watched darkness absorb into the guard's brownish alligator scales.

Charles wasn't the only one with dangerous skin.

A fearsome scream rent the air, nearly deafening her in the process because she couldn't cover her ears.

The scaly skin under her hands swelled, but not with melanoma this time. Giant, pus-filled boils smoothed the scales, then erupted hot, yellowish liquid under

Abby's hands. The fluid stung, but it fortunately wasn't too caustic, otherwise she might have just killed herself and doomed the world, all because she'd used the dark side of her power — and wouldn't that just be the cherry on top of this dirty, rotten week?

At first, the demon tightened his grip by reflex rather than retaliation, nearly fracturing some of her lower ribs. However, once enough boils ruptured, she became too slippery to hold — which was a whole new realm of yuck, but she wouldn't have been a good nurse if she couldn't handle yuck, and she wasn't beneath using pus as a lubricant to get herself out of a tight spot.

Abby ducked out of the demon's arms. As the demon reeled, his hood fell back. The boils extended to his face as well, covering even his eyelids with filmy flesh bubbles. When the guard swiped blindly at her, she poked her fingers in his eyes, causing the boils there to burst. Mimicking The Three Stooges didn't often work well during normal human interaction, but their slapstick was sometimes surprisingly useful in a fight.

Before she did anything else, she freed Charles by grabbing the face of one of his guards. Charles went for the other one, kicking the guard's legs out from under him, then twisting his neck until it snapped. The guard whose face she touched shrieked — startling her into one of her own — as both of his legs spontaneously shattered and he collapsed like tumbling firewood.

Under other circumstances, saying that all hell broke loose might have been overly dramatic. But in Meridian, during a ritual to raise a child-eating demon prince, it seemed appropriate.

In the plus column, Abby and Charles had broken the circle with panic and fury, so Maggie and Kara were safe for a while longer. On the less bright side, seventeen acolytes advanced upon them at Moloch's command, his demonic lip curled with barely contained contempt.

"Kill the incubus. Imprison the girl. We must not be interrupted again. I want my children!"

Abby peeled up her sodden tank top and tore off the small knife she'd duct-taped to her belly—small, but she'd always been able to get a good grip on it. From her hip, she ripped off the silver knuckles and slid them on. The knuckles were for demons, the knife for humans, and any part of her skin could act as a conduit for her power. She didn't like what she could do, but now wasn't the time to get squeamish.

She filled her mind's eye with the image of Maggie and Kara lying on the hospital beds, their bellies massive domes under the hospital gowns. These were the people she was doing this for. She was using her dark side, but dark didn't always have to mean evil. After all, darkness helped a headache, nighttime gave her a job and shadows helped her sleep.

I'm looking at evil, she told herself as she raised her fist and knife. *I'm not the evil one.*

With Charles free to fight on his own, Abby ran toward Maggie and Kara, aiming for the demon guard near the monitors.

Dodging him as he tried to sweep her into his arms, she shoved the knife into his side. It slipped through a gap between the ribs and popped his right lung. Then she whirled around, swinging her silvered fist backhand as she spun so that she hit the demon's face with all her strength, plus a little purifying metal. The demon fell to the side in surprise, his face sunken and singed.

"Stop her!" Moloch's limbs groaned like ancient trees in a hurricane as he stood from his throne once more. The replacement priest cut his chant short as well to join the advancing fray, all focused on keeping Abby from the comatose women.

Charles had extricated a thick, wooden table leg from somewhere and proceeded to enthusiastically beat anyone who came at him where he stood in front of Abby. She hoped he could keep up his batting average, because while she was healing, she wouldn't be able to infect any of her attackers. She was also vulnerable from behind, but she hoped Zekiel had her back, wherever he was. Whatever happened, though, Maggie and Kara getting out of here was more important than Abby's life, so she was willing to sacrifice her kidneys to the cause.

Abby laid her hands on Maggie's shoulders near the base of her neck, where the hospital gown exposed the calligraphy of her collarbone. She shut out all admittedly alarming distractions and closed her eyes, homing in on the permissive glow she sensed in Maggie that called to the glow within her.

Then she pulled, like a fisherman drawing in a bobbing line. The flesh under Abby's skin burned hot, but she couldn't stop yet.

There was more to heal than just the brain damage that had caused the coma. There was the shortening of her ligaments and tendons, atrophy of muscles, disorientation, and that didn't even address the problems after the healing. Abby could fix her, but she couldn't keep Maggie from waking up to a nightmare, since she'd be as viable a vessel for the sacrifice awake as comatose, albeit less cooperative.

Maggie twitched under Abby's hands.

Just as Maggie's eyelids flew open, Abby leaned over her and covered them again.

"I don't know if you know me from these last few months," she whispered, "but my name is Abby, and I'm here to help."

"You sound familiar," Maggie said with a slight Hispanic accent.

"Whatever you see, I need you to stay strong for me. When I take my hand away, I need you to run for the stairs. You're kind of very pregnant. I don't know whether you know that."

"I knew, but not this much. How long—"

"I can answer all your questions as soon as we get out of here. We'll run up these stairs, then we need to stay to the sides and find the stairs to the roof. Got it?"

"Not the front door?" Maggie asked.

"Blocked. Hold on. You're not alone, and I need to wake up your friend. I'm going to take my hand away from your eyes, but I want you to keep them shut until I tell you to run. I need to hurry here. Can you do that, Maggie?"

Abby's urgency must have gotten through, because Maggie nodded against Abby's hand.

"Okay. I'll be right back. Hold on for me."

Abby darted over to Kara and did the same thing, finding the glow in her and connecting it with her own. Unlike Maggie, she found no damage, no illness, nothing that a medical team would have been able to measure with all their modern technology—just a cloud of darkness in her brain, as insidious as any cancer but supernatural in origin. Abby tightened her grip on Kara's shoulders, but now wasn't the time to get angry at Charles for something she'd already known he'd done.

It didn't take nearly as long for Kara to twitch, as though falling onto the hospital bed, and she didn't take to Abby covering her eyes at all. She thrashed against the hospital sheets and the bars holding her in bed, scrabbling her unevenly cut nails on Abby's skin. Abby grunted as Kara drew blood.

"Kara, Kara, Kara, I'm not going to tell you that everything's okay, because it's not. My name is Abby, I'm a registered nurse, we're kind of in a dangerous situation and as soon as I take my hand from your eyes, we need to *run*. I'll hold your hand, and you need to follow me, which means you need to trust me. You have no reason to trust me, but I need you to, or else you, me or Maggie are going to get seriously hurt. We're going to go to the stairs, then we need to find our way to the roof. Whatever you see, whatever you feel, you need to run to protect you and your child. Yes, you're pregnant. I'll explain what I can, but now is not the time."

Abby finally allowed herself to glance up from her healing. Charles was still fighting the good fight, but he was just one incubus, and he wasn't used to fighting the way Zekiel was.

Where is *Zekiel anyway?*

She could understand him leaving Charles to the wolves, but she really didn't think he'd leave her or the cult's victims.

"Please, Kara. Do you trust me?"

"Get me the fuck out of here."

"With pleasure. Ready? Maggie, ready?"

Kara nodded, and so did Maggie, her eyes clenched tightly shut and her hands fists in the sheets.

"On three, climb off the beds. It's going to take more effort than you anticipate, but I'll cover you. No matter what you see, you *run*. One. Two. Three. *Go*." Abby pulled her hand away from Kara's eyes and grabbed her forearm to help her off her barred hospital bed, then reached for Maggie's hand to help her as well.

Maggie had the harder time rolling over and reaching the floor, but she was smart and kept her eyes downcast, although she screamed at the commotion in her peripheral vision.

Kara didn't give herself time to be scared. She'd taken Abby's promise for an explanation to heart and immediately recognized that the priority within the hell around her was to get out of it as soon as possible. She helped Maggie get to her feet, but she was the first to pull them toward the stairs, holding her pregnant belly as though to lift its burden so that she could run more normally. Although tears slipped down her cheeks, she didn't bother wiping them away.

When Abby felt that Maggie and Kara knew where they needed to go, she finally released them so that she at least had her silver knuckles at her disposal. She couldn't use her knife anymore, not when she might need a hand to help the other women.

Maggie paused at the base of the stairs, because more women were shaking the bars and pounding the desk in reception, begging for rescue behind the muffling spell.

"Go!" Abby pushed Maggie forward. "We'll get them. You go!"

"But they're in danger like us," Maggie protested.

Abby spun around and flung her fist up into the shadow of an acolyte's hood. The flesh hissed and crunched. She kicked his abdomen, knocking him back. His hood fell away from a smoking, dissolving face and sharp broken teeth.

Maggie screamed.

"*You're* the ones they're after, not them. You're the ones they need right now. Move!"

Abby shoved her again, and this time Kara grabbed her to help pull her up the stairs. Neither of them could run the same way that Abby could, especially up stairs, but between the three of them and adrenaline, they managed.

Charles, instead of Zekiel, had Abby's back, blocking the bottom of the stairs as he brandished his table leg. His shirt was torn and stained red, but he held his ground, so Abby thought – prayed – that he hadn't been hurt too badly.

Once they'd all made it to the top of the stairs, Abby took both women's hands to draw them around the edge of the second floor.

A shriek like a hawk rent the air, and a giant stone arm shot at them through the remaining rows of empty shelves.

All three women shouted, but Abby yanked Maggie and Kara hard enough to strain muscles, just enough for them to evade Moloch's grasp.

Only for him to try again a few rows down. They outmaneuvered him once again, limited as he was by his statued form.

Then Moloch leaped onto the second floor. The floor groaned and dipped under his weight, but he paid structural integrity little mind. His golden eyes burned with a forger's fire directly at Maggie. No, not at Maggie – at her pregnant belly.

"You're not going anywhere." Moloch hunched into a gargoyle crouch beneath the second-floor ceiling. "You're mine. You were meant for me."

Both Maggie and Kara screamed at the sight of him. They'd seen what could have been a man with his face burning a few minutes ago, but this time they got an eyeful of what a real demon looked like and had no way to dismiss what they saw. Beautiful though he was, he was also giant, with the wings and horns and wickedness that marked him as a demon. He didn't have the luxury of blending in.

Abby darted in front of the other women, but she still didn't have a clue how to stop him. Her silver knuckles were woefully inadequate for a demon of his size. She didn't even know if they would work against the stone of his body, different than Zekiel's living stone that moved like ordinary flesh.

"Give me my sacrifice, breeder."

"Over my dead body." Abby was too scared for bravado. She'd substituted hate for bravado instead. It made her declaration stronger.

"I would never be so merciful. But I will see your body broken while my acolytes each take you in turn to ensure a most bountiful harvest, my dear."

She held up both her bare and silver-knuckled fists. "They touch me, they die. You touch me, you die."

"The silver won't do you a bit of good if I tear off your hand. You don't need that for childbirth."

"No, but I can grow a new one." She was guessing on that one, but she couldn't think of any reason why not. "And they can't take me to your satisfaction if I give them a heart attack every time one of them touches me. Or weren't you paying attention to what I've been doing to your acolytes so far?"

Moloch lowered his head—not in shame or defeat but to present his horns. "They're doing wonders with pharmaceuticals these days. You won't be able to move or talk or even think."

"That wouldn't be nearly as satisfying, though, would it?"

"If you're the healer you say you are, then you should be able to put yourself back together after I fucking tear you apart."

Moloch was in front of her. Maggie was freaking out behind her. Kara wasn't screaming anymore but still cowered against the wall because there wasn't anything else she could do, and there wasn't anywhere for Abby to go, either. Her hands trembled so hard she could see them vibrating like loose guitar strings in front of her. She could barely swallow what little spit was left in her mouth as Moloch crawled forward on his knuckles like a gorilla.

Oh God.

A crunch like the splitting of a geode was followed by Moloch's miserable howl. He arched his back and grabbed behind him, but he couldn't reach the blade buried in his spine halfway to the hilt.

Zekiel clung to the ridge of Moloch's spine, avoiding the grasping fingers. He yanked the blade out, then dropped to the floor on the edge of the hole, which crumbled wherever Moloch struck it as he turned.

"You're dead, twixt dweller!" Moloch bellowed. "You're dead and damned!" His entire body contorted in fury, as though he were made of writhing serpents.

"I live," Zekiel replied, as composed as Moloch was crazed. "But you do not, prince of the dark realm. Your stone heart doesn't even beat."

"If I do not live, then I cannot die. You can. I will rip off your wings and throw them through the rose window of the church you haunt, you miserable, treasonous bat!" Moloch lunged after Zekiel.

Zekiel launched back, flapping his wings to rise to the ceiling before slashing his sword across Moloch's shoulder. Broken stone pattered on the floor like gravel. Abby tried to urge Maggie and Kara forward toward the stairs to the roof, but Moloch backed over the only path there.

He lashed out at Zekiel like a lumbering dinosaur trying to swat a sparrow. Zekiel easily dipped and swooped out of reach, swinging his sword to cut through the stone like a lathe, but Moloch was too thick to just slice off a limb.

Charles backed, limping, along the edge toward the women. "We've got company!"

"Zekiel!" Abby shouted as he ducked again under Moloch's fist. Zekiel met her eyes in unspoken apology for his delay, but he couldn't spare her more than a moment. Moloch had crossed the line from frustrated to furious at his own limitations in his idol form, which was precisely why he'd wanted to incarnate in the first place.

Abby growled in her own frustration and ran straight for Moloch.

"What the fuck are you doing, lady?" Kara shouted.

While Moloch was distracted with the gargoyle flying around his head, Abby slammed her silver-knuckled fist into Moloch's leg. Reverb juddered all the way up her shoulder and neck and rang the gong in her skull. The silver made a dent, though — little more than a pockmark to a giant demon, but his stone steamed like a hot spring in limestone.

He twisted his head on his great creaking neck to stare down at the insect that had hurt him.

Zekiel landed on Moloch's shoulders, sitting on him as a child might sit on his father's shoulders in a crowd. He closed his hands over the tip of his sword and the handle and brought it against Moloch's throat. Then he yanked it back, sawing in jagged zigzags under the edge of the golden face while Moloch bellowed and futilely clawed at Zekiel's legs.

When the sword made it through the column of Moloch's neck, Zekiel flipped back. The golden head toppled from its trunk and rolled down the sagging floor to the opening that led to the inverted pentagram.

The statue body fell forward, crumbling into soulless dust.

"Go!" Zekiel gestured Abby, Maggie and Kara to run through the mess. Maggie flinched from him, but he paid her no mind. "Get to the roof and stay there. I'll take care of the rest down here. Charles, guard them until I'm through. I need to hunt down every acolyte and burn the altar. Then I must hide the head. But I will return. Go *now*!"

Holding up his sword, he pushed past Charles to chase after the fleeing acolytes.

Abby wasted no time arguing. She grabbed Maggie's and Kara's hands again, and they trampled through the dust to run upstairs toward the dome of the night sky, the cold air crisp, clean freedom on their faces.

Chapter Sixteen

On the roof, Abby wrapped Charles' jacket that she'd discarded earlier around Maggie's shoulders. Abby could afford the cold, but Maggie was approaching panic, shivering and clutching her abdomen as though it would fall off if she let it go.

"Over here, both of you." Abby led them to the edge of the roof to sit against the low wall—out of sight, a block against the cold breeze, and it gave them both a chance to rest, although they would be hard-pressed to jump to their feet if anyone came through the door after them.

Charles reached to help Kara down, but Abby glared at him and pointed him away. He raised his hands in mock defeat, then retrieved his table leg to guard the roof access.

"This is a nightmare. That's all this... Just a nightmare. Going to wake up. Not crazy. This is... I'm... This is..." Maggie shook her head and rocked and cringed.

"It's not a nightmare, is it?" Kara said. "And we're not crazy, are we?"

"I can't speak to either of those things," Abby said. "But everything that happened was real, if that's what you're asking."

"And what about him?" Kara looked up at Charles. "What kind of monster is he?"

Abby rubbed Maggie's back, just holding her against the shaking and sending what healing she could to stave off the worst of the panic. "You were in a coma. It's not exactly like sleep. As far as we know, you're not supposed to dream, but some people remember things happening around them as though they were dreams. And your coma wasn't exactly normal. What do you remember?"

Kara stroked her abdomen — not out of any maternal warmth or pride, but as though reminding herself over and over that it was there, as real as the goosebumps on her arms. "I had the most vivid dreams. He was in every one of them. It feels like I've known him for years…. Did he do this to me? All of this?"

Abby didn't have any excuses for him. Her silence was all the answer Kara needed.

"Like some kind of vampire, except…" Kara touched her neck, searching for scars and finding nothing.

"Similar, but not the same," Abby said. "He won't hurt you anymore."

"But I still have *this*. What am I supposed to do with a baby conceived in my dreams?"

"I don't know." Honesty was all Abby could offer her, because it wasn't as though Abby was aware of any support groups for demon victims. Most of the people she saved either didn't get a good enough look at what tried to abduct them, or Abby distorted their memory. There was definitely a market for it here, but heaven knew where to find one. And the support group for people impregnated by demons was probably even harder to find, although Abby thought that might be easier to come by—or just create, given the prison cell below.

If they could deprogram the ones who had participated in the circle without coercion, maybe that would solve the problem of not having anyone to talk to. It would not, however, solve the problem right in front of them, which was a child inside of Kara that she'd never really asked for with a man she'd never really known—a child that wasn't human and wasn't even hers, just using the womb.

"Look… When we get out of this, you and I can sit down with a hot chocolate at Holy Grounds, and I'll explain everything I can and help you go over your options," Abby said. "But you've gone through a lot tonight, and that's probably enough to process for now."

Charles thankfully kept his distance the entire time, although he sometimes cast furtive glances in their direction. None of the cult acolytes tried to come through the door, which meant that Zekiel was more than making up for the time Abby couldn't account for him. She knew he must have been waiting for just the right moment to strike, but that didn't change how alone she'd felt and how much she'd had to depend on Charles, putting herself and the other women in the hands of an incubus when two of the three of them were his victims.

Zekiel flew over the roof wall.

Maggie turned her face into Abby's shoulder and refused to look. Abby stroked her hair, letting her. Some might have considered her denial unhealthy, but Abby believed it was probably the healthiest thing for her. She'd justify and rationalize her way out of having to accept that a monstrous demon had wanted her nearly born child or that she'd been surrounded by people whose faces had smoked like skillets when Abby's silver had struck them. If she could dismiss it as residual brain damage, if she could wake up tomorrow and it all seemed like a bad dream, she might be able to appreciate how she was awake rather than dwell on the circumstances of that awakening. It might just help her recover faster.

Kara was steadier, although just as shaken. Being more grounded in reality — as terrible as it could be — wasn't necessarily a bad thing.

"I took the demon head to a safe place." Zekiel flexed his arms as though they pained him.

Abby had never seen him exhausted before, but the golden head must have weighed a ton, not to mention having to single-handedly neutralize the rest of the mixed cult. Abby would have been exhausted, too. *Oh, wait, I am.*

"Did you happen to drop it into the fires of Mount Doom, by any chance?"

That at least earned her the slightest smile from Kara.

"I cannot say where I left it, but it will be melted and the remains consecrated," Zekiel said. "I also released the prisoners. Some of them resisted, but I bound them so that they couldn't hurt themselves, me or the other women in revenge. The other women, those who could help, aided me in taking the prisoners with them to an abandoned building a block away. I told them to stay there until help came, then closed the door. It was a heavy door, the rest locked or boarded over. My contact will call the hospital to let them know that the women are there. I should take the two of you as well, so that you will be retrieved with them and in the best of hands after your ordeal—well, the second-best hands." He rested his on Abby's shoulder.

If Kara had been wary of him after spending this long on the roof with the man who'd harmed her, the warmth between him and Abby eased her tension. "So that's it? We go to a hospital, they give us a clean bill of health and we just go about our lives as though none of this happened? You don't have some official *Men in Black* story for us to make sure we all tell the police the same thing when they ask?"

"There are too many of you for that," Abby said. "We aren't going to be able to control this narrative. You can tell them whatever you like. I'd prefer it if you left my name out of it entirely, because having to make a statement would make my life much more complicated than it already is. But if you want to tell them the truth about what happened, that's your choice."

"They're not going to believe it, though, are they?" Kara replied. "Coma, pregnancy, hormones, brain damage... Even if some of the other women agree, they'll just say it's mass hysteria among weak-minded women and go with the more likely scenario anyway."

"Pretty much. But I do want you to contact me when things calm down. I'm Abby Stone. Some of the nurses there know my number, but you can also find me at the Cemetery Grove clinic during the occasional graveyard shift."

"Yeah. Okay."

Abby didn't know whether Kara ever wanted to see her or hear her voice again, which panged in Abby's heart, but this was her life, and if she wanted to leave this kind of chaos behind, more power to her.

Maggie refused to be moved by Zekiel, so Abby helped Kara stand, then helped Maggie while Zekiel kept Kara steady on the way to the roof access door.

"Don't be a stranger, Zekiel." Charles backed well away from the door when Kara refused to approach with him there, but he still gulped in the sight of her, as though knowing he would never see her again. "We'll be just fine back here alone. I'll keep Abby warm for you."

Zekiel hurried the women inside from the cold, but he hesitated at the door.

Abby glared at Charles this time instead of just staring at him in irritation. She'd given him a little slack for saving her skin when he could have just handed her over and had her for himself after Moloch had risen, with the demon's blessing. But taunting Zekiel like that as though nothing had changed quickly burned through any goodwill she might have had.

Then she blinked at the glint in Charles' eyes.

She faced Zekiel with her back to Charles. "Go on."

"Something must be done about him," Zekiel murmured. "We cannot just let him go."

"Why not? You swore to it." Charles' smirk permeated his words. "And anyway, haven't I proven that I don't actually want either of you dead? So I played a few games. Both of you already knew I played them. It's what I am. But I saved you. I saved the other girls, even though it hits me right here to let mine go. And I'm firmly cured of apocalypse cults."

"There might be hope for you yet," Abby said.

Zekiel raised a quizzical eyebrow. "I think you overestimate his redemptive qualities."

"Maybe. But I can handle myself."

"I'll bet you can," Charles muttered, still smug as a cat with feathers in its mouth.

"*Trust me*," she mouthed. Then she stood on her tiptoes and kissed Zekiel's cheek.

"I will return soon," he said, "before the dawn."

"What about the dead people below?" Abby asked. "You know, I never thought about what happens to the bodies afterward. You never hear about them on the news or anything. After all the demons I leave dead in that alley, it's always clear the next night for the next set."

"The ones the demon hunters don't find and burn, the pestilence demons dispose of."

Charles shuddered. "Those give me the creeps."

"Why? Because they remind you that immortality doesn't mean you're unkillable?" Abby asked.

"No. They're just disgusting."

"I thought that's what I was supposed to become."

"Not *that* kind, believe me, sweet thing."

"Are you sure?" Zekiel asked Abby.

"I'll be fine. The worst he'll do is make me roll my eyes right out of their sockets." She nodded Zekiel away, then backed up to sit on the floor of the roof again, shivering and rubbing her arms.

Zekiel closed the door behind him.

"You wouldn't know it from the square he's become, but Zekiel used to be quite the beast." Charles sat on the roof wall beside her, close enough for her to curl her arm around his legs—but she didn't.

"He still is," Abby said. "He just grew up."

"Got boring, you mean. I've grown since he left me, but you don't see me thinking I can single-handedly ensure world peace with my fists. I know my place."

"Really? Fighting against a demon prince from the dark realm? Because I'm pretty sure you and Moloch are technically on the same side."

"Doesn't mean we agree how the world ought to be right now—just how it's going to end up." He slid off the wall to crouch next to her. "Hey, your teeth are chattering like joke dentures, love. Let me warm you up. You know I can."

"I think you've done enough damage." Although she was sorely tempted to burrow under his shoulder and wrap her arms around him. Some of his heat reached her across the short distance between them, but she recoiled slightly at the reminder of the tearing and bloodstains on his shirt. "And had enough damage done to you. When did that happen?"

"Don't know. It could have been when I was heroically distracting the demon cult, or it could have been when I was heroically saving your hot ass. It doesn't hurt much."

Abby stood both of them up to get him into moonlight. She was careful with the folds of his shirt, pulling it away from his skin so that she could inspect the cuts more closely. Through the tears in the fabric, Abby glimpsed a series of angry, still-bleeding claw marks. She winced with a hiss.

"Here." She tugged at his shirt. "Get this off."

After all his light, mocking banter, his expression turned unexpectedly serious. Tilting his head a little, he unbuttoned his shirt and shrugged it off, heedless of the cold.

"I can—" Abby reached out to touch him, then stopped as though her palms hit an invisible wall.

"That's right. I was wondering whether you'd realize your dilemma. You want to heal me? You'll have to release me from my oath." He ghosted his bare fingers a fraction of an inch from the line of her jaw like a caress, guiding her to meet his glittering eyes.

Her gaze drifted down to linger on his lips, then to the marred white marble of his chest, so close to her. So much exposed for the both of them. The little hairs on her arms stood up on end—not from the cold but as though they wanted to draw her closer to him. It would be so easy. Less than a second, and he could be touching her. She could be touching him.

"I didn't save you just to kill you," he said, barely a whisper. "Do you trust me?"

"Never."

Charles tightened his jaw in frustration.

"But I release you from your oath."

For a few moments, there was no movement but for the rise and fall of Charles' chest. Then he grabbed her waist to pull her hips against his, and her arms collided with his chest. The contact between them was the most intense spark of static electricity Abby had ever experienced, except instead of making her jerk away, he drew her even closer to him with his charm, which wrapped around her like the silk of a spider's web.

He paused just short of her lips. "Abigail," he breathed, like a groan. He slid hands more sensuous and smooth than the leather of his gloves up her bare arms. She couldn't believe it when she felt him tremble.

She took his face in her hands and pulled him down to claim her mouth. She'd been stalked by an incubus before, and she'd had the last week to show her what being close to an incubus was like. But nothing could have prepared her for the experience of his skin on hers.

It was the difference of a pitch-black, silent walk on a shore at midnight and taking a stroll by an ocean alit with phosphorescence and the reflection of stars, enhanced by a symphony of night insects and whale song. It was the Yellowstone caldera to the Great Plains, a tornado to a draft.

Charles drank her moans, consumed her, dominated her, wrested control of her kiss, her embrace, her thick, thrumming arousal nestled in the cradle of her hips and keenest where the bulge of his cock pressed against her.

But he moaned, too, clutching her tight against him with artlessness that Abby would not have expected from a sex demon. The man carried all knowledge of every desire, probably knew positions and pleasure points that the authors of the Kama Sutra couldn't have begun to imagine, had encountered fantasies from which even the Marquis de Sade would flinch in shock and horror.

So why did it seem like he'd succumbed to her in his very domination?

As she ran her hands over his chest and grasped at his shoulders, dried blood crackled under her palms — the reason why she'd destroyed her last bit of protection against him.

Charles broke the kiss and gasped against her mouth as she took the glitter she'd seen in his eyes from him. The demon claw marks sewed themselves back together to form an invisible seam.

"I don't know everything you've done," Abby said. "I only really know what you've done to me. But you did help. And you let Kara go, even though you knew Zekiel and I would never let you touch her again. I genuinely think there's a heart in there, under all the cold, selfish stone."

His heart pulsed steady and quick under her fingertips. He covered her hand with his. "This won't kill you," he murmured. "I promise you'll like it."

Abby glanced up at him. The guilt must have shown, because Charles tensed.

"I didn't say I was done," she whispered.

She reached inside of him and pulled, draining the steady glow around his darkness like a vampire—except the light she took wasn't the good kind of light, never had been, brilliant in the way that Lucifer was the morning star. She kept pulling at that bad light like a needle and thread in embroidery, extracting each strand of the poison and accepting it into herself, where it became harmless—at least until the day she chose to let it out again.

Charles tried to withdraw, but her power kept him attached. Shock made his face appear younger, revealing how—after all his years and no matter how sophisticated he could seem—he was still juvenile, a petulant, self-gratifying teenager scratching itches.

The flesh under her hand grew cold. Grayish veins shot through the white skin and extended up his neck to his face, where his teeth went sharp as they were exposed in his silent scream. The tips of his ears narrowed to points. His black hair absorbed into his scalp. Wings burst from his shoulders in a final attempt to flee, but the feathers fused, thinned into membranes and froze as though in ice as the stone reached his wing claws.

"I'm so sorry, Charles. I guess you were ready, whether you knew it or not." Abby stroked his creamy marble cheek, struck by the odd juxtaposition of such a horrified visage in such beautiful stone. "Don't you worry about your baby—or Kara, if you actually ever gave a damn about her. Zekiel and I will keep a close eye on them. It'll be the only baby in the world with a guardian gargoyle, which *do* exist, because I say so."

"Cabrera's truly outdone herself."

She spun around, pressing a hand to her heart to hold it in.

Zekiel stepped down from the roof wall. "She worked herself nearly to death when she first came here. I guess her quality's improved now that she can pace herself with new residents. It's okay if you loved him a little. I did. It speaks to your capacity for compassion, not your failure."

"I'm sick and I need help."

But Abby allowed Zekiel to wrap his wind-chilled arms around her and draw her against the warmth of his chest, despite how gross her clothes were from being slimed with demon pus. It hadn't bothered Charles, either. She didn't quite cry, but tears leaked down her flushed cheeks.

"But he's not quite like you, is he?" she said, wiping the tears away. "He's not moving."

"He might have repented in his heart, but his head needs to catch up. He'll have decades to realize what must be done." Zekiel studied the statue. "Until then, he will have nothing but the world moving on without him, left only with his thoughts and memories."

He broke away from Abby to approach his former lover. He whispered something in Charles' ear, then tenderly pressed his lips to the stone neck.

"I told him I'd be waiting for his return," Zekiel said. "Does that bother you?"

"Oddly enough, it doesn't."

"We unfortunately don't have enough time for me to fly you home." He slipped an arm around her waist. "You'll have to go there yourself, and I left the jacket with Maggie. I apologize."

"Have they been found by the people who needed to find them?"

"They're all safe, either headed to the hospital or in the care of someone who knows how to deal with people who've been taken in by cults—demon or otherwise. I'm sorry I can't be any clearer on this. My contact is protective of both his charges and his process. There's nothing dangerous about it. It's just delicate—and legally considered kidnapping."

"Fair enough." She guided Zekiel to the edge of the roof behind Charles. She couldn't stop him from hearing them, but she wanted a little privacy, nevertheless. After nudging Zekiel to sit on the roof wall, his wings furled and hanging off the edge, she stepped between his legs. "Have I thanked you yet for slaying the dragon?"

"I would have saved them sooner if I had found the right opportunity to surprise Moloch without his followers easily coming to his aid." Zekiel lowered his head. "And if I hadn't been under my lover's spell for so long that I missed them taking you."

Abby lifted his chin and smiled. "We just saved the world for a little while. I think we deserve a few minutes without self-loathing. What do you think?"

She slid her hand down his abdomen to the cloth over his cock as she kissed him. She was still juiced from the arousal wrought by Charles' kiss, but she figured he would understand. His hips jerked slightly on the roof's edge. Grasping him through the fabric, she stroked him into half hardness, until he jerked her down and took her mouth the way he clearly wanted to take her.

As the first rays of subtle warmth struck her head, she pulled away with a small smile. She bent down so that she and Zekiel were eye to eye as he too went rigid to the touch.

"I don't mean to be a tease...really." She kissed his cold lips. "I'll call in sick for the next shift when I get home. After what happened earlier this evening, they'll understand, and God knows I need it. Tonight will probably catch up with me in the bath."

She kissed him again, stroking the bulge that she'd made and that had frozen in an almost fully erect state. At least this time it was covered.

"See you tonight," she whispered. "Think nice thoughts."

* * * *

Abby couldn't know what Zekiel thought behind that stone face before the sun set once more.

She *could* guess what Charles thought.

Fortunately, she didn't have to hear it. She would wait a few months before informing him that she hadn't necessarily chosen to do this to him. She was but an instrument, like Cabrera, like Zekiel. She had chosen to accept that responsibility, but Charles was the one who'd made the choice that had changed the trajectory of his life, whether he'd been aware of it at the time or not.

Maybe she should come and read to Charles the way she'd read to Kara and Maggie. It didn't seem right to just...leave him there.

However, he could stand to wait a week or so for her to return and give him attention. Right now, she sat on her heels with her hands on Zekiel's knees, staring up at a stone face trapped in an expression of pained pleasure. It really had been cruel to work him up like that again. But she planned to make up for it as best as she could.

Abby rested her cheek where the cloth draped over his cock. The weather was too cold for her to lick it.

She smiled when the stone fabric became cotton and the erection warmed as the dying light faded behind the skyline, surrendering to the studded blue velvet from the east.

"You wicked little minx." Zekiel threw his head back and groaned when she lifted his covering, wasting no time getting her mouth around the tip, circling the slit with her tongue. "Why do you torture me so?"

"Because it makes me happy." She grinned up at him as she wrung his shaft, shining with his pre-cum and her saliva. "I know it was so bad of me. I just couldn't resist."

"Neither can I."

Zekiel grabbed her arms and hauled her to her feet, then stood and spread his wings—just enough to shield her from prying eyes, which made her grin broaden and nipples harden as he removed her peacoat. She quickly kicked off her boots and wriggled out of her jeans and underwear. Zekiel hoisted her up for her to wrap her legs around his hips, his cock slotted against her ass. He kissed her first, forcing her to hold onto him as he brought his hands under her shirt and pushed her bra up over her breasts.

Then he slid his hands down to her waist to lift her up more and close his hot mouth over one nipple, leaving the other to tighten painfully in the cold. She felt her cooled moisture against his abdomen, where she smeared it as she rocked against him. When he moved to the other nipple, his mouth burned even hotter to the cold flesh and the nipple he abandoned seemed even colder from being wet.

"Now who's being cruel?" she gasped.

His chuckle vibrated through her. "I cannot begin to repay you for what you have put me through, woman. Twice! Perhaps when we have more privacy, we can discuss suitable punishment."

"I have a few ideas." She heard Charles' laughter echo in the back of her mind. "They might surprise you," she admitted with some bitterness.

Zekiel paused his wordless ode to her breasts and leaned her back. "I was an incubus, too, remember? *Nothing* you request will surprise me. You would be far more shocked at some of the fantasies I indulged within my victims' dreams — and sometimes while they were awake."

"I think you're just trying to titillate a girl." Now that she imagined Zekiel engaging in any number of libertine scenarios, she squirmed against him.

"I can do that, too." He shifted his hips so that the head of his cock pressed against her entrance, teasing her. He returned his mouth to her breasts until the clenching muscles of her pussy practically tried to drag him in.

"As much as I'd love to play," Abby said, "we don't have all night."

"No?"

"Fuck me, and I'll tell you the itinerary."

"You drive a hard bargain."

"Your turn."

Zekiel playfully nipped her lip with his sharper canines at the pun, but he cut her giggle short when he pulled her down by her waist, plunging into her cunt in one rough motion that made her clench around him with a surprisingly intense wave of arousal.

He encircled them both with his wings, shutting out the world except for the night sky above them. Then he worked her over his cock, but she rocked over him, too, enthusiastically engulfing him over and over. He joined his fingers with hers at her clit, stroking the pulsing little nub, and where their bodies met, her folds stretched around his girth.

"I thought about this all day, too," she said, panting. "And in my dreams. His touch, yours... I was wet all the way here, imagining you hard the entire day. You didn't suffer alone. Yes. Fuck, yes. Faster. Just like that."

Zekiel captured her mouth and reduced her pleas to inarticulate moans. She rode him hard to drive her pleasure forward. His kiss muffled her cry as her climax shuddered through her, and he pounded tirelessly through it. Then again, a man who could fly any distance with a giant golden head must have had unimaginable strength and endurance. The thought made her eyes roll back again through a mini-orgasm that clung to the coattails of the first.

Zekiel tore himself from her mouth and pressed his face against her neck as his thrusts became erratic.

"My light," he whispered, almost too soft for her to understand, and maybe she wasn't supposed to.

Awfully intimidating, knowing what he thought of her. Something for her to strive toward, perhaps. She dwelled in the night like him, like darker and much viler creatures, but she always found the light eventually with the dawn.

She gently wrapped her arms around his neck and stroked the smoothness of his head and the rippling, flexing muscles of his back until he stiffened and came. He murmured her name against her skin with every jerk of his cock inside her. She kissed his ear until he spread his wings once more and helped her down.

Abby wriggled as she grabbed her panties, then laughed. "Now my nethers are all cold."

"You're the one who keeps insisting on outdoor trysts." Zekiel crossed his arms and watched her dress, amused. Lucky man only had to readjust his covering. She had all these layers, and most of those layers had some kind of fastening.

She thought of Charles' apartment, the room, the privacy, the toys. She wondered how much rent had been paid up and whether Miranda would let her and Zekiel use it until the end of the lease. Taking him back to her house again was out of the question, at least on a regular basis.

"You said we had places to be tonight?" he asked.

"I did. No fighting. No dark alleys, no oil slicks, no demon limbs. Does that sound like a good plan?"

"I don't object thus far, although I need to return to my duties soon."

"So do I. It's just... I called my mom about finding Dad in Cemetery Grove, and she called me late this afternoon to say she was flying in. She's missed him more than she tells me. She thinks she hides it, but she doesn't. She had this spark of hope in her voice when I told her I'd found him again, poor fool."

"We are all of us fools and madmen, Abby, where love is concerned," Zekiel said gently.

"Oh, believe me, I'm aware. Why do you think I searched for him for so long? Anyway, she arrived at DFW earlier, and she's going to meet me at the cemetery with Chinese takeout and a blanket. We're going to have a family picnic with him behind the gravestones. A little unorthodox, but I wanted to invite you. I mean, I don't know if you can eat, but I still want you there. I want you to meet my dad."

He smiled. "A statement of dread for so many young men — but not so for me."

"I want you to meet my mom, too, of course, but she'll be thrilled with you. Unless you're going to disappear on me in ten years without warning."

"I'm not under the same limitations as the stone angels. I have been transported before, but as you can see, I'm far more mobile. And I know how to work a payphone."

"Like the ancient demon that you are, thinking there are even any payphones left. Up for dinner?"

He rested his hand, heavy and promising, on her shoulder. "I would be honored, if your father and his brethren will have me."

"I'll make sure of it." She'd pull out the Bible verses if she had to. Something about angels rejoicing at the salvation of just one. "Let's go. Bye, Charles. See you in a week. I'll bring something fun to read."

Abby climbed onto Zekiel's back as he tried to conceal his grin. She spread her own wings briefly to overlap with his, a declaration that made him close his eyes against the swell of emotion they shared to which she could not put words. When he stepped up on the roof wall, she pulled her wings back in again and held on tight.

Then Zekiel leaped off the edge.

Want to see more from this author?
Here's a taster for you to enjoy!

Meridian: Fever & Fray
Aurelia T. Evans

Coming April 2023

Excerpt

She'd only taken her sweater off because she was too warm.

Now she wrapped it around her like a cross between a cloak and a shield as she stood in front of the receptionist, waiting for the young work-study student to acknowledge her from whatever she was scrolling through.

"Yeah? What?" the student said, still not looking up.

Nova shifted on her wedge heels. "Father Marcus told me to wait in his office."

The assistant rolled her eyes and shrugged toward the line of offices for interdenominational staff. "The door's open. You don't need my permission."

Nova nodded, even though the girl couldn't see her, then hurried to the office labeled with Father Marcus Canc's name. The hall was modern in design, but the office had been paneled in dark wood and decorated in the vein of an old-school study. The scents of woven hardcover books and leather from the chairs entombed her.

She lowered herself into the chair nearest the door, right under the air vent. Although she tucked her sweater even more tightly around her, it wasn't thick enough to block the cold.

Anything to keep her sweater on.

The room where they did their Saturday evening worship services was sometimes too cold during the summer months, but once the weather started to cool down, there was that awkward set of weeks in autumn and spring when it wasn't cool enough to turn on the heater but too cool for the air conditioner to kick in.

When a modest college crowd crammed into a too-small room with no air circulation, it was bound to get too warm before someone decided to manually turn on the air.

While the worship band had played the seventh praise song in their set, everyone had stood, those freer with their bodies waving their hands in the air like Pentecostals while the frozen chosen of the Methodist and white Southern Baptist set had awkwardly swayed. The Saturday evening service served primarily a Catholic crowd, with a Catholic Communion — the Protestants took theirs during Wednesday and Sunday services — but they remained casual enough to welcome anyone who wanted to come in evenings instead of having to wake up early on Sunday morning. They used the same praise band for both Wednesday and Saturday services and borrowed music majors for the more traditional choir on Sunday.

All that body heat, all that closeness, with the chairs crammed together... It had been a perfectly natural thing for Nova to remove her thin sweater. It wasn't like she'd had a spaghetti-strap T-shirt underneath. The tank top straps were at least three fingers wide. She'd checked before she'd bought it. The neckline was modest enough, although she always had some cleavage. Short of a turtleneck, there was nothing she could do about that, and it wasn't cold enough for her turtleneck sweaters. Her skirt passed a high school dress code's muster by a whole foot of fabric, but there wasn't much of a dress code in college, where as long as you weren't naked, they wouldn't kick you out. Still, she was practically nun-like in comparison to what some of the other girls in the makeshift sanctuary wore.

It wasn't that nobody had noticed the boy trying to slip his hand over her ass during the praise songs or the way he'd kept acting like she took up too much space and his elbow just couldn't help but brush the side of her breast. Everyone beside and behind them had probably witnessed that. But when she'd slapped his hand, that's when the situation had become a problem—and only because the slap had been so loud in the otherwise-silent crowd during the homily.

One of the counselors—volunteers from the University of Texas-Meridian campus staff—had made the boy move, but Father Marcus had stood and actually interrupted Father William's message to tell Nova to see him after the service.

Her chest had ached as she'd lowered her head and nodded, crossing her arms over her breasts—not that that helped at all. She'd just wanted them all to stop looking at her.

Always the eyes... Nova couldn't walk down the street alone in a bulky coat that covered her whole body without feeling the eyes. She'd consider herself paranoid, but it wasn't always just eyes. Ever since twelve years old, she'd been inundated with wolf whistles and catcalls. The years before puberty had hit were a distant dreamlike memory to her—a time when strangers had called her 'pretty girl' and given her little extra treats and attention but had never ogled her as though their gazes were fingertips.

A girl got tired of it after a while. Free drinks or desserts now and then were nice, but people seemed to expect that they paid for something else.

At twelve, her parents had yelled at the people who'd scammed on her. Around the time she'd turned fourteen, something had changed. Her mother and father had sat her down and told her she was growing up and needed to start taking responsibility as she became a woman. Her father wouldn't let her out of the house unless she'd been suitably covered. *Modesty*, they'd called it—no jeans that showed the shapes of her legs, no tight-fitting or low-cut tops, no tank tops. They'd have put her in a Catholic school with ill-fitting uniforms if they could have afforded it.

Perhaps she would have been less resentful of their totalitarian rule over her closet if it had done anything to dissuade the gazes, the hands, the taunts that had made her afraid to leave the house alone. Perhaps that was why, once she'd enrolled in UTM, she'd started buying clothes to wear that didn't wear her, although she still stayed relatively modest. If people were going to bother her anyway, she might as well let her skin breathe. If people—if *men*—were going to tell her how good she looked, she might as well look good to herself. Right?

All those justifications she'd made in her head for her shopping spree once she'd settled into the dormitory, away from her parents' control, suddenly seemed weak and small...like her.

She sat in the office with the door open, her legs pressed together instead of crossed. Her father had once told her that when women crossed their legs, it made them look like *those* kinds of secretaries. Her skirt hem rested well below her knees, even while sitting, although it was thinner and flowier than her old skirts had been.

Shivering under the air vent, she hugged her stomach, which was playing cat's cradle with itself. She hadn't done anything wrong, so why did it feel like she'd been sent to the principal's office?

She'd been sent home from high school twenty-one times for skirts that were too tight in the rear, according to her teachers, and the dress code had specified no super-tight clothing—although it had failed to clarify what constituted 'tight'. She'd tried to explain that if she didn't tie them tight enough, they'd fall right off, but she'd been sent home anyway for being a disruptive influence. Other times, she'd been told her shirts were too low cut, even though there'd been girls around her with lower-cut tops, as though her real crime was having bigger boobs.

She'd never been rebellious, had always tried so very hard to please, but since her first major adolescent growth spurt, she'd still developed a reputation as a troublemaker. She'd eaten her lunches alone and made straight As, but she didn't think any one of her teachers remembered her report cards—just the number of times they'd ignored her raised hands in class, the times they'd told her to go home to change or go to the office for one of the oversized T-shirts they kept to shame dress code violators.

All her friends, girls as well as boys, had dried up in middle school. She'd had a few boyfriends, the kind she couldn't bring home because her father always said she was too young to date and needed to focus on school. But a pair of people found a way, anyway.

However, the boys never stayed long. Either they got what they wanted from her and were done, or she didn't give them what they wanted, hoping they'd stay under the assumption that she'd give it to them eventually.

Girls seemed to think she was competition, particularly when it came to boys, including all the ones she didn't want. Nova was always a threat, even though she tried to be as unthreatening and fairy-princess nice as she could. It never got her anywhere, and middle school had been a special brand of hell, so she'd stopped trying to make friends by high school.

She and her roommate didn't even talk, despite having majors and church services in common. Nova might as well live alone in the miniscule dorm.

This was her life. This had always been her life. It was as normal for her as brushing her hair and putting on lip balm in the morning.

Other girls had long-term boyfriends who, even in their horny teenage years, didn't paw at them all hours of the day. Girls could be friends with other girls, even whole groups of them, without claws coming out. Boys could hang out with other girls without incessantly asking if they wanted to make out behind the gym or if she wanted to drive home with them.

There was something wrong with her, something wrong that she was doing. She just hadn't figured out what it was yet. She was afraid to talk about it with anyone, even during confession, where she detailed how she got in trouble but never asked the priests *why*, afraid they'd have no other answer for her than 'Eve's sin', which was no help to her.

She couldn't help having been born a woman. She just wanted to know how to survive it.

Maybe Father Marcus could explain it to her when he arrived. And if he knew that she *wanted* to be good, *wanted* to be pure, *wanted* to be everything short of a nun for the rest of her life, maybe he wouldn't punish her for being the reason why he'd interrupted the homily.

As the clock hand inched toward thirty minutes after the hour when the service should have concluded, Nova closed her eyes and prayed an Our Father. She didn't feel comfortable with Hail Marys anymore — prayers to a maiden when she wasn't technically a maiden. She'd say them when she was told to, but in secret, whenever she thought of Mary, her soul seemed to shrink in fear.

Although why she thought she could go straight to God when she couldn't even go through a saint was beyond her — all those women celebrated for going to such great lengths to preserve their virginity unto death. And she'd just given hers up in a fruitless attempt to get a guy to finally like her for more than her body, get it out of his system so that maybe he'd see her for what she really was.

It never worked. Maybe it did for some girls, but not her. Once the boys tasted what they wanted from her, she was chewed-up gum, mucky and unsticky tape, if you believed the sex education videos their health teacher had made them watch when they'd reached the reproductive unit. The boys were completely sated, and she was left wanting — wanting more, wanting deeper. Was it such a terrible thing to want to be held, to be touched, to be loved, to feel like she was important? But they used her as though she wasn't even there at all.

If she'd been lonely in her preschool and elementary days, Nova thought she wouldn't be quite so lonely now. As it was, she'd never gotten used to having people around her who were only after one thing.

"What are you doing here so late, Ms. Harvey?" Father Marcus asked out in the hall.

"Just waiting for you to come back, sir, to see if you needed anything else from me," the receptionist said.

"Go on home. I'm sure you have other things to do tonight."

"Thanks. Oh, you have someone in your office. She said you told her to be here. Should I stay?"

"No. This shouldn't take long. Thank you, Ms. Harvey. Have a good night."

"You, too, Father Marcus."

The receptionist's footsteps, muffled on the carpet, headed away, while a stronger gait made its way to the office door. Shadow blotted out the light from the hall.

"Have you been sitting here in the dark this whole time?" Father Marcus said in surprise when Nova stood up at his entrance. He switched on the standing bank lamp next to her chair. It didn't cast out all the darkness, but it illuminated Father Marcus' weathered face and a gentler expression than he'd given her during the service.

"Yes, sir."

"Why? I wouldn't penalize you for wasting electricity or anything."

"I don't mind the dark," she said.

"No, I suppose you don't. Please, join me at my desk."

Nova picked up her satchel purse and followed Father Marcus to the two wingback chairs in front of his desk. She took the left. She expected Father Marcus to settle behind the desk and stare disapprovingly at her, but he leaned against the front of his desk instead. The lamplight reflected in his glasses, concealing the direction of his gaze

"You're not wearing a nametag," he said. "What's your name, young lady?"

Nova and nametags were time-honored nemeses. When she put one on her chest like everyone else, an adult usually gave her a stern look and told her to stop calling attention to her breasts. When she put it on her stomach like some of the girls who didn't like to grope their own boob, they told her to stop calling attention to her midriff. When she put it on her skirt, they told her to stop calling attention to her legs or her lady parts. When she put it on her forehead, they told her to stop being a clown and grow up. At this point, she'd given up and hoped that people wouldn't notice or care that she refused to wear nametags anymore.

She stared down at her hands. "Nova Mendez."

"And you're a freshman this year, am I right? I can't remember seeing you in services last year."

She nodded.

"How old are you? Seventeen, eighteen, nineteen?"

"Almost nineteen, sir. I'm old for my year."

"Almost nineteen," he murmured, as though savoring the word. "Well, at your age, I'd expect you to know better."

"Excuse me, sir?"

"Oh, you're demure now, aren't you? So you know what I'm about to tell you. Stand up, Ms. Mendez. I want you to take off that sweater. Go on. I'm going to demonstrate something to you."

"Father?" In spite of the chill in the room, her body flushed hot underneath all her clothes. The sweat under her arms smelled sour to her when she shifted.

"Please, Ms. Mendez, take off your sweater and stand up for me. There's a point I need to make that's important for you to learn."

Nova slowly stood up and pulled her arms out of the sleeves of her sweater. Father Marcus held his hand out, then snapped when she hesitated. Nova dropped her sweater into his hand. He set it on the desk behind him.

"Now, I know that girls — young women — your age like getting attention, any kind of attention. The world tells young women that their only power is in their sexuality, then they act surprised when women flaunting their bodies ends badly. I know it seems like an undue burden forced upon you to adequately cover your body when the world only gives you so many options to do so. But it is your duty, as a woman of God, to not deal in matters of pride and vanity, to preserve your purity, to maintain your modesty. There's a reason why adultery is written into the Ten Commandments as one of the most devastating betrayals that a person can engage in with another person. Do you know why we tell young women to be modest?"

Nova nodded, struggling to swallow past the obstruction in her throat. "Because we belong to God first and our husbands second. We dress modestly to respect God, respect our husbands and respect our brothers in Christ, to help them not to stumble."

"See?" Father Marcus stood with a warm smile. He was well into middle age, but it was a good smile, taking the edge off the storminess of his bushy brows and deepening the lines at the corners of his eyes. "You understand perfectly. It's especially difficult for teenage boys and young men. The slightest glimpse of certain accentuated areas of your body are enough to make them commit adultery in their mind with you, and because you invite their eyes, you commit adultery with them in your mind. So tell me, Ms. Mendez... I know our services are less formal than you might be used to, but why did you choose to wear something like *this* to Mass, of all places?"

He passed his hand over her shoulder. Where his fingers met bare skin, the little hairs on her body stood up with a localized shiver that only made her flush harder. He trailed his touch down her bare arm.

"Even the tightness of your shirt is enough to make a man stumble." He stepped even closer so that she felt his heat as he loomed over her. Nova was petite in stature. Father Marcus was tall, easily twice her size.

And he smelled…different. He didn't have the scent that had clung to the boys back in high school — gym socks, corn chips, wet hair, whatever they'd eaten last. There was an aged quality to him, as though he'd absorbed some of the dusty, leathery odors of his office.

Nova leaned forward, her eyelids fluttering as she breathed him in. It was completely involuntary, but once she'd done it, it couldn't be undone. She entered into the pocket of his heat, where the scent intensified. He was one of those people who seemed to burn from the inside. Her mother always said Nova was one of those people, too, but it didn't feel like it most days. Tonight, it did. She gasped as her heat met his.

His black shirt over his chest filled her vision, the white collar calling her gaze up as a reminder. She raised her eyes to his. At this angle, she could see them through the reflected light, his pupils wide in the dark room, expression as solemn as though he were dispensing the Host.

"It leaves little to a man's imagination, Ms. Mendez," he said. "I can practically see down your shirt. This was how close the young man was to you, yes?"

"He was next to me."

"He could still see what I'm seeing now. I'm a man of the cloth, promised to the Father, my service to the church, and what I see now makes me stumble. Now, this situation is less than organic. I created it as an illustration. But the young man next to you didn't know what this would do to him."

Father Marcus ghosted the tips of his fingers over her collarbone. Then, swallowing thickly, he lowered them down her sternum to the swells of her breasts over the neckline, the deep shadow of cleavage from the low light in the room.

She couldn't help it. She dragged in a breath, her chest expanding, bringing his touch closer. He scalded her where their skin met. She was aware of everything about him — the blue-gray of his scholar's eyes, the glimmer of silver in his eyebrows and the short, thick hair on his head, the duskiness of late-night stubble, the pores on his nose, the slightly parted lips, the ivory of his teeth between them, the wet undulation of his tongue before he spoke.

"The way you're dressed now, you might as well not bother with the shirt." His fingers trembled before he slowly drew the neckline of her tank top down, down, until the shine of her plain black bra was visible over the top.

"You mean I might as well walk around with nothing on but my bra?" She didn't know why she did it, but she took the hem of her shirt and drew it up. Everything was so sharp, yet dreamlike. This couldn't possibly be happening. It *shouldn't* be happening. Yet her breath quickened, and the sweat dripping down her back had nothing to do with fear.

Father Marcus could have — should have — stopped her. She gave him enough time. But when he didn't, she wriggled the tank top over her head, flipping her ponytail.

He opened his mouth to speak but stopped to swallow. His Adam's apple bobbed above his collar.

"You think a bra is enough to block out a man's fantasy? Really, Ms. Mendez, it's an insult to think that little slip of material conceals anything. Look at you. It doesn't even hide the shape of your nipples."

He pinched them through the bra cup. She didn't realize just how close the two of them were until she jumped and her hips brushed against his erection through his loose-fitting black trousers.

Father Marcus stepped back, as though shocked at himself. But he couldn't tear his gaze away.

When she looked down, she saw that he was right. The bra cups were structured and thick to contain her, practical rather than fanciful in construction, yet the shapes of her hard, tight nipples were clear. Underneath the bra, they rubbed uncomfortably against the fabric.

No, not uncomfortable...unbearable. She didn't want the bra on her skin any longer. She wanted skin on skin, the velvet of heat, the softness of a mouth. She wanted it so badly that she nearly doubled over, wrapping her arms around her belly and whimpering at the sensation of her forearms brushing the skin there.

Father Marcus fumbled behind him for a pair of scissors near his blotter. He raised them in front of his glinting eyeglasses. For one terrifying second that did nothing to stifle her need, Nova thought he might stab her with it.

For some reason, the old Exodus verse surfaced in her head — *Thou shalt not suffer a witch to live.*

But she wasn't a witch. She wasn't actively doing anything.

Am I?

The evening ran around her like a river, drawing her along as helpless as a kitten. It might have seemed like she was moving of her own accord, but she felt as though there was another person inside her doing these things instead.

However, it also felt like that person had been there all along.

"God will forgive me for your temptation," he whispered.

"Is that what I am?" Nova looked up just as the priest clipped the straps to her bra before grabbing the cups and yanking them down. The scissors clattered to the floor as he slid his palms back up, cupping her, holding her high and close. Then he withdrew his hands to watch their weight settle.

Father Marcus passed the back of his hand over his lips. "All women are a temptation to men. Man has been giving in to woman's temptation ever since Adam. But you, Ms. Mendez? My God. Every part of you tempts a man, and you do nothing to save them from the curse of their desire for you."

He grabbed the front of her bra again and whirled her around with him to shove her against the desk, where the lamplight illuminated more of her. He found the clasp in the front and ripped the bra off her, the set of his jaw angry but the rest of his face captivated — utterly enchanted.

The desk edge dug into the small of her back. She gripped it, caught in a whirlwind of uncertainty, fear and lust. "What am I supposed to do? I can't help the way I look. And this evening, I didn't take my sweater off to seduce anyone. I was just warm. I don't try to do this. I try to wear things that cover me. This skirt…"

"The way it clings to you, hugging your hips, your…" Father Marcus swallowed again. "It swirls around your legs like a caress every time you move. And what do you think a skirt really hides? We know what's under everything you wear. Whether you're in sackcloth and ashes or a bathing suit, nothing hides what you are."

"I know what's under all this." Nova bit her lip as she closed a fist in the front of Father Marcus' black shirt and drew him toward her. "Does that mean you might as well not be wearing any of it?"

She started at the middle and worked her way up. His abdomen and chest seemed to leap away from her every time he exhaled, but he couldn't help but inhale again so that her knuckles brushed his chest.

When she reached his clerical collar, he batted her hand away with a sharp slap. Then he slapped her face.

Nova leaned back against the desk, holding her hand to her cheek where it tingled from his blow. For a moment, she was shocked out of her haze, shocked by her behavior, shocked by his.

Father Marcus clutched at the loose clerical collar, pressing it against his chest like a man holding on to the top of a cliff. He dipped his gaze from her wide eyes to her bare breasts enhanced by the golden light, the broad, dark nipples and their tips, shifting and quivering slightly with every movement, every breath.

"I'm sorry, Ms. Mendez," he said, tentatively reaching out to stroke her other cheek. "There's nothing you can do."

A groan escaped his lips when he touched her. Suddenly, he crowded her against the desk, pushing her against it until there was nothing for her to do to save her back except to lift herself up to sit on its edge. She spread her thighs wide as he pushed between them, her skirt riding up her legs to expose more bare skin. His collar fell onto her thigh and tumbled to the side. It hit the floor with a muffled whisper.

"They say the devil was the most beautiful angel of all," he murmured as he leaned over her and kissed down her neck. He cupped the underside of her breast to lift it to his mouth.

It didn't matter that there was a window in the door or that the blinds to the large windows were open, that anyone who might walk in for late-night counsel or to clean the offices would see Father Marcus face-deep in Nova's breasts. And even if they didn't see anything, they would be able to hear Nova as she moaned her pleasure.

She nearly fell back on the desk blotter, except Father Marcus had his arm around her, and she clutched at his neck to cling him closer. Lust vibrated through her, keen as fear, strong as a cocktail of adrenaline and caffeine. As Father Marcus thrust his hips against her, dry-humping with his clothed erection, she wished she could spread her legs even more, but that would mean not wrapping them around his. Liquid heat dripped from her pussy, as hot and wet as Father Marcus' mouth around her nipple, sucking her with all the enthusiasm of a drunk with his bottle.

He pressed his forehead against her breastbone and dragged his mouth from the peak of her breast. It gleamed in the low light and chilled in the air.

"I can't..." he whispered. "I can't..."

He fumbled with the front of his trousers while she stroked his chest, falling back on his desk at last, feeling sick, feeling free, feeling twisted like a knot of bread, feeling like if she didn't get his cock inside of her right now, she might spontaneously implode into a shriveled mummy of a girl. With contact, her spirit arched like a cat against a hand over its spine. It was better than anything she'd ever had with those fumbling boys in high school. She might actually get what she wanted this time, what she *needed*.

He knocked her hands away from his chest as he lifted her skirt away from her underwear.

Nova whined, shaking her head against the blotter. Without him touching her skin, she knew he still wouldn't be enough, that he was using her...but she couldn't grasp what was missing. It slipped through her fingers as soon as he nudged her underwear away from her folds.

"God forgive me." Father Marcus clutched his deeply flushed, short, full cock in his hand, the tip leaking thin fluid that made the head shine and her mouth water. With his shirt askew and his pants open, she saw the reality that so many priests like him would deny to the world with their shapeless clothing — that he was a man, thick and alive and desirous, hungry to surround himself with her.

"God forgive me," he pleaded again, but he spoke to her breasts, as though they were the idols from which he sought forgiveness. He brought his cock to her folds, coating the head with her wetness. There was no way she could ever claim that she didn't want this. The proof stained his desk underneath her. "God forgive me, I can't stop her."

"Now, that's just pathetic, Padre," a man said from behind Father Marcus, his voice dripping with disgust. "Where's the accountability?"

Father Marcus stumbled away from Nova.

She pounded her fist against the desk when the head of his cock was taken away just a fraction of an inch from entering her, a fraction of an inch from satisfying her — at least a part of her. Not enough, but it would have been better than nothing.

Now Nova was just incredibly aware of the fact that she sat there with her legs wide, her cunt exposed and her skirt hiked up. Her bare torso seemed somehow more obscene with her skirt still on.

She felt dirty—horny and dirty and confused and dead angry that Father Marcus had the audacity to be ashamed of her, to call her the only sin in the room and give her no hope to be otherwise, the hope for forgiveness only for him. She'd done some of the damage, even though it all seemed like a dream. She'd admit that. But she'd far from done it all.

The man emerged from the shadow of the corner as though he hadn't been in the corner at all but the shadow alone. He slouched out, his thumbs in the belt loops of his jeans, no shirt—somehow especially naked in this stuffy office, where even Father Marcus was mostly dressed, albeit disheveled. The man's tousled sandy hair and dark bedroom eyes made him appear even more naturally sexual and carnal than Father Marcus with his erection unabated. He certainly looked as though he knew better the ways of the world than a priest in denial.

"Look at you. She's a ripe plum of a girl, probably tastes as good as she looks, but let's face it, Padre. She'd just a college girl, and you're a priest."

Father Marcus gaped at him, holding the sides of his placket together as though he'd forgotten that he could close it.

"*Her* priest, in fact. Yet here you are, half-undressed, ready to fuck her like a sailor, and you're really going with the 'I couldn't help it' defense?"

"Sh-she seduced m-m-me....with her cl-clothes. And-and she t-took off her shirt. I can't be e-expected to—"

"You can't lie to me," the man said. "I saw the whole thing. Damn pitiful. I know you don't get a lot, Padre, so all the tension probably builds up like a bitch, but haven't you ever heard of foreplay? As long as you're blaming everything on her and abusing your authority, couldn't you have given her a smidgeon of consideration in return? A nice, long kiss, say...or perhaps you could have fallen to your knees for a taste of the unholy bread and wine."

Father Marcus finally got enough of his wits about him to button his trousers. Then he started after the stranger, attempting to intimidate, to tower over him. "Who are you to come into *my* office and spout these blasphemies and accusations? You have no idea the context of the situation."

Just before Father Marcus reached the stranger, the stranger advanced upon him in turn, his arms spread to invite a fight if the priest wanted one. The man was shorter but younger, his body tight and fit, buzzing with kinetic energy and an odd grace as he moved. Father Marcus staggered back a step, hopelessly confused behind glasses that no longer made him appear mature and learned. Instead, he looked almost feeble as he fell back into one of the chairs.

"The context of the situation..." The stranger glared down at the priest. "It doesn't matter how fucking sexy this woman is, doesn't matter the magic she carries in her veins. You're still the responsible party here. Don't get me wrong. I'm not judging. I didn't interrupt because I was morally offended and shocked, I tell you, shocked. I interrupted this inept, fumbling bout of despair because I wanted better for her. Judging by the way she took everything you dished out without complaint, she's probably had a steady diet of shame, abuse and guilt slung her way by mindless, depraved animals like yourself."

The stranger grabbed the priest's shirt collar like he was going to pick a fight, but his lips were curved in a smile, his eyes alight with amusement.

"I'll bet she's not the first, is she, Padre? No, you don't have to answer that. I can tell the difference between dreams and memories. You've tasted forbidden fruit while wearing that pious costume before. It's true that Nova isn't a normal girl, but it's hard to really blame her when a normal girl still gets your motor revving so hard that you think you can't control yourself."

"God forgives," Father Marcus said.

"Sure, even a worm like you." The stranger wrenched Father Marcus onto the floor. "Even the things you condemn in others, the Creator forgives. I've always had a few words to say about that. But just because He erases the ledger doesn't mean she'll ever forget the way you treated her, the way it made her feel—or the other 'shes' in your life. What do you say, Nova? Should we leave this shit-stain behind while I show you what you've so sorely lacked all these years?"

Nova nervously smoothed her skirt down her thighs, tried to find for her sweater and her shirt. Her bra was...somewhere. She just wanted to leave. She was still horny as a toad, but she was too nauseated now to want anything to do with anyone except Ben and Jerry.

The worst part wasn't what Father Marcus had been doing to her. It was knowing that he was wrong to do it...and doing it with him anyway. Wanting it—like the whore that everyone believed that she was, the whore that everyone treated her as. All at once, it was as though the clammy hands of every man who'd ever touched her had stuck their hands in mud and caked it on her in slimy handprints. She felt like the mouth of a beer bottle passed around a circle jerk.

"Sweetheart, I would've loved to see you drain this slug dick drier than the Sahara, because then you'd be feeling so much better than you do right now." The stranger absentmindedly kicked Father Marcus' chest when the priest tried to rise from the floor. "No, you stay down there. If I could board you underneath the hardwoods, I'd do it, but for now, I want you as close to where you belong as you can get, Padre."

The stranger held out his hand to her.

"I know who you are, Nova. I've been trolling this campus for years. You're the first of my kind I've found. It's been a real pleasure getting to know you, waiting for the moment you were ready to meet, ready to leave this life behind for everything you were meant for, made for. Do you want to know what that is? Do you want me to show you?"

"You've been watching me?" she asked.

He closed his eyes for a moment. "That voice. I bet you'd kill in a torch song. Yeah, I've been watching. It's either just as creepy or less creepy than it sounds. I haven't quite figured that one out yet. It's just what I am. But everything will be explained by the end of the night. I don't want to delay your progress another second, sweetheart. Will you come with me? I'll show you a better time than any of these slime trails."

Nova slid along the edge of the desk away from his hand. Terror ran cold in her fingers and down her spine, but she somehow couldn't look away from him or convince her legs to run.

The stranger tilted his head, his dark eyes warm in the golden light as he stared down at her with…

Is that compassion?

Had any man ever looked at her like that, like anything other than a test, a trial, an obstacle, a prize, a warm place to sink into, a way to get off, an object of shame, a disgusting piece of trash?

"I'll bet you've only ever had boys and horny old men who don't know the first thing to do with a woman, never once showing appreciation for what you gave them—viewing you as a God-given right or a devil-given demon to lead them astray. Am I right? Boys who haven't learned yet to be men and men who haven't earned their title. I, however, won't leave you unsatisfied."

"It's a sin, Ms. Mendez," Father Marcus said from the floor. "It's a sin to have sex outside the confines of marriage."

Nova crossed her arms over her bare breasts. "Like what you were going to do with me? Putting me down the whole time as though it wasn't a sin *we* were committing, but as though—"

"As though you were the sin itself," the stranger hissed in her ear.

Nova jerked up, startled.

"Well, it's far more complicated than that, sweetheart. Let me show you. Let me show you what you truly are, what you can be. This world will smother you, unable to handle you, until you learn who you are and how to control it—control *them*. Come with me."

He offered his hand to her again.

She continued to hold her arms over her breasts, but she wasn't trying to avoid his hand anymore. She was just self-conscious in a whole new way. It was as though this stranger was the first person to see her—really *see* her—as something other than a living flesh sleeve.

"Don't worry about something as common as nudity, love," the stranger said. "Where we're going, it won't matter anymore."

"Ms. Mendez, the consequence of sin is death," Father Marcus urged.

"Everything dies," the stranger said. "But you'll be dust in your grave before we do. Come with me, Nova. Come with me."

She slowly brought her arms away from her breasts.

"God, you're beautiful," the stranger breathed. "The Creator did truly exceptional work with you."

The world spun around her at an ever-increasing pace — or maybe that was just her head. "I don't know you."

"Call me Jules. Actually, call me anything you want, sweetheart. I'll answer to just about anything for you."

"God will never forgive you!" Father Marcus shouted at her as she raised her hand to Jules.

"God doesn't have to forgive her," Jules said. "He made her perfect just the way she is."

A hunger she hadn't realized she suffered for those words reared up like a serpent. She was practically starved for them. Her lips parted to breathe them in, taste them. She couldn't get enough.

Nova slipped her hand into his.

About the Author

Aurelia T. Evans is an up-and-coming erotica author with a penchant for horror and the supernatural.

She's the twisted mind behind the werewolf/shifter Sanctuary trilogy, demonic circus series Arcanium, and vampire serial Bloodbound. She's also had short stories featured in various erotic anthologies.

Aurelia presently lives in Dallas, Texas (although she doesn't ride horses or wear hats). She loves cats and enjoys baking as much as she dislikes cooking. She's a walker, not a runner, and she writes outside as often as possible.

Aurelia loves to hear from readers. You can find her contact information, website details and author profile page at https://www.totallybound.com

Home of Erotic Romance

Sign up for our newsletter and find out about all our romance book releases, eBook sales and promotions, sneak peeks and FREE romance books!

www.ingramcontent.com/pod-product-compliance
Lightning Source LLC
Chambersburg PA
CBHW020213260626
47156CB00002B/361